The
CHESAPEAKE BAY
Book

A Complete Guide

Once seriously endangered, the osprey has come back, and nesting pairs can be seen throughout the Bay area. The bird shown here is not yet fully grown.

THE
CHESAPEAKE BAY
BOOK

A Complete Guide

Fifth Edition

Allison Blake

Berkshire House Publishers
Lee, Massachusetts

On the cover: *View of Annapolis and the State Capitol.* Photo © by David Trozzo.

THE CHESAPEAKE BAY BOOK: A COMPLETE GUIDE
FIFTH EDITION — 2002

*Permission to use historic photographs was courteously granted by the Maryland State
Archives, Annapolis.*

ISBN 1-58157-053-8
ISSN 1056-7968

Editor: Kathryn Flynn. Managing Editor: Philip Rich. Design and composition: Dianne
Pinkowitz. Cover design and composition: Jane McWhorter. Index: Diane Brenner.

Berkshire House books are available at substantial discounts for bulk purchases by
corporations and other organizations' promotions and premiums. Special personalized
editions can also be produced in large quantities. For more information, contact:

Berkshire House Publishers
480 Pleasant St., Ste. 5; Lee, Massachusetts 01238
800-321-8526
E-mail: info@berkshirehouse.com
Web: www.berkshirehouse.com

Manufactured in the United States of America
10 9 8 7 6 5 4 3 2 1

*No complimentary meals or lodgings were accepted by the author and reviewers in gathering
information for this work.*

Berkshire House Publishers'
Great Destinations™ travel guidebook series

Recommended by NATIONAL GEOGRAPHIC TRAVELER and TRAVEL & LEISURE magazines.

. . . a crisp and critical approach, for travelers who want to live like locals.
USA TODAY

Great Destinations™ guidebooks are known for their comprehensive, critical coverage of regions of extraordinary cultural interest and natural beauty. The authors in this series are professional travel writers who have lived for many years in the regions they describe. Each title in this series is continuously updated with each printing, in order to insure accurate and timely information. All of the books contain over 100 photographs and maps.

Neither the publisher, the authors, the reviewers, nor other contributors accept complimentary lodgings, meals, or any other consideration (such as advertising) while gathering information for any book in this series.

Current titles available:
The Adirondack Book
The Berkshire Book
The Charleston, Savannah & Coastal Islands Book
The Chesapeake Bay Book
The Coast of Maine Book
The Finger Lakes Book
The Hamptons Book
The Monterey Bay, Big Sur & Gold Coast Wine Country Book
The Nantucket Book
The Napa & Sonoma Book
The Santa Fe & Taos Book
The Sarasota, Sanibel Island & Naples Book
The Texas Hill Country Book
Wineries of the Eastern States

If you are traveling to, moving to, residing in, or just interested in any (or all!) of these enchanting regions, a **Great Destinations™** guidebook is a superior companion. Honest and painstakingly critical, full of information only a local can provide, **Great Destinations™** guidebooks provide you with all the practical knowledge you need to enjoy the best of each region. Why not own them all?

Contents

CHAPTER ONE
"A Very Goodly Bay"
HISTORY
1

CHAPTER TWO
Of Ferries & Freeways
TRANSPORTATION
20

CHAPTER THREE
A Capital Destination
ANNAPOLIS
32

CHAPTER FOUR
Decoys, Docks, and Lazy Days
THE UPPER BAY
100

CHAPTER FIVE
Time and Tides
MIDDLE EASTERN SHORE
132

CHAPTER SIX
Water, Water, Everywhere
LOWER EASTERN SHORE
180

CHAPTER SEVEN
Virginia's Treasures: Rambling Roads and a Home to History
NORTHERN NECK/MIDDLE PENINSULA
226

CHAPTER EIGHT
Urban Bay Neighbors
BALTIMORE & OTHER URBAN ATTRACTIONS
261

CHAPTER NINE
The Right Connections
INFORMATION
277

Acknowledgments

Over the years, numerous colleagues, acquaintances and friends have helped to ensure *The Chesapeake Bay Book's* authenticity and reliability to its readers. This edition, my fifth, is no different.

Thanks begin with editorial assistant Jan Callahan, a foodie and traveler whose background was especially valuable on the Upper Eastern Shore. Deep in Virginia's Lower Shore, Nancy Drury Duncan added a local's knowledge to that area's research, while Baltimore writer Gary Gately covered his hometown.

Editor Kathy Flynn ensured every detail, and Chesapeake photographer David Trozzo once again brought his flair to the project. Thanks also to fact-checker Heather Adams. At Berkshire House, thanks again to Publisher Jean Rousseau, Managing Editor Philip Rich, and Marketing Director Carol Bosco Baumann, all of whom, as usual, were great.

One of the best parts of this project is being in touch with friends who join me in dining at local restaurants before profiling them — which means readers can rest assured they are in good hands. On the Northern Neck, Kay Kahler Vose of White Stone and Washington, D.C., contributed profiles as well as plenty of valuable local insight reflected throughout that chapter. Ida Lee Wooten of Charlottesville and Deltaville contributed her culinary wisdom, as did brother Murray Blake, world traveler, who weighed in on a daytrip from his home in Richmond. Dr. Rania Lisas of Mechanicsville, Md., contributed south of Annapolis. In Annapolis, Beth Rubin's signature wit marks her profiles. Joanna Sullivan of Baltimore, with husband Michael, covered Baltimore's best. Pat Vojtech covered portions of the Upper Shore and the Kent Narrows area. On the Middle Eastern Shore, thank chef Gwyn Novak for her knowledgeable additions, Pete Nelson, with his Kent Island-area eye, and Easton writer Anne Stinson, with husband, writer John Goodspeed, who settled in at more than one table. Eric Mills, who spends his days as an Annapolis-based editor, visited one of his favorites on a lunch break. On the Lower Eastern Shore, Tracy Sahler and Carolyn Blakeslee Proeber, well-traveled in the region's culinary circles, ensure that visitors to that area aren't steered off course.

In addition, thanks to Chris Conner, Director of Communications at the Chesapeake Bay Program, for his advice and review of the natural history section, John Neely for his advice on fishing details, and Jeff Holland and Carolyn Sullivan for their Annapolis-area insights. Also, my parents, Miriam and Waldo Blake, helped me to chronicle their second home in Williamsburg.

I also must thank my niece, ten-year-old Shannon "Shea" Rust, who had just completed her fourth grade Maryland studies when we struck out to explore the stuff kids would enjoy. A more enthusiastic kid consultant, readers could not have found.

As always, thanks also goes to my mate, Joshua Gillelan, for being patient amid the endlessly interrupted and delayed plans and also eating out so much, as well as other friends and family who cheerfully ate out with us to profile the restaurants. And thanks to the many, many people I've known for years or just interviewed briefly — the B&B operators, the restaurant owners, the kayaking outfitters, the state park operators — for their help. You will enjoy them, and your visit to Chesapeake Country.

Introduction

Crossing the eastbound span of the Chesapeake Bay Bridge is kind of like watching the orange slit of day break up ahead on a transatlantic red-eye. The promise of adventure brings a twinge of excitement

Mainland suburbia melts away as the bridge arcs toward the Eastern Shore. White wakes and white sails mix on the Bay below. Bright mornings bring a splat of reflected sunlight edged in yellow, that accompanies the drive, rippling broadly across the water below.

"But you get that same feeling when you pull up to Point Lookout or arrive in Solomons Island," says my husband.

He's got a point. Point Lookout is land's farewell to the Potomac River. At Solomons, the Patuxent River joins the Bay. Here in Chesapeake Country, territory riven by Bay-bound creeks and rivers, it seems the traveler is always crossing from land to water, sometimes via terrain that isn't quite either.

Consider other Chesapeake crossings that bring anticipation, like traversing a tended country drawbridge. On the Eastern Shore, there's one at Knapps Narrows going to Tilghman Island, or another, a just-passing-through kind of bridge over the Sassafras River above Chestertown on the Upper Eastern Shore. Or you could clank aboard one of the Bay area's small ferries, like the Whitehaven Ferry south of Salisbury, to take the scenic route back home. Not far from the mouth of the Rappahannock River deep in tidewater Virginia, a long bridge links two peninsulas, passing from the Northern Neck to the Middle Peninsula between White Stone and Urbanna.

There's no mistaking the charm of Bay travel: possibilities always exist on the other side.

At least, that's my soul-nurturing explanation of the excited feeling I always get crossing the Bay Bridge. My foodie friend Amy says it's all just nature — the residual memory of soft-shell crabs and Eastern Shore tomatoes.

Allison Blake
Annapolis, MD

THE WAY THIS BOOK WORKS

ORGANIZATION

This book focuses on the Chesapeake's small cities and rural towns, which are covered in six geographically arranged chapters that circle the Bay in clockwise fashion starting with Annapolis. Readers will find Annapolis and its adventures south of town to the Potomac River — an area known as both the Western Shore and Southern Maryland — in one chapter. Baltimore & Urban Bay Neighbors come at the end of the book, corralling the region's more populated areas in one chapter.

Lodgings and restaurants within the chapters are all organized geographically.

Every effort was made to ensure the information in this book was correct as of publication time, but, as always, prices and policies change. It's always best to call ahead. In particular, we suggest you talk with your innkeeper about any specific needs or requests you may have — and ask if policies on children, handicap access, or smoking have changed.

PRICES

Because prices change, we guide readers via a price range system. Lodging rates include a high-season rate for double occupancy, but one inn can easily offer different rates for in season and off season, then slice the pie further with weekday and weekend rates in either season. Two-night minimum stays are common, especially in high season (and in the high traffic tourism areas), and specific rules regarding deposits and their return in the event of cancellation often apply. Always check ahead. In addition, ask ahead if a third person is allowed in the room; this is often frowned upon in B&Bs . . . but not always.

Restaurant prices include the cost of an appetizer, entrée and dessert *sans* drinks, tax and tip. In cases such as a small breakfast joint or general store or sandwich shop where one simply doesn't eat in formal fashion, price codes reflect the restaurant's norm.

Single price codes for Lodging and Restaurants govern the entire book in order to ensure consistency, but the Chesapeake region varies widely in terms of price. Travelers will find the rural areas are often priced well below Annapolis and the tourism centers in the Middle Shore and Upper Shore, as well as Baltimore.

Price Codes	Lodging	Dining
Inexpensive	Up to $75	Up to $15
Moderate	$75 to $120	$15 to $25

| Expensive: | $120 to $150 | $25 to $35 |
| Very Expensive: | Over $150 | Over $35 |

Credit Cards are abbreviated as follows:

AE — American Express	DC — Diner's Club
CB — Carte Blanche	MC — MasterCard
D — Discover	V — Visa

For year-round tourist information, see the sources at the end of the Information chapter.

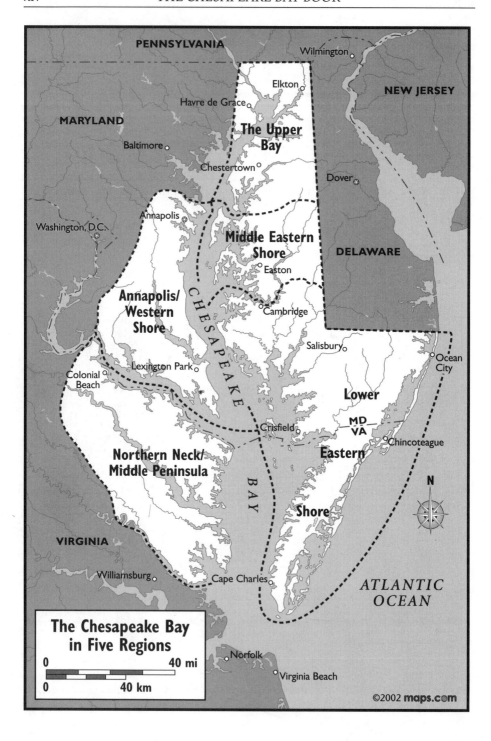

PENNSYLVANIA

Wilmington

Elkton

NEW JERSEY

MARYLAND

Havre de Grace

The Upper Bay

Baltimore

Chestertown

Dover

Annapolis

Middle Eastern Shore

DELAWARE

Washington, D.C.

Easton

CHESAPEAKE

Annapolis/ Western Shore

Cambridge

Salisbury

Ocean City

Lexington Park

Lower

Colonial Beach

MD VA

Crisfield

Chincoteague

BAY

Eastern

Northern Neck/ Middle Peninsula

Shore

N

VIRGINIA

Williamsburg

Cape Charles

ATLANTIC OCEAN

The Chesapeake Bay in Five Regions

0   40 mi

0   40 km

Norfolk

Virginia Beach

©2002 maps.com

CHAPTER ONE
"A Very Goodly Bay"
HISTORY

There is but one entrance by Sea into this Country, and that is at the mouth of a very goodly Bay, 18 or 20 myles broad. The cape on the South is called Cape Henry, in honour of our most notable Prince. The North Edge is called Cape Charles, in honour of the worthy Duke of Yorke. Within is a country that may have the prerogative over the most pleasant places. Heaven and earth never agreed better to frame a place for man's habitation. Here are mountains, hills, plaines, valleyes, rivers, and brookes, all running into a faire Bay, compassed but for the mouth, with fruitful and delightsome land.

Capt. John Smith, 1607

David Trozzo

Breathtaking views like this one at Blackwater National Wildlife Refuge in Cambridge, Md., draw many visitors to Bay Country.

Archaeologists digging in this cradle of U.S. history have unearthed countless remnants of an even deeper past. Layered in sand and clay along Chesapeake Bay shores are oyster shells, some thousands of years old. The largest cache was a thirty-acre Indian shell midden spread across Pope's Creek, off the Potomac River. Long before Chesapeake watermen took up their tongs, the Bay was feeding her people.

The native inhabitants called her Chesapeake Bay, "the Great Shellfish Bay." In the sixteenth century, a Jesuit priest sailed through the Virginia capes described by John Smith and bestowed a second name: La Bahía de la Madre de Dios — the Bay of the Mother of God.

The Chesapeake has always looked after those who lived here. Just as the Native Americans thrived on Bay oysters, so early European settlers grew crops in rich Bay soil. As the indigenous peoples paddled canoes from encampment to encampment, so ferries linked later settlements.

Today, the waters of this ancient river valley fan out into a complex network of urban bridges and rural lanes. Here endures the heart of the modern Mid-Atlantic megalopolis and the soul of nineteenth-century fishing villages. U.S. history here is old; geological history is young.

The Chesapeake Bay is bookended by two major metropolitan areas in two states: Baltimore, Maryland's largest city, and Norfolk-Newport News-Hampton Roads in Virginia's Tidewater. Both are major Atlantic ports. Near John Smith's Virginia capes, now spanned by the 17.6-mile Chesapeake Bay Bridge-Tunnel, Naval Station Norfolk presides over the Navy's strong Tidewater presence.

Much of Maryland's Western Shore life looks to urban centers, as city dwellers willing to endure the hour-plus commute to Washington, D.C. or Baltimore increasingly flood Annapolis or nearby Kent Island, drawing these former Bay outposts into the region's suburbs. For their highway-bound hours during the week, these government types are repaid with long sails on the Bay or afternoons anchored in secluded "gunkholes," shallow coves where green or great blue herons fly from nearby marshes. On the Eastern Shore, fishing, farming, tourism, and the retirement business spur local economic life.

Up the Bay's major tributaries stand the region's major cities: Washington, D.C., on the Potomac; Richmond, Virginia, on the James; and Baltimore, Maryland, on the Patapsco. Maryland's capital, Annapolis, stands at the mouth of the Severn River, near where the William Preston Lane Memorial Bridge — better known simply as "the Bay Bridge" — links the Eastern and Western Shores.

Even as the Chesapeake is defined by her waters, so she is defined by her history. A stop at Maryland's Statehouse in Annapolis, where George Washington resigned his Continental Army commission, is as integral to a Chesapeake country visit as a charter boat fishing trip from Tilghman Island. In 1607, America's first permanent colonial English settlement was established at Jamestown, Virginia. The first Catholic settlers landed farther north, on the Potomac River, and established Maryland at St. Marys City in 1634. Washington and his peers used the Bay first to transport their tobacco, the region's first sizable cash crop, and then to their military advantage as they plotted their navigational comings and goings during the Revolutionary War.

For all of the Bay's history and enduring navigability, however, she shares a problem with virtually every other heavily populated estuary. A confluence of pressures has threatened the health of her rich waters since European settlers first chopped down forests to create fields to farm. Soil from the fertile lands lining the Bay's shores has slipped into the water, silting in harbors and obscuring marshy invertebrate nurseries. Damage has been compounded by twentieth-century wastes: fertilizers, air pollution, and sewage bringing phosphorous and nitrogen, nutrients that damage the Bay.

Many say the magnificent Chesapeake is at the most crucial crossroads of her most recent geological incarnation. A massive assault against pollution has been under way since the late 1970s, and is producing some good results. Perhaps, like the estuary's flushing by fresh water from the north and by saltwater tides from the south, the diverse mix of urban and rural can maintain a beneficial balance in La Bahía de la Madre de Dios.

NATURAL HISTORY

Cargo ships journeying the 200-mile length of the Chesapeake Bay travel in a deep channel that more than 10,000 years ago cradled the ancient Susquehanna River. The mighty river flowed south to the ocean, drawing in the waters of many tributaries but for one independent soul: the present-day James River. Then came the great shift in the glaciers of the last Ice Age, when the thick sheets of ice that stopped just north of the Chesapeake region — in what is now northern Pennsylvania and New York state — began to melt under warming temperatures. As the Pleistocene Era ended, torrents of released water filled the oceans. The Susquehanna River Valley flooded once, twice, and probably more, settling eventually within the bounds of the present-day Chesapeake Bay.

A 1990s discovery may cast new light on evidence of an even earlier event that helped to shape the Bay. Apparently, an asteroid or comet hurtling 50,000 miles per hour left a mile-deep, 56-mile-wide crater near what is now the mouth of the Bay. Scientists call this largest impact crater in the United States the Chesapeake Bay Impact Crater.

The shifts of the Earth and the remnants of space have left behind North America's largest estuary. Estuaries are schizophrenic bodies of water, mixing the fresh waters of inland mountain streams and rivers with salty ocean currents. The undulating brew of fresh and salt stirs a habitat that supports a huge range of creatures. Clams, crabs, oysters, American shad, striped bass (known hereabouts as rockfish), menhaden, and more have always thrived in these waters, living a solitary life in the deep as bottom dwellers, bedding down in the shallows, or navigating to the fresh water to spawn.

The Susquehanna River, supplying fifty percent of the Chesapeake's fresh water, flows into the head of the Bay. The Potomac River adds another twenty percent. Even the renegade glacial-era James River finally joined other Chesapeake tributaries, bringing fresh water that helps to nourish the vast mix of species living in the Bay.

Solid evidence of a prehistoric past lies layered along the Western Shore of the Bay, perhaps most famously at Calvert Cliffs, located eighty miles south of Annapolis. In a swath traveling from here south to the Virginia side of the Potomac River, sharks' teeth and other fossils still wash up from time to time. These are twelve- to seventeen-million-year-old forebears to the Bay's crab, menhaden, and oysters that lived in a Miocene Era sea that stretched to present-day Washington, D.C. Crocodile, rhinoceros, and mastodon lived along the cliffs that were once the uplands of the ancient Susquehanna River Valley.

WHERE LAND & WATER MEET

Consider the Chesapeake's considerable statistics: a 2,200-square-mile surface that expands mightily when the surface area of her 150 tributaries, including all manner of coves, creeks, and tidal rivers, are added. The shoreline is 4,400 miles; if you add wetlands and tidal tributaries, it could reach as many as 8,000 miles. The total system is filled by 18 *trillion* gallons of water, the fresher water in the upper Bay, the saltier farther south.

The Bay's width ranges from four miles at Annapolis to thirty miles at Point Lookout, Maryland, where the Potomac River meets the Bay, dividing Maryland and Virginia. Despite the enormity of this expansive body of water, the Chesapeake is surprisingly shallow. Its average depth is twenty-one feet, although at the so-called "Deep Trough" off Kent Island, just over the bridge from Annapolis, depths reach 160 feet.

Beyond the waters of the Bay, within her six-state, 64,000-square-mile watershed, is geological diversity: the metamorphic rock of the Appalachian plateau, the weathered, iron-rich soil of the Piedmont, and the low-lying coastal plain.

A shoreline that seems to snake forever along marshes, creeks, or rivers provides ample habitat for thousands of species of resident or migratory wildlife and aquatic dwellers. Rookeries of great blue herons and colonies of terns nest on isolated islands, and even brown pelicans appear in the southern reaches of the Bay, increasingly traveling north to locations such as Virginia's Tangier Island, near the Maryland border.

Overhead each fall come the migratory waterfowl — tundra swans, Canada geese, brant, and of course, ducks: mallards, pintail, canvasbacks, and teal — all following the Atlantic Flyway. The mighty osprey is common, back from its severely depleted numbers after the insecticide DDT was banned in the early 1970s. Visitors can easily see their nests upon navigational markers and buoys throughout the Bay. And don't be surprised if that other distinctive raptor with a white head glimpsed near a marsh turns out to be a bald eagle. Numbers of the formerly endangered birds are so improved that it might soon lose its scaled-back "threatened" standing.

Deep on the Eastern Shore, in the lowlands of Dorchester County, the brackish marshes of the Blackwater National Wildlife Refuge welcome the red-cock-

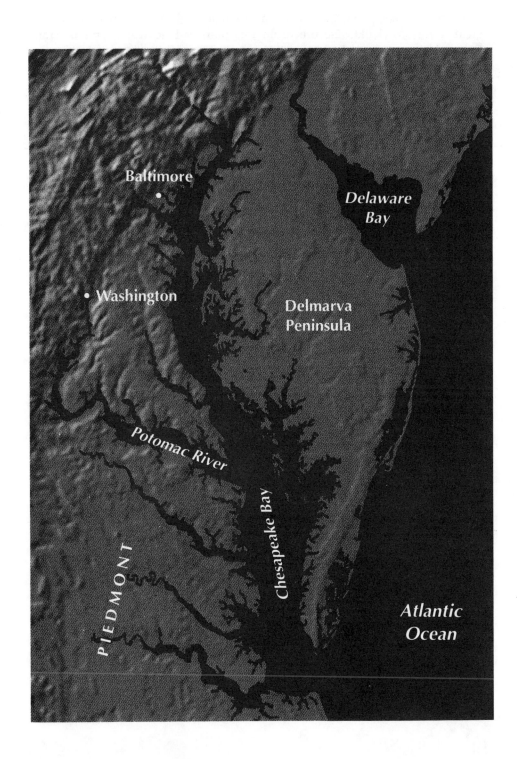

aded woodpecker, peregrine falcon, and the bald eagle, which breeds here. The great horned owl likewise breeds in this marshy blackwater, and the rare Delmarva fox squirrel also makes this area its home. Secretive river otters can occasionally be spotted; more likely, you've seen a muskrat. But it's nutria, a large and invasive South American species of rodent that apparently escaped a fur-breeding operation in the early '40s, that makes its presence especially known. By digging in wetlands, these animals feed the destruction of this critical habitat.

David Trozzo

Canada geese are just one type of migratory waterfowl that call the Chesapeake region home.

Just as it's a surprise to see the pelicans this far north, so it seems surprising that bald cypress exist this far north. Sharp-eyed hikers in the mid-Bay region will spot cypress knees along some wetland trails. In Calvert County, Maryland — not far from the fossils of Calvert Cliffs — stands the Battle Creek Cypress Swamp, where a low boardwalk winds through this mysterious blackwater habitat.

But far more common are the Chesapeake's tidal wetlands, crucial creature nurseries once thought to be no more than mosquito breeding grounds. Saltwater grasses adapted to this habitat between land and sea once grew profusely, sheltering critters such as molting crabs and protecting the sea from the land.

Talk to a salty waterman who has worked the Bay and her rivers for a few decades, though, and he'll tell you the once-prolific underwater Bay grasses are nothing compared to what they once were. Bay environmentalists consider this "submerged aquatic vegetation," or SAV, as a sort of clarity gauge of the Bay. Sediments and nutrients from pollution feed algal blooms, which then block the sunlight so the grasses can't grow. Efforts to bring back these protectors have been somewhat successful in recent years, helping to return an important nursery to young creatures such as rockfish or crabs.

Officially, 350 species of fish live in Bay waters; only some of these create reliable fisheries. Finfish including striped bass, bluefish, American shad, croaker, Atlantic menhaden, and alewives are among those who live here. But most famed among the Bay's aquatic residents are the blue crab and the oyster. Both are the focus of considerable attention in the ongoing, longtime effort to restore the ecological health of the Bay.

SAVING THE BAY

Time and tide have sent shoreline crumbling into the Bay, but the debris of human development has followed, speeding the Bay's decline. In addition to chemical fertilizers from farms and suburban lawns throughout this vast watershed, waste discharged from even vastly improved, modern sewage treatment plants continues to flow in. Air pollution from cars and coal-fired power plants funnels more nitrogen into the Chesapeake.

Efforts to bring back the Chesapeake's historical health stretch back to 1977, when formal federal and state programs allied to launch a massive Bay research and cleanup program. Interestingly, in 1964 President Lyndon B. Johnson announced the federally supported start to a cleanup of the famed Potomac River, a Bay tributary. The $1 billion project is considered a great success story, inspiration to the many agencies now devoting millions of dollars and countless hours to a Baywide cleanup.

Research launched in 1977 culminated in a landmark agreement that established a nuts-and-bolts plan to renew the Bay's deteriorating habitat. This accord, the Chesapeake Bay Agreement of 1983, was signed by Maryland, Virginia, Pennsylvania, the District of Columbia, the federal Environmental Protection Agency, and the Chesapeake Bay Commission, a group of area legislators. When the agreement was launched, the focus was on cleaning up the Bay per se. Two updates have followed. In 1987, additional focus was placed on conserving Bay flora and fauna. Chesapeake 2000 guides the process further, taking it to a new step aimed at improving water quality and protecting living resources in a more interdisciplinary effort. This brings new attention to local action and "Smart Growth" efforts to contain sprawl. The goal? To see the Bay removed from a federal roster of impaired waters by the year 2010.

Results are mixed. Apparent improvements began with submerged aquatic grasses. In places such as Tangier Sound, alongside Crisfield, Maryland, the spread of grasses means more nursery space for the many blue crabs that dwell in that area. Crabs serve as a significant source of income for the crabbers of nearby Smith and Tangier Islands, the Bay's last inhabited islands. On the other hand, in certain areas, SAV improvement has stalled.

The blue crab, mainstay of a Chesapeake summer diet, has become a source of concern throughout the Bay region, where both Maryland and Virginia tightened harvesting regulations starting in 2001 in an effort to ensure the continued future availability of this astronomically popular crustacean. Officially, the crabs are considered to be fully exploited following up-and-down populations during the 1990s. This doesn't mean they aren't available — tables fill at crab houses throughout the Chesapeake all summer long — but do *Callinectes sapidus* a favor when dropping your crab net in the water, and take only as much as you'll need for dinner. And return the females to the water. (And don't be surprised if crabs are imported from North Carolina at Memorial Day — the season doesn't get rolling until midsummer and the best are often available in fall, when prices drop.)

Perhaps signaling a brighter future for the crab are the success stories behind the return of the rockfish and the American shad. Commercial fishermen enjoyed steady rockfish catches of five million pounds annually, then watched as rockfish stocks dropped to two million pounds in the late 1970s. By 1985, Maryland put a temporary moratorium in place. Virginia followed in 1989. Stocks were officially declared restored in 1995, and scientists monitoring the rockfish report continued good news. Habitat restoration and the two fishing moratoria are given credit for bringing back the rockfish, a great success story, but the numbers still fall far below historic stocks.

David Trozzo

Efforts are under way to protect and replenish the diamondback terrapin, Maryland's state reptile, and other Chesapeake wildlife.

More recently, the historic American shad, source of shad roe, has been the beneficiaries of efforts to install fish passages to help this migratory species get upriver to breed. At the Conowingo Dam on the Susquehanna River, where scientists count the annual shad run, more than 200,000 fish passed through in 2001, by far the best year since the 1970s.

Meanwhile, visitors can expect to see enthusiastic local support for the Bay, from residents participating in everything from organized SAV-planting canoe trips to the annual Bay Bridge Walk near Annapolis in late spring (followed by early summer's annual Chesapeake Bay Swim). In both Maryland and Virginia, cars sport Chesapeake Bay specialty license plates, and in Maryland you can check off a box on your state tax return to give money to clean up the Bay.

In the years since the cleanup began, the Bay's health has slowly improved, but caution remains the watchword. Sailing and boating thrive; recreational fishers still go after striped bass. The central effort for all Bay lovers (and residents) is to help restore the estuary and nurture it as the Mid-Atlantic region continues to grow. The balance, though tough to strike, is the fulcrum of efforts to bring back the Bay.

SOCIAL HISTORY

The first settlers of the Chesapeake region lived here during the last Ice Age. These Paleo-Indians were hunters, following mammoth and bison on their migrations. The melting of the glaciers marked the beginning of the Archaic period, when these forebears of the Piscataway and Nanticoke tribes convened in villages and began to eat oysters and other shell- and finfish from the Bay. About 3,000 years ago, they began to farm these shores, raising maize, ancestor to the stacks of corn found at farm stands throughout the region come August, and tobacco, which the English settlers later converted into the region's early economic foundation.

EARLY SETTLERS

Dutch and Spanish explorers of the sixteenth century were reportedly the first Europeans to sail into the Bay, although Vikings may have visited even earlier. The first Europeans to settle permanently, however, were the English. In 1607, Capt. Christopher Newport left England, crossed the Atlantic to the West Indies, then sailed north into the Bay. He navigated up what would come to be called the James River. Those aboard Newport's three-ship fleet, the forty-nine-foot *Discovery*, the sixty-eight-foot *Godspeed*, and the 111-foot *Susan Constant*, settled Jamestown.

Bringing Back the Oyster

For decades, the oyster breathed economic life in to the Eastern Shore. Indeed, the bivalve incited a gold-rush-like boom in parts of the Bay in the 1880s. Then came the century-long bust. Overfishing first devastated stocks, followed by a combination of threats including disease, habitat destruction, and pollution.

Oyster farming and the construction of reefs are helping to boost the Bay's oyster population.

David Trozzo

Now, scientists in Maryland and Virginia are working to renew oyster stocks. This includes rebuilding oyster reefs in the three-dimensional fashion they were found when Capt. John Smith first sailed into the Bay, and when reefs reportedly were so big they posed a hazard to navigation. The idea is to nurture the young — known as spat — in sanctuaries where the oysters can grow large. The larger the oyster, the more eggs it produces. The more eggs, the more potential for a boost in the oyster population.

Back in 1996, for example, an experimental reef was built in Virginia's Great Wicomico River. Nearby, density of seed spat had been 200 per square meter that year. A year later, the nearby reefs saw a nearly 600 percent increase in density.

If you're lucky, you may see this work in progress. Along the Rappahannock River in Virginia, for instance, a barge building one of these reefs is visible from shore through the early-morning mist. Eventually, nine one-acre reefs will be built here in this historically productive area. Each sanctuary reef, which cannot be fished, will then be surrounded by dozens of acres of restored shell bottom.

These oyster reefs are expected to help oysters overcome disease over time, but, perhaps most important of all, provide the Bay with the oysters' historic filtering mechanisms that help purify the water. Scientists say the Bay's oysters filtered all of its water in three days back when John Smith first came here, and now it takes something closer to a year.

As scientists work to build reefs, waterfront residents are taking up the new hobby of oyster gardening, in which locals grow seed destined to move on to life at the sanctuary reefs. Those interested in learning more about oyster gardening should contact The Chesapeake Bay Foundation, 1-800-SAVEBAY.

The new colony, chartered by the Virginia Company, proved to be a near disaster. Hostiles and disease either drove off or killed many of the original settlers. Among the survivors was Capt. John Smith, by all accounts an adventurer. It was here that Smith's fabled rescue by the maiden Pocahontas took place — an event recorded in Smith's journal, but questioned by scholars. As the story goes, the young captain was captured and taken to a village where the old "powhatan," or chief, was to preside over Smith's execution. Even as the warriors threatened with raised clubs, the chief's young daughter threw herself upon the English captain, thus saving him from a brutal fate. Smith was also the first Englishman to explore the Bay and indeed charted it rather accurately. He set out from Jamestown on his exploration in 1608, accompanied by fourteen men on an open barge. They sailed first up the "Easterne Shore," where sources of fresh water proved poor. While still in what came to be called Virginia, Smith wrote, ". . . the first people we saw were 2 grimme and stout Salvages upon Cape-Charles, with long poles like Javelings, headed with bone. They boldly demanded what we were, and what we would, but after many circumstances, they in time seemed very kinde . . ." Smith learned from them "such descriptions of the Bay, Isles, and rivers, that often did us exceeding pleasure." The party then went on across the Bay to its Western Shore, sailing as fast as they could ahead of a fearsome storm. "Such an extreame gust of wind, rayne, thunder, and lightening happened, that with great danger we escaped the unmercifull raging of that Ocean-like water," wrote Smith.

Early Jamestown survived as Virginia's colonial capital to the end of the seventeenth century. Meanwhile, English migration across the Atlantic continued. In 1631, William Claiborne established his trading post at Kent Island, mid-Bay, setting himself up to become arguably the first settler of Maryland. In ensuing years, on behalf of the Virginia Company, he provided ample rivalry for Maryland's "proprietors," or royal grant holders, the Calverts.

George Calvert, the first Lord Baltimore, hoped to settle his own "Avalon." He first sought to establish a colony in Newfoundland, but soon abandoned the harsh northern land. A second grant for a new colony passed to his son, the second Lord Baltimore, Cecil Calvert. The younger Calvert, a Catholic, knew that Virginia would not welcome the new settlement and feared that enemies in England would try to undermine his colony. He put his younger brother, Leonard, in charge of the settlers who boarded the ships *Ark* and *Dove*, and sailed off to found Maryland, named in honor of Charles I's queen, near the mouth of the Potomac River at St. Clement's Island. Visitors can still take a weekend boat out to the island, shrunk from 400 acres to about 40.

The 128 hardy souls aboard the two ships landed on March 25, 1634, after taking a route similar to that taken by Christopher Newport. Upon landing, Leonard Calvert, as governor, led a party of men up the river to meet the "tayac," or leader, of the Piscataways. The tayac gave the settlers permission to settle where they would; their village was to become Maryland's first capital,

A reproduction of a Piscataway Indian hut at St. Mary's City, Md.

David Trozzo

St. Marys City. These Native Americans also taught the English settlers how to farm unfamiliar lands in an unfamiliar climate.

Among the Marylanders' first crops was tobacco, soon to be the staple of a Chesapeake economy and already being harvested farther south along the Virginia Bay coast. In the years that followed, farmers would discover just how damaging tobacco proved to be in costs to both the land and humans; the crop sapped the soil's nutrients. Without fertilizers, a field was used up after a couple of seasons, so more land constantly had to be cleared and planted. This called for labor. While some Englishmen indentured themselves to this life in exchange for transatlantic passage to the colonies, tobacco farming was nevertheless responsible for the beginnings of African slave labor along the Chesapeake. By the late seventeenth century, wealthy planters had begun to "invest" in slaves as "assets."

Up and down the Chesapeake grew a tobacco coast, fueled by demand from English traders. From its beginnings as a friendly home to new settlers, the Bay grew into a seagoing highway for the burgeoning tobacco trade. Soon came fishing and boatbuilding.

A rural manorial society grew up around St. Marys City, which was never itself very large. Perhaps a dozen families lived within five square miles. Planters raised tobacco, a fort was established, and government business eventually brought inns and stables. In 1650, a settlement named Providence was established about 100 miles to the north, near what is now Annapolis. In 1695, the new governor, Francis Nicholson, moved Maryland's capital near the mouth of the Severn River to Annapolis. By 1720, St. Marys City was gone. That colony's heyday has been re-created, however, in a living museum complete with wild Ossabaw pigs. Archaeological work continues on the site. In recent years, three lead coffins holding the remains of members of the Calvert clan were unearthed and authenticated.

Nicholson's Annapolis, considered America's first baroque-style city, remains

The Maryland Statehouse is the nation's oldest state capitol in continual use.

David Trozzo

evident to any visitor. Two circles, State Circle and Church Circle, form hubs from which the streets of today's Historic District radiate. Inside State Circle have stood three statehouses, the most recent begun in 1772. This was the building used as the national capitol during the period of the Articles of Confederation and is the nation's oldest state capitol in continual use. From the center of Church Circle rises the spire of St. Anne's Church, the third on the site since 1696.

Known also as "the Ancient City," Annapolis grew into a thriving late seventeenth- and eighteenth-century town, renowned as the social gathering spot for colonial gentlemen and ladies. Here, the Provincial Court and the Legislature met. Planters "wintered" here amid fashionable society; among social clubs, the most famed includes the witty men of the Tuesday Club, whose members, such as the colonial painter Charles Willson Peale, gathered at the homes of its members for music and poetry.

Elsewhere along the Chesapeake, seaport settlements were emerging. Chestertown was established as a seaport and Kent County seat in 1706. Near the head of the Bay, "Baltimore Town" was first carved in 1729 from sixty acres owned by the wealthy Carroll family. Those who couldn't survive the fluctuations of the tobacco market turned to tonging for oysters, fishing for herring, or shipbuilding.

THE CHESAPEAKE IN WARTIME

During the Revolutionary War, Annapolis' central port location drew blockade-runners and Continental colonels alike. Both Americans and British used the Bay to transport troops. War meetings that included George Washington and the Marquis de Lafayette were held beneath the Liberty Tree, a 400- to 600-year-old tulip tree that stood on the St. John's College campus until dealt a final blow by a hurricane in 1999.

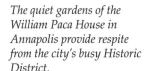

The quiet gardens of the William Paca House in Annapolis provide respite from the city's busy Historic District.

David Trozzo

Three Annapolitans, Samuel Chase, William Paca, and Charles Carroll of Carrollton, signed the Declaration of Independence in 1776; their colonial-era homes have been preserved and are open for public tours. The fourth Maryland signer, Thomas Stone, later took up residence here, too, in what is now known as the Peggy Stewart House. The war finally ended in 1781 at Yorktown, Virginia, near Jamestown. Reinforcements traveled south along the Bay to meet up with Washington's gathering troops, and French Admiral de Grasse barricaded the mouth of the Bay. Lord Cornwallis, the British commander, surrendered.

In 1783, during a meeting of the Continental Congress in the Maryland Statehouse in Annapolis, George Washington resigned his Army commission; visitors may still see the chamber where this occurred. This is also where the Treaty of Paris was ratified in 1784, formally ending the war. Likewise, Annapolis itself saw an end to its glittery social role. The city soon fell quiet, awakened only by the 1845 establishment of the U.S. Naval Academy, which overshadowed much of city life for at least the next century.

Peace with the British after the Revolution was short-lived. Soon came the War of 1812, the final time hostile British troops reached the new nation's shores. The British established their operations center at Tangier Island, and many battles and skirmishes ensued upon the Bay. Visitors to the island will learn about the Methodist "Parson of the Islands," Joshua Thomas, who predicted their defeat when he preached to the British before they sailed up the Bay to Baltimore. The citizens of the young nation were not eager to bow to the British, including those at the shipbuilding center of St. Michaels. Blockade-runners routinely left the Eastern Shore port, and hostility ran high. Late on the night of August 9, 1813, amid rumors of an impending British attack, the good citizens of St. Michaels blew out their lanterns. Just before dawn, the British attacked a nearby fort. The wily Shorefolk were ready. They hoisted their lanterns into the treetops, the British fired too high, and the town, except for the now-renowned "Cannonball House," was saved. For this, St. Michaels calls itself "The Town That Fooled the British."

A year later came the war's decisive battle. In September 1814, a man watched the fire of cannons and guns as the Americans successfully defended Fort McHenry, which guards the entrance to Baltimore Harbor. The next morning, Francis Scott Key saw a tattered U.S. flag flying and, inspired, penned the words to "The Star-Spangled Banner," thus creating what would become the U.S. national anthem in 1931.

NINETEENTH-CENTURY LIFE

Once this second war ended, the denizens of nineteenth-century Chesapeake country turned to building their economy. Tobacco declined; shipbuilding grew. Smaller Chesapeake shore towns, such as Chestertown and Annapolis, lost commercial prominence to Baltimore, which grew into the Upper Bay region's major trade center. Steamships were launched, and the Baltimore & Ohio Railroad more speedily connected the region to points west. Exported were Eastern Shore-grown wheat and the watermen's catch of oysters, menhaden, and more. By all accounts, there was no love lost between the landed gentry, who controlled the region, and the Chesapeake watermen. These scrappy individualists may have been one-time small farmers down on their luck, or descendants of released indentured servants who had once served the wealthy class.

During this era, Chesapeake's shoals saw their first aids to navigation erected as lightships were sent out to warn passing ships of the worst sandbars. In 1819, Congress made provisions to set two lightships in Virginia waters. This experiment in safety was popular, and by 1833, ten lightships stood sentinel at the mouth of the Rappahannock River and elsewhere in the Bay. The mid-nineteenth century saw construction of the distinctive screw-pile lighthouses, with pilings that could be driven securely into the muddy bottom of the Bay. Today, only three stand — two at maritime museums at Solomons and St. Michaels, Maryland, and one in action in the Bay just southeast of Annapolis, off Thomas Point. The Thomas Point Light was manned until automation came in 1986.

As the Bay became easier to travel, the people who spent the most time on the water discovered perhaps her greatest wealth. In the nineteenth century, demand increased for the famous Chesapeake oysters. Watermen went after them in an early ancestor to many "Bay-built" boat designs, the log canoe. Boats like the fast oceangoing schooners known as "Baltimore clippers" already were being built, but oyster dredging and tonging required boats that could skip over shoals, run fast, and allow a man to haul gear over the side. Log canoes have unusually low freeboard; crab pots and oyster tongs can be worked over their sides. These successors to dugout canoes were given sails and shallow-draft hulls to navigate shoals. With their top-heavy sails and low sides, log canoes now present one of a yachtsman's greatest challenges. Shifting their weight just ahead of the wind, sailors race log canoes most summer weekends in St. Michaels on the Eastern Shore.

The Bay's 120-year steamboat era arrived in 1813, seven years after packets first carried passengers on a ship-and-stagecoach journey from Baltimore to Philadelphia. The steamboat *Chesapeake* paddled out of Baltimore Harbor on June 13, 1813, for Frenchtown, Maryland, a now-extinct town at the head of the Bay. Within a week, a trip was offered to Rock Hall, on Maryland's Eastern Shore, for seventy-five cents. By 1848, the steamship company that came to be called the Old Bay Line ran the 200-mile length of the Bay, from Baltimore to Norfolk. Steamships ran in the Bay into the 1960s.

THE CIVIL WAR & SLAVERY

Even as the Chesapeake Bay fueled a growing nineteenth-century economy, these were the years of growing North-South hostility. The Chesapeake region was largely slaveholding, although the nearby Mason-Dixon Line (the southern boundary of Pennsylvania) to the north beckoned many slaves to freedom. Historical accounts say this tended to moderate the behavior of many Maryland slaveholders who feared their slaves would run away.

The history of slavery here had started with tobacco farming in the late 1600s; by 1770, tobacco exports reached 100 million pounds in the Western Shore region. When the tobacco trade declined in the nineteenth century, the services of many slaves were no longer needed. Abolitionist Quakers living in the Bay area campaigned to free many slaves, and free blacks were not uncommon in Annapolis and Baltimore in the first half of the nineteenth century. Many Eastern Shore watermen were free blacks who mixed with white watermen in mutual contempt for the wealthy.

In 1817, abolitionist and writer Frederick Douglass was born into slavery in Talbot County, Maryland. As a boy, he worked at the Wye Plantation, owned by Edward Lloyd V, the scion of a political dynasty in Maryland. Following alternately civil treatment in Baltimore and brutal treatment as an Eastern Shore field hand, Douglass escaped to Philadelphia at age 21 and became a free man.

Because the upper reaches of the Bay were so close to freedom, the Underground Railroad thrived here. The best-known local conductor was Harriet Tubman, an escaped slave from Dorchester County, Maryland, who became known as "the Moses of her People" as she led nearly 300 slaves north during her lifetime.

When the Civil War broke out in 1861, the Virginia half of the Chesapeake quickly turned to Richmond, located at the head of navigation of the James River. Maryland struggled over its political loyalties, and many Chesapeake families would be divided by North-South rivalries.

Naval warfare changed forever on the waters of the Civil War Bay, when the ironclads *Monitor* and *Merrimack* met at Hampton Roads. The *Merrimack*, having been salvaged, rebuilt as an ironclad, and renamed *Virginia* by the Confederates, had already rammed and sunk the Union *Cumberland* and disabled the *Congress*, which burned and sank. The next day, the ironclad *Monitor*, with her two guns protected in a swiveling turret, arrived to engage the *Merrimack's* fixed guns. Neither ship sank the other; neither side won, but the encounter was the first battle between armored battleships.

Ironically, when the Emancipation Proclamation went into effect in January 1863, slaves laboring on the Virginia shores of the Chesapeake were freed where federal law — via Union occupation — prevailed; slaves in Union Maryland were not. The Proclamation freed only those in the states "in rebellion against the United States." It wasn't until September 1864, when Maryland voted for its own new constitution, that those in bondage in the state were freed.

THE OYSTER BOOM

In the years before the war, shrewd Baltimore businessmen had opened oyster-packing plants. With the war over, enterprising Chesapeake business was renewed. The fertile oyster bars of the Bay's famed shoals fueled a much-needed economic burst on the Eastern Shore.

The star of menus all across the Chesapeake region: blue crabs.

David Trozzo

Chesapeake oyster production peaked at 20 million bushels a year in the 1880s, the height of the great oyster boom that started after the Civil War. The Eastern Shore Railroad snaked through the flatlands to Dorchester County, where one John Crisfield, former Maryland congressman, set about capitalizing on his new railroad. At the head of Tangier Sound, where watermen dredged or tonged millions of oysters from the rich waters, Crisfield built his namesake town, which now calls itself the "Crab Capital of the World." The town was literally built upon millions of oyster shells. An enormous wharf stretched along Somer's Cove, and the railroad depot stood nearby. Shuckers and packers set to work once the daily catch was landed; the cargo was shipped out on the railroad line, and newly developed refrigeration techniques kept it fresh on its way deep into the nation's interior.

Like Crisfield, Solomons, Maryland, on the Western Shore, sprang from the oyster rush. Isaac Solomon came from Baltimore, taking his patented pasteurizing canning process to the tiny village, where he set up a successful packing plant.

From this gold mine grew greed, and the famed Chesapeake Oyster Wars ensued. Virginia and Maryland oystermen — the tongers and dredgers, known as "drudgers" — battled over rights to oyster beds; tempers ran high, and shots were fired. Maryland authorities, already funding an Oyster Navy to maintain some measure of decorum on the Bay, were angered that Virginia was less than helpful when it came to keeping its watermen within their boundaries, whatever exactly they were.

The Oyster Wars proved to be the catalyst that finally forced Maryland and Virginia to define their disputed Bay border. Three years of negotiations at the federal bargaining table set the boundary in 1877 about where it is today. The southern shore of the Potomac was always the boundary between the two states, but how far down that shore the river ended and the Bay began, from which point to draw the line east across the Bay was subject to dispute. The two states agreed to draw the line across Smith Point to Watkins Point on the Eastern Shore's Pocomoke River. Today, the boundary has been further refined: Maryland extends to the low-tide line of the river on the Virginia shore. Present-day Virginians at Colonial Beach accept this arrangement with ingenuity, playing the lottery of their own state in town and betting on their neighbor's jackpot at the end of a long pier — the same device they resorted to decades ago when gambling was legal in southern Maryland.

CHESAPEAKE TOURISM

The late nineteenth century brought the first tourists to the Bay, lured by clever investors who built the first resorts. Vacationers from Baltimore and Philadelphia turned to the Chesapeake, staying at new hotels built at Betterton and Tolchester on Maryland's Eastern Shore. On the Western Shore, Chesapeake Beach, just south of the Anne Arundel–Calvert County line, was carved from the shore by businessmen from the Pennsylvania Railroad. A new train station built there gave easy access to people from Baltimore and Washington, D.C.

Until about 1920, the Bay and its tributaries were the region's highways. Ferries connected to railroad lines crisscrossed the network of water and land, and steamships traveled everywhere. Farming and fishing supported much of the rural Western and Eastern Shores in both Maryland and Virginia.

Following World War II, the Chesapeake region mirrored the rest of the country, as industry and shipping propelled Baltimore and Norfolk into a new prosperity.

The automobile, too, fueled change, and by the mid-twentieth century the time had come to span the Bay by highway. On October 1, 1949, construction of the Chesapeake Bay Bridge began. Less than three years later, on July 30, 1952, the $112-million, 4.3-mile bridge opened. Over the next thirty years, travelers "discovered" the Eastern Shore as never before. As far south as Salisbury, Maryland, towns saw growth; Talbot and Kent counties in particular became home to many retirees from the cities — and, increasingly, Washington or Baltimore commuters.

In 1964, the other end of the Bay was spanned. The spectacular Chesapeake Bay Bridge-Tunnel was more than three years in the making, at $200 million, and in the late 1990s, its multimillion-dollar twin span was opened. Two mile-long tunnels and twelve miles of trestled roadway alternately soar above, then dive beneath, the Chesapeake Bay. Four constructed islands serve as supports between bridge and road, as the bridge-tunnel spans the entryway through which early explorers first found the Chesapeake.

What is the future of the Bay area? Apparently, it depends on the self-control of those who live here — and of those within the watershed that spreads all the way to upstate New York. The debris of their lives ultimately trickles into the Bay. Annapolis, with ties to Baltimore and Washington, D.C., increasingly is caught in the region's web of urban growth, yet manages to maintain its colonial charm. The Bay area still retains its rural places. Along the Northern Neck of Virginia, travelers find only a couple of convenience stores. Across the Bay, on the Eastern Shore, the old shipbuilding ports of Oxford and St. Michaels have new lives as quiet, colonial-style villages for people who have escaped the city.

The first English settlers, Protestant and Catholic, brought diversity when they came to live among the Native Americans already here. So it is today, as city dwellers and those who fall in love with "the land of pleasant living" move in among the old families whose forebears long ago planted and fished along the Chesapeake Bay.

CHAPTER TWO
Of Ferries & Freeways
TRANSPORTATION

David Trozzo

Baltimore's skyline, as seen from the water along the Inner Harbor.

The history of Chesapeake transportation is intimately tied to this vast inland sea, plied in ancient days by dugout canoes, later by indigenous sail craft, and today, by massive steel cargo ships or yachts.

For centuries, native inhabitants — the Susquehannock, Wicomico, or Nanti-coke — had the Bay to themselves. Then came the Spanish explorers and, in 1607, the Englishmen who settled first at Jamestown, Virginia. Soon after the vessels *Ark* and *Dove* delivered Maryland's first settlers in 1634, commerce drove the development of a ferry system across the Bay's rivers and creeks.

By the late 1600s, ferries crossed the South River south of present-day Annapolis to deposit traders at London Town, where they swapped furs for supplies. In 1683, what is said to be the oldest passenger ferry service in the country launched its run between Oxford and Bellevue on Maryland's Eastern Shore — and still makes the crossing.

Later came the steamship era, ultimately symbolized by the Baltimore Steam Packet Company, known as the Old Bay Line, which launched in 1839 with wooden, then steel, paddle wheelers and steamships that operated into the

1960s. Visitors will increasingly find local museum exhibitions devoted to those days, especially in small towns, formerly served by steamships, which have been rediscovered.

Even as boat routes linking small towns spread across the Bay, ambitious plans connected the Chesapeake with the young nation's expanding interior. In 1850, the 184.5-mile Chesapeake and Ohio Canal opened after twenty years of construction. The canal was built alongside the nonnavigable section of the Potomac River above Washington, D.C., which in turn is strategically linked to the Bay via the navigable waters of the lower Potomac. Just about the time this marvel of modern engineering opened, the first rails were laid for the Baltimore & Ohio Railroad.

The B&O was the first railroad to connect Bay country to the "outside," but others soon followed. Working in tandem with packet and steamship lines, railroads dramatically opened up the area. Passenger and freight stations ran deep on the Eastern Shore to places like Crisfield, which boomed from oyster exports in the late nineteenth century.

A bridge didn't span the Bay until 1952, when the 4.3-mile William Preston Lane Memorial Bridge (known locally as the Chesapeake Bay Bridge) replaced a ferry, first with a single span, and later, a second span. Travel to the Shore and Atlantic beaches by tourists and city dwellers boomed. In 1991, a new bridge replaced an aging drawbridge at Kent Narrows, just east of the Bay Bridge, greatly easing beach-bound traffic over the busy Narrows.

The 4.3 mile William Preston Lane Memorial Bridge, better known as the Bay Bridge, frames a familiar seascape for Chesapeake anglers.

David Trozzo

Soon after the Middle Eastern Shore was opened up to cars, a feat of engineering did the same at the mouth of the Bay. Where Vikings once may have sailed, the Chesapeake Bay Bridge-Tunnel now stands. The massive, 17.6-mile span alternates bridge and tunnel across four constructed islands to Cape Charles from the Virginia mainland, and not long ago opened a span headed in the other direction. For those who haven't crossed the bridge-tunnel since the last millennium, this means traffic moves through four lanes going north and south, except when lanes converge back to a two-lane highway as the road dips beneath the Bay's shipping channels. At that point, traffic funnels through two one-mile tunnels.

Travelers can reach the gateway cities to the Chesapeake — Washington, D.C., Baltimore, and Norfolk-Hampton Roads — by air, bus, or train. Mass transportation outside the cities is limited, although some connections can be made. To get the most out of your visit, rent a car to explore the small towns and back roads of the largely rural, rambling Chesapeake region. For a taste of local adventure, wander back roads and cross tributary creeks and rivers the same way European forebears did as early as the late 1600s — by ferry.

GETTING TO THE CHESAPEAKE BAY AREA

Unless you plan to spend your entire visit in Baltimore or Annapolis, the area's rambling country roads and tidewater lanes are best explored by car. Rent one at the airport, or tool into town in your own.

BY AIR

Washington, D.C.–Baltimore Metropolitan area

Four major airports serve the region — in Baltimore, Washington, D.C., outside D.C. in nearby northern Virginia, and in the Norfolk-Hampton Roads area. In addition, regional airports in Salisbury, Md., and in the Newport News–Williamsburg, Va., area offer commuter service. Check airport web sites for important information subject to change, such as ground transportation schedules.

Baltimore-Washington International Airport (800-435-9294; 410-859-7111 Baltimore area, 301-261-1000 Washington area; www.bwiairport.com; P.O. Box 8766, BWI Airport, MD 21240) BWI lies an easy 25-mile drive north of Annapolis via I-97, and fewer than fifteen minutes from Baltimore's Inner Harbor. Over the coming years, a massive expansion project will bring new parking lots and larger terminals to BWI.

Ronald Reagan Washington National Airport (703-417-8000; www.metwashair ports.com; Ronald Reagan Washington National Airport, Washington, DC 20001) Located at the edge of the city, with easy access to highways leading to Annapolis.

Washington Dulles International Airport (703-572-2700; www.metwashair ports.com; Washington Dulles International Airport, Dulles, VA 20166) Thirty miles to the west in northern Virginia; a hike from Annapolis, especially given the D.C. area's hideous traffic.

Baltimore Washington International Airport offers convenient service to Bay visitors.

David Trozzo

The airports' web sites provide information on ground transportation or security questions. Among your options at each of the three airports is the SuperShuttle, which circulates through all airports every 15 minutes between 6 am and 2pm (but be forewarned: hour-long waits during these hours are not unknown). Service is on a first-come, first-served basis, and destinations served are determined by ZIP code. For further information: 1-800-BLUEVAN, 410-859-0800; www.supershuttle.com, or check with the SuperShuttle representative stationed at the service's counter on the lower level of each airport.

Travelers trying to get between Dulles and Washington may want to contact the *Washington Flyer* at 1-888-WASHFLY, or www.washfly.com. The shuttles stop at Union Station, with its easy access to the city's Metro subway system (202-637-7000; www.wmata.com) and connections to Amtrak. In addition, Baltimore-bound travelers can hop aboard the MARC (Maryland Area Rail Commuter) trains (410-539-5000 or 800-325-RAIL). Finally, weekday travelers may want to use the commuter bus that runs into Washington from Kent Island and Annapolis in the morning, and back out in the evenings. For information, contact Dillon Bus Service (800-827-3490, 410-647-2321).

Urban Tidewater, Va.

Norfolk International Airport (757-857-3200; www.norfolkairport.com; 2200 Norview Ave., Norfolk, VA 23518) Tidewater's aviation hub. To catch a ride from the airport, try the Norfolk Airport Shuttle (757-857-1231), which offers transport every half-hour throughout the Norfolk-Hampton Roads area, and (for a per-mile fee) will also drive you throughout the region, including the Eastern Shore. Costs vary according to distance and the size of your party.

FROM REGIONAL AIRPORTS

COMMERCIAL SERVICE

Newport News–Williamsburg International Airport (757-877-0221; www.nnw airport.com; 900 Bland Blvd., Newport News, VA 23602) The military's former Camp Patrick Henry hosts service to larger airports in the Mid-Atlantic via United/United Express, USAirways and its attendant Express, and AirTran Airlines. For wide-ranging ground transportation throughout the area, contact Williamsburg Limousine Service (757-877-0279).

Salisbury-Ocean City; Wicomico Regional Airport (410-548-4827; Airport Manager's Office, 5485 Airport Terminal Rd., Unit A, Salisbury, MD 21804) Deep into Maryland's Eastern Shore, this airport offers USAirways Express shuttle service (USAirways Express/Piedmont Airlines; 410-742-4190) to Baltimore, Washington, D.C., Philadelphia, and Charlotte. Also, find National car rental offices here.

PRIVATE PLANES

Pilots with their own planes can check out these regional airports:

Bay Bridge Airport (410-643-4364; 202 Airport Rd., Stevensville, MD 21666) Flight school, tie-downs, and repairs. Can arrange shuttles.

Easton Municipal Airport (800-451-5693; 29137 Newnam Rd., Easton, MD 21601) Tie-downs, ground support. Charter service based here.

Freeway Airport (301-390-6424; 3900 Church Rd., Bowie, MD 20721) Fuel available daily 8 a.m. to dark. Tie-downs and maintenance.

Lee Airport (410-956-2114; Old Solomons Island Rd./P.O. Box 273, Edgewater, MD 21037) Tie-downs, no charters. Located two miles south of Annapolis.

Cambridge-Dorchester Airport (410-228-4571; 5223 Bucktown Road, Cambridge, MD 21613) Tie-downs and other support, including a restaurant.

BY RENTAL CAR

Three airports clustered in the Baltimore-Washington, D.C. area mean that rental car agencies often let you rent a car at BWI, for example, and return it to National or Dulles without an extra drop-off cost. Call to inquire.

Alamo (800-327-9633).
Avis (800-452-1494).
Dollar (800-800-4000).
Hertz (800-654-3131).
National (800-227-7368).
Thrifty (800-847-4389).

CHESAPEAKE BAY AREA ACCESS

Some interstates in both Maryland and Virginia — including portions of I-95 — post 65 mph speed limits. Here are approximate distances and driving times, calculated at 50 mph, from the following major cities to Annapolis:

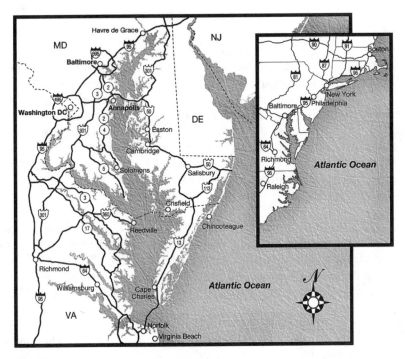

City	Miles	Hours
Atlanta	631	12.75
Boston	425	8.5
Chicago	706	14.0
Cincinnati	504	10.25
New York	216	4.5
Norfolk, VA	204	4.25
Philadelphia	120	2.5
Richmond	133	2.5
Raleigh, NC	277	5.5

BY BUS

Travelers with a slim wallet or a sense of adventure may want to reach the Bay area by bus, but service is limited and schedules may change. As always, call ahead. For information: **Greyhound** (800-231-2222 or 202-289-5154; www.greyhound.com); or **Trailways** (800-343-9999, 410-752-0868, or 202-484-2510; www.trailways.com).

BY CAR

From New York and points north: Take I-95 south to Delaware, and cross the head of the Chesapeake at the Susquehanna River at Havre de Grace. Your most straightforward path through Baltimore means staying on I-95 via the Fort McHenry Tunnel. Circling the city via I-695 (the Baltimore Beltway) takes perhaps 20 minutes more, but crosses a high span with a spectacular view of the city and its harbor, guarded by Fort McHenry in the fork of the river to your right. From Baltimore, it's a smooth ride to I-97 south to Annapolis. For a scenic alternative, pick up Rte. 896 south toward Middletown after crossing the Delaware Memorial Bridge, then take U.S. 301 south through the Delmarva Peninsula. Journey through the Shore on Rte. 50 east. To reach Annapolis, cross the 4.3-mile-long William Preston Lane Memorial Bridge.

From Pittsburgh and points west: The Pennsylvania Turnpike connects with I-70 at Breezewood, Pa., your quickest route to the Bay region. (For a scenic route through rolling farmland, take alternate U.S. 40, which reconnects with I-70 just east of Frederick, Md.) Reach Annapolis and the Eastern Shore via I-70 by way of Baltimore, or I-270 via Washington, D.C. Then take U.S. Rte. 50 into Annapolis.

From western Virginia and Dulles Airport. Take I-66 east. The road connects with the Washington Beltway (I-495) seven miles east of Vienna, Va. Take the Beltway's inner loop north to I-95 to Baltimore; take the outer loop south to reach U.S. 50 and Annapolis.

From points south: To go directly to the tip of Virginia's Eastern Shore, pick up U.S. 13 in North Carolina to the Norfolk area and follow the signs for the Chesapeake Bay Bridge-Tunnel. Or, continue on I-95 to Richmond and take I-64 east down the historic peninsula between the James and York Rivers. At the end of the peninsula, the highway tunnels under the mouth of the James River to Norfolk. Pick up the Bridge-Tunnel to the Shore.

If you're headed to Annapolis, take I-95 to I-495, the Washington Beltway, and circumnavigate the eastern side of the city. Go east on Rte. 50. Since the I-95/I-495 intersection south of the city in Northern Virginia often is traffic-choked, consider turning off I-95 thirty miles north of Richmond for a scenic ride that's not all that much longer. Follow Va. 207 northeast to Bowling Green and pick up U.S. 301 north across the Rappahannock and Potomac Rivers and into Maryland. Expect a twenty-mile stretch of stop-and-go traffic around Waldorf, Md. The road merges with U.S. 50 east twelve miles west of Annapolis.

If you want to visit the Northern Neck, take U.S. 301 until it intersects with Va. Rte. 3. Bear right on U.S. 360 to Reedville, or stay on Va. Rte. 3 to Kilmarnock.

If you're headed to Southern Maryland, cross into the state on Rte. 301 from the only bridge downriver from Washington, D.C. About twenty-five miles later, Md. 234 connects to Md. 5 south to Leonardtown and St. Mary's City, from which you can wend your way up the Bay on Md. Rtes. 235, 4, and 2 past Solomons and Prince Frederick to Annapolis.

Travel Tips for Drivers

Circumnavigating Washington, D.C.: Washington's famed **Capital Beltway** is more than a political concept for the pundits. It's the major artery circling the city. The eastern half of the elliptical roadway is known as I-95 north and south — even as it proceeds east and west. The western half is called I-495. Travelers headed clockwise will find the road referred to as west, north, and east. Locals refer to the clockwise lanes as the Beltway's "inner loop," the counterclockwise route is known as the "outer loop." It's often crowded, even when it's not rush hour.

Meanwhile, an anachronism rules the Beltway's southeastern corner — a draw-bridge. The **Woodrow Wilson Memorial Bridge** across the Potomac, while offering a spectacular view of the river, opens occasionally, so travelers weary of the highway may want to avoid the possibility. Construction of a replacement is under way. **Baltimore's Harbor Tunnel** can get backed up during rush hour or the weekend rush to the Atlantic beaches. To bypass, take I-695 east to the **Francis Scott Key Bridge**. The trip is a bit longer, but the view is much better. And as long as we're talking summer weekends, consider crossing the William Preston Lane Memorial Bridge (aka the **Bay Bridge**) at Rte. 50 near Annapolis sometime other than east-bound at 5 pm on a Friday in July, or westbound at 4pm on a Sunday in August. Construction on the Bay Bridge will mean off-season or nighttime closures (although not on summer weekend nights) until 2006. No daytime lane closures in summer.

For information call 877-229-7726 or visit www.mdtransportation authority.com.

BY TRAIN

Amtrak's classic train stations operate in fully renovated pre-World War II-era elegance: In Baltimore, Pennsylvania Station (1500 N. Charles St.), and in Washington, Union Station (Massachusetts & Louisiana Aves.). Amtrak also operates a rail station at BWI Airport, a short ride from the terminal, on the line connecting Washington, D.C. and Baltimore (800-USA-RAIL; www.amtrak.com).

GETTING AROUND THE CHESAPEAKE BAY AREA

BY BUS

The Washington Greyhound terminal (202-289-5154; www.greyhound.com) is located at 1005 First St. NE. To get from Washington, D.C. to Annapolis, board the Washington Metro at Union Station, ride the Red Line to Metro Center, change to the Orange Line, and head for New Carrollton, Md. During the workweek, take the Dillon Bus Service commuter bus into Annapolis (800-827-3490, 410-647-2321). From Baltimore's bus station at 210 W. Fayette St. (410-752-7682), find Trailways connections to the Eastern Shore. For Greyhound schedules and fares: 800-231-2222, or 800-229-9424 English, 800-531-5332 Spanish; www.grey hound.com.

Maps

Virginia and Maryland offer among the best maps, gratis, which highlight scenic routes or historical tidbits. Pick up the Maryland Dept. of Transportation's highway or scenic routes map by contacting: MD DOT State Hwy. Admin., 410-545-8747; 707 N. Calvert St., Baltimore, MD 21202, or the MD Office of Tourism Development, 800-543-1036, 410-767-3400; 217 E. Redwood St., Baltimore, MD 21201.

Virginia's Dept. of Transportation also gives away a very detailed highway map. Contact: VDOT Admin. Services Division, 804-786-2801; 1401 E. Broad St., Richmond, VA 23219.

For a few well-spent dollars, you can also buy an excellent map of the Chesapeake Bay region that includes historic markers and eliminates the need to switch maps if you cross state lines. The Alexandria Drafting Co., aka ADC Maps, puts out this gem that's available at area stores. Or buy directly from the company: ADC Maps, 800-232-6277; 6440 General Green Way, Alexandria, VA 22312.

Maryland

Greyhound offers daily service from Baltimore and Washington, D.C. to Easton (410-822-3333; Rte. 50 at Cordova Rd.), Cambridge (410-228-5825; 2903 Ocean Gateway Dr.), and Salisbury (410-749-4121; 350 Cypress St.). The Baltimore to Salisbury run operates five times a day. For fare and schedule information on public bus service around Annapolis, contact the city's Department of Public Transportation, 410-263-7964.

Virginia

Trailways makes three trips a day from Norfolk to Exmore, on Virginia's Eastern Shore, and back again, and four trips daily on Fri. and Sun. Contact

Greyhound-Trailways at 757-625-7500; 701 Monticello Ave., Norfolk, VA 23501. For municipal service around Virginia's Urban Tidewater (Hampton-Newport News-Norfolk), Hampton Roads Transit offers service throughout the region. Call 757-222-6100.

BY CAR

To ease confusion for road trippers: U.S. 301 runs north-south from the Potomac River to U.S. 50 at Bowie, Md., where it turns east with U.S. 50. The northbound road becomes Md. Rte. 3 to Baltimore. South of the Potomac toll bridge, Rte. 301 traverses Virginia's northern Tidewater area to Richmond. Drive southeast along intersecting Va. Rte. 3 or Rte. 17.

David Trozzo

George Stubbs tends the drawbridge at Georgetown on Route 213 in the Upper Eastern Shore, one of several drawbridges throughout Bay Country.

U.S. 50, meanwhile, is the eastbound thoroughfare from Washington, D.C. toward Annapolis, and picks up a Rte. 50/301 designation at Bowie. Soon after crossing onto the Eastern Shore, the road splits. Rte. 50 heads south, providing the Shore's major north-south artery, then east after crossing the Choptank

River at Cambridge. North of the split, Rte. 301 goes solo again past the far Upper Eastern Shore. U.S. 13 is the other major north-south highway on the Shore, running all the way up Virginia's Eastern Shore from the Chesapeake Bay Bridge-Tunnel at Kiptopeke, through the middle of Maryland's Lower Shore, and up the Delmarva Peninsula through Delaware.

BY RENTAL CAR

If you failed to pick up a car at the airport and need one once you arrive in Chesapeake Country, here are some local offices.

ANNAPOLIS/WESTERN SHORE

Budget (410-266-5030; 2002 West St., Annapolis).
Enterprise (410-268-7751; 1023 Spa Rd., Annapolis; or 410-224-2940; 913-A Commerce Rd., Annapolis).
Hertz (301-863-0033; 22711 Three Notch Road, Lexington Park).

LOWER EASTERN SHORE

Avis (Salisbury-Ocean City, Md.: 410-742-8566; Wicomico Regional Airport).
Hertz (Salisbury-Ocean City, Md.: 410-749-2235; Wicomico Regional Airport).
U-Save (410-957-1421; 1727 Market St., Pocomoke City, Md.).

BY FERRY

The 300-year-old ferryboat tradition remains in this region of snaking rivers, creeks, and you-can't-get-there-from-here roadways. For assistance, check your maps or ask around for exact locations of these low-load ferries suited to the moseying motorist.

NORTHERN NECK/MIDDLE PENINSULA

Merry Point Ferry (804-333-3696) The Merry Point, in Lancaster County, offers trips across the Corrotoman River. Free. Except for extreme high tides/bad weather, open year-round, Mon.–Sat. 7–7.
Sunnybank Ferry (804-333-3696) Near Smith Point at the mouth of the Potomac River in Northumberland County, this small ferry crosses the Little Wicomico River at Ophelia. Free. Except for extreme high tides/bad weather, open year-round, Mon.–Sat. 7–7.

MIDDLE EASTERN SHORE

David Trozzo

The famed Oxford-Bellevue Ferry, sentimental favorite on the Middle Eastern Shore.

Oxford-Bellevue Ferry (410-745-9023; www.oxfordmd.com/obf) The oldest, continuously operating private ferry in the country was launched on November 20, 1683, allowing easy access between Oxford and St. Michaels in Talbot County. Open March through November. (June–Labor Day, Mon.–Fri. 7am–9pm; Sat.–Sun. 9–9; remaining months, Mon.–Fri. 7–sunset, Sat.–Sun. 9–sunset) Car and driver: $5.50 one-way; $9 round-trip; $.50 each passenger each way. Bicycles: $2.50 one-way; $4 round-trip. Walk-ons: $1.25. Closed Dec.–Feb.

LOWER EASTERN SHORE

Whitehaven Ferry (410-548-4873) This tiny ferry crosses the scenic Wicomico River about eighteen miles southwest of Salisbury on Rte. 352. Free. Open year-round, 6am–7:30pm in summer, 7–6 in winter. Also in Wicomico: the **Upper Ferry** (410-334-2798). Free. Open year-round, 6am–7:30pm in summer; 7–6 in winter.

Several ferries also operate out of Crisfield to Smith and Tangier Islands. Check full listings in the Smith and Tangier Islands section of Chapter 6, *The Lower Eastern Shore.* For year-round service to Smith Island (for adventurers only; be sure that you've arranged accommodations in advance if you intend to stay overnight), contact *Captain Jason I* and *II* (410-425-4471, 410-425-5931).

CHAPTER THREE
A Capital Destination
ANNAPOLIS

Sailboats vie for first place in Annapolis Harbor during summer's Wednesday night races.

On a clear day in early September, station yourself near City Dock and look out to the water. White sails catch the wind on a gentle breeze. Or go to nearby Sand Point State Park Bayside, to watch sailboats and power boats, or huge container ships, pushing through the channel. For all the historic charm of this 300-year-old capital city, its downtown clustered with good restaurants, fun shops, and, no doubt, the house you wish you owned, it's these sparkly days that make folks fall in love with Annapolis.

Clean, waterfront light shines briskly from the top of Duke of Gloucester Street, only steps from where the first colonial capitol building was constructed. That came in 1699, soon after royal governor Francis Nicholson moved the seat of government north from St. Marys City on the Potomac to this town along the Severn River, and built the Baroque-style streets early colonists would easily recognize today. From these early beginnings spring tales of patriots passing through Annapolis, where Maryland's four signers of the Declaration of Independence owned homes that still stand. Three remain open to the public. For a brief time — November 1783 to August 1784 — Annapolis served as the new nation's capital city. In the current Statehouse, George Washington resigned his commission from the Continental Army, and patriots signed the Treaty of Paris, which ended the Revolutionary War.

Evidence of the city's colonial and post-colonial Golden Age remains. St. John's College, the intellectual home of the "Great Books" program, descends from King William's School, founded in 1696. This makes St. John's the nation's third-oldest school after the College of William & Mary and Harvard University. Benjamin Franklin sent cousin Jonas Green from Philadelphia to become the city's printer in 1738; visitors seeking true colonial accommodations can stay in his house, now a B&B operated by direct descendants. It's considered one of the two oldest houses in this city of old houses, where Colonial Georgian, Federal, and even Greek Revival structures line the streets. By 1845, the U.S. Naval Academy was established, renewed by stunning Beaux Arts buildings after the Civil War — during which the academy and St. John's College were taken over as hospitals.

Recent times have brought the sailors and the city refugees who may get to the office aboard a daily commuter bus that takes workers into Washington, D.C., only 40 or so traffic-free minutes away. State legislators continue to bring present-day politicking to this Chesapeake city, and residents fill the Historic District's old homes — just note the two-hour parking zones, and pay heed.

Across the Spa Creek Bridge from Annapolis sits the maritime area of Eastport, giving working credence to the city's claim of "America's Sailing Capital." The city annexed this former workingman's neighborhood decades back. From yacht brokers and other boating industry businesses on the far side of Spa Creek has come a fine group of restaurants — perhaps the city's reliably best —and plans for a maritime museum.

Take a walking tour of the Historic District or Eastport (signs posted throughout the district direct walkers), although neither takes in all of Annapolis, which increasingly sprawls outward from its colonial Severn River start.

Also: parking in the city is notoriously difficult; ask your innkeeper for assistance. If the parking garages in town have filled up, parking at the Navy-Marine Corps Memorial Stadium on Rowe Blvd. costs $3 on weekdays, $4 on weekends. Pay between 7am and 5pm. Shuttle service into town Apr. 1–Oct. 31, Mon.–Fri. 6:30–8, Sat. & Sun. 10–6 (FYI — it's an easy mile-long walk into town).

Visitors to Annapolis also should check the Middle Eastern Shore chapter of this book for ideas for exploring, including Kent Island. Closely associated with the Eastern Shore, the island is but a quick hop across the Chesapeake Bay Bridge.

LODGING

Members of the Annapolis Bed and Breakfast Association (www.annapolis bandb.com) have worked out a half-price discount deal for parking in city garages. You can't come and go during the period without repaying, but it's easiest to walk the Historic District anyway. Many good B&Bs are not association members, but those that are refer to member establishments. In addition, Annapolis Accommodations, Inc. operates as a reservations service for hotels, inns, vacation homes, and B&Bs: 410-263-3262, 800-715-1000, or www. stayannapolis.com.

Lodging prices often vary from weekend to weekday, and according to the time of year. We've done our best to give you an idea of costs, but please check, as they are likely to change. In addition, check on cancellation policies, as most inns and B&Bs have them. Also, unless noted, smoking and pets are prohibited. Ask about other policies that can change. Prices range as follows:

Inexpensive: Up to $75
Moderate: $76 to $120
Expensive: $121 to $150
Very Expensive: Over $150

Credit card abbreviations are: AE, American Express; CB, Carte Blanche; D, Discover; DC, Diner's Club; MC, MasterCard; V, Visa.

1908 WILLIAM PAGE INN
Owner: Robert Zuchelli.
800-364-4160, 410-626-1506.
www.williampageinn.com.
8 Martin St., Annapolis, MD 21401.
Price: Expensive to Very Expensive.
Credit Cards: MC, V.
Handicap Access: No.
Restrictions: No children under 12.

Well located on a quiet street just around the corner from the Historic District's hustle and bustle, this shingled, 1908 house offers five rooms. They include the Marilyn Suite on the top floor, with a big sitting area and TV. Two rooms share a bath (robes supplied), and two others have their own, including one with a whirlpool. While reproductions and antiques add flavor to the turn-of-the-century, cedar-shingled home, they don't clutter. For a treat, ask for the private Fern Room, which opens onto the wraparound porch. Zuchelli, long active in the local B&B industry, opened the inn in the mid-1980s and knows how to run a classy operation, providing luxury and privacy without a fuss. Off-street parking; full breakfast.

ANNAPOLIS INN
Innkeepers: Joe Lespier and Alex De Vivo.
410-295-5200.

It's hard to overstate the upscale level of Cupid-and-Psyche romance at this renovated 1770s home. Gilded rosette moldings crown the down-

www.annapolisinn.com.
144 Prince George St.,
  Annapolis, MD 21401.
Price: Very Expensive.
Credit Cards: AE, MC, V.
Handicap Access: No.
Restrictions: No guests
  under 18.

stairs salons, and etched glass doors separate bedroom from sitting room in an upstairs suite. King-sized beds are dressed up in the finest cotton linens; tapestries hang from walls; and French and English reproductions or antiques furnish the house. Three accommodations total include the Murray Suite, which has a heated marble bathroom floor, and the third-floor room, with its bath of three kinds of marble, remote-controlled whirlpool tub, and easy access to the roof deck. Breakfast starts at 8am. This one-time home to a doctor to Thomas Jefferson fills a top-tier niche in this luxe city's growing diversity of B&Bs. Plan to tuck in to a pampered good time.

**ANNAPOLIS MARRIOTT
  WATERFRONT**
800-336-0072, 410-268-7555.
80 Compromise St.,
  Annapolis, MD 21401.
Price: Very Expensive.
Credit Cards: AE, D, DC,
  MC, V.
Handicap Access: Yes.
Special Features: Smoking
  rooms available.

This hotel offers an Annapolis commodity: the Historic District's only waterfront rooms, with views over mast-filled Spa Creek and out to the Severn River. A total of 150 rooms include water and city views, with irons, cable TV, hair dryers and coffeemakers. Valet parking costs $12 per night. Room rates are based on whether or not there's a water view. Suites, king-sized beds, a small on-site fitness room, and concierge service are available. Visitors also will find a fine location for a cold one at Pusser's Landing, a pub right on the waters of Ego Alley, so named for the parade of boaters showing off their craft.

**THE BARN ON
  HOWARD'S COVE**
Innkeepers: Graham and
  Mary Gutsche.
410-571-9511.
www.bnbweb.com/
  Howards-Cove.html.
500 Wilson Rd., Annapolis,
  MD 21401.
Price: Expensive.
Credit Cards: No; personal
  checks OK.
Handicap Access: No.

Ordinarily, we skip accommodations offering only two rooms — even if one is a suite. However, the Barn on Howard's Cove is a particular find for many reasons. You can bring the kids (even infants!), park easily just two miles outside the Historic District, and, best of all, put a canoe or kayak in a Chesapeake tributary on the property. Plus, the place is a good value. Your hosts have renovated this waterside 1850s barn to ensure a lovely year-round view out to Howard's Cove, and the rooms, with quilts and floral wallpaper, are very comfortable. One large room, one suite with sitting room, and amenities such as VCRs and ceiling fans. An excellent choice for families. Full breakfast. A country feel with comfy grounds.

CHEZ AMIS
Owners: Don & Mickie
　Deline.
888-224-6455, 410-263-6631.
www.chezamis.com.
85 East St., Annapolis, MD
　21401.
Price: Expensive to Very
　Expensive.
Credit Cards: MC, V.
Handicap Access: No.
Restrictions: No children
　under 10.

This cute and cozy former corner store comes with a pressed-tin roof downstairs and breakfast at the Stammtisch, named for the German table where family and friends gather. Four rooms in all start with a downstairs suite (king-sized bed and trundle bed) suitable for a family. Upstairs, the Capital Room salutes both the Maryland Statehouse visible out the window and the nation's capital, where Mickie was once a tour guide (husband Don was a longtime Army lawyer). Photos of politicians line the walls, just as judge's photos hold forth in the Judge's Chambers — where guests can sleep in a queen-sized sleigh bed. The smaller red, white, and blue Captain's Quarters is the only room whose private bath requires a brief trip down the hall; the others are attached to the guest rooms. A kind of nook-and-cranny quality marks the two-toned, rose-colored house, with its collection of bunnies and bears and a handmade quilt hanging from the stairwell wall.

**THE DOLLS' HOUSE BED
　& BREAKFAST**
Owners: Barbara & John
　Dugan.
410-626-2028.
www.annapolis.net/dolls
　house.
61 Green St., Annapolis,
　MD 21401.
Price: Expensive.
Credit Cards: No.
Handicap Access: No.
Restrictions: No children
　under 6.

If it's high Victorian you're after, you can't do better than this classic, trimmed out in tiger oak and home to innkeeper Barbara Dugan's extensive collection of dolls — which means the frat crowd might want to stay elsewhere. Three suites make this a good bargain for traveling companions; sitting rooms are separate in two while the third, the Master Suite, divides its sitting room and bedrooms via the boxed-in chimney. TVs are in the sitting rooms, and each suite comes with an attached bath. Great fun is the Victoria Suite featuring Queen Victoria in print, while upstairs is the ultra-eaved Nutcracker Suite, with two double beds in a large bedroom and a pullout couch in the comfortable sitting room. Add the big bath with its long claw-foot tub and stall shower, and this is one of the city's best options for families with older children (per-person charges for more than two). Out back, relax under the magnolia and enjoy this shaded garden retreat just a short block from the City Dock bustle. Churchill the collie is sociably in residence.

**EASTPORT HOUSE BED
　AND BREAKFAST**
Host: Susan Denis.
410-295-9710.
www.eastporthouse.com.
101 Severn Ave., Annapolis,
　MD 21403.

Looking to Orvis, or maybe L.L. Bean for inspiration, this recently renovated house one block from the water in the Eastport maritime neighborhood creates a clean Chesapeake theme with rooms to match: The Fish Room, The Duck (not decoy) Room, The Captain's Quarters, The Sailboat Room,

Eastport House B&B sits one block from the water in Annapolis' Eastport maritime district.

David Trozzo

Price: Moderate to Expensive.
Credit Cards: No; personal checks OK.
Handicap Access: No.
Restrictions: No children under 8.

and The Maryland Blue Crab Room. The Captain's Quarters may be the most muted, with white and blue accenting original 1860s floors. The Duck Room comes in green and white, replete with a half-canoe shelf, while wooden Costa Rican fish mark their namesake room. TVs in some rooms, guest refrigerator, and a nice backyard porch. Breakfast is served at the oak dining table. All rooms have attached baths except for the two on the uppermost floor (with a sink in each), which makes this a good choice for traveling companions. Street parking.

55 EAST
Innkeepers: Tricia & Mat Herban.
410-295-0202.
http://annearundelcounty.com/hotel/55east.htm.
55 East St., Annapolis, MD 21401.
Price: Expensive.
Credit Cards: MC, V.
Handicap Access: No.
Restrictions: No children under 12.

"Handsome" leaps to mind to describe this tucked-away B&B, which manages to marry worldly aplomb with enough tradition so you'll still know that you're in the cradle of the nation's colonial history. Guests can relax and listen to music or watch TV in two classic downstairs parlor areas, including one painted the most enviously adventuresome color of blue-green you ever saw. Out French doors stands a treat: a New Orleans-inspired courtyard, with a handmade brick fountain and roses blooming in pots. A second-floor balcony overlooks the scene, accessible from two guest rooms. In all, three rooms come with either queen beds or a king that converts to twins, and attached baths — two with full-body spray showers. The rooms are uncluttered, with original drawings or Vermont Casting stoves, and cedar suit hangers in the closets. Breakfast is served on china and crystal. Sophisticated, upscale taste.

Flags from the home country or state of its guests fly from the Flag House B&B's front porch in the thick of the Annapolis Historic District.

David Trozzo

FLAG HOUSE INN
Owners: Charlotte & Bill
    Schmickle.
410-280-2721, 800-437-4825.
www.flaghouseinn.com.
26 Randall St., Annapolis,
    MD 21401.
Price: Very Expensive
Credit Cards: MC, V.
Handicap Access: No.
Restrictions: No children
    under 10.

Located less than a block from the U.S. Naval Academy's main gate, the Flag House offers a central location and sociable innkeepers who have sent a son through the academy. The Schmickles also have recently redone the public rooms in this five-guest-room gem in clubby, comfortable style. Four round rust-leather chairs cluster around a parlor table, with yachting and arts magazines stacked alongside. Guests will find the rooms quite comfortable, with quilts covering the king-sized beds, TVs, and European-style split bathrooms in some. A two-room suite may suit families, and for a fun and different choice, ask for the gorgeous purple toile wallpapered room. A friendly industriousness seems to be at work here; last time we pulled out of the driveway, Bill was adjusting the clever irrigation system he'd created for the plants that hang from the wide front porch, where the state or national flag of each guest in residence flies. Full breakfast is served in the dining room downstairs. Off-street parking.

HARBOR VIEW INN
Innkeepers: Andrea and
    Chuck Manfredonia.
410-626-9802.
www.harborviewinnof
    annapolis.com.
1 St. Mary's St., Annapolis,
    MD 21404.
Price: Expensive to Very
    Expensive.

A wide-open contemporary home hides behind the gray siding and bright blue shutters of this downtown B&B. The architectural detail here is terrific. An oval opening cuts through the tiled foyer leading to a second-floor guest room, allowing even more light to filter downstairs. Three rooms are in residence here, two with patios and two with attached baths. A cobal-blue-highlighted room, with

Credit Cards: No. Personal checks OK.
Handicap Access: No.
Restrictions: No children under 14.

a built-in wainscoted "headboard" and deck looking toward the water is a favorite, and guests need only step briefly into the hall to reach the accompanying bath. The gardens out back change with the seasons, and you can hide from life in a hammock tucked into a far, shaded corner. A change from much of what you'll find in the Historic District, the Harbor View harbors nary an Oriental rug.

HISTORIC INNS OF ANNAPOLIS
Owned by Remington Hotels.
800-847-8882, 410-263-2641.
www.annapolisinns.com.
58 State Circle, Annapolis, MD 21401.
Price: Expensive to Very Expensive.
Credit Cards: AE, DC, MC, V.
Handicap Access: Yes.
Special Features: Smoking rooms available; valet parking; includes the Maryland Inn, Governor Calvert House, and Robert Johnson House.

With three inns set on two circles, the historic inns create a unique setup. No matter where you're staying, you'll check in at the Governor Calvert House on State Circle, directly across from the Statehouse. Management does its best to efficiently shepherd guests through the process, down to a valet in a minivan to take you to your room. Guests may request a favorite inn, although it's possible the inns may not be able to comply. In all, 124 rooms are available, and each is different. The 1720 Governor Calvert House is the most modern of the three, given an extensive 1983 renovation. Archaeologists discovered a 1730 hypocaust, a central heating system originally engineered by the Romans, now preserved in a Plexiglas-covered floor. The Robert Johnson House is probably the quietest inn. The Maryland Inn, part of which dates to the pre-Revolutionary era, started life as an inn in 1784 and remained so until a post-World War I hiatus as an office/apartment complex. Visitors will find a concierge to answer questions or to redirect them for check-in. The Maryland Inn is a sentimental favorite among many Annapolitans and visitors, with its jazz club, the King of France Tavern, and the Treaty of Paris restaurant. Renovations slated for 2002 promise a face-lift (including upgraded bathrooms). At about the same time, a designation of Historic Inns as a Crown Plaza is planned.

JONAS GREEN HOUSE
Owners: Randy and Dede Brown.
410-263-5892.
www.jonasgreenhouse.com.
124 Charles St., Annapolis, MD 21401.
Price: Moderate to Expensive.
Credit Cards: AE, D, MC, V.

Stand in the nineteenth-century dining room and look back through the eighteenth-century hallway that connects to the seventeenth-century kitchen: this house is the genuine article for visitors seeking colonial accommodations. Widely considered one of the two oldest homes in Annapolis, the Jonas Green House is operated by its namesake's great-great-great-great-great-grandson and wife. Green himself was the colony's printer, taught the

Handicap Access: No.
Special Features: Children and pets allowed with prior notice.

trade by cousin Ben Franklin. The current owners renovated the old house in the early 1990s and can offer complete tours to architecture buffs. The home's décor is carefully reproduced, with white walls and colonial wainscoting. Three guest rooms offer antique beds with modern, custom-made mattresses and spare, period accents — like a spinning wheel in one room. Pine floors and fireplaces in each room, full breakfasts in the morning. Easygoing, uncluttered atmosphere; off-street parking, and a short walk to the thick of the Historic District's offerings.

LOEWS ANNAPOLIS HOTEL
General Manager: Terri Ryan.
800-526-2593, 410-263-7777.
www.loewsannapolis.com.
126 West St., Annapolis, MD 21401.
Price: Moderate to Very Expensive.
Credit Cards: AE, D, DC, MC, V.
Handicap Access: Yes.
Special Features: Smoking- and pets-allowed rooms available.

Considered perhaps the city's finest hotel, Loews provides all of the amenities in a brick courtyard-style hotel located just blocks from the Historic District. A total of 217 guest rooms and suites offer it all, with mini-bars, fax machines, hypo-allergenic pillows, fresh-smelling herbal bath amenities, and a spare phone in the bathroom. Rooms are comfortable and handsome, with coordinated earth tone bedding and window treatments. Terraces open onto two upper floors. A wide range of services includes child care, complimentary van service (probably a good idea at night), a fitness room, and lounge. Plans to update the restaurant in 2002 include regional cuisine served at an establishment called Breeze. Valet parking costs $13 per night; self-parking is $10 per night. Lovely meeting and party spaces, include those in the complex's brick Powerhouse Conference Center. Ideal for visitors seeking well-located lodgings with all the amenities.

SCHOONER WOODWIND
Innkeepers: Ken and Ellen Kaye.
410-263-8619.
www.schooner-woodwind.com.
P.O. Box 3254, Annapolis, MD 21403.
Available Fri. & Sat., early May–late Sept.
Price: Very Expensive.
Credit Cards: AE, D, MC, V.
Handicap Access: No.
Restrictions: No children under 16.

Sleep aboard the Schooner *Woodwind* and see what it's like to wake up with the sun peeking through the porthole. The boat stays docked at its berth alongside the Annapolis Waterfront Marriott through the night. Guests will share heads (aka bathrooms), and those in the two forwardmost cabins can even open the hatch. Double berths; breakfast on deck. A two-hour sail goes along with your stay; please discuss times with the boat's operators. A captain and crew member are on-board with you.

TWO-O-ONE BED AND BREAKFAST
Innkeepers: Graham Gardner and Robert A. Bryant.
410-268-8053.
www.201bb.com.
201 Prince George St., Annapolis, MD 21401.
Price: Expensive to Very Expensive.
Credit Cards: AE, D, MC, V.
Handicap Access: No.
Restrictions: No children.

This elegant Georgian home, furnished with English and American period antiques, also comes with a surprisingly large yard for the Historic District. Your hosts have beautifully landscaped this back area, creating garden rooms large enough to offer a measure of privacy to their guests. Expect this same sensibility to extend to the guest rooms, which are spacious and comfortable and come with enough towels to last the weekend. Four suites total, including two with whirlpool tubs. Fun antique finds include a "Beau Brummel," which is, essentially, a vanity for gentlemen of a certain era, which came from Pickfair. This well-located B&B offers a full breakfast and on-site parking. Two dogs live here as well.

RESTAURANTS

From the colonial taverns ringing City Dock to more adventurous Pacific Rim cuisine in well-appointed bistros, Annapolis offers a range of restaurants. An Irish invasion has left three Irish pubs in town, and steak-lovers hungering for a clubby atmosphere, New York strip, and a hearty glass of good red wine won't be disappointed. While crab cakes aplenty (and crab imperial, or crab dip — best served on French bread) show up on local menus, those with a hankerin' for hard-shell crabs spilled across brown-paper-lined tables will find their best bets are just outside town.

Restaurant pricing follows this range for entrée, appetizer and dessert:

Inexpensive: Up to $15
Moderate: $15–25
Expensive: $25–$35
Very Expensive: Over $35

Credit card abbreviations are: AE, American Express; CB, Carte Blanche; D, Discover; DC, Diner's Club; MC, MasterCard; V, Visa.

Annapolis

AQUA TERRA
410-263-1985.
164 Main St.
Open: Daily.

Ask the downtown locals where they eat these days, and you're likely to hear about Aqua Terra. Focused on fashionable world-beat Pan-

Price: Expensive.
Cuisine: New American/
  Asian Fusion.
Serving: L Wed.–Sun.; D
  daily.
Credit Cards: AE, MC, V.
Reservations: Yes.
Handicap Access: Yes.

Asian food and looks, the restaurant nevertheless makes sensible use of its storefront quarters. The old-fashioned pressed-tin roof matches the grayish slate-blue walls, creating stylish uniformity. Two window areas jut out toward the street. But better than its looks, the restaurant's food is terrific, a nice change of local pace. For summer, pan-seared tuna over couscous with tropical veggies and plantain, a tuna tartar appetizer, and — for the A+, another appetizer, arborio-crusted oysters served over a honey lime barbecue with fermented black beans — made for a fine dinner. We were only sorry we couldn't make room for Kobi beef. A nice by-the-glass wine list is priced in the $5–$8 range, and the brief dessert menu leans on ice cream, cheesecake, and a crème brûlée touched with lavender. In addition, there's a healthy list of apres-dinner drinks, including a decent selection of single-malt Scotches. Candles flicker between the mirrors lining one wall, while the chefs sear tunas and blow-torch crème brûlées behind a counter in the open kitchen across the room. Service is prompt, friendly, and nonintrusive.

CAFÉ GURUS
410-295-0601.
601 Second St. in the
  Eastport district.
Open: Daily 7-5.
Price: Inexpensive.
Cuisine: Light Fare.
Serving: B, L.
Credit Cards: AE, MC, V.
Reservations: No.
Handicap Access: No (stairs
  into the building).

Ready for a break from the tourist life? Check out Café Gurus, ensconced in a far corner of the down-home but yachty Eastport district and serving great coffee and creative wraps, soups, salads, and sandwiches. Ingredients are fresh, the price is right, and you can easily park on the street if you've opted not to stroll. Opens at 7am for folks in search of an early-morning "red sunrise wrap" (a sun-dried tomato tortilla rolled with scrambled eggs, red peppers, tomatoes, cheddar, provolone, and salsa), but don't forget it for lunch. Occasional Sat. evening performances by local musicians.

CAFÉ NORMANDIE
410-263-3382.
185 Main St.
Open: Daily.
Price: Moderate to
  Expensive.
Cuisine: French.
Serving: L, D.
Credit Cards: AE, D, DC,
  MC, V.
Reservations:
  Recommended on
  weekends.
Handicap Access: Yes.

Long before the word "Provence" appeared on best-seller titles, Café Normandie was delivering country-French style to upper Main Street. Wood-backed booths downstairs look to a fireplace, and a row of tables upstairs peers out over the street. The menu caters to different tastes, offering higher-priced entrées (filet mignon, veal) for serious appetites and a good selection of moderately priced meals for those who want less. Portions are plentiful. The Caesar salad here is one of the city's best, and the crepe selection is legendary, delivered in regular or buckwheat batter and served with a good-sized side salad of fresh greens. Like so many restaurants in town, Café Normandie names one of its signature dishes for its locale (even though none of the ingredients are local to the Bay): the Annapolis Crepe, at $10.95, rolls shrimp, scallops, mushrooms, and dill into a tasty lobster sauce, big enough to microwave for lunch the next day.

Steamed crabs at Cantler's Riverside Inn in Annapolis: a must-do summertime tradition.

David Trozzo

CANTLER'S RIVERSIDE INN
410-757-1467.
458 Forest Beach Rd.
Open: Daily.
Price: Inexpensive to Very Expensive.
Cuisine: Seafood.
Serving: L, D.
Credit Cards: AE, D, DC, MC, V.
Reservations: No.
Handicap Access: Limited; not to bathrooms.

Nobody comes to Annapolis for corned beef. You want to pick steamed Maryland blue crabs, right? Family owned and operated, Cantler's, a twisting ride out of town, is located on scenic Mill Creek, and rakes in awards year after year. Have it your way: hot from the pot and laden with spices, as a soft-shell sandwich, mixed with seasoning and filler in a crab cake (sandwich or platter), or stuffed in your favorite fish. Despite scanty harvests and escalating prices (up to $45 for a dozen large in 2001), visitors from all over the world hunker down with mallet and knife at these famed paper-covered tables, both indoors and out. Which explains the backup waiting to get into the parking lot. You'd think this place was a religious shrine. For many, it is. And, for the few who don't eat crabmeat, there's fresh fish, fried shrimp and chicken, light fare, even hamburgers and hot dogs. We must warn you, however: ordering the last two at Cantler's might land you in jail. If you've got kids in tow, walk down to the dock to see the peeler crabs and the diamondback tortoise nursery. Try to come on a weekday or at off times on weekends and holidays. For directions: www.cantlers.com.

CARROL'S CREEK CAFÉ
410-263-8102.
410 Severn Ave., Annapolis
  City Marina.
Open: Daily.
Price: Moderate to
  Expensive.
Cuisine: Seafood/New
  Cuisine.
Serving: L, D, SB.
Credit Cards: AE, D, MC, V.
Reservations: Accepted Fri.
  night, Sat. & Sun., and
  Wed. in summer.
Handicap Access: Yes.
Special Features: Waterside
  deck and view.

From its menu staples to its sleek blond-wood dining room on Spa Creek, Carrol's Creek has been known over the years for easy parking, one of the city's best restaurant water views, a good glass of wine, and a nice meal. The menu is solid and always good, featuring favorite fish such as rockfish or mahi-mahi, the first over polenta and the second encrusted with macadamia nuts, served in loop-de-loop presentations. Seafood-lovers should consider the menu's crab and Bay dinners, worthy bacchanals of Bay bounty, the first with cream of crab soup, a salad, fat lump crab cakes, and dessert; the second with the soup, salad, a rockfish, and dessert. A back room (no water view) seats the Sat. overflow. The outdoor deck is the place to watch the Wednesday night sailboat races.

CHICK AND RUTH'S DELLY
410-269-6737.
165 Main St.
Open: Daily, except
  Thanksgiving and
  Christmas.
Price: Inexpensive.
Cuisine: American/Kosher-
  style.
Serving: B, L, D.
Credit Cards: No.
Reservations: No.
Handicap Access: Limited.

Check out the Formica décor and dip into the kosher pickles at this centrally located Annapolis institution where state politicians, locals, and out-of-towners all come to sample the diner food, reasonable prices and ambiance that hasn't changed a whit since Chick & Ruth's opened in 1965. Celebrity photos blanket the walls and, yes, those are bagel light pulls. Comfort is the operative word here, as in comfort food served in *comfort*able surroundings. Fall into the delly for the breakfast platters, served all day, with delly fries. The peppery, onion-laden potatoes (actually home fries) are among the best we've ever tasted. Maybe you prefer your potatoes French-fried or mashed and swimming in gravy. Come here also for the homemade soups, hamburgers, and generous sandwiches named for state lawmakers. When in doubt, go for the No. 1, the Main Street — corned beef, coleslaw, and Russian dressing on rye. You'll need a bath when you finish, or at least a moist towelette. The soda fountain drinks are treats indeed. Slurp a milkshake or malted, or spoon a sundae or banana split. The waitstaff is cheeky and pleasant, if slow at times. Kid-sized portions, with appropriately adjusted prices, are available for rugrats. For the most part, the prices are more reflective of the "Leave it to Beaver" era than the new millennium. In most cases, you can eat for less than $10. Expect a line on weekends, especially for breakfast, when locals and boaters join owner Ted Levitt in the Pledge of Allegiance at 9:30am. Weekdays, when the politicians and tourists are in town, make that 8:30.

GALWAY BAY IRISH RESTAURANT AND PUB
410-263-8333.
61-63 Maryland Ave.
Open: Daily.
Price: Moderate.
Cuisine: Authentic Irish.
Serving: L, D, SB.
Credit Cards: AE, D, DC, MC, V.
Handicap Access: Yes.

L et it be noted at the outset that this is *not* some generic, prefabricated, faux-Irish theme eatery concocted to capitalize on Celtic Chic. With Galway Bay, Annapolis is lucky to have a warm and welcoming establishment as authentically Irish as anything this side of County Cork. The owner-manager, the affable Michael Galway, is a recent emigre from Erin's lovely shore, as is his entire top management staff. Since it opened in 1998, Galway Bay has garnered regional awards as well as a devoted, repeat-business following. Its popularity can be attributed both to atmosphere and cuisine. The feeling is inviting and evocative: exposed brick walls, a high ceiling, vintage Irish art and soft strains of Irish music put you right in the mood. The menu sports a handsome array of great Hibernian fare, both no-frills and fancy. Starters include Oysters O'Reilly (a flavorful way to enjoy a regional favorite), cockles and mussels (naturally), and charbroiled lamb tenderloin marinated in Guinness Stout. Whatever choices one makes, however, any meal here should begin with a sampling of the hearty, therapeutic potato-and-leek soup, and a basket of Galway Bay's famous soda bread, homemade from coarse whole-meal flour imported from Ireland. For the main course, all of Ireland's greatest hits — corned beef and cabbage, shepherd's pie, Irish stew, fish and chips, etc. — are prepared here in expert fashion. Higher-end offerings include chicken breast Cashel blue, pork tenderloin Armagh, Jerpoint oatmeal trout, and steak Tullach Mor. Portions are generous. Many regular diners never diverge from the Irish Reuben, a splendid Old World antecedent to the New York deli version. Separate from the dining room area, and worth a visit in and of itself, is the cozy pub — entering it is like stepping off the streets of Annapolis and into the heart of Dublin.

HARRY BROWNE'S
410-263-4332.
66 State Circle.
Open: Daily.
Price: Very Expensive.
Cuisine: New American.
Serving: L, D, SB.
Credit Cards: AE, D, DC, MC, V.
Reservations: Recommended.
Handicap Access: Yes.
Special Features: View of Statehouse; outdoor dining (at sidewalk tables).

F or a fine dining experience, it doesn't get much better than Harry Browne's. The ambiance is intimate and sophisticated. Service is attentive and unobtrusive. When making a reservation, request a window table for a picture postcard view of the State House. Bathed in moonlight, it's something to write home about. The clubby Grill Room is open Wed. through Sun. evenings. But enough about atmosphere. The menu changes seasonally and the kitchen seldom, if ever, takes shortcuts. We like to start with the baked oysters Annapolitan (topped with, what else, crabmeat), Caesar or mixed green salad, or cream of crab soup. Fresh fish and seafood shine here, as does the beef, duck, and lamb. Most entrées fall between $21 and $27. If you have room, try the rum raisin bread pudding, bananas Foster, crème brûlée, or house-made ice cream. Lunch is memorable, with a host of soups, salads, sandwiches, and hot entrées in the $7–$12 range. Sunday, line up for the brunch buffet ($12.95) or choose from the a la carte menu ($8-$13). Both include a glass of champagne or wine, or a mimosa.

JOSS CAFÉ & SUSHI BAR
410-263-4688.
195 Main St.
Open: Daily.
Price: Inexpensive to Very
    Expensive.
Cuisine: Japanese.
Serving: L, D.
Credit Cards: AE, MC, V.
Reservations: No.
Handicap Access: Yes.

Sushi continues to make inroads among the city's growing group of Pan-Asian-fusion restaurants, but this is the granddaddy of Annapolis sushi restaurants and never disappoints. A recently added back dining room doubles the space, but retains the same intimacy that long has made the front dining room such fun. Tuck into a corner table and start with a salad, including a terrific sesame-tinged seaweed salad. Follow with any type of sushi you can imagine; our household favorite is the rainbow roll, with salmon, tuna, and flounder topping avocado, all rolled in roe. Japanese food-lovers also will find tempuras, teriyakis, sukiyaki, and other traditional favorites on the menu. It's fun to watch the sushi chefs at work, though a bit of a surprise when they and all the servers shout out "Iras-shai," Japanese for "welcome," as diners arrive. A tip for the dinner crowd: get there at 5:30, because a line is likely to spill from the tiny waiting vestibule onto the street as the evening progresses.

LES FOLIES BRASSERIE
410-573-0970.
2552 Riva Road.
Open: Daily.
Price: Very Expensive.
Cuisine: Regional French.
Serving: L, D.
Credit Cards: AE, D, MC, V.
Reservations: Strongly
    recommended, especially
    on weekends.
Handicap Access: Yes.

Don't let the institutional exterior put you off. Inside Les Folies (a 10-minute drive from City Dock), you find earth tone stucco walls and slate floors, fresh flowers, French posters, and photographs. The setting and staff encourage leisurely dining, thank heavens. With food like this, who wants to rush? On a recent evening we started with a lump crabmeat flan with lobster sauce and a salad of field greens, pistachios, goat cheese, and roasted bell peppers. With a glass of wine and basket of crusty bread, we could have quit and been sated. But one must go the extra mile in the name of research. So we plunged into soft-shell crabs (provençal *and* amandine) and grilled Chilean sea bass on a bed of fennel and rice. After such a meal, we chose a light dessert — crème brûlée. The creamy custard with caramelized sugar crust equaled any we'd had on the Left Bank or in the French Quarter. Based on previous visits we recommend the bouillabaisse and paella, coq au vin, veal piccata, and fish any way. A three-course dinner with a cocktail and/or glass of wine will set you back $35–$50. Lunch, only served Mon. through Fri., features soups and sandwiches ($5–$8), salads and hot entrées ($7–$14).

LEWNES' STEAKHOUSE
410-263-1617.
401 Fourth St.
Open: Daily.
Price: Very Expensive.
Cuisine: Steakhouse.
Serving: D.
Credit Cards: AE, DC, MC, V.
Reservations: Strongly recommended.
Handicap Access: First floor only.

Lewnes' has the look of a New York or Chicago steakhouse: spare and clubby. We go for the fork-tender prime-aged steaks and generous sides of salad, potatoes and vegetables. Arrive with an appetite and full wallet (most entrées are $23–$24). Leave your caloric cheat sheet and cholesterol counter at home. The beef is cooked to perfection and served with a bit of melted butter. At your request, the kitchen will forego it or add more. Trust us on this, it adds to the flavor. The salads serve two, unless your appetite equals Henry VIII's. We favor the mashed or hash brown potatoes and sauteed mushrooms with a N.Y. strip, leaving with half the meat for a midnight snack or lunch the next day. Nearby on-street parking is usually scarce, so if you're up to it, park in the Historic District and enjoy the ten- to fifteen-minute walk. Go over the Spa Creek Bridge, left at Severn Avenue, and continue two blocks to Fourth Street. Lewnes' is on the corner. The after-dinner walk aids digestion — so maybe you'll have room for ice cream.

MCGARVEY'S SALOON & OYSTER BAR
410-263-5700.
8 Market Space.
Open: Daily.
Price: Inexpensive to Expensive.
Cuisine: American/ Seafood/Pub Fare.
Serving: L, D, SB.
Credit Cards: AE, MC, V.
Reservations: Not accepted on weekends, holidays.
Handicap Access: Limited (not to bathrooms).

Belly up to the mile-long bar for your favorite eye-opener or sundowner at this longtime Annapolis favorite. Polished wood, brass and Tiffany-style lamps create a welcoming atmosphere in the usually packed and noisy bar area. We prefer the less frenetic, natural light-filled back room. Start with half a dozen oysters, steamed clams, or spiced shrimp from the raw bar. Pub fare shines here: smoked bluefish apppetizer served with horseradish cream sauce, bread, and crackers; a smoked turkey Reuben; open-faced filet with bearnaise sauce; soft-shell crab sandwich with coleslaw and fries; good hamburgers; or Nova Scotia salmon-topped Caesar salad. Kick back with an Aviator, the house lager, or Old Hydraulic root beer. (Owner Mike Ashford's passion for biplanes creates the connection between airplanes and beverages.) At dinner the beef and fish entrées ($15–$18) are less inspired and inspiring. Comfort food — meatloaf, turkey, and the like — star on the nightly dinner specials. Service is friendly and reliable. Eat at off times on weekends or plan to wait.

MIDDLETON TAVERN
410-263-3323.
2 Market Space.
Open: Daily.

Located at City Dock, barn-red Middleton Tavern lays authentic claim to tavernhood dating to 1740. Ye olde place houses cozy wallpapered

Price: Inexpensive to
   Expensive.
Cuisine: Seafood/
   American/Tavern Fare.
Serving: L, D, weekend B.
Credit Cards: AE, D, MC, V.
Reservations: No, but offers
   "priority seating" for
   those who call ahead.
Handicap Access: No.

dining rooms suitable for ladies' luncheons in front, or a back bar known for its 99-cent "oyster shooters" where you, too, can drown an oyster in cocktail sauce and chase it with beer. From price to the food, the menu continues the wide-ranging theme. Order Thai and Szechuan-touched side veggies or Italian pastas or soups (Cuban black bean — big thumbs up), or steaks and smoked bluefish. Pay $8 or $9 for a sandwich, or $32.95 for a crab-stuffed rockfish. Over the years, we've tended to come here for lunch or late-night meals, and Middleton is good to keep in mind on Sunday, when they serve the breakfast menu until 2pm. The wide front porch, a great people-watching spot, is almost as much a city landmark as the Naval Academy Chapel dome.

NORTHWOODS
410-268-2609.
609 Melvin Ave.
Open: Daily.
Price: Expensive to Very
   Expensive.
Cuisine: Continental.
Serving: D.
Credit Cards: AE, D, MC, V.
Reservations:
   Recommended.
Handicap Access: Not the
   bathrooms.

Well past age 15, Northwoods continues to reap culinary kudos and a loyal local following, serving fine food via wonderful service in a subdued dining room. You can't do better than the prix fixe, four-course dinner, available any night but Saturday. Choose appetizer, salad, entrée and dessert from the entire menu, all for a mere $29.95. Appetizers recall your trips to Europe, including gambas, sauteed in garlic, red pepper, olive oil, and lemon. For an entrée, bite into a rare tuna steak with its lemony relish of hearts of palm, artichoke hearts, and shrimp, or a king salmon grille topped with tarragon orange buerre blanc. The wine list is well considered; the dessert cart will make your eyes pop. Owners Leslie and Russell Brown (he is the executive chef) have their restaurant details down delightfully pat — duly noted with an award of excellence from DiRoNA, the Distinguished Restaurants of North America. If you need one more excuse to visit, we'll give you two: lot parking is easy, and it's located near Rte. 50's Rowe Blvd. exit, with easy access.

O'LEARYS
410-263-0884.
310 Third St.
Open: Daily.
Price: Expensive.
Cuisine: Seafood/Nouveau.
Serving: D.
Credit Cards: AE, DC, MC,
   V.
Reservations: Yes.
Handicap Access: Yes.

Certainly one of the best restaurants in town, O'Learys is unbeatable for its seafood. The dependably excellent quality of both food preparation and unobtrusive but attendant service may push it into the overall top spot in this restaurant-rich city. The spare dining room lets the food take center stage, although it's always fun to gaze at the black-and-white Annapolis maritime photos lining the mustard-yellow walls. The restaurant's signa-

David Trozzo

Seafood lovers make it a point to dine at O'Learys restaurant in Eastport.

Special Features: No smoking.

ture is six types of fish done in your choice of one of six different ways. That means your Alaskan halibut or Atlantic salmon might be grilled with capers, olive oil and lemon served with warm orzo salad and broccolini, or lightly blackened with Creole crème, black beans and rice alongside broccolini. The lengthy menu also promises creative executions of shrimp or crab, or herb-encrusted lamb chops, roasted, then grilled, or filet mignon. Look for seasonal changes, such as the addition of Muscovy duck come fall, done with a truffled pinot noir reduction, pilaf of brown basmati, dried cranberries, pecans, and haricots verts with applewood bacon. Talk about apropos to the time of year! All you need now is a nice glass of wine, chosen from the long and well-considered list that includes plenty of red and white wines to match your meal. Located in the Eastport maritime district, the restaurant sits along the water in the former home of a waterman who ran a fish market on the property. There's a very limited water view, but seafood-loving visitors to Annapolis would be remiss if they didn't finagle a reservation at this popular establishment, noticed by regional reviewers from the *Washington Post* to *Baltimore* magazine.

RAM'S HEAD TAVERN (AND FORDHAM BREWERY)
410-268-4545.
33 West St.
Open: Daily.
Price: Inexpensive to Expensive.
Cuisine: American/Pub Fare.
Serving: L, D, SB.

Locals remember ten or so years ago when the Ram's Head was a hole in the wall (in this case, the basement), when Naval Academy midshipmen and locals packed the closet-sized brickskeller to munch burgers and drink their way through 300-plus brands of beer. My, how times have changed. After several expansions, the Ram's Head is a happening. Depending on their mood and the weather, diners can opt for the cozy, paneled Tea Room, din-

David Trozzo

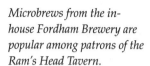

Microbrews from the in-house Fordham Brewery are popular among patrons of the Ram's Head Tavern.

Credit Cards: AE, D, MC, V.
Reservations:
  Recommended.
Handicap Access: Yes.
Special Features: Outdoor
  dining, on-site
  performance space.

ing room (with mostly booths), bustling bar area or, weather permitting, New Orleans-style patio. The food is hearty and eclectic. Hamburgers, sandwiches, soups, salads (try the Greek or Caesar topped with chicken), and seafood dishes anchor the menu. The award-winning chili is just what the doctor ordered on a nippy day — or night. Sunday brunch, with close to a dozen entrées priced below $10, is a steal, especially when enjoyed in the brick courtyard. Under the same roof, the Fordham Brewery turns out better-than-average microbrews also served or sold in the area. See the "Nightlife" section for details about performances in the adjacent theater space. The staff is generally attentive, enthusiastic, and personable. No wonder repeat patrons pack the Ram's Head.

RIORDAN'S
410-263-5449.
26 Market Space.
Open: Daily.
Price: Inexpensive to
  Expensive.
Cuisine: Seafood/American.
Serving: L, D, SB.
Credit Cards: AE, D, MC, V.
Reservations: Fri.–Sat. only,
  for upstairs dining room.
Handicap Access: Limited.

Belly up to the bar at this popular saloon opposite Ego Alley, the tongue of water slipped into City Dock. If you're waiting for a table, enjoy a frosty mug; the pub purveys more than thirty beers. The polished wood bar, brass accents, posters, and Naval Academy and sports memorabilia create a kitschy casual ambiance that nurtures the spirit as well as the stomach. Start with the loaded potato skins, hot crab dip (a meal in itself), or raw bar offering. Burgers and oversized sandwiches with steak-cut fries are available at lunch and dinner. Heartier appetites applaud the baby-back ribs, grilled fish, and pasta entrées. The beef and chicken receive less praise. The Sunday brunch is an Annapolis tradition. Best to arrive early or plan on a wait. Entrées are $7–$10 and include a mimosa or glass of champagne. The child's brunch is only $4.50. Service is consistent and efficient at Annapolis' answer to Cheers.

TREATY OF PARIS
410-263-2641.
Maryland Inn, Church Circle.
Open: Daily.
Price: Very Expensive.
Cuisine: American/Continental.
Serving: B, L, D, SB.
Credit Cards: AE, D, DC, MC, V.
Reservations: Strongly recommended for dinner and brunch.
Handicap Access: Yes, with prior notice.
Special Features: Historic inn; two fireplaces.

The Treaty of Paris, the historic Maryland Inn's intimate dining room, is a favorite, especially on a winter's eve. The two working fireplaces, brick interior, fine food and service, and all that candlelight spell romance. But you don't have to be in love to enjoy it. State pols favor the place, and the conversation makes for good eavesdropping. The kitchen's signature "Treaty of Paris" entrée means scallops, shrimp, fresh fish, mussels, and clams in a tomato-spiked seafood broth, while other dinner entrées include fish, beef, fowl, lamb, and pork. The Treaty serves what could be the best crab cakes in the area, well-seasoned lump crab-meat, no discernible filler and — thank heavens — no cartilage or shell. While the market price prevails at dinner, we could hardly finish a recent $11.95 luncheon crab cake sandwich served with a small portion of coleslaw. Locals lap up the daily soup and half-sandwich or soup and salad special, a steal at $8.95. Whatever else you order, try the popovers. The Sunday brunch is $19.95; less for seniors, much less for children. But make a reservation. A colonial-style tea is served (on the porch in good weather, otherwise in the King of France Tavern) Wed. between 3 and 4.

TSUNAMI
410-990-9868.
51 West St.
Open: Daily.
Price: Inexpensive to Expensive.
Cuisine: New World.
Serving: L, D.
Credit Cards: AE, MC, V.
Reservations: No.
Handicap Access: Yes.
Special Features: Sushi bar open until late; telephone orders available.

Looking for big-city fast-forward fare? Try Tsunami, which brought the Asian-fusion trend to Annapolis. It remains the most visibly hip place in town, with spare décor anchored by near-royal blue walls, top-notch food, and affable service often delivered by one of the four owners. World-beat fare includes fresh executions of Chesapeake favorites, like a rockfish en paillotte with coconut curry sauce, and a version of crab cakes served with a citrus wasabi aioli. Visitors who've had their fill of rockfish and crab (Bay-area blasphemy!) will find tiger prawns (a spring roll appetizer comes with a sake hoisin dip) or a fine wok-seared pepper tenderloin done up with a honey balsamic syrup and horseradish oil. Interestingly enough, the chef creating this globally inspired food is a self-taught local, Jonathan Jaquet, who learned the trade in several of the city's kitchens. He works alongside sushi chef Stanley Hsu, whose offerings hardly lack for takers. The two couples who

Tsunami offers fast-forward fare on Annapolis' West Street, undergoing a renaissance.

David Trozzo

own Tsunami get points for creating a New York-style outpost for locals. An expansion was recently completed, with booths to create intimacy and carpeting and other efforts that will be welcome antidotes to the currently sometimes-loud restaurant. This is also a late-night gathering spot; don't be surprised if a crowd has gathered well into a weekend night.

WILD ORCHID CAFÉ
410-268-8009.
909 Bay Ridge Ave.
Open: Tues.–Sun.
Price: Expensive to Very Expensive.
Cuisine: American.
Serving: L, D, SB.
Credit Cards: AE, D, DC, MC, V.
Reservations: Recommended, especially at dinner.
Handicap Access: Limited.
Special Features: Garden patio; Sunday tea.

With its squash yellow walls, polished wood floors and forest green tabletops, the Wild Orchid is an inviting country inn less than two miles from City Dock. At lunch, locals, business types and out-of-towners fill the dining rooms (one large, one small) and patio. Pique your appetite with the butternut squash crab soup, a delectable variation on standard cream of crab. Half a dozen salads — with eye- and taste-appeal — several sandwiches, and a handful of hot entrées are priced between $8 and $12. While you are welcome to order a la carte, the $30 fixed-price dinner includes bread with spinach/ mushroom/leek spread, soup, salad, any entrée on the menu (seafood, beef, fowl, fish, and vegetarian), and any dessert. Speaking of desserts, try the Chocolate Decadence, a flourless chocolate cake more like fudge. Since the entrées average $25 and the desserts are $6, this could be the best deal since the New Deal. Sunday brunch is served from 9 to 3, followed by tea from 3 to 5. Service is prompt and friendly yet courteous. A side note: We appreciate the Wild Orchid's staff addressing us as ma'am and sir, not "you guys." We hope other restaurants take note.

SEAFOOD SOUTH OF TOWN

Deale

HAPPY HARBOR INN
410-867-0949, 301-261-5297.
533 Deale Rd.
Open: Daily.
Price: Inexpensive to
   Expensive.
Cuisine: Seafood.
Serving: B, L, D.
Credit Cards: D, MC, V.
Reservations: No.
Handicap Access: Yes.

Watching the charter boats come in to their slips on Rockhold Creek just outside the wide glass patio of Happy Harbor is half the fun of eating here. The catch of the day is held high, and witnesses from the dining room can respond by digging in to their own seafood bacchanal: oysters, crabs or fish reliably arrive here in season. On Tuesday nights from Apr.–Oct., stop in for the seafood buffet with steamed shrimp or crab legs. Open year-round, Happy Harbor is one of those places that makes for a good escape from life here in this watermen's village. Note: the restaurant doesn't serve hard-shell crabs.

SKIPPER'S PIER
410-867-7110.
6158 Drum Point Rd.
Open: Wed.–Thurs. 4–10;
   Fri.–Sun. 11:30–11; winter:
   Wed. & Thurs. 4–9,
   Fri.–Sun. Noon–10.
Price: Moderate.
Cuisine: Seafood /Crabs.
Serving: L, D.
Credit Cards: AE, D, DC,
   MC, V.
Reservations: For parties of
   10 or more.
Handicap Access: Yes.

One of the best waterside crab-pickin' spots around, Skipper's does a great job. Every detail seems to have been considered, down to sippee-type cups for the kids, which frees them to explore the waterfront deck and nearby sandbox and kiddie pirate boat without trailing too many pink dribbles. The hard-shell crabs are regularly excellent, but the menu includes much more than that, including fine fat crab cakes. Get here in the late afternoon, and you should have no trouble getting a small picnic table right along the water. In summer, speakers playing oldies are affixed to the Rockhold Creek-side fence, a sensory detail of mixed blessings. If rain threatens, grab an outdoor table beneath the pink canopy, replete with those big outdoor heaters like they have in Parisian cafés. The dock bar, Barnacles, gets loud some weekends, but it provides a great rooftop deck for stargazing, where one July Fourth we even found ourselves witnessing one of the small-town fireworks displays up the river. A charming surprise — but the restaurant's open even in winter. For directions: www.skipperspier.com.

Riva

**MIKE'S RESTAURANT &
   CRAB HOUSE**
410-956-2784.
3030 Old Riva Rd.

We like Mike's and have for years. Located on the outskirts of town, it's easy to meet incoming friends from Washington, D.C. without explaining how to navigate Annapolis' sometimes confus-

Open: Daily.
Price: Moderate to
    Expensive.
Cuisine: Seafood.
Serving: L, D.
Credit Cards: AE, MC, V.
Reservations: For large
    parties only.
Handicap Access: Yes.
Special Features: Outdoor
    waterside deck; dockage.

ing Historic District. It also comes with parking, overlooks the South River, and serves great hard-shell crabs and big seafood platters. It's a lively scene out on the outdoor deck in midsummer, and a wedding or other celebratory gathering always seems to have taken up residence. Even into Oct., the deck stays open if the weather is good, although service can get a little spotty. Boats dock alongside, mallards paddle in, and, with everybody cracking crabs, it's the consummate Chesapeake scene in full glory. The cavernous indoor dining room is as full as the parking lot during summer crab season, but if you come early, during the week or in the off-season, you should have no problems. The menu's steak and rib entrées should make the beef eaters happy, and a fresh but utilitarian salad bar is offered alongside the bar where bands gather and folks boogie on the small dance floor. A popular place.

FOOD PURVEYORS

Sitting down for a fine meal is no problem in Annapolis and environs, but sometimes you're on the run. Here are some local food purveyors who'll do right by you. Stop in for ice cream or pick through the world's best sweet corn before heading to the seafood market for hard-shell crabs.

COFFEE

City Dock Café (410-269-0969; 18 Market Space) Bright, clean, and often packed. A variety of coffees, sandwiches, fat cookies, and pastry. Front windows offer a fine view of City Dock. Open: Sun.–Thurs. 6:30am–10 pm, Fri.–Sat. 6:30am–midnight.

Starbucks The espresso machine operates constantly at these busy branches of the national chain. City Dock location (410-268-6551; 124 Dock St.) open Sun. –Thurs. 6:30–9, 'til 10 Fri. and 11 Sat. Annapolis Harbour Center location (410-573-0076; off Aris T. Allen Blvd.) open Mon.–Thurs. 5:30–10, 'til 11 Fri. and Sat., 6–9:30 on Sun.

FARMERS' MARKETS

Anne Arundel County Farmers' Market, Inc. (410-570-3646; Harry S Truman Pkwy., Riva) A variety of farmers and vendors spread their wares here during the longer summer markets or the shorter "fall" and "Christmas" markets. Always open on weekends, but call for hours, especially if you're interested in attending the summer market midweek. The same number can give you information on farmers' markets in Deale and Severna Park, too.

Pennsylvania Dutch Farmer's Market (410-573-0770; 2472 Solomons Island Rd., Annapolis Harbour Center) Operating weekends. Stalls filled with everything from subs to fresh produce. Quilt shop, restaurant. Open Thurs.–Sat.

HISTORIC MARKET HOUSE

Market House (Market Space at City Dock) As is typical in the region, a dose of history is available, even with your takeout. In a town full of rehabilitated historic buildings, the Market House stands as one of the city's more enduring phoenixes, heir to a long line of city markets that has stood near here since 1788. This particular market was reopened in 1971 following an extensive renovation and is a good place to stop for a quick takeout lunch. White tables outside let you eat on the run in good weather, or sit on the steps across the street at City Dock. Vendors include: **Annapolis Fish Market** (410-269-0490; open 9–6) with a genuine belly-up-to-the-raw-bar; **The Big Cheese** (410-263-6915; open 8–6); **Nick and Dolly's Gourmet** (410-280-1974; open 8–6); **Machoian Poultry** (410-263-5979; open Sun.–Thurs. 9–6, Fri. & Sat. 9–7:30); **Mann's Sandwiches** (410-263-0644; open 7–6); and **Sammy's Deli** (410-263-6883; open 9–6).

ICE CREAM

Ben & Jerry's (410-268-6700; 139 Main St.) Within sight of City Dock; quite popular.

Storm Brothers Ice Cream Factory (410-263-3376; 130 Dock St.) Longtime resident of the City Dock area serves 45 flavors of ice cream and four types of sherbet. Open 10:30am–11pm in summer (midnight on weekends); closes one hour earlier in winter.

NATURAL/WHOLE FOODS

Fresh Fields (410-573-1800; Annapolis Harbour Center, 2504 Solomons Island Rd.) Not that the whole foods giant needs a plug from us, but the locals fill the aisles here. Favorites: focaccia topped pizza-style with artichokes; Coleman's antibiotic-free beef; Arctic char; great buffalo mozzarella. Good takeout if you're off for a day on the Bay. Open: Oct.–May, Mon.–Sat. 9–9, Sun. 9–8; Jun.–Sept., 8–9 daily.

Sun and Earth Natural Foods (410-266-6862; 1933 West St.) Beloved old health and whole foods shop stocks all of the necessities, including Green Goddess sandwiches. Open Mon.–Sat. 9:30–6:30, Sun. Noon–4.

SEAFOOD MARKETS

Annapolis Seafood Market (410-269-5380; Forest Dr. & Tyler Ave.) Longtime, popular local seafood market, beautifully organized from in-season sweet corn to the line at the crab and spiced shrimp counter to the excellent take-out sandwiches for folks on the go (the shrimp salad only takes a minute). All kinds of good and fresh seafood.

CULTURE

CINEMA

Crown Theaters (410-571-2796) operates the Annapolis commercial movie houses, which include the **Crown Harbour Center IX**, the **Crown Annapolis Mall XI** showing first-run fare, and the **Crown Eastport Art Cinemas** weighing in with artier flicks.

DANCE

BALLET THEATRE OF MARYLAND
410-263-2909, tickets;
410-263-8289,
information.
www.btmballet.org.
Maryland Hall for the
Creative Arts, 801 Chase St.
Season: Fall through spring.
Tickets: Children $12,
seniors/adults $24 plus $1
handling fee.

Regional company with its own school and principal dancers, including those formerly with the Bolshoi and the National Ballet of China. Four major productions each year at Maryland Hall generally include a modern production and classic. The annual *Nutcracker* is a holiday sellout (matinee tickets go first).

GALLERIES

The visual arts scene in Annapolis revolves around Maryland Hall for the Creative Arts and the Historic District's commercial galleries. Watercolors of local scenes and marine prints are more likely to hang than cutting-edge abstracts, although interesting work can be found at these galleries.

ELIZABETH MYERS MITCHELL ART GALLERY
410-626-2556.

Your best chance in Annapolis to see major works by major artists. Visiting shows often are curated elsewhere by groups like the Smithsonian Institution's Traveling Exhibition Service or the American

Mellon Hall (attached to the Francis Scott Key auditorium lobby), St. John's College, 60 College Ave.
Open: Tues.–Sun. Noon–5, Fri. 7–8 during school year; hours may vary in summer.

MARYLAND FEDERATION OF ART CIRCLE GALLERY
410-268-4566.
www.mdfedart.org.
18 State Circle.
Open: Tues.–Sun. 11–5.

MARYLAND HALL FOR THE CREATIVE ARTS
410-263-5544.
www.mdhallarts.org.
801 Chase St.
Open: Mon.–Wed. and Fri. 9–5, Thurs. 9–8:30, Sat. 10–1.

Federation of Art in New York. Recent shows: Mayan ceramics from the Palmer Collection, Josef Albers and the New York School. Lectures, gallery talks, and group tours are held in conjunction with exhibitions. Check www.scja.edu ("campus resources") for schedules.

Originally built in the mid-1800s as a storage loft for the Jones and Franklin General Store, the building's exposed brick walls serve as backdrop for changing shows. Paintings, sculpture, wearable art, and photographs by the 300-artist member-roster. Two rooms host monthly exhibitions, which often feature small group shows. A good place to look for a well-priced piece from an unknown. If you're in Baltimore, stop by the MFA's City Gallery (410-685-0300; 330 N. Charles St.).

The city's performing and visual arts center and school houses three galleries showing a variety of work, including pieces by Maryland Hall's twelve artists in residence, as well as students and others. While you're in the building, wander upstairs and see if any of the artists are working in their studios at the former 1932 Annapolis High School building. Performances from pop to bluegrass are held here as well; check www.tickets.com.

HISTORIC BUILDINGS & SITES

Annapolis

CHARLES CARROLL HOUSE OF ANNAPOLIS
410-269-1737.
107 Duke of Gloucester St.
Summer Hours: Sun.–Fri. Noon–4, Sat. 10–2.
Fall Hours: Fri. and Sun. Noon–4, Sat. 10–2; closed from Dec. until May or June.
Admission: Adults $5, seniors $4, students

Four Marylanders signed the Declaration of Independence; all of them, at least for a time, owned homes in Annapolis. This was the birthplace and boyhood home of Charles Carroll of Carrollton, the only Roman Catholic to sign the Declaration. Located on the grounds of St. Mary's Church, his home housed a chapel in which Catholics worshiped during the mid-eighteenth century, when the religion was forced underground. Restoration has been under way for some years, including archaeological digs in the formal gardens that turned up

(12–17) $2, 11 and under
free. Group rates
available.
Handicap Access: Yes.

artifacts, likely from a tavern that once operated on
the property. Construction of the original family
house began in 1721; later additions included a
story, an A-frame room, and a three-story wing in
1770. Call for tour schedule. Public activities include
architectural history tours, complete with hard hats.
In Sept., enjoy the Irish Heritage Festival.

CHASE-LLOYD HOUSE
410-263-2723.
22 Maryland Ave.
Open: Mon.–Sat. 2–4; closed
Jan.–Feb.
Admission: $2.

Samuel Chase, yet another Annapolitan to sign
the Declaration, started this house in 1769 —
before he became one of the new nation's first
Supreme Court justices. Later, he sold the home,
unfinished, to Edward Lloyd IV, member of a
prominent Maryland political dynasty. The brick
mansion is most noted for the spectacular "flying"
stairway, which has no visible means of support.

GOVERNMENT HOUSE
410-974-3531.
State & Church Circles.
Open: By appt. only,
Tues.–Thurs. 10–2; during
legislative session,
Jan.–mid-Apr., only Tues.,
Thurs.

The Maryland governor's home is an 1868
Georgian-style mansion, filled with Maryland
arts and antiques. Arrange tours by appt.

David Trozzo

*Aficionados of colonial architecture can tour the Hammond-Harwood House on Maryland
Avenue.*

HAMMOND-HARWOOD HOUSE
410-269-1714.
19 Maryland Ave.
Open: Mon.–Sat. 10–4, Sun. Noon–4; 45-minute tours on the hour, last tour at 3pm.
Admission: Adults $5, children $3.

Widely considered one of the nation's finest remaining examples of Georgian architecture, this 1770s center-block house, preserved as a museum since 1926, boasts two wings connected by two hyphens, a style known as a five-point Maryland house (a Palladian varietal that turned up only in colonial Maryland). The symmetry is meticulous: false doors balance actual entrances. Inside hang portraits by one-time Annapolitan Charles Willson Peale and furniture by noted Annapolis coffin-maker and cabinetmaker John Shaw. Intricately carved ribbons and roses mark the front entrance. Gift shop; exhibitions. Discount tour tickets for $10 are available for those who also visit the nearby William Paca House.

MARYLAND STATEHOUSE
410-974-3400.
State Circle.
Open: Daily 9–5; tours at 11 and 3.
Handicapped accessible.

The first Statehouse was built on this hill in 1699; the current building is the third. Fire, the scourge of so many colonial-era buildings, destroyed the first building, replaced in 1705. The second lasted until 1766, when the government decided to build a more architecturally distinguished capitol building. Marylanders now boast that theirs is the country's oldest state capitol building in continuous use. From Nov. 26, 1783, to Aug. 13, 1784, the building served as the capitol to a new nation. The Old Senate Chamber where George Washington resigned his commission in the Continental Army in 1783 remains. The Treaty of Paris officially ending the Revolution was ratified here in 1784. Also see Charles Willson Peale's portrait of Gen. Washington with Marylander Tench Tilghman and the Marquis de Lafayette. (Peale lived in Annapolis for a time.) The General Assembly convenes for the annual ninety-day legislative session from winter into spring; a visitors' center in the first-floor lobby offers abundant state travel information.

ST. ANNE'S EPISCOPAL CHURCH
410-267-9333.
Church Circle (Parish House, 199 Duke of Gloucester St.).
Open: Daily; tours by appt.

This is the third church built on this hallowed Annapolis site. Fire destroyed much of the second (1792–1858), but parts of the old building were incorporated when the new church went up in 1859. Many graves in the old churchyard were moved when Church Circle was widened years ago, but the graves of Annapolis' first mayor, Amos Garret, and Maryland's last colonial governor, Sir Robert Eden, remain. Inside is a silver communion service given by King William III, dating from the 1690s.

WILLIAM PACA HOUSE AND GARDEN
410-263-5553.
www.annapolis.org.
186 Prince George St.
Open: Mar.–Dec., Mon.–Sat.
10–5, Sun. Noon–5;
Jan.–Feb., Thurs.–Sat.
10–5, Sun. Noon–4.
Admission: Fee.

William Paca, three-time colonial governor of Maryland and signer of the Declaration of Independence, built his magnificent Georgian mansion between 1763 and 1765. Here he entertained during the era known as Annapolis' golden age. During meticulous renovations here in the 1960s and 1970s, X-rays revealed that two architectural styles found in the main staircase dated to the same era, a mixing and matching apparently chosen by Mr. Paca himself. First-floor antiques date to Paca's residency; liberties, like a nineteenth-century spinet, were taken on the second floor. In 1965, high-rise apartments were slated to replace the building, then a hotel. Historic Annapolis, Inc. bought the house and, in six weeks' time, convinced the Maryland General Assembly to buy the two-acre garden site in back. Archaeologists set about reconstructing the gardens and knew that they had hit pay dirt when they uncovered an original pond — it promptly refilled from a spring beneath. A must-see for any gardener, the formal, terraced Paca Gardens boast a reconstructed pavilion and Chinese-style bridge, and create a favorite respite in the middle of town. Watch for a variety of special events, from music to special plant sales. A discount package is available to those also touring the Hammond-Harwood House. Recorded tours available. The Historic Annapolis Foundation, which owns the Paca House, also operates other historic buildings around town; for information call 410-267-7619.

Edgewater

Youngsters sift dirt at an open dig at London Town, once a Colonial port south of Annapolis, where volunteers can assist with archaeology digs.

David Trozzo

LONDON TOWN HOUSE AND GARDENS
410-222-1919.
www.historiclondontown.com.

Cross the South River Bridge on Rte. 2 south of Annapolis to visit this eighteenth-century Georgian tavern on the riverbank, site of a once-booming town. In addition to eight acres of mar-

839 Londontown Rd.
S. on Rte. 2 from Annapolis;
  1 mi. past South River
  Bridge, left on Mayo Rd.
  (Md. 253), 1 mi. to left on
  Londontown Rd.
Open: Mon.–Sat. 10–4, Sun.
  Noon–4; closed Jan. and
  Feb.
Admission: Adults $6,
  seniors $4, children 7-12
  $3, children 6 and under
  free.

velous gardens and an ongoing archaeological dig, visitors will find the house-turned-tavern built by William Brown in 1764. Traveling colonial-era men of limited means once shared beds upstairs; traveling gentleman professionals — an itinerant dentist, for example — had their own rooms while they stayed in town to do business. Volunteers may assist the archaeological dig monthly.

HISTORIC SCHOOLS

ST. JOHN'S COLLEGE
410-263-2371; for events,
  410-626-2539.
www.sjca.edu.
60 College Ave.

The "Johnnies," as students at **St. John's College** are called, study only the Great Books during their years here, where intellect is greatly valued and humor tends toward plays on Greek or Latin phrases. The college, descended from King William's School in 1696, claims to be the nation's third oldest. The oldest building on campus, McDowell Hall, houses the venerable Great Hall, where a banquet was tossed for the aging General Lafayette in 1824, and a hospital was set up during the Civil War. The 1934 Maryland Archives building now houses the college library. Visitors may walk the campus, but those interested in the school's history should join a tour by an organized tour group. See "Tours" later in this chapter.

UNITED STATES NAVAL ACADEMY
Armel-Leftwich Visitor
  Center.
410-263-6933.
www.navyonline.com.
52 King George St.
Visitor Center hours: 9–5
  Mar.–Dec., 9–4 Jan. and
  Feb.
Tour fees; schedules change
  seasonally.
Enter the academy grounds
  at Gate 1, at the foot of
  King George St., then
  head to the Visitor Center,
  next to Halsey Field
  House.

For many people around the world, "Annapolis" and "U.S. Naval Academy" are synonymous. Locals would beg to differ, but none would disagree that the **U.S. Naval Academy** has had — and remains — a great influence on the city. Founded in 1845 at old Fort Severn, the Academy's long history includes its notable move from Annapolis to Newport, Rhode Island, during the Civil War, prompted by the Maryland city's overwhelming Southern sympathies. During the war, both the Academy and nearby St. John's College became military hospitals. Upon their return, naval officers found the campus in great need of military spit-shine. So commenced plans for a "new Academy," the collection of Beaux Arts buildings designed by architect Ernest Flagg that visitors now see, constructed between 1899 and 1908.

David Trozzo

The Navy's Blue Angels fly over the United States Naval Academy's commissioning ceremony each spring.

For athletic event ticket information: 800-US4-NAVY; www.navysports.com. For community relations/general public inquiries: 410-293-2293; www.usna.edu.

Security requires a photo ID to enter the grounds; no visitor parking. Enter through Gate 1.

Inside the **Academy Chapel**, begun in 1904, is the final resting place of the "Father of the U.S. Navy," John Paul Jones, finally entombed in 1913 after a fantastic journey. He was buried in Paris in 1792, but his grave was lost in the turmoil of the French Revolution as the cemetery, owned by the House of Bourbon, was seized, sold by the Revolutionary government, and later developed. After a concerted search, Jones' tomb was rediscovered 100 years later. Following much politicking, it was determined that the admiral should be laid to rest in the Academy Chapel — then still under construction. The casket arrived at the Academy in 1906, but spent seven somewhat ignominious years beneath the grand staircase leading to Memorial Hall from the giant dormitory, Bancroft Hall. To see the spectacular marble sarcophogus, enter from the outside, beneath the chapel. The names of the seven ships that Jones commanded are inscribed in the floor encircling the tomb.

Lovers of ships and naval history should see the **U.S. Naval Academy Museum** (410-293-2108; www.usna.edu/Museum; Preble Hall, 118 Maryland Ave. Open Mon.–Sat. 9–5, Sun. 11–5). Highlights of the collection (which range from paintings to Naval gear to ship's instruments) include the Beverley R. Robinson Collection of prints depicting naval battles and ships dating back to the 1600s, located in Halligan Hall. The Class of 1951 Gallery of Ships at the museum displays a wide range of fabulous ships' models. Notable is the spectacular Henry H. Rogers Collection of more than 100 ships' models, including some that are well over 300 years old. In addition, the museum shows "dockyard" models of ships built by order of the British Royal Navy, and exquisite ships' cases dating to the Jacobean, William and Mary, and Queen Anne periods. And don't miss the world's largest collection of "bone" models, carved from leftovers from beef rations given French prisoners of war, generally from 1756 to 1815.

Noon meal formations by the Brigade of Midshipmen at full military attention occur at Tecumseh Court Mon.–Wed. and Fri. during the school year, weather permitting.

There's plenty more, too. Call the visitor center for current information.

LIBRARIES

Interested in learning more about the Chesapeake — or maybe your family's genealogical past? Visit the **Maryland State Archives** (410-974-3914; 350 Rowe Blvd.) to peruse thousands of different series of records, from vital statistics to church registers, including many from the Roman Catholic Archdiocese of Baltimore. Here author Alex Haley of *Roots* fame found his African ancestor, the slave Kunta Kinte, after the late historian and longtime archivist Phoebe Jacobsen figured out how to use manumissions and other documents of slaveholders to help African-Americans trace their pasts. Call for hours and registration information.

MUSEUMS

**BANNEKER-DOUGLASS
MUSEUM**
410-216-6180.
84 Franklin St.
Open: Tues.–Fri. 10–4, Sat.
Noon–4.
Admission: Donations
welcome.

Victorian Mount Moriah African Methodist Episcopal Church, built in 1874, stood amid what was the Historic District's black neighborhood dating to the mid-nineteenth century. Named for two prominent black Marylanders — Frederick Douglass, born in the Eastern Shore's Talbot County, and Benjamin Banneker, who helped survey the Federal City, now Washington, D.C., in the 1790s — the museum celebrates Maryland's African-American life. Long-term exhibitions focus on such issues as the recent "African-American Schools in Anne Arundel County: 1865–1965." Expansion is under way, with increased gallery space and a gift shop slated to open in 2003. Visitors with a particular interest in Douglass may want to visit Twin Oaks, his summer home in Annapolis; call the Highland Beach Historical Assoc. to set up an appointment: 410-267-6960.

MUSIC

ANNAPOLIS CHORALE
410-263-1906.
www.annapolischorale.org.
Maryland Hall for the
  Creative Arts, 801 Chase
  St.
Tickets: $20–$30.

This ambitious 150-voice chorale, which has performed at Carnegie Hall, includes the smaller Chamber Chorus and the Annapolis Chamber Orchestra. Up to ten performances each season range from *Die Fledermaus* to Broadway, and include a Christmas concert for kids and a March Bach festival held at St. Anne's Church.

ANNAPOLIS OPERA
410-267-8135.
www.annapolisopera.com.
Maryland Hall for the
  Creative Arts, 801 Chase
  St.
Tickets: $48 for major
  productions.

Stages two major productions, such as *La Bohème*, an annual vocal competition, and a clever array of shorter performances, such as the annual al fresco performance at Quiet Waters Park or holiday Mozart arias.

**ANNAPOLIS SYMPHONY
  ORCHESTRA**
410-263-0907, tickets;
  410-269-1132,
  administration.
www.annapolissymphony.
  org.
Maryland Hall for the
  Creative Arts, 801 Chase
  St.
Season: Sept.–May.
Tickets: Single tickets $23,
  $30, $32; full-time students
  21 and younger $7.
Family concerts
  (recommended for kids 4
  and older): Adults $10,
  children $8.

Ambitious performances include Brahms' Symphony No. 2 or a Mozart clarinet concerto, and pops concerts at Christmas (featuring, of late, Radio City Music Hall's musical director) and in the spring. Call early for tickets; the best go to subscribers.

**MARYLAND HALL FOR
  THE CREATIVE ARTS**
410-263-5544; 410-269-1087.
www.mdhallarts.org;
  www.tickets.com.
801 Chase St., Annapolis,
  MD 21401.

Popular Maryland Hall serves as the center for the city's arts scene, headquarters to the major performing arts companies and classes. Performances by national and local artists range from pop to bluegrass.

**NAVAL ACADEMY
  MUSICAL
  PERFORMANCES**
Tickets, 410-293-TIXS;
  information,

From Glee Club concerts to world-class symphonies, the Naval Academy offers a broad variety of musical performances. Don't pass up a chance to hear an organ concert in the exquisite

410-293-2439.
U.S. Naval Academy Music
    Dept., Alumni Hall.
Prices: Range broadly; best
    to call ticket office for
    information.

Academy Chapel, including the Halloween concert by Juilliard-trained academy organist Monte Maxwell, replete with a laser light show. The annual *Messiah*, performed with the Hood College Choir and noted soloists, is a holiday favorite. In addition, the **Distinguished Artists Series** brings in five productions a year by traveling groups such as the Russian State Symphony or the London City Opera, plus a choral concert by the academy's Glee Club performing with the Annapolis Symphony Orchestra. These are held in the Bob Hope Performing Arts Center in Alumni Hall. Also, the Masqueraders theatrical club is known for an annual winter musical, such as *1776* or *On the Town*. Call early; tickets are heavily subscribed with priority for the Brigade of Midshipmen. Check www.usna.edu/Music for schedules and info.

SUMMER CONCERTS

The **Summer Serenade Concert Series** (7:30 p.m. Tues. from the second Tues. in July through the third week in Aug.) features the U.S. Naval Academy Band at City Dock. Bring a chair, and call 410-293-0263 or check www.usna .edu/USNABand for schedules.

Quiet Waters Park, located at the edge of town at the entrance to the Hillsmere community, offers Sat. concerts from mid-June to early Sept., often featuring groups such as the Annapolis Symphony and the Annapolis Opera. Call 410-222-1777 for hours and schedule.

NIGHTLIFE

Nighttime in *Annapolis* means folks head for City Dock, where places that are quaint colonial taverns at lunchtime open their doors to the music and tourist scene at night. Summer weekends can be mobbed, but even locals try to slip in one night down there to soak up the warm breezes off the water. Over the Spa Creek Bridge is *Eastport*, a hotbed of sailors and some good places to grab a drink.

The hottest live music ticket is the **Ram's Head On Stage** (410-268-4545; 33 West St.), host to the biggest name bands in town, like Suzanne Vega, Roy Clark, or the Iguanas, and also part of the **Ram's Head Tavern**, home to the **Fordham Brewing Co**. microbrewery. A couple of doors up stands **49 West Coffeehouse, Wine Bar and Gallery** (410-626-9796; 49 West St.), a European-style café with regular art openings and jazz or classical guitar music. Martinis? Try **Tsunam**i (410-990-9868; 51 West St.).

A favorite cozy brick pub is located downstairs at the Maryland Inn, the tiny **Drummer's Lot**, a terrific spot for a quiet drink, situated next to the **King of France Tavern** (410-216-6340), which features weekend jazz.

For drinks on the water: **The Chart House** (410-268-7166; 300 2nd St.) in *Eastport*. Big windows onto the water give a great view of Annapolis Harbor, and a copper-topped fireplace dominates the room. Also in Eastport is the bar at **Carrol's Creek Café** (410-263-8102; 410 Severn Ave.), with lots of local camaraderie. Go for drinks on the waterside deck during summer. On the Historic District side of Spa Creek, try **Pusser's Landing** at the Annapolis Marriott Waterfront Hotel (410-268-7555; 80 Compromise St.), with its outdoor deck and terrific black-and-white lobby photos of old Annapolis.

Irish bars have their adherents and, maybe, music: **Sean Donlon Restaurant and Irish Bar** (410-263-1993; 37 West St.), **Castlebay Irish Pub** (410-626-0165; 193 Main St.), and **Galway Bay** (410-263-8333; 61-63 Maryland Ave.), with its authentic pub.

Pubs ring City Dock, and many offer live music. **Armadillos** (410-280-0228; 132 Dock St.) hosts bands and DJs. Just up the street, **Acme Bar and Grill** (410-280-6486; 163 Main St.) has acoustic music, primarily during the week. **McGarvey's Saloon** (410-263-5700; 8 Market Space) brings an uptown saloon flavor, with mirrors backing heavily polished, dark wood bars that are often crowded on weekends; serves late. Nearby **Riordan's Saloon** (410-263-5449; 26 Market Space) is still claimed by the locals, who love the burgers, and it serves late. Also at City Dock are **Griffins** (410-268-2576; 22-24 Market Space) and **O'Brien's Oyster Bar & Restaurant** (410-268-6288; 115 Main St.).

PERFORMING ARTS & THEATER

ANNAPOLIS SUMMER GARDEN THEATRE
410-268-0809.
www.summergarden.com.
143 Compromise St.
Season: Mem. Day–Labor Day.
Tickets: Adults $12, students, senior citizens and large groups $10; no credit cards.

This blacksmith shop near City Dock dates from 1696 and may even have housed George Washington's horses out back — right where the audience sits today. Established in 1966, the theatre offers light musicals and comedies under the stars. Recent productions include Shakespeare's *Much Ado About Nothing* and Sondheim's *Into the Woods*.

CHESAPEAKE MUSIC HALL
800-406-0306, 410-626-7515.
www.chesapeakemusichall.com.
339 Busch's Frontage Rd.
Season: Year-round; Thurs.–Sun., some Wed. matinees.

Located on Rte. 50 and featuring productions like *Showboat* or *The Wizard of Oz* along with kids' shows like *Pinocchio*. Look for special nights featuring a piano bar or Elvis tribute.

COLONIAL PLAYERS
410-268-7373.
www.cplayers.com.
108 East St.
Season: Fall through spring;
shows are Thurs.–Sun.
with some Sun. matinees.
Tickets: $8 Thurs. & Sun.;
$11 Fri. & Sat.; seniors and
students $6 Thurs. & Sun.
Handicap Access: Yes.

Over 50 years old and known for its breadth, theater-in-the-round, and well-priced tickets, Colonial Players does everything from comedies to classics, like *Jacques Brel is Alive and Well and Living in Paris* or *Blood Brothers*, as well as an annual *Christmas Carol*.

SEASONAL EVENTS & FESTIVALS

David Trozzo

Eastport Yacht Club hosts the annual Lights Parade on the first Saturday in December.

A couple of easy rules: oysters in the "R" months and crabs all summer long. Keep an eye peeled for the many festivals, church suppers, and volunteer firemen's association events that include a chance to chow down on these Chesapeake delicacies. For current information about happenings, pick up a copy of *Maryland Celebrates*, an annual calendar of festivals and events, at area visitor centers. Or contact: Maryland Office of Tourism Development, 1-800-MDISFUN; www.mdisfun.org.

If the thought of a gut-busting, all-you-can-eat seafood session leaves you salivating, move the **Annapolis Rotary Club Crabfeast** to the top of your summer must-do list. *National Geographic* has even covered this event. Generally held the first Fri. of Aug. at the Navy-Marine Corps Memorial Stadium. Call 410-841-2841 or check www.annapolisrotary.com.

The **Chesapeake Bay Blues Festival,** held over a weekend in mid-May at Sandy Point State Park, features acts like Keb' Mo', Johnny Lang, R.L. Burnside, KoKo Taylor, or Bo Diddley. Park and shuttle from the Navy-Marine Corps Memorial Stadium. For information: www.bayblues.org, or write 5303 Chrysler Way, Upper Marlboro, MD 20772.

Thousands show up for the annual **Chesapeake Bay Bridge Walk**, held the first Sunday in May after the early morning **Governor's Bay Bridge Run** that fills up far in advance. Shuttles take bridge-walkers from the Navy-Marine Corps Memorial Stadium and other locations. Contact: 1-877-BAYSPAN. Whatever you do, don't plan a drive across the Bay that day. One-half of the bridge is open, but you don't want to deal with the human bottleneck.

Celebrate Maryland's African-American history at the **Kunta Kinte Heritage Festival**, named for author Alex Haley's African forebear in "Roots," who stepped off a slave ship at Annapolis City Dock. Regional entertainment includes dance troupes and steel drum bands, crafts, food, and more. Second weekend in Aug. on St. John's College's lower field. Contact: 410-349-0338.

Held since 1975 at the private Roedown Farm southwest of Annapolis in Davidsonville, the early April **Marlborough Hunt Races** draws hundreds to watch the thoroughbred point-to-point timber race. Contact: Annapolis & Anne Arundel Co. Conference and Visitors Bureau, 410-280-0445.

A knight prepares to joust during a tournament at the Maryland Renaissance Festival, which runs weekends during the fall in Crownsville near Annapolis.

David Trozzo

From its start on the weekend before Labor Day, sixteenth-century England is the order of nine consecutive weekends at the **Maryland Renaissance Festival**, held just west of Annapolis in Crownsville. Bearded men wrestle in the mud, and lovely ladies work the crowd. A roving band of jesters, crafters, jugglers, magicians, and minstrels. Admission. Contact: 410-266-7304.

The crab soup cook-off is a highlight of the Maryland Seafood Festival at Sandy Point State Park each September.

David Trozzo

The **Maryland Seafood Festival** features lots of different music and lots of seafood. Generally held the weekend after Labor Day at Sandy Point State Park near Annapolis. Kids' activities. Call 410-268-7682 or check www.mdsea foodfestival.com.

Every mariner for miles around attends Columbus Day weekend's **U.S. Sailboat Show** at Annapolis City Dock. The very latest in sailboat designs, from racing to cruising vessels, is found in the water along with every imaginable service or sailing gimcrack. In-town parking will be a nightmare (try the shuttle from Navy-Marine Corps Memorial Stadium), but expect bargains, deals, and celebrations among the restaurants and bars. Admission. Contact: 410-268-8828. The following weekend, check out The **U.S. Powerboat Show** at the same location. Here's your chance to see the newest boats for work or play in the water, from yachts to inflatables. Admission. Contact: 410-268-8828.

TOURS

The **Historic Annapolis Foundation** has prevailed upon avid Chesapeake sailor Walter Cronkite to narrate two intriguing tours of this 300-year-old city. The famed newsman tells of the city's colonial or African-American heritage via "Acoustiguide" recordings. Reserve an hour for the African-American Heritage Tour; ninety minutes for colonial history. Tapes rented at the foundation's Welcome Center and Museum Store at City Dock. Available daily; $5 per person. Contact: 410-268-5576.

David Trozzo

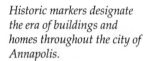

Historic markers designate the era of buildings and homes throughout the city of Annapolis.

Annapolis Tours, also called Three Centuries Tours, means guides in colonial dress lead groups through city streets, point out the highlights, and disclose tales that you'd otherwise miss. Group tours, garden tours, tavern suppers, candlelight tours, and excursions to the Eastern Shore are also offered year-round. Daily walk-up tours leave Apr. 1–Oct. 31 at 10:30am from the city's visitor center at 26 West St., at 1:30 from the City Dock information booth. No reservations required; fee. Contact: 410-263-5401; www.annapolis-tours.com.

Discover Annapolis takes visitors for one-hour bus rides through the city's sights, departing the city's visitor center at 26 West St. Fee; no credit cards. Make reservations at the visitor center. Contact: 410-626-6000.

RECREATION

BICYCLING

Y ou can't cross the William Preston Lane Jr. Memorial Bridge — aka the Bay Bridge — on a bike. Officially, you're on your own to arrange transportation. However, if you get stuck, the police at the Bay Bridge can refer you. Call them at 410-757-1977/78. Check Chapter Nine, *Information*, for state cycling info.

To reach the 13.3-mi. **Baltimore & Annapolis Trail** from town: Cross the Severn River via the U.S. Naval Academy Bridge. At the far side, go straight to the trail, on your left, built along the old railroad bed, which travels north to Glen Burnie. You'll share it with in-line skaters and walkers. For information: 410-222-6244.

Runners jog along the Baltimore & Annapolis Trail, which is also great for biking.

David Trozzo

Quiet Waters Park (south of town on Hillsmere Dr.) is a favorite local destination for family cyclists and in-line skaters. Paved trails of just under six miles wind through woods and open parkland, and end overlooking the South River. Contact: 410-222-1777; closed Tues.

LOCAL CYCLING SHOPS

Bike Doctor (410-266-7383; 150 Jennifer Rd.).
Capitol Bicycle Center (410-266-5510; 300 Chiquapin Round Rd.).

BIRD-WATCHING

Situated along the Atlantic Flyway, Bayside **Sandy Point State Park** offers good year-round birding — but offers particular treats in winter or spring. Northern waterfowl (loons, grebes, and gannets) and all owl species have been spotted in winter. Breeding birds, many of them songbirds, have been spotted in the restricted back acreage of the park, which is a bird sanctuary. Check at the park office (open 8:30–4 Mon.–Fri.) to see if you can get access, or find out about walks hosted by local bird clubs: 410-974-2149; 1100 E. College Pkwy., Annapolis, MD 21401.

BOATING

Deck shoes are de rigueur, and masts fill Spa Creek in the middle of America's Sailing Capital, where everybody can talk a little boat talk. On Wed. evenings in summer, the Annapolis Yacht Club hosts races on Spa Creek — starting gun, approximately 6pm. To watch, stake out a spot at the Eastport Bridge, or visit a creekside restaurant.

CHARTERS, CRUISES & BOAT RENTALS

Annapolis

Annapolis Bay Charters (800-292-1119, 410-269-1776; www.annapolisbaychar
ters.com; 7310 Edgewood Rd./P.O. Box 4604, Annapolis, MD 21403) Since
1980; thirty or more boats up to eighty-six feet, sail or power, captained or
bareboat. Charters also available out of Solomons.

Annapolis Marriott Waterfront (410-263-7827; 80 Compromise St., Annapolis,
MD 21401) Home to both the Schooner *Woodwind* and rental concessions for
small sailboat and two electric boats.

Beginagain (800-295-1422, 410-626-1422; captpaul@erols.com; 1511 Bay Ridge
Ave., Annapolis, MD 21403) This thirty-six-foot sloop operates three-hour
trips three times a day from City Dock. May 1–Sept. 30; $60 per person, plus
tax; maximum six passengers.

Schooner *Woodwind* (410-263-7837; www.schoonerwoodwind.com; Annapolis
Marriott Waterfront dock, 80 Compromise St., Annapolis, MD 21401) Twin
74-foot wooden *Woodwinds I* and *II* ply Annapolis Harbor; the original takes
tourists. On Fri. sunset sails, catch the popular locals, Them Eastport Oyster
Boys, performing their own brand of Bay music. Sails daily; call for schedule.

Stanley Norman (410-268-8816; 6 Herndon Ave., Annapolis, MD 21403) The famed
skipjack belongs to the Chesapeake Bay Foundation, and occasional trips may
include an oyster dredging excursion. Costs are less for CBF members.

Watermark Cruises (410-268-7600; www.watermarkcruises.com; Annapolis
City Dock, P.O. Box 3350, Annapolis, MD 21403) Longtime city business
offers forty- and ninety-minute tours out of Annapolis Harbor and Severn
River, or trips across the Bay to St. Michaels. The range of vessels includes
the 297-passenger *Harbor Queen*. Specialty cruises range from moonlit wine
cruises to a "blues cruise" to others. Also look for their City Dock-based Jiffy
Water Taxis for a quick ride across Spa Creek.

Edgewater

Suntime Rentals (410-266-6020; 2820 Solomons Island Rd., Edgewater, MD
21037) Powerboats (nineteen-footers), Jet Skis, waterskiing equipment, and
wakeboards just south of Annapolis on the South River. Two-hour minimum; daily rates available. May 1-Oct. 1.

Galesville

Hartge Chesapeake Charters & Yacht Sales (410-867-7240; www.hartge.com;
4880 Church Lane, Galesville, MD 20765) Charter fleet of ten twenty-eight-
to thirty-seven-foot sailing vessels south of Annapolis. All bareboat.

LANDINGS AND BOAT RAMPS:

See Chapter Nine, *Information*, for info on free maps of Chesapeake landings.

MARINAS

Annapolis

Annapolis City Marina (410-268-0660; 410 Severn Ave., Annapolis, MD 21403) Right in the midst of the bustle. Transient dockage for boats drawing up to ten feet. Groceries, laundry, showers, fuel, and pump-out station. 87 slips.

Annapolis Landing Marina (410-263-0090; 980 Awald Dr., Annapolis, MD 21403) Transients, fuel, showers, laundry, café, pump-out station, and swimming pool. 120 slips.

Annapolis Yacht Basin (410-263-3544; 2 Compromise St., Annapolis, MD 21401) Transients, fuel, ice, showers, laundry. 107 slips (about 40 for transients).

Bert Jabin's Yacht Yard, Inc. (410-268-9667; www.bjyy.com; 7310 Edgewood Rd., Annapolis, MD 21403) One of the biggest marinas in the area, with about 400 slips and a huge yard with all services. Transients.

Chesapeake Harbour Marina (410-268-1969; www.chesapeakeharbourmarina .com; 2030 Chesapeake Harbour Dr. E., Annapolis, MD 21403) Transients, water taxi to City Dock area. Pool, tennis court. 200 slips.

Mears Marina (410-268-8282, 301-261-1234; www.mearsmarinas.com; 519 Chester Ave., Annapolis, MD 21403) Transient slips fluctuate among the 236 slips, including a few that accommodate boats up to eighty feet. Pool, tennis courts. Call in advance. Headquarters of Severn River Yacht Club.

Petrini, Inc. (410-263-4278; www.petrinishipyard.com; 1 Walton Lane, Annapolis, MD 21403) Range of services on Spa Creek. Biggest Travelift in Annapolis. About 45 slips; transients can find space.

Port Annapolis (410-269-1990; www.portannapolis.com; 7074 Bembe Beach Rd., Annapolis, MD 21403) Bikes. No fuel. 265 slips.

Friendship and Tracey's Landing

Herrington Harbour (North — Tracey's Landing, 800-297-1930; South — Friendship, 800-213-9438) Yacht yard to the north; resort to the south. Herrington Harbour is enormous and a notable presence south of Annapolis. Dining available at both; the resort offers everything from nature trails to a beachfront motel. Hundreds of slips.

Galesville

Hartge Yacht Yard (410-867-2188, 301-261-5141; 4880 Church Lane, Galesville, MD 20765) A favored area marina that's been there since 1865. All services. 280 slips; usually some transient availability.

Severna Park

Magothy Marina (410-647-2356; 360 Magothy Rd., Severna Park, MD 21146) Marina services, swimming pool. Deep-draft slips, 182 total, including some off the seventeen-foot channel. Located on the Magothy River, just north of the Bay Bridge.

SAILING & POWERBOAT SCHOOLS

Annapolis Sailing School (800-638-9192, 410-267-7205; annapolissailing.com; 601 6th St., Annapolis, MD 21403) Classes offered by a venerable, reputable school. Experienced instructors teach classes from "Become a Sailor in One Weekend" to "Bareboat Cruising." Sail the waters off Annapolis, between the Chesapeake Bay Bridge and Tolley Point, and up the Severn River, popular with local sailors. Rentals of twenty-four-foot Rainbow daysailers are available. Also home to KidShip, where sailors as young as 5 learn to tack. Holder 12s and Americas and Barnetts, and the Annapolis Powerboat School with five- and two-day courses.

Chesapeake Sailing School (800-966-0032, 410-269-1594; www.sailingclasses .com; 7074 Bembe Beach Rd., Annapolis, MD 21403) Well-established school offers a wide range of sailing courses, as well as half-day to weeklong charters on vessels ranging from eight-foot Optis for beginning kids to Tanzer 22s for older folks. Also offers the Kids on Boats program for families; the Tiller Club allows sailors to pay a yearly fee to take out Tanzer 22s, and rentals on boats ranging from twenty-two to thirty-eight feet; captain and bareboat charters.

J World (410-280-2040; www.sailjworld.com; 213 Eastern Ave., Annapolis, MD 21403) Begun in Annapolis in the early 1990s, the J-boat-oriented sailing school offers weekend programs for any level. Also, weeklong schools.

Womanship (800-342-9295, 410-267-6661; 137 Conduit St., Annapolis, MD 21401) This reputable school was started by women for women and now has spread to fifteen locations, hosting three-, five-, and seven-day comprehensive classes, including mother-daughter classes and beyond. Daytime classes.

CANOEING & KAYAKING

Wild rice grows with midsummer abandon along Jug Bay, a suburban outpost along the Patuxent River west of Annapolis. Three centuries ago, this was a deepwater harbor, but time, siltation, and an old railroad bed have conspired to create a quiet paddler's paradise for modern times. Studded by marshmallows and home to kingbirds, territorial red-wing blackbirds, and largemouth bass or perch, access to this tidal river includes the **Jug Bay Wetlands Sanctuary** (410-741-9330; 1361 Wrighton Rd., Lothian, MD 20711; open Wed., Sat., Sun.; closed Sun. Dec.–Feb.; call in advance for access) on the east bank in Anne Arundel County, offering guided canoe trips from time to time. **The Patuxent River Park Jug Bay Natural Area** (301-627-6074; 16000 Croom Airport Rd., Upper Marlboro, MD 20772), across the river in Prince George's County, is uncrowded with two landings. Buy a nominally priced permit to paddle and a fishing license to cast. Check for canoe trips, even pontoon boat trips. Canoe and kayak rentals. Call for prices.

OTHER RENTALS

Amphibious Horizons (888-I-LUV-SUN, 410-267-8742; www.amphibioushorizons.com; 600 Quiet Waters Park Rd., Annapolis, MD 21403) operates out of Quiet Waters Park from Apr.–Oct. Singles, doubles, and sit-on-top kayak rentals, plus canoes and paddleboats to folks who venture to the park. All but the most experienced kayakers stay in Harness Creek, since the South River, a quarter-mile away, is known for its heavy powerboat traffic. Kayak classes. No canoe trips, but kayaking trips explore waters from Havre de Grace to Smith Island, from one day to one week.

The Springriver Corp. (410-263-2303, 301-888-1377; www.springriver.com; 311 Third St., Annapolis, MD 21403) has reasonably priced rentals by the half day or full day. Call by Thurs. for weekend reservations. Located on Spa Creek in Eastport.

FAMILY FUN

See the goats, learn to milk a cow, and learn about organic farming at the **Horizon Organic Dairy, Farm and Educational Center** (410-923-7600; www.horizonorganicfarm.com; 1 Dairy La., Gambrills, MD 21054), located

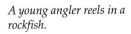

A young angler reels in a rockfish.

David Trozzo

outside Annapolis on 875 acres in **_Gambrills_**. Tours are available; the education center is open Mar. 16–Dec. 31. Mon.–Sat. 10–5, Sun. 12–5; fee.

FISHING

BOAT RAMPS

In **_Annapolis_**, Sandy Point State Park (410-974-2149; 1100 E. College Pkwy.; nominal entry fee) gets you right onto the Bay. Twenty-two ramps launch boaters into Mezick Pond, a little inlet on the Chesapeake. Very popular and reasonable. Spa Creek access is at **Truxtun Park** (410-263-7958; Hilltop Lane; nominal fee to launch; no park entry fee) in the middle of town outside the Historic District.

CHARTER FISHING BOATS

Edgewater

Sportfishing on the Chesapeake Bay, Inc. (800-638-7871, 301-261-4207; www. belindagail.com; P.O. Box 53, Edgewater, MD 21037) Capt. Jerry Lastfogel, former officer for the Maryland Charterboat Assoc., has been running charter boat fishing expeditions for years. Fish aboard the forty-two-foot _Belinda Gail III_. Half-day and full-day trips out of Collins Marine Railway on Rockhold Creek in Deale.

GOLF

Annapolis Golf Club (410-263-6771; 2638 Carrollton Rd., Annapolis) 9 holes. Nice, local course; semiprivate. Located in the Annapolis Roads community.
Atlantic Golf at South River (800-SO-RIVER, 410-798-5865; www.mdgolf.com; 3451 Solomons Island Rd., Edgewater) 18 holes. Challenging public course. Driving range, putting green. Earned 3½ stars in _Golf Digest's_ 2000–2001 "Places to Play."
Bay Hills Golf Club (410-974-0669; 545 Bay Hills Dr., Arnold) 18 holes; semiprivate. Located north of Annapolis.
Dwight D. Eisenhower Golf Course (410-571-0973; 1576 Generals Hwy., Crownsville) 18 holes. Popular public course located just outside Annapolis.

NATURAL PLACES: STATE, NATIONAL AND PRIVATE REFUGES & PARKS

Jug Bay Wetlands Sanctuary (410-741-9330; 1361 Wrighton Rd., Lothian, MD

20711) Seven miles of uncrowded trails; limited hours. On the Patuxent River; if you're lucky, you might — and we mean might — catch a glimpse of the elusive river otter. Open Wed. and weekends in warm weather; small entrance fee. Call for reservations and winter hours.

Kids catch blue crabs with chicken necks tied to a net or a string.

David Trozzo

Sandy Point State Park (410-974-2149; 1100 E. College Pkwy., Annapolis, MD 21401) 786 acres. Located on Rte. 50, near the last exit before the Bay Bridge. One of the few sandy beaches on the Bay. It's fun to hang out here and watch what goes in the Bay — from passing scows or barges to the crisp white sails of the yachting set in summer. Plus, an up-close and personal view of the Bay Bridge. Beach for swimming, fishing, crabbing; marina means boating (rowboats and motorboats for rent), windsurfing; 22 boat ramps; bait, tackle, fuel, and fishing licenses. Costs are $3 to $4 per person. Over age 62 and kids in car seats free.

SPORTING GOODS & CAMPING SUPPLY STORES

Angler's Sport Center (410-757-3442; 1456 Whitehall Rd., Annapolis) The dean of local sporting goods. Hunting and fishing licenses, fishing gear, decoys, outdoor clothing, supplies for archery and hunting. Located between Annapolis and the Bay Bridge, exit 30 off Rte. 50, E. of Cape St. Claire.

Marty's Sporting Goods (410-956-2238; 95 Mayo Rd., Edgewater) Everything for fishing.

SWIMMING

Arundel Olympic Swim Center (410-222-7933, 301-970-2216; 2690 Riva Rd., Annapolis) Olympic-sized pool operated by the Anne Arundel County Recreation and Parks Dept. Nominal entrance fees. Open Mon.–Fri. 6am–10pm, Sat. 8–8, Sun. 10–6.

Sandy Point State Park (410-974-2149; 1100 E. College Pkwy., Annapolis) One of the few sandy beaches on the Bay. Costs are $3 to $4 per person. Over age 62 and kids in car seats free. Take the last exit off Rte. 50 before the Bay Bridge.

TENNIS

In Anne Arundel County, forty-five county parks have tennis courts; eight have lights for nighttime play. Visitors to Annapolis, where court time is harder to find, may want to use courts in nearby towns in less-congested central or rural south county. Contact: Anne Arundel County Department of Recreation and Parks, 410-222-7300.

SHOPPING

ANTIQUES

Annapolis Antique Gallery (410-266-0635; 2009 West St.) An emporium of 40 dealers offering glass, china, and furniture; items ranging from country to Empire. Take the Parole exit off Rte. 50, and you're practically there.

Antiquity Perfection (410-216-9067; 69 Maryland Ave.) Jewelry and linens, glassware and furniture. Eight dealers; perhaps the most browsable antiques shop on Maryland Avenue.

Bon Vivant Antiques (410-263-9651; 104 Annapolis St., West Annapolis) A welcome addition to the West Annapolis shopping corridor, with a wonderful antique shop full of china, silver, and jewelry treasures. Well worth a stop.

Ron Snyder Antiques (410-266-5452; 2011 West St.) Eighteenth- and nineteenth-century furniture, and a devotee of the 100-year rule. Marilyn Snyder says they like to start at 1830 and work back. Right next to the Annapolis Antique Gallery; longtime local dealer.

West Annapolis Antiques (410-295-1200; 103 Annapolis St., West Annapolis) The women tee-heeing over the fabulous hats they found in this browsable shop were worth the stop.

BOOKS

Annapolis

Barnes & Noble (410-573-1115; Annapolis Harbour Center, Rte. 2 & Aris T. Allen Blvd.) Huge and popular, as one might expect. But also a knowledge-able selection of regional and local books, ranging from Bay histories and watermen to literature penned by local writers. Probably the best stock of Chesapeake books around.

Borders (410-571-0923; Westfield Shoppingtown Annapolis, Rte. 50, Jennifer & Bestgate Rds.) The popular chain has recently arrived in a huge two-story emporium in the Annapolis mall. Books and much more.

Briarwood Bookshop (410-268-1440; 66 Maryland Ave.) Good selection of Maryland books and a variety of used tomes on art, military, and other sub-jects of interest to sophisticated, inquiring minds. A good bulletin board, too — worth checking out to see what's going on.

CHILDREN

Be Beep-A-Toy Shop (410-224-4066; Festival at Riva Shopping Center, 2327-C Forest Dr.) Quality toys.

Fancy Frocks (410-626-9711; 216 B Main St.) Wide variety of little kids' wear; cute and different.

The Giant Peach (410-268-8776; 110 Annapolis St., West Annapolis) Probably the most venerable children's clothing shop in town.

CLOTHING

Elanne (410-263-3300; 27 Maryland Ave.) Excellent service from one of the city's longtime specialty women's clothing shops. Recommended if you're looking for something different.

Fashnique (410-268-6778; 181 Main St.) Gauze, imports, 100-percent cotton and rayon clothing for women. Good selection, and the sales at this longtime local shop aren't bad, either.

Hats in the Belfry (410-268-6333; 103 Main St.) Something of an impromptu performance space, because everybody tries on hats: felt hats, straw hats, including genuine Panamas, funky hats, sporty hats, Easter bonnets, and hats to garden in.

Hazel T., Ltd. (410-263-5958; 206 Main St.) Upscale, good-looking women's clothing that's breezily fashionable. Unique jewelry, too.

Hyde Park Annapolis Haberdashery (410-263-0074; 110 Dock St., Harbour Square) Classic men's clothing.

Johnson's on the Avenue (410-263-6390; Maryland Ave. & State Cir.) In the window hang traditional houndstooth wools and other fine classic menswear for civilians; inside, the Italian sweaters are folded on the counter. This Annapolis institution once made uniforms for Navy officers for seven decades and shipped them all over the world. Now their trademark "military covers," or hats, are worn by the actors in the TV series *JAG*. Noted for fine service.

Knits, Etc. (410-280-3400; 88 Maryland Ave.) Worth a stop if you're in search of sweater variety, from light summer pastel tops to multicolored cardigans.

Why Knot (410-263-3003; 162 Main St.) Good-looking women's clothing from one of the historic district's longtime shops.

DESIGN SHOPS

Details (410-269-1965; 80 Maryland Ave.) Design business storefront shop with a nice array of upscale but not overpriced lamps, candles, frames, and other items for the home.

DHS Designs (410-280-3466; 86 Maryland Ave.) Fun to shop; large French or Italian pieces that go along with a design business.

GALLERIES

The Annapolis Pottery (410-268-6153; 40 State Cir.) A well-loved local institution offering a wide array of stoneware and porcelain pieces, from handy pitchers to art platters and more.

Aurora Gallery (410-263-9150; 67 Maryland Ave.) Contemporary design pieces and fine crafts in many media. Good jewelry, too.

Dawson Gallery (410-269-1299; 44 Maryland Ave.) Old-fashioned gallery with worn wooden floors showcases nineteenth- and early twentieth-century American and European paintings.

La Petite Galerie (410-268-2425; 39 Maryland Ave.) Paintings from the nineteenth and twentieth centuries; generally traditional, representational works. Local artists.

League of Maryland Craftsmen (410-626-1277; 216 Main St.) Established upper Main Street commercial gallery focused on Maryland-based craftspeople. Nice turned wood pieces, or crabs done up in any medium at all. Glass, sculpture, paintings.

Main Street Gallery (410-626-1277; 109 Main St.) Nice space; a real mix of work. Represents about forty-five artists, primarily regional. Openings monthly from Apr.–Oct.

Maria's Picture Place (410-263-8282; 45 Maryland Ave.) Small gallery with good frame shop showcases famed Annapolis-based Chesapeake photographer Marion Warren.

McBride Gallery (410-267-7077; 215 Main St.) Longtime local gallery hosts a variety of sixty artists, many from Virginia and Maryland, many with a maritime or shoreside appeal.

Nancy Hammond Editions (410-267-7711; 64 State Cir.) Longtime local silk screen artist creates vibrant cut-paper painted collages, prints and other pieces. Also, limited edition silk screen prints of Bay-related icons like herons, ties, jewelry. Very Annapolis.

West Annapolis Gallery (410-269-5828; 108 Annapolis St.) Great show of watercolor landscapes by a Maryland Hall artist in residence and the gallery's owner last we stopped in. At the time, we picked up a cool copper hanging garden sculpture. Frame shop.

GIFT SHOPS & CRAFT GALLERIES

Easy Street (410-263-5556; 8 Francis St.) Among the best and most enduring of the city's upscale craft and gift galleries. Specializes in blown glass or art glass pieces.

Europa (410-268-4400; 62 Maryland Ave.) Tapestries and brocades, glassware and paintings from abroad.

The Pewter Chalice (410-268-6246; 168 Main St.) Tired of scouring the earth for classic "silver" baby gifts? A nice pewter selection of these and a wide range of other fine pewter pieces.

Plat du Jour (410-269-1499; 220 Main St.) Filled with tempting French and Italian ceramics and fine linens. Among the most unique shops in the Historic District.

JEWELRY

La Belle Cezanne (410-263-1996; 117 Main St.) One of the best windows to shop in Annapolis. Some unique items.

Tilghman Co. (410-268-7855; 44 State Cir.) The fine old Maryland name of this business tells you that this is a traditional jewelry store featuring classic gold and silver pieces and pearls, plus Lenox, Waterford, and fine sterling. In business since 1928; on State Circle since 1948.

W.R. Chance Jewelers (410-263-2404; 110 Main St.) From traditional to contemporary work; fine service. In business more than 50 years.

MALLS & OUTLETS

Annapolis Harbour Center (410-266-5857; Rte. 2 & Aris T. Allen Blvd.) This place has been packed since the day it opened in the early 1990s. Tower Records, Office Depot, Fresh Fields, Starbucks, Barnes & Noble, Old Navy, and many specialty clothing shops.

Westfield Shoppingtown Annapolis (410-266-5432; Rte. 50, Jennifer & Bestgate Rds.) Over 180 stores, with Nordstrom and Lord & Taylor, The Hecht Co., clothing, book, record, shoe, and specialty stores.

MARINE SHOPS

Bacon & Assoc., Inc. (410-263-4880; 116 Legion Ave.) Nifty place for used equipment; noted for a broad array of secondhand sails. In business over forty years. Open during the week only except Sat. 9:30-12:30 in summer.

Boater's World (410-266-7766, 301-970-2073; Annapolis Harbour Center, Rte. 2 & Aris T. Allen Blvd.) Discount marine supplies.

Fawcett Boat Supplies, Inc. (410-267-8681; 110 Compromise St.) Right at City Dock, a local institution for fifty years and a good source of local boating information. Good selection of nautical books.

SPECIALTY SHOPS AND GENERAL STORES

A.L. Goodies General Store (410-269-0071; 112 Main St.) The resident five-and-dime in the trendy City Dock area. Two full floors. Racks and racks of greeting cards, brass weather vanes . . . even peanut butter cookies.

Annapolis Country Store (410-269-6773; 53 Maryland Ave.) The floorboards still creak in this upscale general store, which features Winnie-the-Pooh, Raggedy Ann, Crabtree & Evelyn, and more.

Art Things (410-268-3520; 2 Annapolis St., West Annapolis) Great art supply shop, where the employees are perennially helpful and cheerful. Paints, brushes, papers, and hard-to-find items like oversized mailing tubes.

Avoca Handweavers (410-263-1485; 141-143 Main St.) Avoca has been doing business in Ireland since 1723 and continues to make a splash in the Annapolis Historic District. Exquisite handiwork. Wools, linens, clothing, as well as Irish glass and pottery.

Chadwick's, The British Shoppe, Ltd. (410-280-BRIT; 10 Annapolis St., West Annapolis) Filled with all kinds of imported British things, including many foods and Woods of Windsor toiletries. Books, greeting cards, china.

Chesapeake Trading Company (410-216-9797; 149 Main St.) Books, great jewelry, and outdoor clothing.

Historic Annapolis Foundation Museum Store (410-268-5576; 77 Main St.) Classic children's toys and museum-quality gifts in a restored eighteenth-century warehouse.

Pepper's (410-267-8722; 133 Main St.) Navy T-shirt and sweatshirt central.

A South-of-Town Outing

Crystal, humid-free days have a way of blowing through sultry Chesapeake just as midsummer wanders past, hinting at the coming fall. Now's the time to hit the roads south of Annapolis for **Galesville**, a gentle West River port town about an hour's drive east of Washington, D.C., and only 15 miles south of Annapolis. Annapolitans widely consider this boaters' haven to be an off-the-beaten-path gem. With its couple of restaurants, couple of shops, and the view across the mast-laden river from the tiny waterfront park, Galesville offers a glimpse at old "South County" life, as this area south of Annapolis is known.

Head down Rte. 2 S., and feel free to stop at the occasional antique shop or farm-stand you'll find along the way. Turn left on Muddy Creek Rd. after 4.4 miles, and stay on this winding road through old farmland for another five miles. When you reach Galesville Road, turn left and stay on it into town. You'll pass a few antique shops here, as well.

Closer to the water stands the **West River Market & Deli** (410-867-4844; 1000 Main St.), which has been here over 100 years, replete with horehound candy in a barrel in the back. You'll also find pies ranging from key lime to blueberry, break-fast sandwiches, and dinner specials like crab cakes or BBQ. If it's breakfast or lunch, walk a few hundred feet down Main Street to eat at the waterside park with benches and a collection of boat propellers serving as public art. If it's the week-end, stop next door (leave lunch outside) at the market's former granary-turned-art-gallery. The **River Gallery, Ltd.** (410-867-0954; 1000 Main St) is owned by three artists who show the original artwork, including paintings and crafts, of up to twenty consignors. Open Fri. Noon–3, Sat.–Sun. 11–5, or by appt.

If you're more inclined to tuck into a full meal, two delightful spots fill the bill. **Topside Inn** (410-867-1321; 1004 Galesville Rd.; serving D, L on summer weekends, Sunday B, L; closed Mon.–Tues.) has a second-floor balcony across the street from the river; try to snare a table there. Seafood is highly advised, perhaps with a Mediterranean touch (fresh red snapper with tomatoes and onions, marinated in olive oil and basil, topped with scallions). Prices are Moderate to Expensive, espe-cially if you simply opt for a salad (try the seafood salad with shrimp, scallops, crabmeat, and feta).

Across the street stands **The Inn at Pirate's Cove** (410-867-2300; 4817 Riverside Dr.; serving L, D, SB; Moderate to Expensive), with its seafood-heavy menu and a willingness to charge only $1 to split an entrée. Try the portobello mushroom with gruyere appetizer and the signature Flounder Longhorn, a filet stuffed with crab and garnished with a shrimp, only if you're starved. Ask for a table on the far side of the deck from Big Mary's Dock Bar in summer (unless live music is preferable to conversation), or enjoy the tiled bar area in colder weather. This is also home to a small inn and a marina with transient slips.

There's no need to stop where Anne Arundel County stops, however. Areas fur-ther south, still within Maryland, hold their own treasures. When planning a trip, consider Calvert County, Solomons Island, and St. Mary's County, described in the next sections.

CALVERT COUNTY

The Gov. Thomas Johnson Bridge arcs across the Patuxent River at Solomons Island, where the river flows into the Chesapeake Bay.

David Trozzo

New residents discovered this Western Shore county to the tune of a 45 percent population boost in the 1990s, but not to fret. Fishing and exploring are fine hereabouts, with a touch of prehistoric glamour added by the 30-mile, Bay-front Calvert Cliffs. Public access points are few, but you can still find sharks' teeth and other fossils. At the county's southern tip, the Patuxent River meets the Bay at Solomons Island, a boating center and tourist village. Day-trippers from Washington, D.C. and Baltimore will discover much.

Golfers will be happy to tee off at the **Twin Shields Golf Club** (410-257-7800; 2425 Roarty Rd.) off Rte. 4 on Rte. 260 in *Dunkirk*, an 18-hole, semiprivate course highly praised by an old golf pro friend. Near the county's northern boundary, it's west of side-by-side North Beach and Chesapeake Beach, two towns long overlooked and a tad funky, and now being re-discovered with their small Bayside beaches and boardwalks. Go antiquing in *North Beach* at **Nice & Fleazy Antique Center** (410-257-3044; 7th & Bay Ave.), with a large space that even has a section for slot machines, remnants of Southern Maryland's gamblin' past. Quartered in the same space, **Willetta's Antiques** (301-855-3472; open Thurs.–Sun.) routinely carries good-looking china pieces and furniture that most definitely are not the usual suspects. **Coffee, Tea & Whimsey** (410-286-0000; 9122-B Bay Ave.) across the street has whimsical gifts, especially those with a nautical bent, and a coffee bar in back.

The decades-old **Rod 'N Reel** complex, founded in 1946, is a key attraction in *Chesapeake Beach*, a town first envisioned as a getaway at the turn of the last century. Its notable marina (301-855-8450; Rte. 261 & Mears Ave.) offers sportfishing from May–Nov. Hunt for rockfish or bluefish on a half-day or full-day trip accommodated by a sizeable fleet of Coast Guard-licensed captains, as well as head boats. The complex's signature restaurant (301-855-8351; L, D daily, B, L, D Sat. & Sun.; Moderate to Expensive), with wide windows onto the marina and an expansive stretch of Bay, likely provides the area's best dining option. A seafood-heavy dinner menu scales the price range from a $10.99 seafood-filled potato skins appetizer to a host of platters priced around $25. Choose from an entire section of crab sandwiches at lunch. Out front in summer, the **Boardwalk Café** (410-257-2735) offers a tiny taste of Ocean City along the Western Shore.

Across the street stands the **Chesapeake Beach Water Park** (410-257-1404; 4079 Creekside Dr.) with eight slides, a "dreamland river" where you can tube or swim, and more — including a separate "diaper" pool. Fee. Open Mem. Day–Labor Day.

Five miles south stands the **Breezy Point Beach & Campground** (410-535-0259 from May 1–Oct 31; otherwise, 301-855-1243, ext 225; office: 175 Main St., Prince Frederick, MD 20678), where nets off the beach help protect swimmers from sea nettles. You can also fish, crab, or camp here. Open May 1–Oct. 31, 6am–dusk. Fee.

Farther south, on Rte. 4 at *Huntingtown*, pull into the **Southern Maryland Antique Center** (410-257-1677; 3176 Solomons Island Rd.; open Thurs.–Sat.) when you see the red, white, and blue "antiques" flag flying. Good furniture finds are possible at this large and worthwhile multidealer center. At *Prince Frederick*, see the **Main Street Gallery** (410-535-3334; 486 Main St.; open Wed. –Sat. 11–5, plus Sun. in Nov.–Dec.), where artists Nancy Collery and Jeff Klapper have turned their home's first floor into a gallery that shows regional artists. Still farther south, at *St. Leonard*, the **Chesapeake Marketplace** (800-655-1081, 410-586-3725; 5015 St. Leonard Rd.; open Wed.–Sun.) is a real browsing emporium for those who can't resist flea markets.

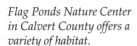

Flag Ponds Nature Center in Calvert County offers a variety of habitat.

David Trozzo

A mix of habitat throughout the county means good bird-watching (herons and kingfishers, American woodcock, bald eagles), hiking, and even beach time. Visit the 100-acre **Battle Creek Cypress Swamp** in *Prince Frederick* (410-535-5327; Grays Rd., off Rte. 506; open Tues.–Sat. 10–4:30, Sun. 1–4:30 Oct.–Mar.; 5pm closing in summer.) to stroll the boardwalk running through the nation's northernmost stand of bald cypress, an intriguing — and unique — Bay-area habitat. Seven miles south, at *St. Leonard*, is 500-acre **Jefferson Patterson Park and Museum** (410-586-8500; 10515 Mackall Rd.; open Wed.–Sun. 10–5), headquarters for much of the state's archaeological work, with a visitor's center highlighting Chesapeake's past. Easy trails through fields and along the Patuxent River pass digs. The old barn has been transformed into a broad picnic pavilion. Just a tad south, perhaps a mile, look to the left of Rte. 2/4 for the sign to Bayside **Flag Ponds Nature Park** (410-586-1477; open daily, Mem. Day–Labor Day; weekends the rest of the year; small fee.) Here's one of the larger Bay beaches you're likely to see, along with a fishing pier, fossil-hunting, visitor center and a friendly nod to the property's former life as a pound-net fishing station. Remainders such as the restored "Buoy Hotel" tell of the fishermen who stayed here for weeks at a time.

If it's time to eat, **Stoney's,** with locations in *Prince Frederick* and *Broomes Island,* can't be beat. Given the choice between the two, we go to the Stoney's on Broomes Island, an isle notable because former state Sen. Bernie Fowler undertakes his "sneaker index" every June to peer down to see if the Bay's clarity has improved. Getting there, down a long and winding tidewater road, is half the adventure, and Stoney's broad deck on the water, one of the biggest around, features a floating dock.

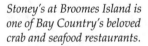

Stoney's at Broomes Island is one of Bay Country's beloved crab and seafood restaurants.

David Trozzo

But sometimes you're on Rte. 2/4 through town and you don't have time to wander down a back road, or worse, it's the dead of winter and the Broomes Island Stoney's is closed. This is when we go to the Fox Run Shopping Center Stoney's in Prince Frederick, with its clubby Chesapeake waterfowl décor and spacious dining room, as well as a full dinner menu, which you won't find on Broomes Island. Either way, the food's great: peppery crab soup, a baseball-sized "baby" crab cake, which, at four ounces, allows substantive crab gluttony — and it comes in an even larger size. On a hot day, the dining room can be sparse. Everybody must be down at the Broomes Island Stoney's, cracking crabs on the waterfront. If its raining, ask for an upstairs table, order the smoked bluefish appetizer to go along with your crabs (or crab cakes), and settle in for a fine time peering out over the water. (410-535-1888; 545 N. Solomons Island Rd., Prince Frederick/410-586-1888; Oyster House Rd., Broomes Island, closed Nov.–early Feb.; both serving L, D daily; Moderate).

If it's the last Sat. in August, consider a stop at the island's 1672 Christ Episcopal Church at 3100 Broomes Island Rd. to celebrate Maryland's official state sport at the **Calvert County Jousting Tournament,** well into its second century. Knights engage in mock battle and a bazaar is set up before the sporting jousts begin. Admission $1; limited handicap access. End the day with a reasonably priced country supper at the church. Contact: 410-586-0565.

Just north of Solomons, in _Lusby,_ sits a famous throwback, where paper umbrellas stud serious drinks (be careful) and the keyboardist has been known to play "Don't Cry for Me, Argentina" — twice. Surely the food's not the only draw at **Vera's White Sands** (410-586-1182; off Rte. 4; open April–mid-Oct., Tues.–Sat. 5–9, Sun. 1–9; serving D Tues.–Sat., L and D Sat.–Sun.; Moderate to Expensive). We once settled into our rattan peacock chair at a table overlooking St. Leonard's Creek as a nearby table ordered. A crème de menthe parfait for her; a shrimp cocktail served in a giant conch shell for one of the men. "Oh, I haven't had one of these in centuries!" we overheard as a piña colada arrived. Who has? Try the crab cake, New York strip, or the seven-boy chicken curry on its carved wooden tray of accoutrements: scallions, almonds, hot chili paste, bananas, coconut, cucumber, and mango chutney. Perhaps the famed Vera will appear at dinnertime. Clad in a wildcat print caftan-like affair (a print more exotic than the leopardskin vinyl that's dressed her barstools for decades), she recently walked us through her restaurant in her gold slings. Appliqued cloth umbrellas hanging above our table came from India; the wooden sculptures along the walls from places like Singapore and Bali, she said. Back in the glass-enclosed Palm-Palm Room, husky metal nautical items came from engine rooms — hardworking relics of the seagoing life in this treasure-filled restaurant. Boaters can still tie up here at reasonable rates, and the rest of you should get here while you can.

SOLOMONS ISLAND

The nineteenth-century oystering village of Solomons Island led a quiet life for decades. It's discovered now, and easily is the tourism center of the Maryland Bay region south of Annapolis, with B&Bs, restaurants, shops, and terrific fishing nearby. Anchoring Solomons is the **Calvert Marine Museum** right near the town's entrance on Solomons Island Rd. (410-326-2042; www.calvertmarinemuseum.com; open daily 10–5; adults $5, children $3). Here, the tale of the Patuxent River and Chesapeake marine life is told in all its chapters, from the recently historic to the prehistoric — down to crocodile jaws and the teeth of mastodons dug from nearby Calvert Cliffs. Kids love the aquariums full of Chesapeake critters, including, believe it or not, seahorses, or blue crabs sidling through their tanks. On a back deck tank, river otters play. Take a spin through the post-war recreational boating scene and view leisure craft built by Solomons' M.M. Davis & Sons Shipyard, or inspect more historic craft. Out back stands the **Drum Point Lighthouse**, one of only three remaining screw-pile lights. Forty-three of these distinctly Chesapeake sentinels once stood in the Bay's soft bottom, warning mariners off dangerous shoals. Kids like these lights. This is one of two screw-pile lights stationed at a Bay-area museum (the other is at the Chesapeake Bay Maritime Museum in St. Michaels), and kids like them in part because it feels fairly safe to climb their ladder-like steps to the first floor. When threatened by wreckers in 1975, Drum Point Light was moved to the museum from its location a few miles north. Clamber up a short ladder-style entry into the cozily re-created lighthouse keeper's home — in this case put together with help from the memory of a former lighthouse keeper's granddaughter, Anna Weems Ewald (1906–1995).

Climb up the Drum Point Lighthouse to take a peek at the past outside the Calvert Marine Museum at Solomons Island.

David Trozzo

Down the street, the 1934 **J.C. Lore Oyster House** shows how oysters moved from tongers' boats to gourmets' plates. While you're enjoying the museum's offerings, take a ride around Solomons' Back Creek and into the Patuxent River aboard a turn-of-the-last-century "bugeye," one of the indigenous oystering craft, called the **William B. Tennison**. Her sail rig was removed in the early 1900s and an engine installed so she could do duty as a "buyboat," motoring among the oyster dredgers and purchasing their catch. Museum staff tell about the passing shoreline. May–Oct., 2pm Wed.–Sun.; additional cruises at 12:30 and 3pm on weekends in July and Aug. Adults $5, children $3. Folks still intrigued by island life also can take a two-hour walking tour with **Solomons Walkabout,** Mar.–Oct. by appt.; closed Mon. Contact 410-394-0775; www.solomonswalkabout.com; P.O. Box 40, Solomons, MD 20688.

Shops along the town's main street include several good gift shops. Check out the **Harmon House** (410-326-6848; 14538 Solomons Island Rd.), an old Victorian offering everything from crab tchotchkes to pottery art bowls by regional artists, **Trendies** (410-394-0165; 14636 Solomons Island Rd.), an upscale design-style gift shop in a nineteenth-century general store, and Sea **Gull Cove Gifts** (410-326-7182; 14488 Solomons Island Rd.) for souvenirs. Also stop by **Carmen's Gallery** (410-326-2549; 14550 Solomons Island Rd.) for watercolors, serigraphs, and Chesapeake scenes, primarily by regional artists, and **Fine Things** (410-326-0546; Avondale Center, 14350 Solomons Island Rd.), a design store with nice prints and attractive home decorating items.

Fishermen will love Solomons, here at its wide, mid-Bay point. **Call Witch Charters** (800-303-4950; 1410 Foxtail Ln., Prince Frederick) to go fly-fishing with Orvis-endorsed charter guide Capt. Bo Toepfer. He trailers his twenty-three-foot custom Maralina yacht to Solomons or any other port. Or contact the **Solomons Charter Captains Association** (888-591-7222, 410-326-2670; P.O. Box 831, Solomons, MD 20688) for year-round charter boat fishing offered aboard more than thirty vessels, all operated by U.S. Coast Guard-licensed captains. **Bunky's Charter Boats, Inc.** (410-326-3241; www.bunkyscharterboats.com; 14446 Solomons Island Rd. S.) has long been the center for Solomons' sport-fishing, with charter boats available for half-day and full-day trips; head boats for groups. You also can rent a sixteen-foot fiberglass skiff. Fishing Apr.–Nov.; bait and tackle shop open year-round. Or rent a fifteen- to twenty-foot power-boat or a sea kayak from **Solomons Boat Rental** (800-535-BOAT, 410-326-4060; www.boat-rent.net; Rte. 2 & A St.).

Or, put your own boat in at the **Solomons Boat Ramp** beneath the Thomas Johnson Bridge over the Patuxent (410-326-8383; fee).

For a treat just north of town, drive down Dowell Road and keep an eye out for colorful ceramic gates to your left, topped by the sculpted echo of waves. This is the entrance to a 30-acre sculpture garden on St. John Creek called **Annmarie Garden.** (410-326-4640; www.annmariegarden.org; 13480 Dowell Rd.; open daily 10–4). A bronze oyster tonger (an oysterman using "tongs," a cross between scissors and a pair of long-handled rakes) greets visitors. Amid the well-landscaped woods, find pieces like "The Council Ring," by B. Amore and Woody Dorsey, quietly inviting reflection, or "The Surveyor's Map," an aluminum "boardwalk" into (and even over) the woods by Jann Rosen-Queralt and Roma Campanile. Enjoy the **ArtsFest** in mid- to late-Sept.

LODGINGS, MARINAS, & RESTAURANTS

Prices are based on high-season rates, but prices are likely to drop midweek or off-season. Also be sure to check cancellation policies, and assume you can't bring your pet or smoke inside unless told otherwise.

Prices for lodgings fall into the following ranges:

Inexpensive: Up to $75
Moderate: $76 to $120
Expensive: $121 to $150
Very Expensive: Over $150

Restaurant pricing follows this range for entrée, appetizer and dessert:

Inexpensive: Up to $15
Moderate: $15–$25
Expensive: $25–$35
Very Expensive: Over $35

Credit card abbreviations are: AE, American Express; CB, Carte Blanche; D, Discover; DC, Diner's Club; MC, MasterCard; V, Visa.

David Trozzo

*Back Creek Inn offers
solitude in Solomons.*

BACK CREEK INN B&B
Innkeepers: Carol Pennock
& Lin Cochran.
410-326-2022.
www.bbonline.com/md/
backcreek/.

You many spend the day in the gardens at this waterside inn, perhaps lounging beside the softly gurgling fountain. Among the perennials and bulbs are irises transplanted from one of the owners' great-grandmother's gardens, blooming happily in May alongside peonies and foxglove.

210 Alexander Lane/P.O. Box 520, Solomons, MD 20688.
Price: Moderate to Expensive.
Credit Cards: MC, V.
Handicap Access: Yes.
Special Features: Deepwater dock (draws 8 ft.).

For a break in the action, wander down to the dock and dangle your feet over Back Creek. Laid-back and comfortable, this B&B is quartered in an 1880s waterman's house and has been in business so long that you'll no doubt reap the benefits of the innkeepers' experience. A cottage in the garden's corner draws its steady stream of return guests; if you can't book it, then any one of six rooms or two suites in the house and annex, named for herbs, will prove comfy for the night. The rooms, all with king- or queen-sized beds, are all different, from the large Thyme room with a fireplace and TV, to smaller rooms at the back of the house upstairs, with garden views. Downstairs, a glassed-in common room with stereo and TV looks out to the water, where a yachtsperson in need of a shower and a bed can tie up at the deepwater dock. Full breakfast is served at individual tables in the breakfast room, where tea is served Thursdays in good china cups.

SOLOMONS VICTORIAN INN
Owners: Helen & Richard Bauer.
410-326-4811.
www.solomonsvictorianinn.com.
125 Charles St./P.O. Box 759, Solomons, MD 20688.
Price: Moderate to Very Expensive.
Credit Cards: AE, D, MC, V.
Handicap Access: Yes.
Restrictions: Only children over age 13.

From a sailor's peaked and varnished top-floor suite to a simple bedroom with a bath, this B&B covers the accommodations waterfront. Five rooms, all with attached baths and furnished in antiques or reproductions, are quartered in the 1906 Victorian home, formerly owned by the locally notable boatbuilding Davis family. Upstairs is the yachty top-floor suite, replete with a blue in-room whirlpool under a skylight and a built-in seating area with matching blue cushions and a small galley. The view of the harbor is enough to make you buy a boat. The 1998 carriage house offers two lovely big rooms, including a classy hideaway upstairs with a king-sized bed across from an in-room whirlpool. Full breakfast (shrimp souffle most Sunday mornings); if the coffee pot's not on by 7am you can fix your own hot drink on the breakfast porch. Prices drop to Inexpensive in the off-season.

HOTELS AND MARINAS

Comfort Inn/Beacon Marina (410-326-6303; 800-228-5150, reservations; 255 Lore Rd./P.O. Box 869, Solomons, MD 20688) Sixty rooms. 186-slip marina. Restaurant, outdoor pool. Moderate to Very Expensive.

Holiday Inn Select (800-356-2009, 410-326-6311; 155 Holiday Dr., Solomons, MD 20688) 326 rooms. Gift shop, waterfront dining, two marinas. Moderate to Very Expensive.

Hospitality Harbor Marina (410-326-1052; 205 Holiday Dr., Solomons, MD 20688) Pool, tennis courts, weight room — all of the amenities from the Holiday Inn next door. About 80 slips, roughly 30-35 slips available for transients.

Spring Cove Marina (410-326-2161; springcovemarina.com; 455 Lore Rd., Solomons, MD 20688) Fuel, laundry, Naughty Gull restaurant. Approximately 250 slips, 40 for transients.

Zahniser's Yachting Center (410-326-2166; www.zahnisers.com; 245 C St., Solomons, MD 20688) Pump-out station, pool, sail loft, yacht brokerage. Reservations recommended. Over 300 slips; transient slips available. Courtesy bikes. Ice, laundry, full-service ship store. Also home to the fine Dry Dock Restaurant, with good seafood and a yachty décor overlooking Back Creek. Call for reservations: 410-326-4817. Dinner nightly; Sunday brunch.

RESTAURANTS

The owner/chefs of the C.D. Cafe provide fresh meals at their popular Solomons eatery.

David Trozzo

THE C.D. CAFÉ
410-326-3877.
14350 Solomons Island Rd.
  (Avondale Ctr.)
Open: Daily.
Price: Moderate.
Cuisine: Creative Regional.
Serving: L, D, SB.
Credit Cards: MC, V.
Reservations: No.
Handicap Access: Yes.

A recent temptation to gobble fast food was tempered by the knowledge that this comfortable café, with one of the tastiest, well priced menus in Bay Country, was nearby. Over the years we've dined here and enjoyed fine roasted veggie sandwiches, salty ham and lima bean soup, and fresh Romaine salads that accompany each dish. This time, we asked for the quickest takeout item. "The chicken sandwich," said our server. Spiced with curry and touched with almonds, we could only regret that a busy schedule kept us from settling in to one of eleven tables with views across the road to the Patuxent River and the arcing Gov. Thomas Johnson Bridge. The café's Cajun dishes are authentic — not, like so many north of the Louisiana border, depressingly faux. Fine pastries, coffee.

LIGHTHOUSE INN
410-326-2444.
14636 Solomons Island Rd. S.
Open: Daily.
Price: Expensive.
Cuisine: Seafood/American.
Serving: L (Sat. & Sun. only), D.
Credit Cards: AE, D, DC, MC, V.
Reservations:
  Recommended for inside dining.
Handicap Access: Yes.
Special Features: Waterfront dining, free dockage available.

With its glass front and back offering magnificent views of the Patuxent River on one side and Solomons' harbor on the other, the Lighthouse Inn is one of the small island's prettiest places to eat. Its cathedral ceilings and skipjack bar (complete with sails), designed and built by local master carver "Pepper" Langley, add to the festive atmosphere. Depending on when you go, you have a number of choices in seating. If you prefer something fairly casual, ask for a table on the Quarterdeck, where you can choose from the usual assortment of appetizers (mozzarella sticks and steamed shrimp), as well as crab cake sandwiches and turkey tortilla wraps, to name a few. Indoors, the menu features somewhat more refined dining, including such selections as the inn's hand-cut, grilled filet mignon paired with a crab cake, or a daily fish selection. Have it baked, fried, broiled, sauteed, spiced Cajun-style or stuffed with crab imperial.

ST. MARY'S COUNTY

Maryland's first colonists stepped ashore in rural St. Mary's County, at **St. Clement's Island** in the Potomac River. Now preserved as a state park, the peaceable island sits out in the river upstream from St. Mary's City, site of the colony's first capital and location of a village that re-creates the original – which is being excavated.

An easy day trip from Annapolis, Washington, D.C. or Baltimore, the county mixes history alongside rural Chesapeake, with good mid-Bay fishing and even beach parkland in places like **Point Lookout State Park** at the county's southernmost tip, where more than 50,000 Confederate troops were imprisoned during the Civil War.

Reach St. Mary's County via Rtes. 235, 5, or 2/4. Off Rte. 235 on the Patuxent River side of the county, in Hollywood, stands a colonial grande dame. From its bluff overlooking the Patuxent River, **Sotterley Plantation**'s architectural treasures have weathered the passing generations in relative obscurity. That, despite an intriguing group of owners. Early Maryland Gov. George Plater III corresponded with his friend George Washington from here. J.P. Morgan's daughter came to live here when her husband Herbert L. Satterlee — a lawyer and writer who penned the lyrics to "Autumn Leaves" — bought the place in

1910. Now an extensive renovation is under way at the manor house, which dates its oldest portion, built of rare post-in-ground construction, to 1727. Tours continue, including restoration plan tours for those who call ahead. The ninety acres, 1.3 mi. of trails, and twenty outbuildings include a rare surviving slave cabin that dates to the 1830s. Annual events: Family Heritage Day, a celebration of African-American life, a quilt show in spring, and a Christmas celebration. Contact: 800-681-0850, 301-373-2280; www.sotterley.com; 9 mi. E. of Leonardtown on Rte. 245. Open: grounds, year-round, Tues.–Sun. 10–4; manor house, May–Oct., Tues.–Sun. 10–4. Admission: Adults $7, children 6-16 $5; ground fee $2; group tour rates.

In quaint _Leonardtown_, antiquers will find the **Maryland Antiques Center** (301-475-1960; Rte. 5 south of Rte. 243), with furniture and nauticals among the specialties. Also in town is an artists' co-op called The **North End Gallery** (301-475-3130; 41625 Fenwick St.; open Wed.–Sun.), offering exhibitions and a range of talent. Open Wed.–Sun. Consider a visit to town on the third weekend in Oct. to enjoy the famed **St. Mary's County Oyster Festival,** held at the county fairgrounds on Rte. 5 past town, and home to the National Oyster Shucking Championship. For info, call 800-327-9023. If it's time for lunch, don't miss the **Do-Dah Deli** (301-997-1604; 22696 Washington St.; open Mon.–Fri.; serving B, L; Inexpensive), a great place to dine in or take out. Fresh-made salads include chicken cobb, macaroni, Greek, Caesar, and taco; the sandwich menu includes create-your-own and Boar's Head meats and cheeses. Particularly good: the Reuben and the crab cake sandwiches. There are fancier restaurants in town, but for taste and value, this is the best.

To reach St. Clement's Island and the **St. Clement's Island/Potomac River Museum** at _Colton's Point,_ on the Potomac River side of the county, follow brown history-marker signs on back roads from Rte. 5. The small but well-considered museum offers a fine review of early Maryland history saluting its English settlers, who arrived just across the channel at St. Clement's Island in 1634. Among the museum's exhibits is an England room that includes the beginnings of the Church of England's separation from the Catholic Church. The Calverts, successive Lords Baltimore and Maryland's founders, were Catholics with political clout with the Stuart kings of England in the first half of the seventeenth century. (Maryland was the first New World colony to actively promote religious tolerance.) Also detailed here: the colonists' journey aboard the *Ark* and *Dove,* their fortunate first meeting with the Piscataway tribe members, as well as Potomac River life. It's a great destination — even for folks who aren't Maryland history buffs — with riverfront picnic tables, a fishing pier (licenses required), and, best of all, a summer weekend water taxi shuttling to the forty-acre island, with its mown paths, narrow beaches, picnic tables and multitudinous osprey. Stay for about an hour, or catch the second boat back mid-afternoon. The boat runs Mem. Day through Oct., Sat.–Sun. 12:30–4, weather permitting, and costs $5 for adults and $3 for children. The ride takes about fifteen minutes. Contact the museum: 301-769-2222; 38370

Point Breeze Rd., Colton's Point; open late Mar.–late Oct., Mon.–Fri. 9–4, Sat.–Sun. Noon–5; winter: Wed.–Sun. Noon–4; $1 for ages 12 and up.

Near the tip of the county stands *St. Mary's City*, home to **Historic St. Mary's City**, the re-created 1634 colonial capital, alongside the small liberal arts **St. Mary's College**, one of only two public honors colleges in the country, with a number of historic buildings and gardens (contact 240-895-4380 for event information; www.smcm.edu; St. Mary's City, MD 20686). The original capital city was gone by 1720, but is the subject of extensive archaeological work. Among tantalizing discoveries: three lead coffins found in the early 1990s. After NASA finished testing the air to see if it dated to the seventeenth century, researchers concluded that the remains inside likely belonged to members of the Calvert family, Maryland's founders. Visitors walking the trails at this riverside site will see framed houses marking a particular dig. In addition, docents, some in costume, explain the re-created elements of the city, from a Yaocomaco Indian village with sleeping furs inside the straw "witchotts," or dwellings, to Godiah Spray's tobacco plantation populated by Ossabaw pigs, a species that first roamed here 300 years ago. The square-rigger *Maryland Dove* (a big hit with kids), a reproduction of one of the two vessels that brought early settlers, docks in the St. Mary's River and is fun to check out. Also on the grounds: a reproduction of the Statehouse, a 1934 chapel, and Farthing's Kitchen, where vending machines are located. Visit the Visitor Center for an overview, and picnic at the riverside tables. Contact: 240-895-4960, 800-762-1634; Visitor Center, 240-895-4990; www.smcm.edu/hsmc; 18559 Hogaboom Lane. Open: fall and spring, Tues.–Sat. 10–5; Sun., only Godiah Spray Tobacco Plantation, Visitor Center and Exhibit Hall are open. Summer hours are Wed.–Sun. 10–5. Adults $7.50, seniors and students $6, ages 6–12 $3.50; prices lower on off-season weekends.

Outdoor-lovers visiting St. Mary's County will find plenty to do. Cyclists drawn to flat tidewater back roads should stop by area tourism departments or visitor centers to pick up a copy of the southern Maryland bicycling map, with its routes plotted through the region and details about traffic. (Note: no crossing major bridges.) Or go bass fishing on the 250-acre lake at **St. Mary's River State Park** (301-872-5688; Camp Cosoma Rd.), a two-site park where the lake, encircled by an 11.5-mi. trail, is off Rte. 5 between Leonardtown and Great Mills. Picnic tables here. Or duck down to **_Ridge_**, home of **Scheible's Fishing Center** (301-872-5185; www.webgraphic.com/scheibles; 48342 Wynne Rd.), where the longtime charter fleet takes fishers in search of striped bass or bluefish. Half- or full-day charters; also head boats. Restaurant, lodge.

Farther south, at the end of Rte. 5 where the Potomac River meets the Chesapeake Bay, stands **Point Lookout State Park** (301-872-5688; P.O. Box 48, Scotland, MD 20687), once a Revolution-era lookout and later a Civil War-era Confederate prison camp. Sun yourself on the beach or surf cast. Swim in designated areas. Hike back along the beach to the ruins of the Civil War's **Fort Lincoln**, and, at the park's tip, check out its lighthouse. Grills, picnic area, and camping. Also, you can cruise to **Smith Island,** one of the Bay's last two inhabited islands, from the park (see Chapter Six, *Lower Eastern Shore,* for more about the island). **Smith Island Cruises** (410-425-2771) departs Point Lookout during the season. Call for prices and schedules.

LODGINGS, MARINAS, & RESTAURANTS

For lodging and restaurant price codes, see page 90.

The innkeepers at the Brome-Howard House have created a comfortable enclave in St. Mary's City.

David Trozzo

THE BROME-HOWARD INN
Innkeepers: Lisa & Michael Kelley.
301-866-0656.
www.bromehowardinn.com.
18281 Rosecroft Rd./P.O. Box 476, St. Mary's City, MD 20686.
Room Prices: Moderate to Very Expensive.
Restaurant Prices: Expensive to Very Expensive.
Handicap Access: For restaurant only.
Restaurant hours: Thurs. 5:30–9, Fri.–Sat. 5:30–10, SB 11-2, Sun. D 5-9.
Cuisine: Seafood/ Continental.
Serving: D, SB.
Credit Cards: AE, D, MC, V.
Reservations: Yes, on warm weather weekends.

Situated on 30 acres of farmland overlooking St. Mary's River near historic St. Mary's City, the nineteenth-century Brome-Howard Inn offers top-notch cuisine, bed and breakfast services, catering, and five miles of hiking trails along the riverbank. Though dining is a bit pricey and formal (classical opera fills the parlors, and the tables are set with hand-painted china and fresh roses from its working gardens), the management and wait staff welcome the more casually dressed diner, and are highly attentive and accommodating. Inside, the décor is comfortable, with fox-hunting scenes and model ships. If the weather invites, request outdoor dining and enjoy the river view.

The menu ranges through selections of seafood, duck, beef, and lamb, and the wine list is extensive. A mixed green salad with apples, goat cheese, walnuts, and an astonishing balsamic vinaigrette is complexly orchestrated to a fine-tuned taste. The miniature crab cakes, an appetizer, are perfectly seasoned. Particularly good is the fisherman's stew, based in a saffron broth with a touch of garlic and filled with shrimp, crab, mussels, and seasonal fish fillets. Save room for dessert, as a large slice of New York cheesecake comes with fresh-picked blueberries from the inn's gardens. As our two-year-old dining companion noted, "Yummy."

Overnight guests will find feather beds on pencil-post beds, as well as bright baths. Four rooms have fireplaces, but ask for a room with view out onto the river. Full breakfasts, bicycles, and a fabulous back porch and garden near the river.

Motels in Lexington Park, deep in the county near the Patuxent Naval Air Station, include a **Days Inn** (800-428-2871, 301-863-6666; 21847 Three Notch Rd., Lexington Park, MD 20653), 165 rooms, Inexpensive to Moderate; and **Hampton Inn** (800-HAMPTON, 301-863-3200; 22211 Three Notch Rd., Lexington Park, MD 20653), 111 rooms, Inexpensive to Moderate.

Marinas with transient dockage are available at **Point Lookout Marina** (877-384-9716, 301-872-5000; www.pointlookoutmarina.com; 16244 Miller's Wharf Rd., Ridge MD 20680) and twelve miles from Point Lookout at **Tall Timbers Marina** (301-994-1508; Herring Creek Rd., Tall Timbers, MD 20690). Both have restaurants, pool, and other facilities for boaters.

CAPTAIN LEONARD'S SEAFOOD HOUSE
301-884-3701.
Rte. 235, Mechanicsville.
Open: Daily except Tues.
Price: Moderate.
Cuisine: Seafood.
Serving: L, D.
Reservations: No.
Handicap Access: Yes.

For folks en route to St. Mary's County or returning home, *the* place to stop is Captain Leonard's. Right on Rte. 235 and the southern junction of Rte. 6, this gem is easy to dismiss if judged by the exterior. Locals know better. Once inside, if you can find a space in the packed parking lot, piles of pickin' crabs and mugs of beer sit in front of folks who make the restaurant ring with laughter and conversation. The service is welcoming if sometimes a bit slow, but it matches the relaxed atmosphere. The crabs are the best, but also consider oysters, scallops, cherrystone clams, snow crab legs, catfish, trout, flounder, spiced or delicately breaded fried shrimp, and even frog legs. Those who prefer turf to surf can find chicken, hamburgers, and New York strip steak. From the appetizer list, the crab balls are prime with lump crab and heartily seasoned, and seasonal raw oysters on the half shell are a fresh favorite. Soup offerings include Maryland red and cream of crab, and oyster stew. A definite Southern Maryland treasure you'll want to share with your friends.

EVANS' SEAFOOD
301-994-2299.
St. George Island.
Open: Tues.–Sun.
Price: Inexpensive to Expensive.

Founded deep in the county in 1963 by waterman Robert "Bugs" Evans, the place was sold outside the family in 2000. Not to fret. Cliff and Cathie Weddington, patrons of the Potomac River-

Cuisine: Seafood.
Serving: D (Tues.–Fri.), L &
   D (Sat. & Sun.).
Credit Cards: AE, MC, V.
Reservations: For parties of
   6 or more only.
Handicap Access: Yes.

side restaurant during the Evans family years, are still using the same family recipes. And the open, rustic dining walls still bear nets, buoys, and other nautical stuff that has seen actual work. Expect genuine Southern Maryland seafood, like local hard-shell crabs at noninflated prices, and fried soft-shells, crab cakes, and seafood platters broiled or fried. Sides include genuine hushpuppies and untrendy veggies, such as beets. Friendly waitpersons stop by often enough to be helpful, but not so frequently they're intrusive. A waterside deck at the back of the restaurant offers a fine weekend crab-cracking spot.

Family Fun: Fossil-Hunting

Eons ago, the Bay was a Miocene Era sea. Remnants of that past turn up along the Calvert Cliffs, as fossils dating fifteen to twenty million years back wash ashore. The cliffs run from the north of Calvert County south, and ancient sharks' teeth are the prize. You also can find ancient sand dollars, scallops, and other shells. Public access points are few. Common wisdom says get there at low tide. Later, we learned that great finds depend on: the weather, luck, whether the beach has been picked over during a run of calm days, or whether you arrive just after a storm's kicked things up. Author Allison Blake took her 10-year-old niece, Shannon, to Calvert Cliffs State Park to look for fossils early one June morning. Here's Shannon's report:

Calvert Cliff's Fossils

"Calvert Cliffs State Park is a nice place to spend the day, but I didn't really find many fossils there. The cliffs are 30 feet long and sort of like a straight walk up. Luckily, when we were at the park, we saw a geologist and he showed us fossilized sand dollars. There's a beach a little north from there called Flag Pond Nature Center where you can find sharks' teeth, but we had no luck there. Flag Pond is more like a beach, I thought.

My aunt went to Brownie's Beach (author's note: now called Bay Front Park) after I left and found seven sharks' teeth. It is at the north end of the thirty-mile range of the cliffs, and the other two locations we went to were on the south. But if you do go to Calvert Cliffs State Park, you should keep in mind that it is a 1.8-mile walk, and if you're going to play at the beach, then you should be ready to walk 1.8 miles back. Also, the bugs are bad so bring bug spray. Also, DO NOT CLIMB ON THE CLIFFS!!! Lastly, you should get there at low tide to look for shells and low tide is according to the position of the moon."

Well, there you have it. The geology buff we encountered at the state park put us on to **Flag Ponds Nature Center.** We also found locals identifying their finds identifying them in a section of the **Calvert Marine Museum** that has lots of fossils. And the museum puts out a good public bulletin, "Fossils of Calvert Cliffs." Digging in Calvert Cliffs is prohibited. Additional fossil hunting haunts:

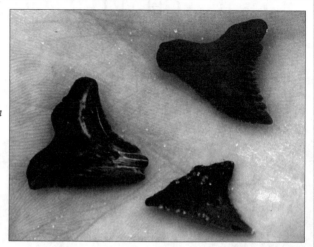

Ancient sharks' teeth wash up along Calvert Cliffs, where beachcombers can spot them in the tide line.

David Trozzo

Bay Front Park (410-257-2230; about .5 mi. S. of Chesapeake Beach) A thin beach widens noticeably at low tide; we found seven sharks' teeth in an hour one afternoon!

Calvert Cliffs State Park (301-872-5688; Rte. 765, Lusby) Thirteen miles of hiking trails include a nice 1.8-mi. walk to the beach that starts out next to a babbling brook, passes a haunting wetland (you can walk out on a boardwalk), then takes you to the narrow beach. No lifeguards. Open sunrise to sunset. Contact the park via Point Lookout State Park, 301-872-5688; P.O. Box 48, Scotland, MD 20687.

CHAPTER FOUR
Decoys, Docks, and Lazy Days
THE UPPER BAY
Havre de Grace around the Head of the Bay to Chestertown and Rock Hall

David Trozzo

Great Oak Manor offers fine accommodations in Chestertown.

Fields of corn and soybeans go on forever as the countryside starts to roll north from the Chesapeake Bay Bridge on the Eastern Shore, toward the stately brick buildings of Chestertown, a major eighteenth-century port, and on to crossroads towns beloved by antiquers, or marinas alongside rivers named Chester, Sassafras, and Bohemia. Rounding the head of the Bay, the traveler salutes the Chesapeake & Delaware Canal at Chesapeake City, a recovered Victorian gem where plaques on the front of each white or purple-trimmed home announce the name of its nineteenth-century founder. Past Elkton and North East (and the top-of-the Bay Elk and North East Rivers), one finally crosses high above the mighty Susquehanna. Here is the prehistoric forebear to the Bay, a wide river whose nearby towns include churches or mansions built of granite, tougher stuff than you'll find in the southern Bay.

Look to the river as you cross to see the Susquehanna Flats, which once drew U.S. presidents and merchants of industry to partake in the sportsman's "gunning" life. Here, the Northeast is coming on; travelers headed north on I-

95 will find themselves on the New Jersey Turnpike in less than an hour. They'd do well to stop in Havre de Grace, "Decoy Capital of the World" and a growing tourist town where the river meets the Bay. From many points in town, you can see the water.

This part of Bay Country looks more to Philadelphia than, say, Baltimore or Washington, but nowhere in Chesapeake does one escape colonial U.S. history. George Washington passed through the Upper Shore as he went about his Revolution-era duties.

Chestertown boasts of being the nation's tenth most popular historic place to visit, owing to its abundant restored eighteenth-century homes. Cross the Chester River into this prosperous town, where shops and restaurants line the streets and the Imperial Hotel and White Swan Tavern, famed restorations, can be found. Washington College dates to 1782 and offers movies and other activities in which the public can partake — or maybe you'd rather just stroll its green grounds. With its wealth of terrific lodgings, central location, restaurants and other amenities, Chestertown makes a central headquarters for exploring the Upper Eastern Shore and Bay area.

From here, you can head straight for the Bay, down Rte. 20 to Rock Hall. This little waterman's town increasingly is claimed by boaters who dock their craft at multitudinous marinas or stay in its pretty B&Bs. Evidence remains that the houses turning into shops on Main Street were family homes not so terribly long ago, as all the buildings haven't been completely gentrified. Open long weekends, the handful of gallery-style shops here offer original work by regional artists and crafters. And don't forget to visit Eastern Neck National Wildlife Refuge, past Rock Hall to the end of Rte. l, where you can walk out a boardwalk and look over the water for shorebirds in summer, or for the famed tundra swans who arrive as cooler days signal the coming of winter.

Antique lovers won't want to miss the crossroads town of Galena, 15 miles from Chestertown up Rte. 213, the most scenic primary route through this part of the shore. Antique shops here make for some good browsing, and you'll find treats like pie safes and pine sinks, sturdy furniture from an earlier era. This little town isn't far from Crumpton, home of Dixon's Furniture, Inc. and the notable Wednesday auction that spans 30 acres.

Farther on up Rte. 213 stands Chesapeake City, famous for the C&D Canal and the Bayard House, a fine dining establishment whose physical rebirth may ultimately be as significant as its food. It was restored in the mid-80s, as this Victorian town's renaissance was under way. Bring your binoculars when you visit, since watching the major ships pass through the canal is a prime Chesapeake City activity. Just outside of town, the C&D Canal Museum even has a TV screen so you can watch the maritime parade.

Havre de Grace, less than an hour west of here across the tip of the Bay, qualifies as one of the more industrious Bay towns when it comes to tourism. Over recent years, city leaders have built a lovely boardwalk along their Susquehanna waterfront and welcomed a variety of cruising craft to town. It is thought that the town's name derives from the Marquis de Lafayette, who compared this with Le Havre in his own France. Dating to 1658, Havre de Grace still feels like a hometown despite the arrival of newcomers and changes along the waterfront. Along Washington Avenue, for instance, antique stores have moved into old department stores. Visitors of a certain age will recognize the feel of old downtowns from childhood.

Travelers along these rolling tidewater roads can't help but notice how many long lanes stretch back from farms or historic homes with names like "Tranquility." It's true that new homes are popping up, but the indelible impression of cornfields and working farms remains. Marinas cluster the edge of the rivers, where boaters enjoy the charms of gentle rivers that flow to the Bay.

LODGING

From reproduction Georgians to old Victorians, the villages and crossroads towns in the Upper Bay region offer lovely B&Bs. Have tea on a brick patio during summer afternoons, or relax in a hot tub alongside the Chesapeake & Delaware Canal. Midweek or fall-to-early-spring rates generally are lower than those of high summer, but are subject to change. Check cancellation policies, and don't be surprised if your inn has a two-night minimum, especially in high season. Assume smoking and pets are prohibited, unless otherwise noted, and ask about other policies that can change.

Lodging rates fall within this scale:

Inexpensive: Up to $75
Moderate: $76 to $120
Expensive: $121 to $150
Very Expensive: Over $150

Credit card abbreviations are: AE, American Express; CB, Carte Blanche; D, Discover; DC, Diner's Club; MC, MasterCard; V, Visa.

Havre de Grace

**LA CLE D'OR
  GUESTHOUSE**
Proprietor: Ron Browning.
888-HUG-GUEST,
  410-939-6562.
www.lacledorguesthouse
  .com.

La Cle D'or looks sturdily prosperous from the outside, but check out the crystal chandeliers and shiny gold wallpaper in the parlor! The 1868 brick house is surprisingly luxurious, and host Ron Browning knows a thing or two about antiques. Guest rooms retain a French flair — this is, after all,

226 N. Union Ave., Havre de Grace, MD 21078.
Price: Moderate to Expensive.
Credit Cards: MC, V.
Handicap Access: No.
Restrictions: No children under 12.

Havre de Grace, the "Harbor of Grace" named by Lafayette — right down to the Napoleanic wallpaper. The Rochambeaux Room comes with an antique double bed and a bath around the corner. Next door find the pleasant La Peu, rented only with the Rochambeaux, making a nice accommodation for traveling couples willing to share a hall bath. Then there's the LaFayette Suite, with a queen-sized bed and a window-lined sitting room above the gardens below. Each room comes with a TV and VCR. A big hot tub sits out among the gardens. Ron is a schoolteacher and books around his schedule.

SPENCER-SILVER MANSION

Innkeeper: Carol Nemeth.
800-780-1485, 410-939-1097.
www.spencersilvermansion.com.
200 S. Union Ave., Havre de Grace, MD 21078.
Price: Inexpensive to Moderate inside the house; Expensive for the carriage house.
Credit Cards: AE, D, MC, V.
Handicap Access: In the carriage house.
Special Features: Kids OK; pets allowed in the carriage house.

"J.N. Spencer, 1896" reads the marble plate surrounding the doorbell at this Victorian, authentic from the turret atop the house to the intricate woodwork in the hallway. A bronze art deco figure even presents itself on the newel post. Original stained glass atop many windows is worth the price of your night's stay, and innkeeper Carol Nemeth has been at it for so many years it's hard to imagine a detail she hasn't foreseen. Not only that, but this is a good bargain. Four rooms inside the house include marble-topped tables or corner cabinets with inset glass. Two enormous front rooms share a bath; two have private baths. Enter one of the private baths, with its two-person whirlpool tub, through stained glass doors. The stone carriage house out back is cozy enough to spend the winter, with a queen-sized bed up the iron spiral staircase in the cozy wood-stained bedroom, replete with a windowseat. Downstairs expect a daybed, whirlpool, TV/VCR, and kitchenette. In a relative rarity, breakfast at the Spencer-Silver is served until 10:30am.

VANDIVER INN

Innkeeper: Susan Moldoon.
800-245-1655, 410-939-5200.
www.vandiverinn.com.
301 S. Union Ave., Havre de Grace, MD 21078.
Price: Moderate to Very Expensive.
Credit Cards: AE, D, MC, V.

The venerable Vandiver, one-time home to the local mayor and Maryland politician of the same name, nearly doubled its longtime accommodations in recent years when it expanded into two houses next door. Now visitors can stay in the 1886 Victorian, nine rooms in all, with elaborate tiled fireplaces or twin flues, clawfoot tubs, and antique full-size beds, or head for the new rooms next door, with queen- or king-sized beds and individual entrances. Either way, your old-fashioned-flavored stay comes

Handicap Access: Ramp into building, but claw-foot tubs.

with modern touches like hair dryers, fat towels and bath salts, and voice mail and dataports. The Vandiver's downstairs rooms often host gatherings, a chef sees to catering, and an enormous broad pavilion out back, painted multiple greens, matches the main house.

Chesapeake City

INN AT THE CANAL
Innkeepers: Mary & Al Ioppolo.
410-885-5995.
www.innatthecanal.com.
104 Bohemia Ave./P.O. Box 187, Chesapeake City, MD 21915.
Price: Moderate to Expensive during the week; Expensive to Very Expensive on weekends.
Credit Cards: AE, CB, D, DC, MC, V.
Handicap Access: No.

Replete with elaborate hand-painted ceiling murals in both the parlor and dining room, this Victorian is still known locally as the Brady-Rees House, after the Bradys who owned and operated tugboats on the nearby canal. Six rooms and a suite reflect the owners' longtime experience in the B&B biz: uncluttered, with easily accessible luggage racks so there's no mystery about where your suitcase is supposed to go. Nice touches include bureaus converted to sinks in the bathrooms and four-poster rice beds. Individual climate control, telephones, and TVs in the rooms, which are good-looking without a lot of fuss. Upstairs find a third-floor suite. Breakfast is served at individual tables, and guests will want to visit Inntiques, located in the former milking room and in a small cottage next door.

OLD WHARF COTTAGE B&B
Operated by The Bayard House.
410-885-5040, 877-582-4049.
www.bayardhouse.com.
10 Bohemia Ave., Chesapeake City, MD 21915.
Price: Expensive to Very Expensive.
Credit Cards: AE, D, MC, V.
Handicap Access: No.
Special Features: Children OK.

This little building along the C&D Canal has had several lives, including an early one as an ice house, and later as a gift shop. Now it's a small cottage-style inn settled across the street from the Bayard House Restaurant, with lots of privacy after everybody else goes home. On the first floor find a sitting room, kitchen and bath, and upstairs, a bedroom with its own balcony. Ceilings are low and floorboards slope, but these unique accommodations should not be missed if you're looking for a true getaway. Continental breakfast, terrific location, and, overall, incredibly cool.

SHIP WATCH INN
Owners: Linda & Thomas Vaughan.
410-885-5300.
www.shipwatchinn.com.

Porches span each of the three waterview floors, allowing ample opportunity to watch the maritime parade along the C&D Canal. A mid-1990s renovation to this 1920s building left pine floors covered with Oriental-style runners and details

401 First St., Chesapeake City, MD 21915.
Price: Moderate to Expensive.
Credit Cards: AE, MC, V.
Handicap Access: Yes.

such as a porthole window cut into a corner room. Eight rooms and suites vary broadly along a comfortably elegant design scale, detailed nicely and furnished with antiques. In Room #6, for instance, a double bed tucks into a built-in, draped alcove. In another room, a lady's secretary, replete with a safe, doubles as a nightstand; the whirlpool bath is just through the door to the attached bathroom.

Small TVs in the rooms, late-afternoon goodies, and an outdoor hot tub. Full breakfast is served on the first-floor porch in good weather. The Vaughans descend from one Capt. Firman Layman, once proprietor of a former inn that's now the fine-dining Bayard House. The family tradition continues.

Chestertown

THE BRAMPTON INN
Hosts: Michael & Danielle Hanscom.
410-778-1860, 866-305-1860.
www.bramptoninn.com.
25227 Chestertown Rd., Chestertown, MD 21620.
Price: Expensive to Very Expensive.
Credit Cards: D, MC, V.
Handicap Access: Yes.
Restrictions: No children under 12.

You'll feel yourself start to relax as you pull up to this 1860 plantation house, fronted with century-old trees and boxwoods set on thirty-five acres between the Chester River and the Chesapeake Bay. Inside, the ceilings are high, the furnishings mix antiques and reproductions, and old wood dominates, from Georgia pine floors to a three-and-a-half-story walnut and ash central staircase. Ten guest rooms, all have private baths and AC, nine have working fireplaces, and five have whirlpool tubs. The second-floor Blue Room, with windows in the trees, is lovely in the fall, while the two-story Fairy Hill Suite, once a kitchen topped by slave quarters, is charming. Full breakfast, afternoon tea, classic videos for viewing, and warm hosts in the business since 1987.

GREAT OAK MANOR B&B
Innkeepers: Don & Dianne Cantor.
800-504-3098, 410-778-5943.
www.greatoak.com.
10568 Cliff Rd., Chestertown, MD 21620.
Price: Expensive to Very Expensive.
Credit Cards: MC, V.
Handicap Access: No.
Restrictions: No children.

Unusual among the many Eastern Shore mansions built in the 1930s, this faithful Georgian reproduction used old brick, probably shipped as ballast in Grace Line ships. Detail and carvings are meticulous, rooms are furnished with Oriental rugs and antiques, and the public rooms are varied and interesting. Everywhere is an atmosphere of friendly comfort. By preserving the original home's flavor, the Cantors created a place that's formal but not stuffy, classical but homelike. All eleven guest rooms are attractively decorated and spacious, many with Bay views and five with fireplaces. The old, illegal third-floor gambling room is high-ceilinged and spacious, with a king bed and sitting area. Set on twelve acres sloping down to a gazebo, Great Oak Manor has 100 feet of private Bay beach and hammocks underneath tall trees. Guests have complimentary access to the nearby Great Oak Landing, with a 9-hole golf course, tennis, and a swimming pool. Full breakfast. Bikes available for rent. Ask for the midweek discount.

IMPERIAL HOTEL
Innkeepers: Jan Macdonald
& Richard O'Neill.
410-778-5000.
www.imperialchestertown.
com.
208 High St. Chestertown,
MD 21620.
Price: Moderate to Very
Expensive.
Credit Cards: AE, MC, V.
Handicap Access: No

A few years back, Jan Macdonald and Richard O'Neill, with successful careers in business and finance, learned that the fabled Imperial Hotel was for sale. With the 1903 hotel's award-winning 1985 renovation to build on, the food- and wine-loving pair are well on their way to creating a first-class hotel. The inn creates intimacy and privacy in its beautifully appointed eleven rooms and two suites of period furnishings. Upscale amenities such as towel warmers ensure guests feel pampered; a clubby double veranda overlooking the historic district makes this unpretentious little hotel a comfortable and quiet place for guests. A lovely courtyard in back of the hotel is available for private parties during summer. In the colder months, the cozy Chester River Lounge, in the hotel lobby area, is an ideal place for a fireside cocktail. For a comfortable escape, you can't do better than the Imperial. See "Restaurants" for more on this landmark

THE INN AT MITCHELL HOUSE
Innkeepers: Jim & Tracy
Stone.
410-778-6500.
www.chestertown.com/
mitchell.
8796 Maryland Pkwy.,
Chestertown, MD 21620.
Price: Moderate.
Credit Cards: MC, V.
Handicap Access: No.
Restrictions: Children
accepted by prior
arrangement only.

This longtime B&B boasts a much older history of welcoming guests. British commander Sir Peter Parker allegedly was brought here after the nearby Battle of Caulk's Field in 1814. When surgery upon the kitchen table failed to save his life, they pickled Peter Parker in a keg of rum and sent him back to England. You'll find your stay here far more pleasant. Located in the country close to Chestertown, Rock Hall, and the once-bustling resort town of Tolchester, this 1743 manor house sits at the end of a long, tree-lined drive by a pond. Inside are five rooms with private baths (a sixth room is rented only as part of a suite), four with fireplaces (fire logs provided). Four more fireplaces stand in the house's public areas with an outdoor motif of mounted waterfowl, marsh grass, and riding hats, which makes for a suitable introduction to rural Kent County. A full country breakfast is served in a dining room decorated with china plates.

THE PARKER HOUSE
Hosts: Marcy & John Parker.

When regulars said the stairs gave them trouble, the Parkers turned their inn's family

410-778-9041.
www.chestertown.com/
   parker.
108 Spring Ave.,
   Chestertown, MD 21620.
Price: Moderate to
   Expensive.
Credit Cards: No.
Handicap Access: Yes.
Special Features: Children
   welcome; well-behaved
   dogs OK in one room.

room into a spacious first-floor guest room with king-sized bed. That gives you an idea of the warm welcome that awaits in this circa 1876 Victorian in the heart of Chestertown. Large common areas are lavishly furnished with antiques. Three guest rooms have private baths, and two upstairs have adjoining rooms to create suites with a shared bath when needed. Marcy's popovers and Amish sticky buns delight guests at the Continental breakfast served in the formal dining room.

Once the home of Kent County's first millionaire, this house had the county's first indoor bathroom and electricity. By the mid-1960s, it was vacant, in disrepair, and called a ghost house by local kids. Now the Parker House is a post-restoration showcase.

THE WHITE SWAN TAVERN

Manager: Mary Susan
   Maisel.
410-778-2300.
www.chestertown.com/
   whiteswan.
231 High St., Chestertown,
   MD 21620.
Price: Expensive to Very
   Expensive.
Credit Cards: MC, V.
Handicap Access: Yes.
Special Features: Children
   welcome.

Perhaps the most authentic, meticulous colonial restoration on the Eastern Shore, the 1733 White Swan is a time capsule. Handsome and dignified, located on the historic district's main street, a collection of people in waistcoats and breeches gathered about in the public rooms would create a perfect time warp. Guest rooms, however, have modern comforts, with private baths, nonworking fireplaces (although the fires blaze in the common areas), and refrigerators. Accommodations range from the John Lovegrove Kitchen room, with its massive fireplace and exposed beams dating to 1705, to the winding T.W. Eliason Victorian Suite, complete with parlor. Even if you can't stay here, stop by for afternoon tea, daily 3–5. Guests also get a full Continental breakfast brought to their room on request, a complimentary fruit basket and a bottle of wine. Check the display cabinet to see artifacts found during the 1978 archaeological dig.

Rock Hall

THE INN AT OSPREY POINT

Manager: Christine Will.
410-639-2194.
www.ospreypoint.com.
20786 Rock Hall Ave., Rock
   Hall, MD 21661.

Newly built in 1993, this white brick Colonial is modeled after the Coke-Garrett House in Williamsburg, Va. Seven pretty rooms with colonial-style furnishings and décor have private baths, AC, cable TV, and other pleasantries of the early twenty-first century. Family-friendly rooms are large enough to accommodate a pullout couch or a cot. Located on

David Trozzo

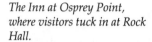

*The Inn at Osprey Point,
where visitors tuck in at Rock
Hall.*

Price: Expensive to Very
  Expensive.
Credit Cards: D, MC, V.
Handicap Access: No.
Special Features: Children
  welcome.

thirty lush Swan Creek acres overlooking a marina
with swimming pool, volleyball, horseshoes, nature
trails, and complimentary bicycles, this is more like a
small resort than an inn. Management can arrange
sailing, fishing, or horseback riding; the restaurant
serves dinner Thurs.–Mon. Continental breakfast.
Restaurant regulars know to order the cream of crab
soup, served with the traditional sherry.

SWAN HAVEN
Innkeepers: Diane Oliver &
  Harry Newman.
410-639-2527.
www.swanhaven.com.
20950 Rock Hall Ave., Rock
  Hall, MD 21661.
Price: Moderate to
  Expensive.
Credit Cards: AE, MC, V.
Handicap Access: No.
Restrictions: No children
  under 10.

At various times a temporary hospital and a
waterman's home, the century-old Swan
Haven, a Victorian cottage, is a handy resting place
for people in town for sailing, biking, kayaking, or
bird-watching. Seven modern rooms, all with private baths and cable TVs, are pretty and comfortable
without being overly fancy. Beds are mostly king
and queen. The second-floor Cignet Room features a
whirlpool tub for two, king-sized bed, and a grand
view of Swan Creek and the marina through double
doors that open onto a screened-in porch. After a
self-serve Continental breakfast, take advantage of
the free bikes (also rented to nonguests, along with
kayaks, canoes, small boats, windsurfers, and fish-
ing rods), the sprawling deck, and the pier, a perfect place to take in the sunset or
watch the boats and waterfowl come and go. Walk to local restaurants.

MOONLIGHT BAY INN
Innkeepers: Dotty and Bob
  Santangelo.
410-639-2660.

Settle in to your Queen Anne-style room in this
romantic Victorian along the water, with lush
wallpaper and afternoon high tea to boot. Ten rooms
total mean you're almost assured a water-view

www.rockhallmd.com/
moonlightbay.
Lawton Dr., Rock Hall, MD
21661.
Price: Expensive to Very
Expensive.
Credit Cards: D, MC, V.
Handicap Access: Yes.
Special Features: Two
rooms suitable for very
young children.

room. Five in the newer "west wing" have balconies and single whirlpools; four of five rooms in the main house have water views. Private whirlpools in many. Sailors ready to get off the boat for a night can dock at one of the marina's fifty transient boat slips. Two comfy parlors.

HOTELS/MOTELS

Comfort Suites (410-810-0555; 160 Scheeler Rd., Chestertown, MD 21620) Located off Rte. 213 just outside of town. Fifty-three rooms, indoor pool, nonsmoking rooms available. Moderate to Expensive.

Inn at Black-eyed Susan (410-778-3200; www.black-eyedsusan.com; 601 Washington Ave., Chestertown, MD 21620) Recently renovated and a reasonable option for families. Twenty-five rooms, one whirlpool suite. Some rooms have pullout couches. Continental breakfast on Sat. and Sun., outdoor swimming pool. Summer rates: Inexpensive to Moderate during the week; Moderate during the weekend.

Mears Great Oak Landing and Lodge (410-778-5007, 800-LANDING; www.mearsmarinas.com/greatoak.html; 22170 Great Oak Landing Rd., Chestertown, MD 21620) Boaters arriving at the accompanying marina will be especially happy to find a bed in one of twenty-eight rooms. 9-hole golf course. Restaurant overlooking the water. Open seasonally. Moderate to Expensive.

RESTAURANTS

As always around the Bay, dining options are varied and the seafood can't be beat. Restaurant price ranges, which include entrée, appetizer, and dessert, are as follows:

Inexpensive: Up to $15
Moderate: $15 to $25
Expensive: $25 to $35
Very Expensive: Over $35

Credit card abbreviations are: AE, American Express; CB, Carte Blanche; D, Discover; DC, Diner's Club; MC, MasterCard; V, Visa.

Havre de Grace

Look out over the Susquehanna River while dining at The Tidewater Grille in Havre de Grace.

David Trozzo

TIDEWATER GRILLE
410-939-3313.
300 Foot of Franklin St.
Open: Daily.
Price: Moderate.
Cuisine: Authentic
    Regional American.
Serving: L, D.
Credit Cards: AE, DC, MC, V.
Reservations: Not accepted.
Handicap Access: Yes.

Take advantage of this longtime staple along the upper Susquehanna River reaches of the Chesapeake Bay, where the food and service have remained at a high if casual level for years. Long windows open the modern dining room onto the Susquehanna and its passing railroad bridge, while an ample deck outside accommodates the al fresco crowd. For a recent early afternoon lunch, we waited approximately one minute until a waterside window table was cleared, and not much longer before our server swooped in to take our order and returned with a fat lump crab cake sandwich topped by a blood-red seasonal tomato. Chesapeake-inspired stained-glass panels of leaping fish or ducks top the long windows, a lovely but nonintrusive touch — just like the food and service. The rest of the well-considered menu includes seafood dishes, pastas, and beef.

Chesapeake City

BAYARD HOUSE RESTAURANT
410-885-5040, 877-582-4049.
11 Bohemia Ave.
Open: Daily.
Price: Expensive to Very Expensive.
Cuisine: Seafood/Continental.
Serving: L, D.

In an earlier life, this 1829 brick establishment served the builders of the C&D Canal. Now, the green Victorian painted lady welcomes diners in cozy fireplace-centered dining rooms or a long, glassed-in canal-side patio with candy-striped fabric draping the inside wall. Food here focuses on Chesapeake-area seafood with some fusion touches (watercress with a char-grilled summer salmon; a crab spring roll appetizer), but depend on crab

The Bayard House offers fine dining along the Chesapeake and Delaware Canal topping the Bay at Chesapeake City.

David Trozzo

Credit Cards: AE, D, MC, V.
Reservations: Suggested.
Handicap Access: Yes.

cakes and a veggie Maryland crab soup on the menu, too. A noted specialty is the Tournedos Baltimore, one topped with a crab cake, one with a lobster cake, finished with a Madeira cream and seafood champagne sauce for $26. The most recent chef, Brandon Gentry, brings country club kitchen experience and a degree from the Culinary Institute of America. Downstairs find the historic Hole in the Wall pub. Located at the end of Bohemia Avenue, Bayard House is popular with diners in Chesapeake City.

Kennedyville

KENNEDYVILLE INN
410-348-2400.
11986 Augustine Herman
  Hwy. (Rte. 213).
Open: Wed.–Sun.
Price: Moderate to
  Expensive.
Cuisine: Regional
  American.
Serving: D Wed.–Sat.; L
  Sun. 1–6.
Credit Cards: D, MC, V.
Reservations: For parties of
  6 or more only.
Handicap Access: Yes.
Special Features: Private
  parties up to 24
  accommodated; children
  welcome.

Upon one thing locals agree: the Kennedyville Inn is the best restaurant in Kent County. Former owners of Chestertown's Ironstone Café, chef/owner Kevin McKinney and his wife, Barbara Silcox, operate a superb eatery. The focus is on creative cuisine, rather than the Saturday evening, where-to-be-seen reservation. Come as you are, as it's a friendly place with a young, energetic staff. The eclectic menu features several barbecued rib specialties, flavors to rival any you'd find in Memphis. Australian lamb chops roasted with oregano and garlic, or beef filet with horseradish, lovage and cream cheese mousse showcase this talented chef's menu. Crab steak, a signature dish, is two crab cakes formed into one very large "steak," delicately prepared with virtually no filler. Truly a cut above the traditional offering, these are not comprised of more bread than crabmeat. Daily seasonal soup specials and McKinney's own warm, crusty bread are a meal unto themselves. Prices range from $3 to $9 for the ever popular oyster fritter, offered only in winter, and $16 to $24 for entrées. "Centrally located in the middle of nowhere," this exceptional restaurant is worth the eight-mile drive from Chestertown into the hamlet of Kennedyville.

Chestertown

The popular Blue Heron Cafe in Chestertown.

David Trozzo

BLUE HERON CAFÉ
410-778-0188.
236 Cannon St.
Open: Mon.–Sat.
Price: Expensive to Very Expensive.
Cuisine: Traditional and Innovative American.
Serving: L, D.
Credit Cards AE, D, MC, V.
Reservations: Strongly advised.
Handicap Access: Yes.

Chestertown is blessed with a number of good eating establishments and the Blue Heron Café is no exception. This is a favored spot of the town's "in crowd," who quickly fill the choice tables on any given Saturday night. So try the Blue Heron dining during the week, or perhaps for lunch.

High ceilings affixed with quietly spinning fans and soft music are a part of the casual dining atmosphere. The star is clearly the superbly prepared fare, which has remained consistent since it opened in 1997. The menu focuses on the freshest ingredients found locally, with strong emphasis on creative but classic preparation. There's a nice selection of seafood, including Maryland crab cakes and gently sauteed softshell crab in season. For those wanting the more hearty of choices, the roasted rack of lamb rubbed with rosemary and garden lavender accompanied by a fresh mint demi-glace, or the grilled filet mignon with roasted onion and sage should more than satisfy. For starters, the oyster fritters in a lemon butter sauce are a favorite requested by the loyal patrons — famous enough to get a mention in *Time* magazine a few years back.

Management has added six outdoor tables in the courtyard out back, and it's the ideal spot to enjoy your culinary options, a sip or two of wine from a terrific wine list, and the friendly, easy pace of historic Chestertown.

IMPERIAL HOTEL
RESTAURANT
410-778-5000.
208 High St.
Open: Wed.–Sat. from 5:30;
 Sun. Noon–3.
Price: Expensive to Very
 Expensive.
Cuisine: New American.
Serving: L (Sun. only), D
 (Wed.–Sat.)
Credit Cards: AE, MC, V.
Reservations: Suggested.
Handicap Access: Yes.

Formality reigns in the Imperial Hotel's two intimate dining rooms, where diners tread a lush green rug and sit down to tables topped with crisp white linens with flickering votives. Alongside one dining room wall stands a dark wood antique sideboard. Very Victorian; dig out your manners. But contemporary cooking drives this notable Eastern Shore grande dame. Executive Chef Eliza Abbey works her magic in the Imperial's kitchen, and her cuisine can best be described as unpretentious, eclectic, and regional, drawing upon only the freshest in-season ingredients. Roasted tomato orange vinaigrette on a bed of local field greens, or fresh salmon and scallop phyllo are just two samples of her inventive offerings. Rack of lamb with rosemary and garlic may be delicious, but try the toasted pecan and peanut encrusted rack and you'll get a sense of this talented chef's range. Imperial service, too — friendly, efficient, and gracious. The wine list is a wine-lover's paradise, and the knowledgeable owners are available to assist with choices. Restaurant food is only as good as the folks who prepare it; let's hope that Eliza Abbey's name continues to appear on the bottom of the menu for a long time to come.

THE OLD WHARF
410-778-3566.
Cannon St., next to Kibler's
 Marina on the Chester
 River.
Open: Daily.
Price: Moderate.
Cuisine:
 American/Chesapeake.
Serving: L, D, SB.
Credit Cards: AE, MC, V.
Reservations: Not accepted.
Handicap Access: Yes.

While Chestertown has several great restaurants, The Old Wharf is the only one accessible by water, and with plenty of depth at the dock for even the biggest sailboats. Landlubbers find a panoramic water view through a long wall of windows. If you happen to find a line when you arrive (not uncommon on weekends), step outdoors to view several historic vessels docked alongside.

Fresh seafood dominates the menu, though you'll find chicken and steak as well. Normally, seafood dishes are simple yet tasty. Recently, we arrived late on a busy holiday weekend and ordered two similar crab dishes, which tasted very different. But given the delicious cream of crab soup, the scarcity of local crabs over the Memorial Day weekend we visited, and the restaurant's usual quality, we can't fault them too much.

Rock Hall

BAY LEAF GOURMET
410-639-2700.
5757 Main St.
Open: Tues.–Sun.
Price: Inexpensive.
Cuisine: Light fare and
    desserts.
Serving: B, L, takeout D.
Credit Cards: AE, MC, V.
Reservations: No.
Handicap Access: Yes.

Increasingly, outsiders are discovering Rock Hall, a long-ensconced waterman's town with a bustling harbor at the edge of town. But let's keep it in perspective. As we gazed out the window over a bleu cheese and apple quiche lunch here one late-July Tuesday, a man rode his riding lawn mower down the middle of this cute but not entirely re-made Main Street with nary a vehicular competitor in sight. For its part, the Bay Leaf creates a wel-come development along Main Street. Open throughout the week year-round, the gourmet café offers homemade soups, design-your-own sand-wiches, desserts, and quiches, such as the aforementioned bleu cheese and apple, eggy and wonderful — and a tough choice over the wild mushroom and leek option. Morning coffee carafes sit out late alongside muffins and pas-tries, and chatter in the kitchen regarding the day's best special wafts out from behind the counter. Owner Christine Burgess has cooked in kitchens around the area, and she's created an airy, clean dining room with a menu to match.

Hammer into a dozen blue crabs at Waterman's Crabhouse, Rock Hall.

David Trozzo

**WATERMAN'S
    CRABHOUSE**
410-639-2261.
Sharp St.
Open: Daily.
Serving: L, D.
Price: Moderate.
Cuisine: American/
    Chesapeake.

Located in one of the few remaining waterman enclaves on the Bay, casual Waterman's Crab-house gives diners a front seat on a working har-bor. Inside, continuous windows let the outside in, or dine on the restaurant's spacious deck. If you arrive by boat, tie up free at Waterman's while you eat. The great view is augmented by great food, cold beer, and live entertainment most summer

Credit Cards: AE, D, MC, V.
Reservations: Suggested but not required.
Handicap Access: Yes.

nights. Expect traditional Bay dishes, including crabs done every way possible, steamed shrimp, clams, and oysters. The fresh catch of the day comes off the workboats puttering up to the harbor. The menu also includes traditional Eastern Shore dishes such as steak and chicken. Even without the tasty main courses and one of the best cream of crab soups we've sampled, the fresh potato salad is worth the trip. For your money's worth, try the all-you-can-eat crab feasts on summer Tues. and Thurs. when crabs are available. A band plays outside Thurs.–Sun., early May through Oct.

FOOD PURVEYORS

COFFEE HOUSES

Java by the Bay (410-939-0227; 118 N. Washington St., Havre de Grace) Café-style coffeehouse sells teas and morning Danish, biscotti and pastries. Easy to find in tourist shopping district. Open Mon.–Sat. 7:30–6 (closes Sat. at 5), Sun. 8:30–4.

Play It Again Sam (410-778-2688; 108 S. Cross St., Chestertown) Coffee bar with baked goods, sandwiches, and desserts inside an old store with a wood floor and pressed-tin ceiling. Open Mon.–Sat. 7–5:30, Sun. 9–4.

CRAB HOUSES AND SEAFOOD MARKETS

E&E Seafood, Inc. (410-778-6333; Kent Plaza, Chestertown) Open daily. Fish, crabs, sandwiches, smoked fish.

J&J Seafood (410-639-2325; 21083 Chesapeake Ave., Rock Hall) Steamed hard-shell crabs and live soft-shell crabs, rockfish, perch, and oysters; bait and ice. Closed Jan. and Feb.

Price's Seafood Restaurant (410-939-2782; 654 Water St., Havre de Grace) Established in 1944, this is where Havre de Grace cracks crabs. Open Apr.–Nov.

ICE CREAM AND CANDY

Bomboy's Home Made Candy (410-939-2924; 329 & 322 Market St., Havre de Grace) Family-owned since 1978, now moved across the street (which smells deliciously of chocolate!). Ice cream at the original location. Both closed Mon.

Durding's Store (410-778-7957; 5742 Main St., Rock Hall) Folks still come for ice cream at this soda fountain installed in this 1872 pharmacy in 1923. Rotating favorites include Moose Track (vanilla with fudge and Reese's peanut butter cups) and Muddy Sneakers (vanilla with chocolate caramel). Also cards and some gift items.

NATURAL FOODS

Chestertown Natural Foods (410-778-1677; 214 Cannon St., Chestertown) Natural foods, organic produce, vitamins and supplements, bath products, and snacks.

SANDWICH SHOPS

The Feast of Reason (410-778-3828; 203 High St., Chestertown) Sandwiches made on specialty breads for lunch. No credit cards. Open Mon.–Sat. 10–4.

CULTURE

CINEMA

First-run fare is screened at the new **Chester 5 Theatres** (410-778-2227) at Washington Square on Rte. 213 in _Chestertown_. Washington College in Chestertown offers a free weekly film series that brings high-quality movies and foreign films to campus in the **Norman James Theatre** (410-778-7849) at 7:30pm on Fri., Sun., and Mon. during the school year.

Chestertown

CHESTER RIVER ARTWORKS
410-778-6300.
Artworks@dmv.com.
Rtes. 291 and 20.
Call for hours and workshops.

Radcliffe Mill at the edge of town has found new life as a fledgling arts center. Five studios are devoted to clay, visual arts and design, woodworking, writing, and textiles. Classes, including some for kids, and exhibitions. Day, weekend, or longer workshops.

CONSTANCE STUART LARRABEE ARTS CENTER
800-422-1782, ext. 7849;
410-778-7849.

Thanks to the rebirth of Washington College's one-time boiler plant, its fine arts department has expanded studio space for painting, drawing, pottery, sculpture, printmaking, and photography. Largely academic space, the center also shows stu-

Washington College, 300
   Washington Ave.
Call for hours.

dent artwork. Chestertown resident Larrabee was one of World War II's first women photojournalists. Her work has been exhibited at the Smithsonian and Corcoran Galleries in Washington, D.C. Also on campus: the Gibson Performing Arts Center gallery.

HISTORIC BUILDINGS & SITES

Chestertown

GEDDES-PIPER HOUSE
410-778-3499.
101 Church Alley.
Open: May–Oct., Sat. &
   Sun. 1–4; Nov.–Apr.,
   weekends by
   appointment. Self-guided
   tours available year-
   round Tues.–Fri. 10–4.
Admission: $3 donation
   requested.

Designed in the "Philadelphia style," this three-and-a-half story brick townhouse was built in the late 1700s. Now the museum headquarters of the Historical Society of Kent County, the home was owned by a series of merchants, including William Geddes, customs collector for the Port of Chestertown. Geddes claims a notorious local fame — his was the brigantine ravaged during the 1774 Chestertown Tea Party, still celebrated. He sold the house to merchant James Piper. It now features eighteenth- and nineteenth-century furnishings, maps, china, and library.

Havre de Grace

The Concord Point Lighthouse stands sentinel at Havre de Grace.

David Trozzo

**CONCORD POINT
LIGHTHOUSE**
410-939-5108.
Lafayette & Concord Sts.
Open: Apr.–Oct., Sat. &
    Sun. 1–5.

The Susquehanna River, Chesapeake's prehistoric precursor, flows into the Bay at Havre de Grace. Perhaps the best view — though hours are limited — is from here. Visitors to the 1827 lighthouse will notice the boardwalk that ends out front. The half-mile-long promenade rounds the point along the Susquehanna, affording an exhilarating view.

HISTORIC SCHOOL

Chestertown

Our country's father gave express permission for use of his name, contributed fifty guineas to its 1782 founding, and served six years on the Board of Visitors and Governors of **Washington College** (410-778-2800; 300 Washington Ave., Chestertown, MD 21620). Now it's known for its creative writing program and the notable undergraduate literary prize, the Sophie Kerr Prize (just about $62,000 in 2001). Beautiful grounds.

MUSEUMS

Chesapeake City

C&D CANAL MUSEUM
410-885-5621.
815 Bethel Rd.
Open: Year-round,
    Mon.–Fri. 8–4.
Admission: Free.

The fourteen-mile-long Chesapeake & Delaware Canal severs the top of the Delmarva Peninsula from the mainland, linking the Upper Chesapeake Bay with the Delaware River. In so doing, the grand old C&D shaves 300 miles off an otherwise roundabout journey from Philadelphia to Baltimore by way of Norfolk and the Virginia capes. Discussed for 150 years before it was finally dug by 2,600 men in the 1820s, the canal cost a whopping $2.5 million and opened in 1829. Photos, models, maps, and a thirty-eight-foot, nineteenth-century waterwheel, at the time considered a marvel of engineering, are on display at the tiny museum — the former pump house for the old locks. Interactive exhibits and a TV monitor track the ships headed through the canal. It's awe-inspiring. Run by the U.S. Army Corps of Engineers, who operate the canal.

Havre de Grace

**HAVRE DE GRACE
DECOY MUSEUM**
410-939-3739.

So you want to know about decoy carving? This is the place, a proud piece of the past in this growing tourist/sailing town that calls itself

www.decoymuseum.com.
215 Giles St.
Open: Daily 11–4; closed
major holidays.
Admission: $4 adults, $3
seniors and students
9–18.
Handicap Access: Yes.

America's Decoy Capital. The museum is dedicated to preserving the Bay's old "gunning" tradition, the art of hunting with decoys. Works by noted carvers R. Madison Mitchell, Bob McGaw, Paul Gibson, and Charlies Joiner and Bryan are shown, as well as tools of the trade and displays recalling the early twentieth-century days when carvers gathered around the stove. Perhaps most intriguing is a peek into why conservation measures have become so important: the sinkbox. This clever contraption was outlawed in the mid-1930s — "because it was too effective," chuckled a longtime Chesapeake outdoor enthusiast. Shaped like a bathtub with square wings weighted down with flat-bottomed decoys, the sinkbox held a hunter who took to the duck hunt at the nearby Susquehanna Flats, which drew rich and famous hunters from Baltimore, Washington, D.C., and Philadelphia. Out back stands the workshop of local decoy carver Mitchell.

**ROCK HALL
WATERMAN'S
MUSEUM**
410-778-6697.
Haven Harbour Marina,
20880 Rock Hall Ave.
Open: Daily 8–5 (honor
system: pick up key at
the marina's Ditty Bag
store).
Admission: Free.

Rock Hall, a sailing and boating center to many, has roots as a watermen's community, celebrated at this charming museum in an old waterman's shanty. Inside find tools of the trade for oystering, crabbing, and fishing, photographs, local carvings, and boats.

MUSIC

Chestertown

**WASHINGTON
COLLEGE CONCERT
SERIES**
410-778-7839.
Season: Sept.–early May.
Tickets: Call for ticket
prices and schedule.

The popular Washington College Concert Series, pushing 50, is an annual five-concert series featuring such performers as Peter Schickele (aka P.D.Q. Bach), The American Boychoir, and the madrigal group Chanticleer. Held in the college's Gibson Performing Arts Center.

NIGHTLIFE

Chesapeake City has always enjoyed an interesting paradox. It's small and seemingly remote, but ships from all corners of the globe pass by on the bustling C&D Canal. Applaud the Caribbean flavor brought by calypso combos that play from Mother's Day to Labor Day at the dockside terrace of **Schaefer's Canal House** (410-885-2200; off Rte. 213 on the north side of the canal). Open Wed.–Sun.

Around _Chestertown_, visit **Andy's** (410-778-6779; 337 1/2 W. High St.), a small, friendly, popular club that regularly hosts live jazz, bluegrass, rock, and blues.

PERFORMING ARTS & THEATER

Chestertown

WASHINGTON COLLEGE
410-778-7849, Special Events Office.
310 Washington Ave.

Drama majors fulfill their "senior obligation" by staging a full dramatic production in Tawes Theatre — your evening entertainment. Student musical ensembles, from the Concert Band and Jazz Band to the Early Music Consort, perform throughout the year. For a monthly listing of performance events and prices, contact the Special Events Office.

Church Hill

CHURCH HILL THEATRE
410-758-1331.
103 Walnut St. (Md. 19) off Md. 213 btw. Centreville & Chestertown.
Tickets: Prices vary.

This 1929 building has gone full circle, from town hall to movie theater to decline and, finally, rescue. With its restored 1944 Art Deco theater interior, the Church Hill Players' home maintains a lively performance schedule that has included _The Seven-Year Itch_ and _Steel Magnolias_. Look for a range: touring performers and a Young People's Series offering theater, magic, and puppetry.

SEASONAL EVENTS

Chestertown

Chestertown commemorates its pre-Revolutionary War radical politics on the Sat. of Memorial Day weekend in the **Chestertown Tea Party Festival.** The townwide celebration features colonial parades, music, festivities, historical re-enactments, boat rides for children, and food recalling the 1774 Chestertown Tea Party, where the townspeople rose up against Port Collector William Geddes, whose brigantine _Geddes_ was plundered, Boston-style, by the locals. (Maybe it's apocryphal, but some say that they saved the shipment's rum.) Free admission; handicap access. In early Sept. enjoy the **Chestertown Jazz Festival** (410-348-5528; www.kentcounty.com), with Fri. evening and Sat. afternoon music in Wilmore

Park. In Sept. and Dec., it's worth checking out candlelight walking tours through this delightfully old-fashioned town. Contact: 410-778-0416.

Rock Hall

Blues, bluegrass, and Irish folk music are featured at the **Rock Hall FallFest** in early Oct., a celebration of music and mariners. Artists, children's theater, food, and regional favorites like oysters shucked before your eyes. For information: **Kent County Tourism Office**, 410-778-0416.

TOURS

Chesapeake City

Chesapeake Horse Country Tours offers a private, narrated walking tour of this canal town's historic district, featuring multicolored nineteenth-century homes that prospered with the C&D Canal. A van takes visitors on a tour to see private horse farms nearby. $20; three hours; reservations required. Contact: **Uniglobe Hill Travel**, 800-466-1402, 410-885-2797; 200 Bohemia Ave., Chesapeake City, MD 21915.

Chestertown

Learn about the Georgian, Federal, Italianate or Queen Anne-style buildings that mark the chapters in the life of pretty Chestertown. The "Walking Tour of Historic Chestertown" brochure, with architectural and other highlights, is easy to follow, with stops at the Courthouse or the famed White Swan Tavern, where George Washington supposedly supped. Contact the **Kent County Tourism Office**, 410-778-0416; www.kentcounty.com; 400 High St., Chestertown, MD 21620. Also at the tourism office is the "Driving Tour of the Kent County Peninsula," which guides drivers through rural and historic highlights.

RECREATION

BICYCLING

The Shore's user-friendly topography moves from pleasantly rolling hills at its upper extreme to sprawling flatland farther south, giving cyclists a mix of riding conditions on lightly traveled roads through great coastal scenery. In *Kent County*, the tourism office offers a booklet detailing bike-tour options.

Distance and difficulty levels range from the eleven-mile "Pomona Warm-Up" to the eighty-one-mile "Pump House Primer," which takes in Chesapeake City and Cecil County's rolling horse country. The Baltimore Bicycling Club developed the routes. For a copy of "The Kent County Bicycle Tour," contact: **Kent County Tourism Office**, 410-778-0416; www.kentcounty.com; 100 N. Cross St., Chestertown, MD 21620.

LOCAL CYCLING SHOPS

Bikework (410-778-6940; 208 S. Cross St., Chestertown) Closed Thurs.
Swan Haven Rentals (410-639-2527; 20950 Rock Hall Ave., Rock Hall) Bicycles, boats, and fishing gear.

BIRD-WATCHING

Eastern Neck Wildlife Refuge (410-639-7056; www.easternneck.fws.gov; 1730 Eastern Neck Road, Rock Hall, MD 21661) lies at the end of the peninsula that includes Chestertown and Rock Hall. It's a favored birding ground, with 244 species recorded here, including a bountiful collection of wintering migratory birds like pintails, old-squaw, and other sea ducks. Other times of the year, look for threatened bald eagles, osprey, terns, gulls, woodcock, woodpeckers, and other migrants.

BOATING

CHARTERS, CRUISES, & BOAT RENTALS

Chesapeake City

Miss Clare (410-885-5088; 64 Front St., Chesapeake City, MD 21915) This classic Chesapeake deadrise — a crab boat design — started life in Cambridge and did duty as a charter fishing boat in the charming Atlantic town of Lewes, Del., before Capt. Ralph H. Hazel brought her back to the family hometown to do history tours of the C&D canal. Hour-long cruise, April–Oct. 31. Adults $10, children $5. Departs from the dock at Chesapeake City. Fri. and Sat., two-hour cruises to Turkey Point Lighthouse, where you can view all five rivers that empty into the head of the bay. $25 per person; half-price for children.

Chestertown

Schooner *Sultana* Projects (410-778-5954; www.schoonersultana.com) The 97-foot floating classroom *Sultana*, launched in 2001, re-creates a 1767 Boston-built vessel that spent time as a British Royal Navy dispatch boat and revenue cruiser. The original patrolled the Chesapeake Bay from 1769–1771. Now, her namesake teaches schoolkids about history and aquatic science. Although *Sultana's* homeport is Chestertown, she sails the Chesapeake — so you may catch her in another port, or maybe at home for a public cruise. Keep an eye out.

Southern Cross Charters (410-778-4460; www.kentcounty.com/southerncross; Great Oak Landing Marina Resort, P.O. Box 426, Chestertown, MD 21620) Day, sunset, and overnight cruises on the Chesapeake Bay in a forty-one-foot Morgan Out Island ketch-rigged sail yacht. Food service. Overnight cruises to Baltimore's Inner Harbor, Rock Hall, Annapolis, and Georgetown.

Havre de Grace

Applegarth Cruises (Capt. Paul Thomas, 410-879-6941; 2524 Ady Rd., Forest Hill, MD 21050) Charter this miniature skipjack from a professional captain who can drop you off at one of four nearby islands to explore, picnic, or hang out at the beach. Or, go for a sail. Hourly costs drop with each additional hour.

Lantern Queen (410-287-7217; Foot of Congress Ave., Havre de Grace, MD 21078) Take a cruise aboard a Mississippi-style riverboat. Thurs. & Fri., May-Sept., starting at $30.

Martha Lewis (410-939-4078, 800-406-0766; www.skipjackmarthalewis.org; Chesapeake Heritage Conservancy, 121 N. Union Ave., Havre de Grace, MD 21078) This skipjack, restored in 1994, offers public cruises in the summer and fall. They depart Lighthouse Pier in Havre de Grace; Sat. & Sun., noon, 1:30 and 3 (when in port, so call ahead); $10 per person, $5 for children 10 and under. Daylong oyster cruises show the public how it's done and cost $150. Call for departure information.

Rock Hall

Gratitude Yachting Center (410-639-7111; 5990 Lawton Ave., Rock Hall, MD 21661) Charter Island Packets, Nauticats; captained or bareboat.

Haven Charters (410-639-7140; www.havencharters.com; 20846 Rock Hall Ave., Rock Hall, MD 21661) Bareboat only twenty-nine- to thirty-nine-foot sailboats.

Marinas

Bohemia Bay Yacht Harbor (410-885-2736; 1026 Town Point Rd., Chesapeake City, MD 21915) Full service, transients. 299 slips on the Bohemia River.

Chestertown Marina (410-778-3616; 211 Front St., Chestertown, MD 21620)

Mechanic on premises, fuel. 60 slips; transients welcome. Located on the Chester River in the heart of historic Chestertown — restaurant adjacent, walk to everything.

David Trozzo

Boats line Georgetown Yacht Basin on the Upper Eastern Shore.

Georgetown Yacht Basin (410-648-5112; 14020 Augustine Herman Hwy./P.O. Box 8, Georgetown, MD 21930) More than 300 open and 100 covered slips here; 156 more slips at Granary Marina directly across the Sassafras River.

Haven Harbour Marina (410-778-6697, 800-506-6697; 20880 Rock Hall Ave., Rock Hall, MD 21661) Large marina with many amenities. Two pools, bar and grill. 217 slips; 50 to 60 available for weekend transients.

Osprey Point Marina (410-639-2663; 20786 Rock Hall Ave., Rock Hall, MD 21661) Floating docks, bathhouse, pool; 160 slips on Swan Creek. Alongside full-service restaurant and inn.

Rock Hall Landing (410-639-2224; 5657 S. Hawthorne Ave., Rock Hall, MD 21661) Closest marina to town, along the Chester River. Pool, 77 slips. Open Apr. 15–Nov. 15.

Sailing Emporium (410-778-1342; 21144 Green Lane, Rock Hall, MD 21661) Laundry, lending library with liberal policy, 150 slips, pool, pump-out station, barbecue grills, picnic tables. On the Chester River.

Skipjack Cove Yachting Resort (410-275-2122; 150 Skipjack Cove Rd., Georgetown, MD 21930) Tennis courts, Olympic-sized pool. 20 moorings, 20 lifts, 360 slips on the Sassafras River.

Tidewater Marina (410-939-0950; Bourbon St., Havre de Grace, MD 21078) 160 slips. Fuel, haul-outs, repairs, discount marine store, showers, laundry, courtesy car. Where the Susquehanna meets the Chesapeake.

SAILING & POWERBOAT SCHOOLS

Havre de Grace

BaySail School and Yacht Charters (410-939-2869; www.baysail.net; Tidewater Marina, Bourbon St., Havre de Grace, MD 21078) American Sailing Association-certified courses, beginner to advanced; private instruction aboard your boat (hourly rate). Charters Hunters and Catalinas, bareboat or captained.

CANOEING & KAYAKING

The Upper Bay region provides often protected, quiet rivers and creeks. View osprey, blue and green herons, kingfishers and terns, and catch a few perch or rockfish in summer. See "Landings & Boat Ramps" in Chapter Nine, *Information*, to find out how to order a free map of Bay access points.

Some good paddles: In *Queen Anne's County*, put in at the **Corsica River** at *Centreville* and poke around upstream or downstream on a pretty stretch of water with homes along the bank. Turner's Creek, which flows northwest into the **Sassafras River** in *Kent County*, affords some scenic canoeing past stunning sixty- to seventy-foot-high bluffs.

For those without their own boat (or just some local advice), the following outfitters can help.

Chester River Kayak Adventures (410-639-2001, 410-639-2061; www.rock-hallmd.com/crkayak; 5758 Main St., Rock Hall, MD 21661) Kayak rentals, tours available. Tours start with fifteen minutes of instruction.
Starrk Moon Kayaks (877-KAYAKS1, 410-939-9500; 502 Warren St., Havre de Grace, MD 21078) Lessons, trips and rentals; check out one of the islands in the river, or paddle the town's coastline. Prices: $25–$45 for four-hour rentals; $25–$90 for trips.

FISHING

BOAT RAMPS

In *Cecil County*, try the Fredericktown boat launch on the Sassafras River; call **Cecil County Parks and Recreation** (410-392-4537, 410-658-3000) or **Elk Neck State Park** (410-287-5333). Easy-to-find ramps in downtown *Havre de Grace* include those at **Jean Roberts Memorial Park** (410-939-0015; $5 fee on weekends and holidays) on the Susquehanna River, and at the end of town at the city yacht basin at **Tydings Park**. To obtain a free map of Bay access points, check "Landings & Boat Ramps" in Chapter Nine, *Information*.

FISHING CHARTERS

The Kent County Office of Tourism (410-778-0416; www.kentcounty.com; 400 High St., Chestertown, MD 21620) The county lists fishing charters in its visitor's guide; check them out.

GOLF

Brantwood Golf Club (410-398-8848; 1190 Augustine Herman Hwy., Elkton) 18 holes; semiprivate. Located on Rte. 213.

Bulle Rock (888-285-5375; www.bullerock.com; 320 Blenheim Lane, Havre de Grace) One of sixteen five-star courses in North America, and rated #1 in Maryland by *Golf Digest* in 2000. Public, locker room attendant, fine-dining restaurant, Bay views.

Mears Great Oak Landing Resort and Conference Center (800-LANDING, 410-778-5007; Great Oak Landing Rd., Chestertown) 9 holes; executive course. Open to the public.

NATURAL AREAS: STATE, PRIVATE, FEDERAL PARKS

Chesapeake Farms Wildlife Habitat (410-778-8400; 7319 Remington Dr., Chestertown, MD 21620) Features a free driving tour through its 3,000 acres of wildlife and agricultural management demonstration area. The drive is open April–Oct. 10. Privately owned, located between Chestertown and Rock Hall.

Eastern Neck National Wildlife Refuge (410-639-7056; 1730 Eastern Neck Rd., Rock Hall, MD 21661) 2,300 acres of island with walking trails of up to 1.2 mi. Located at the mouth of the Chester River in Kent County, this is the Bay's only undeveloped island with Bay access. Go past Rock Hall until the road ends. Four trails, a boat ramp, and a boardwalk to an observation deck overlooking the Bay.

Elk Neck State Park (410-287-5333; 4395 Turkey Point Rd., North East, MD 21901) 2,188 acres. Located on Rte. 272, 9 mi. S. of North East. Where the North East and Elk Rivers meet. Swim, hike five different trails, launch a boat or canoe, or stay in one of nine small cabins or campgrounds. Walk the trail to see Turkey Point Lighthouse, where the Elk River meets Bay. Diverse terrain at this 2,000+ acre park includes steep bluffs, forests, marshland, and beaches.

Millington Wildlife Management Area (410-928-3650; 33626 Maryland Line Road, Massey, MD 21650) Located off Rte. 301 along the Delaware border. Nature trails, ponds, woods. 3,800 acres. Hunting in season.

Susquehanna State Park (410-557-7994; 3318 Rocks Chrome Hill Rd., Jarrettsville, MD 21084) Five miles north of Havre de Grace; 2,639 acres. Good for hiking, with fifteen miles of trails; boating, fishing. Check out the Susquehanna River, source of the fresh water in the Bay estuary.

HORSEBACK RIDING

Fair Hill Stables (contact Tailwinds Farm, 410-620-3883; 41 Tailwinds La., North East) Five hour-long trail rides in summer; fewer in the off-season. Located in the Fair Hill Natural Resource Management Area. Kids and adults; $22–$26.50.

HUNTING

Not every quarry is fowl or afoot — **sporting clays** are growing in popularity. In Kent County, try **Alexander Sporting Farms** (410-928-3549; 13503 Alexander Rd., Galena, MD 21635) or **Hopkins Game Farm** (410-348-5287; Rte. 298/P.O. Box 218, Kennedyville, MD 21645), which also has quail and pheasant. Five stands, golf driving range, lodging. If it's true waterfowl you're after, one of the best-known hunting guides is Floyd Price (410-778-6412) of Kennedyville, with his sizable operation.

SPORTING GOODS & CAMPING SUPPLY STORES

Toy's Outdoor Store (410-778-2561; 6274 Rock Hall Rd., Rock Hall).
Vonnie's Sporting Goods (410-778-5655; Rt. 213, Kennedyville) A complete hunting and fishing center with licenses, clothing. See Miss Kay, a local institution, or join the hunters at 5:30am for coffee at Vonnie's restaurant.

SWIMMING

Betterton Beach (contact Kent County Parks and Recreation, 410-778-1948; Rte. 292, Betterton) Deep in the Upper Bay, where freshwater dominates. Noted for reliable swimming conditions devoid of stinging nettles. Picnicking, fishing jetty, bathhouse, beach. Free. Lifeguard only on Sat. & Sun., Mem. Day–Labor Day. Picnic pavilion available for group rental.
North East Beach (410-287-5333; Rte. 272, North East) Picnicking, bathhouse. $2 per carload on weekdays; $2 per person on weekends and holidays; open April through mid-October. Along the North East River.
Rock Hall Public Beach (410-639-7611; Beach Rd., Rock Hall) From this tiny beach you can watch the giant container ships make their way from the Bay Bridge up to Baltimore. No lifeguard at this no-frills beach.

SHOPPING

ANTIQUES

Folks with a penchant for antiques (or collectibles, as so many cast-offs are known) find themselves in fine browsing territory on the Upper Bay, with its wealth of antique shops (don't miss Galena, not far from Chestertown) and unique auctions.

Residing on the Upper Shore for decades now is a marvel known alternatively as **"The Crumpton Auction"** or **"The Dixon Auction"** (Dixon's Furniture Inc., 410-928-3006; Rtes. 290 and 544, Crumpton, MD 21628). Reputed to be 30 acres, the auction starts at 9am sharp each Wednesday. You can check out everything in the "$5 field" on Tuesday, but that doesn't include furniture auctions. Year-round. Also: Rudnick's in nearby Galena, with 9am auctions every second and fourth Saturday (410-648-5601, 800-772-5601). Finally, check out the big auction at **American Corner** (410-754-8826; six miles north of Federalsburg on Auction Rd.). Every Thursday at 5pm, buildings full of stuff go on the block. Find everything from outboard motors to furniture.

Chesapeake City

Black Swan Antiques (410-885-5888; 219 Bohemia Ave.) Particularly good stop for those inclined toward Bay-related items. Nauticals include binnacles, prints, and oyster cans, from Maryland Beauties to the McReady Brothers of Chincoteague. Weekends only.

Havre de Grace

Bank of Memories (410-939-4343; 319 St. John St.) A range of goodies housed in the town's former First National Bank.

Franklin Street Antiques (410-939-4220; 464 Franklin St.) Cookie jar central, for sure. But glass drinking straw dispensers also line one shelf at this chockablock shop. Keep an eye out for decoys, the local pride and joy.

Havre de Grace Antique Center (410-939-4882; 408 N. Union Ave.) Likely the best antique shop in town — filled with shelves aplenty. A second location at 230 N. Washington St. (410-939-9397) has multiple dealers and great browsing.

Seneca Cannery Antiques (410-942-0701; 201 St. John St.) The enormous space, with granite walls, is almost as interesting as the wares provided by twenty-one plus dealers — which on one recent visit included a stuffed rooster for $95.

Thorofare Antique Mall (410-942-1110; 220 N. Washington St.) About twenty dealers stationed in a former downtown department store; antiques and old hand-painted furniture. Open daily year-round.

Washington Street Books & Antiques (410-939-6215; 131 N. Washington St.) Wonderful used bookshop well worth the stop. Knowledgeable proprietor.

Blue Heron Antiques & Collectibles (410-778-8118; 204 High St.) A good place to start if you're looking for collectibles, china, crystal, or Oriental treasures.

Galena

The Cross Street Station (410-648-5776; 105 Cross St.) On your right just before you hit Main Street coming from Chestertown, this large emporium brings nice furniture (blanket chests, an ancient pie safe) and a fun attitude.

Firehouse Antiques Center (410-648-5639; 102 N. Main St.) Multidealer shop focuses on high-quality (and not inexpensive) period furniture and accessories. Gorgeous American furniture.

Galena Antiques Center, an emporium among the antiques shops in the tiny town of Galena.

David Trozzo

Galena Antiques Center (410-648-5781; 108 N. Main St) The granddaddy of Galena antique shops, a large multidealer stop and home to a custom "barnwood" furniture workshop, where turned porch balustrades become custom table legs at amazingly low prices. *Life* magazines going way back. Open daily 10–5.

BOOKS

The Compleat Bookseller (410-778-1480; 301 High St., Chestertown) This fine store has a range of titles that you won't find in the big discount places.

Corsica Bookshop, Books, Beans and Beyond (410-758-1453; 101 S. Commerce St., Centreville) The Upper Eastern Shore's longtime bookstore, a good stop for travelers passing through en route to Chestertown and environs, is well-supplied. In addition, a gift shop and nice coffee bar have been added.

CLOTHING

Chester River Knitting Co. (410-778-0374; 306 Cannon St., Chestertown) Hand-made sweaters, from turtlenecks to crewnecks, from alpaca to cashmere.

Pride & Joy (410-778-2233; 321 High St., Chestertown) Children's apparel and gifts, for new arrivals up to older children.

GALLERIES

Capt. Bob Jobes Decoys (410-939-1843; www.jobesdecoys.com; 721 Otsego St., Havre de Grace) A paint-stained shed with its ceiling papered in decoy posters might not seem like a "gallery," but a similar shed, where famed Upper Bay carver Madison Mitchell once held forth, is now tucked behind the nearby Havre de Grace Decoy Museum. Decoys are America's water-front folk art, and Jobes, the eldest son of carver Capt. Harry Jobes, once earned $1 an hour working for Mitchell. In his workshop: swans, mallards, canvasbacks, blue herons and miniatures, plus the requisite friendly black lab wandering through in search of a pat. Jobes also sells and appraises his forebears' old decoys. Open daily; just stop by.

Carla Massoni Gallery (410-778-7330; www.massoniart.com; 203 High St., Chestertown) Fine art, from realism to abstract. Original paintings, prints, photography, and sculpture.

Reuben Rodney Gallery (410-639-2494; 5761 Main St., Rock Hall) Co-op of fourteen regional artists. Some unique stuff.

Vincenti Decoys (410-734-7709; 353 Pennington Ave., Havre de Grace) Not only will you find gorgeous decoys, from Patrick Vincenti's to historic col-lectibles, but decoy-carving materials, too. Where else are you going to find little plastic packets of glass eyes and pewter duck feet?

GIFT SHOPS & CRAFT GALLERIES

The Finishing Touch (800-292-0457, 410-778-5292; 311 High St., Chestertown) Fine framing, gifts, cards, candles, photo frames, and some truly nice handi-work from local painters and potters.

Kerns Collection Ltd. (410-778-4044; 210 High St., Chestertown) Whimsical crafts and pottery, unique clothing and jewelry.

Maren's (410-885-2475; 200 Bohemia Ave., Chesapeake City) Christmas shop and floral gifts.

JEWELRY

Forney's Jewelers (410-778-1966; 106 S. Cross St., Chestertown) Diamonds, gold, silver, pearls, colored gems, and watches, as well as silverware, pewterware, china, and brass.

MALLS & OUTLETS

Prime Outlets at Perryville (410-378-9399; 68 Heather Lane, Perryville) Smallish outlet center with thirty-three shops including OshKosh, Mikasa, L.L. Bean and Nike.

MARINE SUPPLY

Chester River Marine Services Ltd. (410-778-2240; 7501 Church Hill Rd., Chestertown) Full-service marine store.
Tidewater Marina Store (410-939-0950; Bourbon St., Havre de Grace) Marine books and hardware. Keep going past the big boatyard to find it.

SPECIALTY SHOPS & GENERAL STORES

Back Creek General Store (410-885-5377; 100 Bohemia Ave., Chesapeake City) Circa 1861 general store, with Cat's Meow items, Bennington & Lang Pottery, etc.

Unique offerings can be found at The Shoppes at Oyster Court in Rock Hall.

David Trozzo

Shoppes at Oyster Court (Oyster Court behind Main St., Rock Hall) A cluster of relocated watermen's buildings houses artists and crafters and some small boutiques. It's open year-round, Thurs.–Sun., more days from spring to fall. Telephone numbers of the artist-shopkeepers are on the doors, so if you come when a store is closed, call.
Twigs & Teacups (410-778-1708; 111 S. Cross St., Chestertown) Specialty bath products, dishes, tea things, children's books and toys, clothing, and textiles make this a difficult gift store to leave.

CHAPTER FIVE
Time & Tides
MIDDLE EASTERN SHORE

Expect to see plenty of water-fowl, like this wood duck, on the Eastern Shore.

David Trozzo

There's a livin'-is-easy mix on the Middle Eastern Shore, where updated trends make careful inroads in a place where old ways stay strong. Traditional oysters, for instance, a declining Bay staple, nonetheless can always be had during their cold-weather season. At old pine-paneled restaurants, they arrive in thick, milky stews. In fancier dining rooms, with buffed-glass halogen lighting and exposed ductwork, champagne and puff pastries infuse the ol' bivalve.

With its hundreds of miles of snaking shoreline, the Mid-Shore area is less marshy than the Lower Eastern Shore, yet somewhat diminished of the upland you'll find further north. We define the area broadly, to include the Shore's gateway, Kent Island. The Mid-Shore extends east to the Delaware line, and south to the Choptank River, promising crossroads towns as well as more established tourist draws.

The island ends at the waterway known as Kent Narrows, technically on the Eastern Shore, although Kent Island and the Kent Narrows area, which includes the town of Grasonville, are often viewed together as a kind of gateway to the Shore. On the island, the historic enclave of Stevensville has seen a few artists and artisans set up shop. The powerboat crowd gathers at the Kent Narrows' marinas (August's big race: "Thunder on the Narrows"), and along the area's south side, a cluster of venerable waterside seafood restaurants reside.

To the east, in Talbot County on the Eastern Shore proper, the village of Wye Mills promises peeks at the past via nature and commerce. Maryland's biggest white oak, 450 years and counting, dominates its own state park here. Schoolchildren gather 'round to hear ground grain clatter through square wooden chutes en route to the millstone, as flour-making demonstrations take place at the mid-eighteenth-century mill, which replaced a 1671 forebear. George Washington's troops at Valley Forge obtained their ground flour from the mill. This is a good day (or half-day) stop, with picnic tables behind the mill, settled, of course, alongside a lovely stream.

Farther south come better-known towns to which travelers increasingly flock: busy Easton, the county seat; low-key Oxford, with its Tred Avon-side beach known as "The Strand"; St. Michaels, the county's biggest tourist town; and Tilghman Island, where inroads by visitors seem unlikely to dislodge the sturdy breed of watermen who live here.

Centered around its eighteenth-century courthouse, Easton is the business center powering this part of Bay Country. The town's roots go back to the late seventeenth century and construction of the Third Haven Meeting House, an early Quaker structure visited by William Penn and still open to visitors. Highlights here include the renovated Art Deco Avalon Theatre, with its continuous fare including notable touring musicians, the Academy Art Museum's exhibitions, antique shops, and the new march of contemporary dining establishments along Goldsborough Street. This is a central location with a Federal - and Victorian-filled historic district — though, it must be said, one without a waterfront. A finger of the Tred-Avon River pokes into the southwest corner of town; kayak rentals and a small marina reside there.

South of Easton, via "the Oxford Road," as the locals call Rte. 333, sits the hamlet of Oxford. A prettier waterside village you won't find. White picket fences, clapboard and grand old manses alternate along Morris Street, the main road into town. This was a Colonial deepwater seaport, designated the Eastern Shore's official "Port of Entry" in 1694. An international trade in tobacco, grown here, bustled for a time. The so-called "Financier of the Revolution," Robert Morris, lived in Oxford, his former home a long-standing landmark restaurant and inn that still bears his name.

Yet another remnant of that era, the Oxford Bellevue Ferry, trundles across the Tred Avon River from March through November, creating a considerable shortcut to St. Michaels. Begun in 1683, this is believed to be the nation's oldest privately operating ferry, and is a favorite of cyclists looping the county's flat roads. The frontage stretching along the waterfront, known as The Strand, includes a beach, a good place for visitors of all ages to dip their toes in the water. Afterward, walk up to the Oxford Market & Deli on Morris Street for a hand-dipped ice-cream cone. In Oxford come the sweet pleasures of small moments unencumbered by much too much.

Cross on the ferry and wind through back roads on the way to St. Michaels. In Bellevue sits the kind of surprise explorers often find in the Bay's scratch-in the-sand-sized towns: a weaver's studio and gallery, open only by appointment. Farther on up the road, through Royal Oak, sits The Oaks, a rambling country inn operated by the folks who run 208 Talbot, a St. Michaels restaurant that's been winning raves for at least a decade. Indeed, Talbot Street is the main drag through this tourist town, lined by shops selling aromatic candles or Chesapeake T-shirts, fine-crafted gold pins or women's jackets made of hand-woven fabric. Fine restaurants and plentiful B&Bs are tucked along town streets.

St. Michaels was first developed in 1778, created from auctioned-off land grants, and its historic claim to fame is the incident during the War of 1812 that led to its reputation as "the town that fooled the British." One August night in 1813, as rumor circulated of an impending British attack, the people of St. Michaels darkened their homes, hoisted lit lanterns into the treetops, and tricked the enemy into firing too high.

Perhaps now its greatest claim to fame emerges from the town's shipbuilding heritage, and, indeed, that of the Chespeake region. The extensive Chesapeake Bay Maritime Museum, a multibuilding complex at Navy Point, offers a seemingly endless collection of Bay boats, from the skipjack *Rosie Parks* to the *Thor* pilothouse on the museum grounds — a magnet for curious kids. The museum's small boat collection also shows the evolution of the log canoe, from Native American conveyance to oyster tonger's sailboat to the craft with enormous sails raced now in a popular series involving yacht clubs from Rock Hall to Cambridge. Given their slender shape — and springboards that hold crewmembers balancing the proceedings — this can be exciting racing. On a weekend you might get lucky and see the log canoes along St. Michaels' Miles River. For info: www.logcanoes.com.

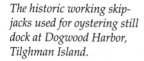

The historic working skipjacks used for oystering still dock at Dogwood Harbor, Tilghman Island.

David Trozzo

For a peek at the working version of Chesapeake's most famed workboats, continue down Rte. 33 to Tilghman Island, also called Tilghman. This is home to a skipjack fleet, the nation's last all-sail workboats, used for oystering. You'll see them at the Knapps Narrows before crossing onto the island, and again not far down the island, to your left, at Dogwood Harbor. Although the skipjacks carry the blue-ribbon reputation, keep an eye out for the distinctive low sides — "lowboard" — of Bay-built workboats used by crabbers and dredgers, with their pretty lines and sturdy, flat wheelhouse roofs. These are the tools of the working watermen who live on Tilghman and around the Bay. But don't be fooled: there's upscale cuisine to be had and fine lodgings available, too. Tilghman mixes old and new Chesapeake as well as any town.

LODGING

From in-town suites with quilts and whirlpool tubs to rooms just off the golf course, Mid-Shore visitors will find a range of accommodations. Off long lanes are former farms — and maybe a manse — that's been turned into a B&B or inn. These offer best-of-both-worlds lodgings, often on the water. Sail in and tie up at the pier, or perhaps launch a kayak.

Prices for the same lodging can vary widely. Expect two-night minimums on weekends during the high season; prices often drop during the week. Winter rates are often lower than in summer. Ask about other limitations, including policies regarding the return of deposit checks if you cancel. Assume smoking and pets are not allowed inside, and ask about other policies that can change.

Lodging rates fall within this scale:
Inexpensive: Up to $75
Moderate: $76 to $120
Expensive: $121 to $150
Very Expensive: Over $151

Credit card abbreviations are: AE, American Express; CB, Carte Blanche; D, Discover; DC, Diners Club; MC, MasterCard; V, Visa.

Kent Island

KENT MANOR INN
Owners: David Meloy &
   Alan Michaels.
800-820-4511; 410-643-5757.
500 Kent Manor Dr.,
   Stevensville, MD 21666.
On Kent Island, U.S. 50 to
   Md. 8 S.

Kent Manor is a faithful restoration of a large plantation house. There's a lovely garden house, a pier on the shallow headwaters of Thompson's Creek, paddle boats, bicycles, and a 1 1/2-mile trail winding through the extensive property. All twenty-four rooms are tastefully furnished

Price: Very Expensive.
Credit Cards: AE, D, MC, V.
Handicap Access: Yes.
Special Features: Children
welcome.

in period style, some with porches and French marble fireplaces; Chesapeake waterfowl and workboat prints decorate the walls. Ask for a garden view instead of Bay view; the Bay is close, but not close enough to actually see from your room. The restaurant serves fine cuisine in a romantic Victorian setting. A quiet, dignified getaway.

Queenstown

PINTAIL POINT MANOR
Innkeepers: Jane and Walt
Johnson.
410-827-6130, 877-897-6130.
www.pintailpoint.com.
911 Pintail Point Ln.,
Queenstown, MD 21658.
Price: Very Expensive.
Credit Cards: MC, V.
Handicap access: No.
Special Features: Kennel
on-site.

Originally purchased as 280 acres in 1979, Pintail Point now comprises 1,000 acres on a working farm that smartly uses its riverside fields and buildings as a country retreat, with a nationally ranked sporting clay range, a fishing charter, and golf. The farm also features two B&Bs: an English Tudor-style "Manor House" along the Wye River, and a typical Maryland farmhouse done up in "art ducko." The latter, called the Irishtown Bed & Breakfast, rents as a whole for up to $500 per night for up to six people; ten people max. The Manor House provides the finest accommodations, with a patio open onto the Wye (one of the lovelier Bay tributaries), and clubby common rooms. Hunting trophies decorate the game room, with its pool table, air hockey and shuffleboard games. The back Wye Room, open along the waterside deck, is the spot for a gourmet breakfast. Guest rooms run from a cottage with floral-covered queen beds and kitchenette to large, traditional suites in the house with sitting rooms (one opens onto a balcony). Bikes and golf carts for rent. Kids staying at the complex can even peek at the Holsteins and their calves in the farm's working portions.

Easton

THE BISHOP'S HOUSE
Innkeepers: Diane Laird-
Ippolito & John B.
Ippolito.
800-223-7290, 410-820-7290.
www.bishopshouse.com.
214 Goldsborough St./P.O.
Box, 2217, Easton, MD
21601.
Price: Moderate to
Expensive.
Credit Cards: No.

Home to the bishop of the Episcopal Diocese of Easton for much of the twentieth century, this 1880 home serves up Victorian style of the highest order. From the plaster ceiling medallions to the claw-foot tubs, the longtime B&B offers antique furnishings, vintage hats filling the walls, and a wraparound porch. The five guest rooms all have private baths, although you'll run up the stairs to reach one. Whirlpool baths and fireplaces available. All but one bed are carved antiques fitted

Handicap Access: No.
Restrictions: No children under 12.

with queen-sized mattresses — and the lone reproduction is a beautiful, comfy king. Along with the downstairs parlors, guests will find an upstairs sitting room with fridge and microwave. Guests can watch TV in their own rooms while planning to rent an inn bike or walk into downtown Easton after a full hot breakfast.

THE INN AT EASTON
Hosts: Andrew and Liz Evans.
410-822-4910, 888-800-8091.
www.theinnateaston.com.
28 S. Harrison St., Easton, MD 21601.
Price: Moderate to Very Expensive.
Credit Cards: AE, MC, V.
Handicap access: Restaurant only.
Restrictions: No pets or kids under 9.

With bright yellow and aubergine walls and a Balinesque bust on the mantel, this inn's front sitting room instantly signals that this is not your typical Eastern Shore B&B. Recently redone from top to bottom, the inn boasts seven guest rooms (including four suites) sitting atop a much-heralded restaurant downstairs (see "Restaurants," later in this chapter). Stylishly painted and decorated guest rooms are hung with original paintings by Luis Orozco and Dorlies Schapitz, brightly colored pieces that recall the tropics. Consider the Parisian Room, with its plaid vanity skirt and fleur-de-lis on the lamps, the Garden Suite's cozy dormer sitting room just through the bath, or the Holiday Suite, with bright red, yellow, and maroon "Arabian Nights" drapery acting as a headboard. Luxe details prevail throughout, ranging from dimmer lights to feather beds, Aveda bath products to clock radio/CD players. Handsome white rockers sit on a second-floor veranda overlooking the street, easily accessed by two accommodations in the front of the house. Continental breakfast and a lovely outdoor dining patio centered by a fountain. Settle in and breathe.

Oxford

1876 HOUSE
Owners: Eleanor & Jerry Clark.
410-226-5496.
www.bbhost.com/1876 house.
110 N. Morris St./P.O. Box 658, Oxford, MD 21654.
Price: Moderate.
Credit Cards: No.
Handicap Access: No.

Fans of old houses will like this one on Oxford's main street. The stairs curve so sharply that there's a handhold to grab as you make your way up to your room. That's in no way a criticism of the house, where three rooms (one of them a two-room suite) are neatly decorated in Queen Anne style. All have private baths, though one is across the hall. A Continental breakfast is served in the formal dining room. Guests who want to avoid driving to their weekend getaway can arrange for a ride from Jerry, who operates a limousine service.

COMBSBERRY
Innkeeper: Cathy
   Magrogan.
410-226-5353.
www.combsberry.com.
4837 Evergreen Rd.,
   Oxford, MD 21654.
Price: Very Expensive.
Credit Cards: AE, MC, V.
Handicap Access: Yes.
Special Features: Pets OK in
   the cottage.

A classic long colonial lane leads to stately Combsberry, circa 1730 and centerpiece to this nine-acre waterside estate, joined by a new brick Carriage House and the cute Oxford Cottage. All are done up in updated English country style, with the seven guest rooms inclined toward floral chintz-covered furniture, floral wallpaper, whirlpool tubs, and water views. The manor house's downstairs features sitting rooms where guests relax in leather chairs in wood-paneled rooms with fireplaces. Guest rooms feature such luxury as the Magnolia Suite upstairs, with its huge second-floor patio and windows onto the water from the bath with a whirlpool tub. The Carriage House, often leased as a whole, offers two guest rooms (cathedral ceilings, whirlpool tubs, luxe bedding) on either end of a broad living/kitchen area with TV/VCR and gas fireplace, and open windows onto Brigham's Cove. Oxford Cottage has a galley kitchen and fainting couch in near the queen bed. Full breakfast is served in a contemporary sunroom in the back of the main house. Brick patios settle in under magnolias, and two canoes are available to launch from the dock, where guests arriving via water can tie up. All in all, this is as luxurious as you'll find in the area, comfortably situated just outside Oxford

The "financier of the Revolution" is namesake to this fine dining and lodging establishment, The Robert Morris Inn, once his Oxford home.

David Trozzo

ROBERT MORRIS INN
Owners: Wendy & Ken
   Gibson.
410-226-5111.
www.robertmorrisinn.com.
314 N. Morris St./P.O. Box
   70, Oxford, MD 21654.

George Washington may or may not have slept here, but his pal owned the place. Robert Morris Jr. helped finance the Revolution, and, besides signing checks, he put his signature on the Declaration of Independence, the Articles of Confederation, and the Constitution. The inn's

Price: Expensive to Very
  Expensive.
Credit Cards: AE, MC, V.
Handicap Access: Yes.
Restrictions: No children
  under 10.

thirty-five rooms, all with private baths, are split between the mustard-colored clapboard building by the Oxford-Bellevue Ferry landing and the secluded Sandaway nearby, where rooms provide spectacular Tred Avon River views. Visitors also will find newer accommodations at the Sandaway — including suites and a small cottage — than those in the historic inn. There, rooms ooze historical atmosphere, only fitting given that the inn has stood here since 1710. The inn's restaurant closes in the winter, but its rooms remain open at a reduced rate on some Dec. and Mar. weekends. Both are closed in Jan. and Feb. Continental breakfast.

Royal Oak

On a tidewater road outside St. Michaels, The Oaks, once a farm, offers country hospitality.

David Trozzo

THE OAKS
Innkeepers: Shawn and
  Heather Maloney.
410-745-5053.
www.the-oaks.com.
Rte. 329 at Acorn Ln.; P.O.
  Box 187, Royal Oak, MD
  21662.
Price: Moderate to Very
  Expensive; Inexpensive
  in the annex.
Credit Cards: MC, V.
Handicap Access: No.
Restrictions: No kids from
  Mem. Day–Labor Day.

Located on the grounds of an original land grant deeded by Lord Baltimore about 1680, this is a former farm with a long history as a country inn. Most recently, it has been renovated as The Oaks. A swimming pool, shuffleboard, and a couple of canoes to put in at Oak Creek set the stage for an easygoing respite off this country road winding south from St. Michaels. The inn hosts fourteen rooms, while another eight live across the street in serviceable quarters the management says are "like summer camp with running water." Give them points for honesty. The fancier inn rooms come with queen- or king-sized beds, the former sometimes accompanied by an antique full-bed headboard. Three rooms have decks, and some come with gas fireplaces and whirlpool tubs. Settle in on white wicker furniture on a side screened porch, or at a deckside table along Oak Creek. If you're inclined toward the less-expensive rooms, they're clean, straightforward, and available only during summer months.

St. Michaels

FIVE GABLES SPA AND INN
Innkeeper: Lynsey Rochon.
877-466-0100, 410-745-0100.
www.fivegables.com.
209 N. Talbot St., St. Michaels, MD 21663.
Price: Expensive to Very Expensive; spa packages available.
Credit Cards: AE, MC, V.
Handicap Access: No.
Restrictions: Children discouraged.

Yellow toile and whimsically painted furniture are among the touches guests will find in the smart, well-appointed rooms here on St. Michaels' main street. In all, fourteen rooms are located in two buildings, each with a gas fireplace, whirlpool tub, and CD/clock radios — not to mention a porch. Cobalt blue tiles line the brick indoor courtyard-style pool. Visitors who want the spa treatment can partake of facials, herbal baths, massage therapy, steam and sauna. Continental breakfast is served, as well as afternoon refreshments. This is a good-looking inn that takes a contemporary approach to Eastern Shore style.

HARBOURTOWNE GOLF RESORT & CONFERENCE CENTER
800-446-9066, 410-745-9066.
www.harbourtowne.com.
P.O. Box 126, St. Michaels, MD 21663.
On Martingham Dr., just W. of St. Michaels off Md. 33.
Price: Very Expensive.
Credit Cards: AE, D, DC, MC, V.
Handicap Access: Yes.

Drive through a community surrounding an 18-hole Pete Dye–designed golf course to reach Harbourtowne, with its manicured public areas and 111 rooms, all with water views. Each also comes with terraces or covered porches. Twenty-four rooms have wood-burning fireplaces. It's a true resort, so there's a beach on a shallow little inlet from the Miles River, lawn games, tennis, swimming, trails for walking and jogging, biking, softball, volleyball, badminton, horseshoes, and a fitness center. Harbourtowne also has two restaurants and three lounges. The water view from most of the resort is spectacular.

THE INN AT PERRY CABIN
General Manager: Stephen Creese.
800-722-2949 (reservations); 410-745-2200.
www.perrycabin.com.
308 Watkins Lane, St. Michaels, MD 21663.

Absolute luxury draws many visitors for a first-class stay on the Miles River. This 1820 house was a landmark for years, then Sir Bernard Ashley of the Laura Ashley fabric and fashion empire bought it in 1988. Now it's owned by Orient Express, but is still a showplace and lovely English country inn with lots of pinks, golds, chintz and plump pillows — and even a secret doorway to the

Price: Very Expensive.
Credit Cards: AE, DC, MC, V.
Handicap Access: Yes.
Special Features: Children and pets welcome; please notify in advance if bringing a pet.

"morning room" behind a bookshelf in the next-door salon. Each of the forty-one rooms comes with a shape and décor all its own. Service here is at the highest level. The inn has an indoor heated pool, steam room, small exercise room, secluded courtyards and porches, 24-hour room service, and the ability to arrange guest activities, such as boat charters. A bar and lounge has recently replaced the game room. Don't pass up the chance to dine in the restaurant, where the food is as good as the inn — and that's very good indeed (see "Restaurants").

KEMP HOUSE INN

Owners: Diane & Steve Cooper.
410-745-2243.
www.kemphouseinn.com.
412 S. Talbot St./P.O. Box 638, St. Michaels, MD 21663.
Price: Moderate.
Credit Cards: D, MC, V.
Handicap Access: Yes.
Special Features: Children OK.

For historical surroundings at a reasonable price, the 1807 Kemp House offers a best bet. There's no TV, no public sitting room, and you'll have to pick up your Continental breakfast at the front desk. But working fireplaces, carved mantelpieces, original pine floors on two floors (brick ones on the first) and reproduction rope beds that may include a trundle for a child offer comfortable authenticity. Seven rooms in all, plus a cottage out back. One of the rooms has a private terrace. Sleeping here puts you in good company: A young Robert E. Lee stayed two nights here as builder Col. Joseph Kemp's guest. You can even stay in the room that he used, identified with his name.

THE OLD BRICK INN

Innkeeper: Martha Strickland.
410-745-3323.
www.oldbrickinn.com.
401 S. Talbot St., St. Michaels, MD 21663.
Price: Moderate to Very Expensive.
Credit Cards: AE, MC, V.
Handicap Access: One room.
Restrictions: Children 12 and older.

And now for something completely different: the "Guinevere Suite," featuring exposed brick walls and a suit of armor in the corner. Chesapeake, this room is not. But it's one of three fun theme rooms at the Old Brick Inn, a twelve-room operation in the middle of town. Guests stay in the historic house or a 1985 carriage house, in rooms with newer baths thanks to a 1998 renovation. Although the Arthurian era gets a nod, most rooms are more on the traditional, updated side. There's a small pool outside in a brick courtyard. Continental breakfast.

PARSONAGE INN

Owner: Will Workman.
800-394-5519, 410-745-5519.
www.parsonage-inn.com.
210 N. Talbot St., St. Michaels, MD 21663.

Dr. Henry Clay Dodson, pharmacist, postmaster, and businessman, opened the St. Michaels brickyard after two fires devastated the town. He built this place in 1883 as a testament to the permanence of brick. It went on to serve as the Methodist

Price: Expensive to Very Expensive.
Credit Cards: MC, V.
Handicap Access: Yes.
Restrictions: Children not encouraged, but allowed.

Church parsonage for sixty years, and became a B&B in 1985. All eight rooms have private baths and king or queen brass beds, except the suite, which has a private entrance, porch, and sitting room with TV and two twin beds. Behind the brick house, a building added with the restoration offers large, ground-level rooms popular for their size and convenience. Some rooms have fireplaces, breakfast is gourmet, and afternoon tea is served for guests who are around to partake. Bikes for guests.

VICTORIANA INN BED AND BREAKFAST

Innkeepers: Maria and Charles McDonald.
410-745-3368, 888-316-1282.
www.victorianainn.com.
205 Cherry St./P.O. Box 449, St. Michaels, MD 21663.
Price: Very Expensive.
Credit Cards: MC, V.
Handicap Access: No.
Restrictions: No children under 15.

The white Adirondack chairs stay full on the St. Michaels Harbor side of this updated Victorian, where the fuss factor is well under control. Guest rooms are painted stylishly in light shades of yellow or similar airy tones, the wing chairs are new, and the redone wooden floors are fabulous, covered with Oriental rugs. Fireplaces and harbor views are available, as is a first-floor junior suite entered via French doors. There's a TV and VCR in a parlor, a sunroom opens onto the water. Considerable updates have gone into this longtime St. Michaels B&B near the Chesapeake Maritime Museum.

Between St. Michaels and Tilghman Island

INN AT CHRISTMAS FARM

Innkeepers: David and Bea Lee.
800-987-8436, 410-745-5312.
www.innatchristmasfarm.com.
8873 Tilghman Island Rd., Whitman, MD 21676.
Price: Expensive to Very Expensive.
Credit Cards: MC, V.
Handicap Access: Yes.
Restrictions: Children during the week only.

Exploring St. Michaels' shops and sampling its ever-better restaurants appeal to many visitors to this increasingly popular getaway, but staying outside of town on the road toward Tilghman's waterfront delights offers the best of all worlds. The forty-seven-acre Inn at Christmas Farm is among the best of the growing out-of-town bunch, with a spring-fed freshwater pond you can swim in, a small beach along the cove, and an upscale yet farmy offering of seven guest suites. Book a place in the old farmhouse — perhaps in the affixed (and fixed-up) former waterman's shed — or one of two suites in the 1893 St. James Chapel trucked over from nearby Sherwood. Whirlpools, king-sized beds, wet bars, sitting rooms, a two-mile walking trail, and waterviews are available here — along with five dogs, one miniature horse, a goat, and peacocks. Not to mention David's fine paintings. The place is captivating.

THE MOORINGS BED AND BREAKFAST

Innkeepers: Pete and B.J. Raynor.
800-316-6396, 410-745-6396.
www.mooringsbb.com.
7857 Tilghman Island Rd./P.O. Box 45, Sherwood, MD 21665.
Price: Expensive to Very Expensive.
Credit Cards: MC, V.
Handicap Access: No.
Restrictions: No children.

This is pure Eastern Shore, from the country breakfast served each morning to the farms next door. Harris Creek runs alongside the inn (itself a former farm), and your innkeepers keep a rowboat and canoes for guests. Quilts and white wicker furniture mark the older rooms in the farmhouse; reconstruction means nouveau farm-style accommodations, where a bare brick chimney acts as a divider in a new bath not far from an octagonal porthole window. In all, five rooms include three with whirlpools and the kind of relaxation you've traveled to find. Or go dawdle by the pool. Harris Creek Kayak is set to launch from this easygoing spot off the road between St. Michaels and Tilghman in 2002 (www.harriscreekkayak.com).

WADE'S POINT INN ON THE BAY

Owners: Betsy & John Feiler.
888-923-3466; 410-745-2500.
www.wadespoint.com.
P.O. Box 7, St. Michaels, MD 21663.
Five miles S. of St. Michaels on Wade's Point Rd., McDaniel.
Price: Moderate to Very Expensive.
Credit Cards: V, MC.
Handicap Access: Yes.
Restrictions: Children welcome, but no facilities for infants.

A longtime sentimental favorite, this old inn sprawls along Eastern Bay and includes a "Victorian summer wing" with non-air-conditioned rooms with screen doors. More modern, upscale accommodations are available in a newer complex, and you can't beat the glassed-in breakfast room. There's also an old-fashioned farmhouse, which can be rented as a whole. It's even fun to get here: you drive down a lane, passing chickens as you go. This place has it all.

Tilghman Island

BLACK WALNUT POINT INN

Innkeepers: Tom & Brenda Ward.
410-886-2452.
www.tilghmanisland.com/blackwalnut.
P.O. Box 308, Tilghman Island, MD 21671.
Price: Expensive to Very Expensive.

On a clear day, you can see Cambridge to the east and Chesapeake Beach and North Beach to the west from the spread on this spectacular mid-Bay point. There's nothing overly fancy about the rooms in the 1840s house or the two cottages (one with two accommodations), what with quilts on the beds and basic baths, but that's the point. If you can watch sunset from across the Chesapeake Bay and sunrise from across the Choptank River, swim in the pool, settle into the hot tub, play a game of ten-

Located at the tip of Tilghman Island, Black Walnut Point Inn provides a haven surrounded by water.

David Trozzo

Credit Cards: D, MC, V.
Handicap Access: No.
Restrictions: No children under 12.

nis . . . what more could you want? Maybe just outstanding fishing, especially for migrating rockfish in the fall. Add the extra $25 for a third person, and a family's stay in one of the cottages of this former farmhouse/hunt club complex is a bargain for this part of the Eastern Shore. Among the common areas is a sitting room with a TV and VCR, and a series of stuffed sea ducks bagged by Brenda's grandfather on Hooper's Island, deep in Dorchester's wilds. Continental breakfast at this marvelous retreat is served until 10am.

CHESAPEAKE WOOD DUCK INN

Innkeepers: Kimberly and Jeffrey Bushey.
410-886-2070; 800-956-2070.
www.woodduckinn.com.
P.O. Box 202, Gibsontown Rd., Tilghman Island, MD 21671.
Price: Expensive to Very Expensive.
Credit Cards: MC, V.
Handicap Access: No.
Restrictions: No children under 14.

This Dogwood Harbor-side B&B has taken a turn for the culinary, with Chef Jeffrey Bushey in residence. The six-room Victorian is comfortably furnished in low-key but upscale Eastern Shore fashion, with queen- or king-sized beds, and there's a great sitting room looking out on the water. Out back stands a contemporary cottage, with a CD player and a fun collection of antique doorknobs. And check out breakfast: a pie made from jumbo lump crab, sweet corn, and spinach is just one specialty of the house. Equally inventive dinners are available as well; call for details.

LAZYJACK INN

Innkeepers: Mike & Carol Richards.
410-886-2215, 800-690-5080.

Pink roses line the oyster-shell drive here come early August, a color nearly the same as this home's broad front porch floor. It's a cheery touch to this longtime B&B along Dogwood Harbor and a

www.lazyjackinn.com.
5907 Tilghman Island Rd./
   P.O. Box 248, Tilghman
   Island, MD 21671.
Price: Very Expensive.
Credit Cards: AE, MC, V.
Handicap Access: No.
Restrictions: Children over
   12 only.

heads-up regarding some fun details in the large rooms. Painted furniture, including a headboard created from an old piano (truly!), makes an appearance in the Garden Suite, with its private first-floor screened porch. The Nellie Byrd Suite, named for a skipjack, offers harbor views through cathedral ceiling-high windows. The inn offers two rooms and two suites with whirlpool tubs. In-room AC. Full breakfast is served at 9am This is also home to the *Lady Patty*, a forty-five-foot Bay-built ketch that takes folks on two-hour sails Apr.–Oct., including one at sunset.

**TILGHMAN ISLAND
INN**

Owners: Jack Redmon and
   David McCaloum.
410-886-2141, 800-866-2141.
www.tilghmanislandinn
   .com.
21384 Coopertown Rd.,
   Tilghman Island, MD
   21671.
Price: Expensive to Very
   Expensive.
Credit Cards: AE, D, DC,
   MC, V.
Handicap Access: Yes.
Special Features: Pets
   allowed for additional
   fee; advance
   arrangements required.

With twenty attractive rooms upstairs, a terrific restaurant downstairs, and the Knapps Narrows flowing alongside, you may decide to settle in for the long run at this fun inn. The rooms are contemporary looking, with cobalt bottles of Saratoga water at the ready. Ten look out on the water and come with whirlpool tubs, including those being updated with Ultra spas. Two suites have sitting rooms. A pool sits at one end of the inn, an outdoor deck bar is open in summer, and kayak rentals are available. The piano bar is a fun place to find yourself on a winter Saturday night. Plan to dine at the restaurant; see our profile under "Restaurants" in this chapter.

HOTELS/MOTELS

The Tidewater Inn (410-822-1300; www.tidewaterinn.com; 101 E. Dover St., Easton, MD 21601) Georgian-style 1949 hotel with 114 guest rooms in Easton's town center. Notable for its Sun. brunch in the Crystal Room. Moderate to Very Expensive.

Days Inn (410-822-4600; 7018 Ocean Gateway Dr., Easton, MD 21601) Swimming pool. Continental breakfast. Moderate to Expensive.

Comfort Inn Kent Narrows (410-827-6767, 800-828-3361; 3101 Main St., Grasonville MD 21638) Water-view location next to the Kent Narrows. Indoor pool, hot tub, sauna, exercise room. Continental breakfast. Moderate to Very Expensive.

Best Western (410-745-3333; 1228 S. Talbot St., St. Michaels, MD 21663) Located before you get to the thick of the town's offerings. Clean and comfy. Suites

The Tidewater Inn has stood in Easton's center for decades.

David Trozzo

available. Continental breakfast in-season, in-room coffee, pool. Moderate to Expensive.

Harrison's Chesapeake Country Inn and Sport Fishing Center (410-886-2121; www.chesapeakehouse.com; 21551 Chesapeake House Dr., Tilghman, MD 21671) Venerable waterside lodgings, renowned among fishers who can eat breakfast early before heading out on a charter boat from the Harrison's fleet. Moderate to Expensive. Packages available. See "Restaurants" and "Recreation" in this chapter for dining and fishing details.

RESTAURANTS

A culinary awakening is well under way on Easton's Goldborough St. in the heart of Talbot County, which also encompasses St. Michaels, Tilghman Island and Oxford — in short, the Eastern Shore's trendiest tourist areas. But you can still have your crab cakes, crab imperial, and oysters on the half-shell, old-style. Price ranges, which include entrée, appetizer, and dessert, are as follows:

Inexpensive: Up to $15
Moderate: $15 to $25
Expensive: $25 to $35
Very Expensive: Over $35

Credit card abbreviations are: AE, American Express; CB, Carte Blanche; D, Discover; DC, Diners Club; MC, MasterCard; V, Visa.

Kent Island/Grasonville/Kent Narrows

THE NARROWS
410-827-8113.
3023 Kent Narrows Way S., Grasonville.
Open: Daily.
Price: Inexpensive to Expensive.
Cuisine: New American.
Serving: L, D.
Credit Cards: D, DC, MC, V.
Reservations: Recommended on weekends.
Handicap Access: Yes.

In an area where restaurants cater to the informal crab picking crowd with picnic tables, plastic utensils, and brown paper as table coverings, The Narrows stands out as a touch of elegance at the Kent Narrows. Yes, they do serve steamed crabs, but if you prefer your crabmeat already picked, you'll find this Chesapeake delicacy served in many different dishes with flavorful sauces. Besides the Chesapeake staples of crab, oysters, clams, and rockfish, you'll also find great tuna and catfish dishes, as well as shrimp. The Narrows can be a bit pricey, with meals averaging close to $20 before you add drinks and appetizers, but they do offer a light fare menu, which is tasty, more affordable, and less filling for those watching their figures. The Narrows overlooks the busy Kent Narrows and, if you're lucky, on a breezy evening you can dine out on the deck and watch the boats pass by.

HOLLY'S RESTAURANT
410-827-8711.
108 Jackson Creek Rd., Grasonville.
Open: Daily.
Price: Inexpensive.
Cuisine: Eastern Shore.
Serving: B, L, D.
Credit Cards: MC, V.
Reservations: No.
Handicap Access: Yes.

It's déjà vu every time we settle into a knotty pine booth at Holly's. My husband tells me about his dad bringing him here when he was a kid for a real chocolate milkshake. Or he waxes over bringing his own daughter when she was young, and how they filled time waiting for real chocolate milkshakes by filling out the placemat quiz, "Can you name the states and their capitals?" However, more than nostalgia has kept Holly's thriving for 45 years at its prime Eastern Shore entry locale on Rte. 50. The prices couldn't be more reasonable, and the homemade food means carrots in a spicy Maryland crab soup were likely chopped right in the kitchen. Likewise, the mashed potatoes and the turkey in an open-faced hot turkey sandwich boast home-cooked roots. Alert diners passing through the dining room will note the abundance of fried chicken being consumed by their fellow diners, folks clued into a Holly's signature. Except for the market price for crab dishes, the most expensive item on the menu is lasagna at $11.95. The children's menu is well-priced and highly sensible (hot dogs, for example), which must tempt even organic moms after the long and fussy drive back from the beach. The real chocolate milkshakes, by the way, cost $3 — and are worth every dime.

ANGLER'S RESTAURANT
410-827-6717.
3015 S. Kent Narrows Way, Grasonville.
Open: Daily.
Price: Moderate.
Cuisine: Chesapeake Seafood.
Serving: B, L, D.
Credit Cards: D, MC, V.
Reservations: No.
Handicap Access: Yes.

Painted yellow with a huge, retro sign on its roof, this place is impossible to miss. Besides, Angler's has been here since 1933 and everybody within a fifty-mile radius knows how to get here — which is why there's often a line out front for breakfast on weekends, pretty much year-round. This is hearty food, solid waterman's fare heavy on old-fashioned Chesapeake recipes, served by waitpeople who can be brusque when they get busy. But they're sharp and efficient, and they'll keep your coffee mugs and your water glasses full. Angler's does its crab cakes up right, with a time-tested recipe older than you are. Don't neglect oysters in the "R" months, or the crab soups — and how about the catfish or grouper? Or even shrimp, fried or stuffed. Keep in mind that Angler's does not serve hard-shell crabs, the Chesapeake mainstay. Apart from the seafood: anyone for sauteed liver and onions with gravy (over a baked or mashed potato), or meatloaf and gravy? Elegant, Angler's ain't. The dining rooms are fake wood paneling, vinyl, and Formica. Remember, though, this is still watermen's territory, so sit down and enjoy a family-run restaurant with all its rough-hewn charm.

HARRIS CRAB HOUSE
410-827-9500.
S. Kent Narrows Way (Exit 42 off Rte. 50/301), Grasonville.
Open: Daily.
Price: Moderate to Expensive.
Cuisine: Seafood.
Serving: L, D.
Credit Cards: MC, V.
Reservations: No.
Handicap Access: Yes.
Special Features: Public docking; shops in season.

Harris Crab House is the Kent Narrows' fun place for food, where diners join others at long picnic tables downstairs, or at smaller individual tables inside on the "upper deck" or on the outside deck. Both decks overlook the northern end of the Narrows. Fresh steamed crabs (priced according to size: jumbo, extra-large, large, or medium), Bay fish, and soft-shell crabs, much of it netted by local anglers, are the Harris specialty. "For the Rebel," as the menu reads, come nonseafood entrées, such as barbecued chicken and ribs (that's "and," not "or"). Parents, look for a kids' menu. This is Chesapeake Bay food at its most genuine, plentiful, and moderately priced, and so popular we once, no kidding, stood in line behind a man who'd driven all the way from New Jersey to eat crabs here.

KENT MANOR INN
410-643-5757, 800-820-4511.
500 Kent Manor Dr. (off Rte. 18, near Bay Bridge), Stevensville.
Open: Daily.
Price: Very Expensive.

For nearly fifteen years, this historic inn has been delighting diners throughout the Annapolis-Baltimore-Washington, D.C. area with favorite regional dishes as well as enough innovative creativity to keep them surprised. Although lunch and dinner menus are similar, differences ensure a

David Trozzo

The Kent Manor Inn, with its fine dining and lodging, welcomes visitors to Kent Island, located between Annapolis and the Middle Eastern Shore "mainland."

Cuisine: Eclectic (Nouvelle, European, Bay Regional).
Serving: B, L, D, SB.
Credit Cards: AE, D, DC, MC, V.
Reservations: Suggested.
Handicap Access: Yes.

unique experience during either meal. For example, luncheon guests will find the intriguing buffalo mozzarella with young eggplant, while only at dinner can you find smoked trout mousse — each delectable in its own right. Regardless of when you visit, Chef Dennis Shakan's entrées need careful perusal before making your selection. At dinner, his potato and turnip-crusted salmon is one of the most enticing. Most popular may be the fire-roasted rack of lamb, served with a shiitake mushroom compote and minted orzo, completed with a pomegranate glaze. In keeping with the circa 1820 history of the inn, the dining area's décor is elegantly simple and understated. The most pleasant section is a narrow glassed-in porch with a half-dozen tables for two or four overlooking the inn's carefully maintained lawns and gardens, its large gazebo, and its dock on Thompson's Creek. A meal at the Kent Manor Inn is an experience beyond reproach; see "Lodgings" for information about its twenty-four rooms and suites.

TAVERN ON THE BAY
410-604-2188, 410-604-1933.
500 Marina Road (off Rte. 18, on the Bay, near the Bay Bridge), Stevensville.
Open: Daily.
Price: Expensive.
Cuisine: Regional.
Serving: SB, L, D.

The Chesapeake Bay Beach Club, visible from the eastern end of the Chesapeake Bay Bridge, boasts this restaurant that affords guests enviable Bay views to Annapolis through wall-to-wall windows. Its vaulted cedar-plank ceilings enhance the spacious dining room without compromising the intimacy of its booths and tables. Extensive lunch and dinner menus offer regional and national

Credit Cards: AE, MC, V.
Reservations: Suggested.
Handicap Access: Yes.

dishes, with the occasional import. Starters are epitomized by imaginative items such as the tuna tower, twin rolls of fresh tuna, wonton-wrapped with wasabi-cilantro sauce, flash fried and served with a soy-lime dipping sauce, or a brie-mango quesadilla topped with mango and brie between red chile tortillas with jicama and tomatillo salsa. Seafood entrées include sesame-encrusted tuna, halibut or mahi-mahi, while the kitchen's "Signature Specialties" unroll duck breasts served over sweet corn and roasted red pepper coulis, or applewood bacon-wrapped sea scallops. Meanwhile, presentations of pasta and meat abound. The menu also includes a small children's section and raw bar offerings. Sunday brunch means smoked salmon with the scrambled eggs. Uncle Mike's Sunset Theatre, an open-air cocktail lounge, continues to celebrate the vista from the dining room.

Easton

EAGLE SPIRITS RESTAURANT
410-820-4100.
28449 Clubhouse Dr.
Open: Daily.
Price: Inexpensive to Expensive.
Cuisine: American.
Serving: L, D.
Credit Cards: AE, D, DC, MC, V.
Reservations: Recommended.
Handicap Access: Yes.

Located in the Easton Club's golf course clubhouse off Oxford Road (Rte. 333) at the western edge of town, this restaurant can be recommended for the following: its gourmet food (the chef is Ron Brown), its bar (Michelle Gannon supervises preparation of a classy martini), its ample parking lot, and its chairs, some of the most comfortable on the Eastern Shore. The lunch menu includes appetizers like smoked cheddar and chicken crepes, and various soups of the day, salads, sandwiches, an oyster poor boy, and a clubhouse burger. Flounder is your best bet among the entrées. The regular dinner menu offers seven appetizers, notably fried calamari, and seven entrées, including roast duckling, oysters stuffed with crab imperial, and a New York strip steak. Desserts run from lemon tarts to ice cream. A $16.95 fixed-price dinner, served from 5 to 6:30, offers a choice of two appetizers and two entrées.

GENERAL TANUKI'S RESTAURANT
410-819-0707.
25 Goldsborough St.
Open: Tues.–Sun.
Price: Expensive.
Cuisine: Pacific Rim.
Serving: L, D.
Credit Cards: D, MC, V.
Reservations: Recommended.
Handicap Access: Yes.

While Easton has always had its share of nice restaurants, lately there has been something of a culinary renaissance taking place in this small Eastern Shore town. And the heart of that movement seems to be centered on Goldsborough Street. The latest addition is General Tanuki's, a Pacific Rim restaurant that features the flavors of California, Hawaii, Thailand, and Japan all rolled into one. With its chic New York looks (exposed duct work and dark-gray walls), General Tanuki's pres-

Special Features: Smoke-free.

ents a friendly, relaxed atmosphere for those who are looking for something a little different from the usual crab cakes and filet mignon. Instead, hungry diners can choose from such illustrative entrées as The Evil Devil Prince, curried chicken with a spicy coconut sauce and rice, or the Drunken Duck, grilled duck breast basted with plum glaze and served with bamboo shoots, fresh herbs, and a sweet chili sauce. General Tanuki's also offers a complete sushi bar featuring nigiri, maki, veggie rolls, halemaki and sashimi. And don't forget a glass of sake to go with your first course, just one choice from the restaurant's well-designed wine list.

THE INN AT EASTON
410-822-4910.
28 S. Harrison St.
Open: Wed.–Sun.
Price: Very Expensive.
Cuisine: Modern
  Australian.
Serving: D.
Credit Cards: MC, V.
Reservations:
  Recommended.
Handicap Access: Yes.

Through the royal front door in its Federal façade, the Inn at Easton offers diners contemporary comfort and creative cuisine. Under the direction of Chef/Owner Andrew Evans, the inn's menu changes every three weeks and relies on the freshest local ingredients. Take, for example, the Caesar salad composed of Butterpot Farm baby cos topped with crisp pancetta and freshly shaved parmeggiano-reggiano, garnished with homemade garlic crostini as a first course. The conservative dinner palate might want to consider the wonderfully tender Delmonico steak served with pomme frites and a red wine jus. Or, if you're feeling a little more adventurous, try the crispy skinned rockfish over a bed of wild rice floating on a pool of vanilla crème anglaise. Pair that with a bottle of wine from the inn's selection of boutique Australian wines, and you have a meal fit for a king. Order a la carte Wed., Thurs., Sun. On Fri. and Sat., there is no a la carte, simply a $49 prix fixe menu. Either way, you can't go wrong.

MASON'S RESTAURANT
410-822-3204.
22-24 S. Harrison St.
Open: Mon.–Sat.
Price: Expensive.
Cuisine: Creative
  American.
Serving: L (Mon.–Sat), D
  (Tues.–Sat.).
Credit Cards: AE, CB, DC,
  MC, V.
Reservations: Yes.
Handicap Access: Yes.

Now featuring courtyard tables and Executive Chef Chad Scott, Mason's Restaurant is an expansion of this long-established candy store and café, stylishly remodeled and located on one of downtown Easton's most handsome historic streets. It has become very popular, especially at lunchtime, and the bar's jumbo martinis and the kitchen's world-class chili and sandwiches (e.g., corned beef, pastrami, ham and cheese on croissants) explain why. The dinner menu offers seasonal soups and salads, six appetizers (fried calamari, sushi-grade tuna tartar, prosciutto and melon), and eight entrées such as capelli with backfin crab, Chinook salmon with corn and leek fondue, and a rack of lamb with goat cheese and spinach. Mason's wine list includes a fairly extensive list of reds and whites priced between $5.25 and $12 per glass, $20 to $100 for a bottle. A considerable variety of desserts includes some of the region's best chocolate.

OUT OF THE FIRE
410-770-4777.
22 Goldsborough St.
Open: Mon.–Sat.
Price: Expensive.
Cuisine: Mediterranean.
Serving: D.
Credit Cards: AE, D, DC, MC, V.
Reservations: Recommended, particularly on weekends.
Handicap Access: Yes.

Warm and inviting, yet polished as a slick New York City bistro, Out of the Fire is the perfect place to settle in for an evening of good food and great wine. From the overstuffed sofas just off the wine bar to the open kitchen complete with a wood-burning hearth oven, this restaurant makes every attempt to put you at ease. The staff is knowledgeable about both the ever-changing menu selections and the equally diverse wine list. Standard entrées include an array of oven-fired pizzas to tempt your taste buds, while others, such as the filet mignon with crispy gnocchi and roasted shallot sauce, or wild mushroom penne, are more tempered by the changing seasons. The wine list is extensive, and you can also enjoy martinis, cordials, or single-malt Scotches. And if you've timed it well on a weekend evening, you just might be treated to live guitar music wafting from the wine bar.

Restaurant Columbia Chef Stephen Mangasarian at his fine eastery on Easton's Washington Street.

David Trozzo

RESTAURANT COLUMBIA
410-770-5172.
28 S. Washington St.
Open: Tues.–Sat.
Price: Very Expensive.
Cuisine: New American.

Each evening, Restaurant Columbia's chef/owner offers only twenty-four patrons the opportunity to sample his daily creations. The reason for this is simple — everything is made fresh on the premises, from the cloud-like yeast rolls

Serving: D.
Credit Cards: AE, MC, V.
Reservations: Yes.
Handicap Access: Not from
　front entrance.

with whipped butter to the chocolate chip/coconut ice cream for dessert. The menu changes every three weeks and places great emphasis on fresh ingredients from area growers. And while certain entrées come and go, the pistachio-crusted rack of lamb with a raspberry sauce remains the house's signature dish. When it comes to wine, Columbia doesn't disappoint. *Wine Spectator* recently named its cellar one of the best in the U.S. Restaurant Columbia is one of Easton's best-kept secrets. Just be sure to call for reservations.

Oxford

LATITUDE 38
410-226-5303.
26342 Oxford Rd.
Open: Tues.–Sun.
Price: Moderate to
　Expensive.
Cuisine: Creative Regional.
Serving: D, SB.
Credit Cards: AE, D, MC, V.
Reservations:
　Recommended on
　weekends.
Handicap Access: Yes.

Latitude 38 can well be described as the Cheers of Oxford. If they don't know your name when you enter, you can be darn sure they will by the time you leave. A haven for locals and those just sailing through on the weekends, Latitude 38 offers the best of both worlds: multicourse meals for the sit-down crowd, or inexpensive bar dinners for those who just can't face their own kitchens. For the price and the camaraderie, you can't beat the latter. Your only obstacle will be finding a place at this incredibly popular bar, recently expanded to accommodate its growing following. For a mere pittance, you are treated to the chef's daily whims. Bar dinners change every night, while the regular menu varies biweekly.

**PIER STREET
RESTAURANT AND
MARINA**
410-226-5171.
West Pier St.
Open: Apr.–early Nov.
Price: Moderate to
　Expensive.
Cuisine: Eastern
　Shore/Seafood.
Serving: L, D.
Credit Cards: MC, V.
Reservations: Yes.
Handicap Access: Yes.

Pier Street's wide decks sprawl along the Tred Avon River, filled with picnic tables filled themselves with as good a dozen crabs as you'll find on the Bay. With great blue herons and gulls stationed on nearby pilings, and management supplying bread crusts for kids — who, when we visited, roused swan families and rockfish alike — you can ease back and enjoy Chesapeake life at its most sublime. If you don't like hard-shell crabs, go for local seafood. Carryout, dockage for diners, gas for boats available.

ROBERT MORRIS INN
410-226-5111.
314 N. Morris St.

Dating to 1710, the Robert Morris Inn is one of the country's oldest historic inns. Situated along the Tred Avon River in the colonial village of

Open: Daily Apr.–Nov.;
    weekends only Dec.,
    Mar.; closed Jan. & Feb.
Price: Moderate to
    Expensive.
Cuisine: Regional
    Seafood/Continental.
Serving: B, L, D.
Credit Cards: AE, MC, V.
Reservations: Only for
    parties of 8 or more.
Handicap Access: Yes.

Oxford, it is a favorite destination for residents and tourists who appreciate traditional Maryland fare served in a historic atmosphere. Whether seated in the rustic Tap Room, Colonial Tavern, or main dining room, select from the same menu they have been serving for thirty years. Black angus beef, seafood au gratin cakes (a combination of crab, shrimp, Monterey Jack, and cheddar cheeses), and Chesapeake fries sprinkled with the owner's secret seasoning are just a few of the choices. But the real reason you go to the Robert Morris Inn is for the crab cakes, deemed by author James Michener as the best on the Chesapeake (a much jockeyed-over distinction in Bay restaurants, by the way). Made from jumbo lump crabmeat, these creations are held together seemingly by sheer will. It seems the Robert Morris Inn does not know the meaning of the word "breading."

**SCHOONER'S
LLANDING**
410-226-0160.
314 Tilghman St.
Open: Thurs.–Mon.
Price: Moderate.
Cuisine: Seafood.
Serving: L, D.
Credit Cards: MC, V.
Reservations: Not accepted.
Handicap Access: Yes.

This dockside restaurant has gone through a number of iterations over the last few years, trying to establish a clear identity. It's gone from casual to fine dining, none of which has been particularly inspired. But despite the fairly predictable food, Schooner's seems to attract a strong local crowd, which can only be attributed to its very festive atmosphere. Located directly on the water at Oxford's edge, you may want to wait just to sit outdoors and eat on the dock. Whether you come by land or by sea, straight from the boatyard or the brokerage house, Schooner's Llanding is simply a comfortable place to unwind at the end of the day. Dockage for boaters.

St. Michaels

BISTRO ST. MICHAELS
410-745-9111.
403 S. Talbot St.
Open: Thurs.–Mon.
Price: Expensive.
Cuisine: French Provençal.
Serving: D.
Credit Cards: AE, CB, D,
    DC, MC, V.
Reservations:
    Recommended.
Handicap Access: Yes.

Conveniently located on the Mid-Shore's left bank in the heart of St. Michaels, this lively and spirited restaurant is the next best thing to dining in France. Whether you choose to sit indoors or out, the Bistro's Art Deco furnishings, French theater posters, and crisp white tablecloths transport you to another place. The seasonally changing menu is small (lunch often features no more than five items), but don't be deceived. Chef David Stein is a master at soups, and his mussels, a standard on each menu, are fabulous. And if neither of those tickle your fancy, try one of his cleverly designed pizzas — barbecued chicken, pine nuts, and spinach, for example — that differ by the day. True to its French roots, the Bistro's wine selection is extensive. Before you go, bone up on your French. Words like entrecote and choucroute garni appear frequently throughout the menu. Luckily, the knowledgeable and courteous staff is happy to lend assistance.

THE CRAB CLAW RESTAURANT
410-745-2900.
304 Mill St.
Open: Daily, Mar.–early Dec.
Price: Moderate to Very Expensive.
Cuisine: Eastern Shore.
Serving: L, D.
Credit Cards: Not accepted; ATM machine on-site; personal checks accepted.
Reservations: Recommended on weekends.
Handicap Access: Yes.

This is one of Bay Country's most well known seafood and crab decks, settled on prime real estate alongside the Chesapeake Bay Maritime Museum overlooking St. Michaels Harbor. Originally the Eastern Shore Clam Co., a clam and oyster shucking house, the restaurant was launched in 1965 by the Jones family. Plan on a crab feast here.

INN AT PERRY CABIN
410-745-2200.
308 Watkins Ln.
Open: Daily.
Price: Very Expensive.
Cuisine: Continental.
Serving: B, L, D.
Credit Cards: AE, DC, MC, V.
Reservations: Yes.
Handicap Access: Yes.

The owner of this inn, although no longer Laura Ashley's widower, is still British — so the remodeled manor and its restaurant are still quiet elegant. So are the prices. Dinner, for example, costs $69.50 per person, not including tax, tip or beverages. For that you get a gorgeous view of boats on the Miles River and your choice of eight first-course selections that include braised lobster, torchon of foie gras and crab spring roll; four between-course selections, for example, mango and pineapple sorbet or maybe grilled asparagus salad; and eight main course selections. These can range from roasted halibut to a beef tenderloin or glazed shank of lamb. Finally, there's dessert, mostly quite Continental. If you order from Chef Mark Salter's Chesapeake Tasting Menu — "Complete table only, please" — the prix fixe is $95 per person (not including tax, tip or beverage). Regional food includes rockfish and soft-shell crabs, although the crab cakes — prepared with red pepper, jicama, celery remoulade and cider-paprika vinaigrette — have been known to disappoint crab-cake purists. The service and cuisine are generally excellent. Management asks you to "refrain from cellular phone use in the dining room." As noted, the Inn at Perry Cabin is elegant.

One of St. Michaels' favorite restaurants, 208 Talbot.

David Trozzo

208 TALBOT
410-745-3838.
208 N. Talbot St.
Open: Wed.–Sun.
Price: Expensive to Very
    Expensive.
Cuisine: Innovative
    American.
Serving: D.
Credit Cards: D, MC, V.
Reservations:
    Recommended.
Handicap Access: Yes.

It's rare to find a restaurant you can always count on to offer great food and exceptional service. 208 Talbot is one of the Bay's best. The menu is inventive and, while not extensive, covers all the bases. You never have to worry that it won't feature one mouth-watering entrée after another. Chef-owner Paul Milne has been featured on "Great Chefs of the East," and 208 Talbot has often been the recipient of the prestigious DiRoNa (Distinguished Restaurants of North America) award.

The 1871 brick duplex's dining room radiates an intimacy and romance that would melt even the hardest heart. Begin the evening with a plate of the restaurant's signature baked oysters draped with a luscious champagne cream sauce and garnished with julienned prosciutto and chopped pistachios. Another old favorite is the grilled rib eye atop a bed of sautéed wild mushrooms and topped with a cloud of garlic mashed potatoes and frizzled onions that's so tall it seems to reach toward heaven. Not surprisingly, an evening at 208 does come with a price tag, but if the old adage "you get what you pay for" is true, you won't be disappointed.

**TOWN DOCK
    RESTAURANT**
410-745-5577.
125 Mulberry St.
Open: Daily (Apr.–Oct.);
    closed Tues. & Wed.
    (Nov.–Mar.).
Price: Expensive.

Owned and operated by notable Maryland Chef Michael Rork, Town Dock is home to award-winning creations in a casual, relaxing waterfront setting. For his efforts, Rork has become a regular at the Beard House in New York, but you can try his creations right here. Start with the Crab Monterey, a heaping pile of warm, oversized tortilla chips

Chef Michael Rork holds forth at his Town Dock Restaurant, on the water in St. Michaels.

David Trozzo

Cuisine: Creative Regional
   Seafood.
Serving: L, D.
Credit Cards: AE, D, DC,
   MC, V.
Reservations:
   Recommended.
Handicap Access: Yes.

engulfing an overflowing crock of a magical blend of lump crabmeat, fresh tomatoes, and Monterey Jack cheese. Crab bisque is a house specialty. Hearty and rich, the velvety cream base surrounds the lumps of crabmeat, and each bowl is served with its own mini carafe of sherry to pour on as you see fit.

One of the best features about the Town Dock is that you can choose from the interestingly creative (shrimp and grits) to typical Chesapeake selections (crab cakes and rockfish). Before 5:30pm, a selection of entrées is offered at half price — the perfect size for smaller to medium appetites. But perhaps the best part of dining at Town Dock is the finale. To ease the pain of the bill, everyone is presented with a larger-than-life, chocolate-covered strawberry. You almost won't need dessert.

Tilghman Island

**HARRISON'S
   CHESAPEAKE HOUSE**
410-886-2121.
21551 Chesapeake House
   Dr.
Open: Daily.
Price: Moderate.
Cuisine: Eastern Shore.
Serving: B, L, D.
Credit Cards: MC, V.

If your style leans toward waterfront decks with picnic tables full of hot steamed crabs and pitchers of icy beer or freshly brewed tea, Harrison's is the place for you. Or, dine indoors in the expansive, multitiered dining room that overlooks the Choptank River and Harrison's fleet of charter fishing boats, where the Chesapeake surf and turf is a must entrée. Delicately fried chicken breasts are paired with crab cakes thick with backfin lumps.

Reservations: Accepted
  only for parties of 8
  more.
Handicap Access: Yes.

**TILGHMAN ISLAND
INN**
410-886-2141.
21384 Coopertown Rd.
Open: Daily except Wed.;
  closed in Jan.
Price: Expensive.
Cuisine: Creative American.
Serving: L, D, SB.
Credit Cards: AE, D, DC,
  MC, V.
Reservations:
  Recommended.
Handicap Access: Yes.

Both are served with homemade, all-you-can-eat coleslaw, hot rolls and four family-style vegetables. With more than 110 years of experience behind the fryer, Harrison's kitchen is the master at serving Eastern Shore comfort food.

A summer lunch couldn't find a finer setting than this waterside deck overlooking a constant parade of boats using the Knapps Narrows waterway, a shortcut from Annapolis to Oxford. Aside from the traffic of recreational boaters, most of the remaining legendary fleet of skipjacks and traditional workboats call this their home port. Lunch is available only in clement weather on the deck, where food is prepared on a grill. Rain and/or cold drive diners indoors to the bar in the main dining room with a la carte menus, or to a spiffy new addition, the Bay Watch Room, which has a prix fixe menu. The kitchen's signature appetizer, black-eyed pea cake, is a bit of alchemy: humble black-eyed peas are combined with cornmeal and red peppers, fried into a cake and energized with fresh salsa. In season, the soft-shell crabs in tempura explode in intense flavor, a pouf on the tongue with each crispy bite. Tilghman Island is crab-oyster central, with vittles harvested in its own back yard, and regulars swear by the inn's Oysters Choptank, the bivalves gussied up in champagne sauce in a nest of puff pastry. Ignore the feed limits when it's time for dessert; all sweets are made in-house and range from merely fabulous ice cream to wildly seductive pastries. The menu changes frequently, but the quality remains constant. So does the view, with marshes thrashing in the wind or basking in sunlight, osypreys and shorebirds in summer, Canada geese and eagles in winter. Forget your schedule; linger and savor the experience.

FOOD PURVEYORS

COFFEE SHOPS

Coffee East (410-819-6711; 1 Goldsborough St., Easton) All the exotic (and nonexotic) coffees in an open, cheery café that's also fast becoming a favored local luncheon spot.
Blue Crab Coffee Co. (410-745-4155; 211 N. Talbot St., St. Michaels) Fresh pastries, coffees, and teas. Open late Fri. & Sat. in season.

ICE CREAM

Hill's Drug Soda Fountain (410-822-9751; 30 E. Dover St., Easton) Old-fashioned drugstore soda fountain beloved by all.

Justine's Ice Cream Parlour (410-745-5416; 101 Talbot St., St. Michaels) Creative array of ice-cream goodies in the midst of St. Michaels, open daily during its Mar.–Nov. season.

SEAFOOD MARKETS & CRAB HOUSES

Big Al's Market (410-745-3151; 302 N. Talbot St., St. Michaels) Where St. Michaels buys its hard-shell crabs for summer crab feasts. Fresh fish, grocery, deli, beer, wine, and liquor. Hunting and fishing licenses.

Captain's Ketch Seafood Market and Carry-Out (410-820-7177; 316 Glebe Rd., Easton) Picked crabmeat, lobster, and fish, including orange roughy, catfish, and smoked bluefish. Good takeout, too.

Chesapeake Landing Seafood Market and Restaurant (410-745-9600; Rte. 33, McDaniel) People drive all the way from Easton to get seafood here between St. Michaels and Tilghman. Oysters and crabs in season. Once a wholesale business, it's now a thriving retail market and restaurant with reasonably priced takeout.

David W. Wehrs Seafood (410-643-5778; 1819 Little Creek Rd., Chester, on Kent Island) Fresh crabmeat, live or steamed crabs, and clams right off the boat. While primarily a wholesale place — with great takeout — there's a deck over the water where folks can pick crabs. Take exit 39-B (Dominion Rd.) from Rte. 50, 2 mi. to right at the T onto Little Creek Rd., go to end.

Fisherman's Seafood Market (410-827-7323; 3032 Kent Narrows Way S., Grasonville, on Kent Island) Locals know to stop at the seafood market in the midst of this tourist restaurant complex, including its crab deck, for fine fresh fish to prepare at home.

GOURMET AND SPECIALTY MARKETS

The Railway Market (410-822-4852; 108 Marlboro Rd., Easton) Where healthy Shore gourmets shop. Originally located in Easton's old-time railway depot, the store's larger strip mall location offers organic and natural groceries, takeout and café, health and beauty products, books. Open daily.

Chesapeake Gourmet (410-827-8686; 189 Outlet Center Dr., Queenstown) A well-supplied shop with dishes, kitchenware, coffee and tea, wines, microbrew beers, and specialty food products. Good deli for takeout just off Rte. 50 at Prime Outlets. Open daily.

Flamingo Flats (410-745-2053; 100 Talbot St., St. Michaels) An endless collection of hot sauces, as well as cookbooks, jewelry, flamingo stuff, and gourmet condiments and sauces. Hot sauce tasting bar in summer.

Oxford Market & Deli (410-226-0015; 203 S. Morris St., Oxford) All you need, from groceries to ice cream to deli sandwiches.

CULTURE

CINEMA

See movies in *Easton* at **Tred Avon Movies 4** (410-822-5566) in Tred Avon Square on Marlboro Rd.

GALLERIES

Easton

David Trozzo

The Academy Art Museum in Easton plays a central role in the Shore's art scene.

ACADEMY ART MUSEUM
410-822-ARTS.
www.art-academy.org.
106 South St.
Open: Mon.–Sat. 10–4,
Wed. 10–9.

Long the gathering place for the area's artists, this white clapboard former schoolhouse provides 24,000 square feet of studios and gallery space. Exhibits include those by major artists such as Roy Lichtenstein or Ansel Adams, and a growing permanent collection. Other offerings include classes, an afternoon and evening concert series, and lectures. Call ahead for concert and lecture reservations.

Stevensville

**KENT ISLAND
FEDERATION OF ART**
410-643-7424.
405 Main St.
Open: Wed.–Fri., Sun. 1–4;
Sat. 10–4.

Local and regional artists working in media from oils to photography exhibit at this fine Victorian at the edge of town. Monthly exhibits have featured everything from paintings to pottery; a separate member gallery changes its exhibit every two months. Classes.

HISTORIC BUILDINGS & SITES

Easton

**HISTORICAL SOCIETY
OF TALBOT COUNTY**
410-822-0773.
25 S. Washington St.
Open: Tues.–Fri. 11–3, Sat.
10–4. Tours 11:30 & 1:30
Mar.–Dec.; by appt in
Jan. & Feb.
Admission: Free for
museum and garden; $5
for tours.

In the main building, photographs capture Talbot County's rural and maritime history. On the grounds stand historic structures representing different periods of local history. Joseph's Cottage (1795) tells the story of an Easton cabinetmaker. The James Neall House (1810), an excellent example of Federal architecture, shows how life changed for the affluent cabinetmaker and his Quaker family after early nineteenth-century success. The Society's buildings surround a stunning garden based on an eighteenth-century design. An annual antiques fair takes place the first week of October.

**THIRD HAVEN FRIENDS
MEETING HOUSE**
410-822-0293.
405 S. Washington St.
Open: Daily 9–5; services
Sun. 10, Wed. 5:30.

Built from 1682 to 1684, this is the oldest building in Maryland. Originally located in virgin timber (Easton was founded twenty-five years later), the Meeting House is now neatly tucked into a residential street on a seven-acre parcel. Stroll the peaceful grounds and admire a simple building still in use 300 years after Pennsylvania founder and Quaker William Penn preached here.

Tilghman Island

Skipjack sails once numbered in the hundreds on the Chesapeake Bay, so it's a bittersweet pleasure to spot the distinctive outlines of one of the few remaining ladies that ply the Bay in search of oysters. Fewer than a dozen skipjacks still work the water, and many of those dock in Tilghman's Dogwood Harbor. (You'll also find a couple of working skipjacks on Deal Island, and several continue to "work" the Bay as ecotour boats.) Get a sense of life aboard a skipjack, learn the lore, and "dredge" for oysters by taking a cruise on the 1886 *Rebecca T. Ruark*, the oldest skipjack still in service (Capt. Wade H. Murphy Jr., 410-886-2176). Follow Rte. 33 through St. Michaels and over the Tilghman Island drawbridge, then turn left about a half-mile onto the island. You'll see the harbor.

Wye Mill

WYE GRIST MILL
410-827-6909.
Operated by Preservation
  Maryland and Friends of
  Wye Mill.
Rte. 662 off Rte. 50, N. of
  Easton in Wye Mills.
Open: Mid-Apr.–mid-Nov.,
  Mon.–Thurs. 10–1,
  Fri.–Sun. 10–4.
Admission: $2 donation
  suggested.

A gristmill has been grinding cornmeal and flour at Wye Mills since 1671, and you can still see the great stone turn by water power on the first and third Sat. of every month. An exhibit focuses on the mill's glory days, from 1790-1830, when wheat brought prosperity. Buy a bag of freshly ground meal or "The Wye Millers Grind," a 100-recipe cookbook. Wye Mill is a hotbed of historic sites, all within a few hundred yards of each other. Look for the restored, early Episcopal Old Wye Church, circa 1717, and Maryland's official state tree, the Wye Oak, now more than 400 years old — mature when Europeans first explored the upper reaches of the Chesapeake Bay. Call 888-400-RSVP for information on any of these sites.

On a culinary note, Orrell's Maryland Beaten Biscuits (410-820-8090), the world's only commercial beaten biscuit company, makes the small local delights. The result is surprisingly flaky and chewy and certainly worth trying. You'll find the flour flying and can take a tour Tues. & Wed., 7–2, and other days around the busy winter holidays.

MUSEUMS

St. Michaels

**CHESAPEAKE BAY
  MARITIME MUSEUM**
410-745-2916.
www.cbmm.org.
Mill St., Navy Point.
Open: Summer, daily 9–6;
  spring/fall 9–5; winter
  9–4.
Admission: Adults $7.50,
  seniors $6.50, children
  6–17 $3.

The world's largest fleet of indigenous Bay workboats tells the story of the watermen's history — and indeed of the Chesapeake Bay itself. Among the eighty-five vessels are the *Rosie Parks*, a famous skipjack; the *Edna E. Lockwood*, the last log-hull bugeye still plying the Bay; and the *Old Point*, a crab dredger from Virginia. The eighteen-acre complex on the shores of Navy Point comprises twenty-three buildings, nine devoted to exhibits on the Bay's geological, social, economic, and maritime history, from the age of sail and steamboats to the advent of gas and diesel engines. The screw-

Many historic boats like this skipjack are docked or otherwise on display at the Chesapeake Bay Maritime Museum in St. Michaels.

David Trozzo

pile Hooper Strait Lighthouse moved here in 1966. Inside, the lighthouse keeper's late-nineteenth-century life is re-created, and everyone stops for the prime view of the Miles River. Also displayed are the massive punt guns used by the market gunners, as well as a huge collection of the decoys used by all waterfowl hunters. Kids love clambering through the interactive skipjack in the "Oystering on the Chesapeake" exhibit. There's the waterman's work life exhibit in warm weather, Tolchester Beach Bandstand with summer concerts, and many boat-related festivitals (see the heading "Seasonal Events & Festivals"). Also, the gift shop offers a range of nautical items, as well as maritime and Chesapeake books. Maritime scholars may be interested in the museum's library, devoted to maritime and Chesapeake writings and history.

The new vehicle entrance on Talbot St., slated to open in 2002, incorporates another Bay artifact: the Knapps Narrows drawbridge, which served as the gateway to Tilghman Island for sixty-four years, until 1998. The bridge was moved to St. Michaels and positioned partially open so that motorists could see the same view that boaters saw during the bridge's many years of service.

MUSIC

QUEEN ANNE'S COUNTY ARTS COUNCIL
410-758-2520.
206 S. Commerce St.,
 Centreville, MD 21617.
Season: Year-round.

The Arts Council sponsors a variety of regional events at various locations, including summer Concerts in the Park featuring top-grade regional talent. Also, classes and events such as the annual five-county poetry contest.

Easton

EASTERN SHORE CHAMBER MUSIC FESTIVAL
410-819-0380.
www.musicontheshore.org.
Season: Two consecutive weekends in mid-June.
Tickets: Prices vary, depending on venue and program.

Since 1986, J. Lawrie Bloom, principal clarinetist with the Chicago Symphony Orchestra, has brought in a host of top young names on the international concert circuit for two weekends of performances on the Shore. The talent roster is always impressive, and performances have expanded to include one at Washington College in Chestertown. Typical venues include the Avalon Theatre, a private estate, and the Chesapeake Bay Maritime Museum.

NIGHTLIFE

Kent Narrows, where Kent Island and the Queen Anne's County mainland meet, has undergone a real growth spurt in recent years that's spawned its own dock bar night scene, particularly on summer nights when the boating set ties up here. **Red Eye's Dock Bar** (410-827-3937; Mears Point Marina) brings in rock bands and DJs, and generally gets wild and crazy on the weekends (and on some weeknights) during the busy season. For another scene, consider the **Chesapeake Bay Beach Club** (410-604-1933; www.chesapeakebeachclub.com; 500 Marina Club Rd.) in *Stevensville,* in full view of the Bay with its much-welcomed restaurant (see "Restaurants") and **Music Pavilion** with all kinds of activities. (The Pavilion opens at 4 on Thurs. and Fri., 5 on Sat., noon on Sun. during the season.) This place offers it all — including a beach where you might find a volleyball game during the day.

In *Grasonville* you can try the hometown waterfront bar at **Angler's** (410-827-6717; 3015 S. Kent Narrows Way). If the watermen (look for white boots) there are wearing T-shirts with a beer logo, the summer crabs are in; if they're wearing plaid flannel, it's oyster season.

In *St. Michaels,* locals go to **Carpenter Street Saloon**, aka "C Street" (410-745-5111; 113 S. Talbot St.) for conviviality and free popcorn. In *Easton,* the **Washington Street Pub** (410-822-9011; 20 N. Washington St.) can get pretty packed, especially Thurs.–Sat. nights, and even more especially when a DJ or local band plays. **Time Out Tap and Grill** (410-820-0433; 219 Marlboro Rd.) gives Talbot Countians billiard tables and sports-oriented television year-round.

Oxford offers a few good spots to stop and have a drink. **Latitude 38** (410-226-5303; 26342 Oxford Rd.) is out on the road and also is a good place for dinner. **Schooner's Llanding** (410-226-0160; 314 Tilghman St.; closed Tues.) on Town Creek has a deck bar in-season, a restaurant, and a lounge.

PERFORMING ARTS & THEATER

Easton

The Art Deco Avalon Theatre in Easton draws national acts and local performance groups alike.

David Trozzo

AVALON THEATRE
410-822-0345; box office,
410-822-0345.
www.avalontheatre.com.
40 E. Dover St.
Season: Year-round.
Tickets: Prices vary; call
410-481-SEAT.

This beautifully restored and renovated 1920s Art Deco theater is a showplace for all of the performing arts in the area, a well-used community gem. The calendar is packed with classic film screenings, children's theater, poetry gatherings, performances by the Mid-Atlantic Symphony Orchestra, and musicians ranging from Leons Redbone and Russell to New Orleans guitar phenom Anders Osborne — and jazz, classical, Celtic, and folk heroes as well. The alternative Cricket Theatre (Beth Henley, Sam Shepard pieces) performs here, as does the Easton Chamber Orchestra. All of the seats in this intimate theater are good, but come early to enjoy the architecture or capture a prime spot on the main floor in front of the stage.

Oxford

TRED AVON PLAYERS
410-226-0061.
Season: Oct., Nov., Feb.,
Apr., Aug.
Tickets: $8 for matinees, $10
for evening
performances, $30 for
dinner theater.

The established community theater stages musicals, contemporary comedies, and classical dramas featuring thespians from around Talbot County. It's worthwhile to book a ticket if you're going to be in town. Performances at the **Oxford Community Center** (410-226-5904; 200 Oxford Rd.), which also hosts a winter chamber concert and occasional visiting concerts.

SEASONAL EVENTS & FESTIVALS

Easton

During the second weekend in November, Easton undergoes an amazing transformation — and what small town wouldn't if 20,000 visitors showed up? The internationally known, three-day **Waterfowl Festival** features more than 450 of the world's finest decoy carvers and wildlife painters. Since its founding in 1971, the Waterfowl Festival has raised millions for conservation organizations devoted to preserving waterfowl. Exhibits spread across town, showcasing decoy art, paintings, sculpture, retriever demonstrations, the Federal Duck Stamp exhibit, fly-fishing demonstrations, master classes with artists, a sporting clay tournament, and, always a hit, the World Championship Goose-Calling Contest. A fleet of shuttle buses provides free transportation from the parking areas to the exhibit locations. Admission; handicap access. Contact: 410-822-4567; www.waterfowlfestival.org; 40 Harrison St., Easton, MD 21601.

Grasonville

The **Queen Anne's County Waterman's Festival** at Kent Narrows is unique. Where else can you see an anchor-throwing contest, a rowing race, and a docking competition for Bay workboats, all while listening to country music and munching food? Held on the first Sun. in June, 11–6, at Wells Cove Public Landing. Small admission fee; handicap access. Contact: Queen Anne's County Office of Tourism, 888-400-7787, 410-604-2100; 425 Piney Narrows Rd., Chester, MD 21619.

St. Michaels

The **Mid-Atlantic Maritime Arts Festival** is Talbot County's rite of spring, a three-day affair on the third weekend in May, with maritime paintings, prints, photography, waterfowl and fish carvings, ship models, and seafood. But that's just one Chesapeake Bay Maritime Museum fest. The **Antique & Classic Boat Festival** in mid-June features more than 100 classic boats and automobiles. Crab-lovers should catch **Crab Days** on the first weekend in Aug., and **Oyster Fest** comes on the first weekend in Nov. Free with museum admission. Contact: 410-745-2916; www.cbmm.org; Chesapeake Bay Maritime Museum, Mill St., Navy Point, St. Michaels, MD 21663.

Tilghman Island

The annual **Tilghman Island Day** celebration combines demonstrations of the waterman's way of life with a heaping helping of what that way of life yields: seafood. Crab and oyster aficionados come from afar on the third Sat. in Oct. Boat maneuvering and oyster tonging are shown off in folklife demonstrations and high-spirited contests. See the skipjacks race. The celebration benefits the Tilghman Volunteer Fire Company. Contact the Talbot Chamber of Commerce in Easton: 410-822-4653; P.O. Box 1366, Easton, MD 21601.

TOURS

Dockside Express (410-886-2643; www.cruisinthebay.com; P.O. Box 803, St. Michaels, MD 21663) A costumed tour guide takes visitors through St. Michaels, and perhaps other towns, answering questions such as, "Who's buried next to his mule at Mulberry Point?" Call for schedules and costs.

St. Michaels Walking Tour (410-745-9561) Pick up a walking tour brochure at the visitor center in the middle of town and consider a walking tour with the St. Mary's Square Museum, a tiny 1865 dwelling moved to its spot in the center of town in 1964. The museum is only open from 10–4 on Sat., Sun., and holidays, May–Oct., or by appt.

RECREATION

BICYCLING

David Trozzo

The Oxford-Bellevue Ferry is a popular option with Mid-Shore bicyclists.

L ow-lying coastal plains meet rolling farmlands along the Bay and tributaries, where wide shoulders stretch alongside many main roads. Favorite rides include the 31-mile Easton-to-St. Michaels trip, the 10-mile Easton-to-Oxford run, and the 25-mile round-trip from St. Michaels to Tilghman. Many cyclists make a point of riding the Oxford-Bellevue Ferry, which costs $2.50 one-way and $4 round-trip for cyclists. A free map of routes, developed by the Oxford Mews Emporium, can be had by contacting the Mews at 410-820-8222. Also, a 35.4-mile loop from Easton to Oxford, across the ferry to St. Michaels, is available via text at www.eastonmd.org/ebmasite/biking.htm.

LOCAL CYCLING SHOPS

Easton Cycle & Sport (410-822-7433; 723 Goldsborough St., Easton) Can refer cyclists to rental outfits and advise on routes. Full service.

Wheel Doctor (410-745-6676; 1013 S. Talbot St., St. Michaels) Day-only rentals of cruisers, multispeed comfort bikes, recumbent bikes and tandems, from $16 to $30. Shop owner Jude McGloin can recommend routes, and suggests cyclists use the map he distributes, the Talbot County Chamber of Commerce map.

BIRD-WATCHING

S ome of the best birding in the Mid-Shore area, with its limited public water access, is from a boat. Osprey, bald eagles, herons blue or green, and migratory birds passing through are often spotted. The area's not far from Blackwater National Wildlife Refuge on the Lower Eastern Shore, and Sandy Point State Park in Annapolis, where birders like to go.

BOATING

CHARTERS & RENTALS

All Aboard Charters (410-745-6022; Rte. 33, Knapp's Narrows Marina, Tilghman; mailing address: P.O. Box 154, McDaniel, MD 21647) Charter the gussied-up Bay workboat *Nancy Ellen* for fishing trips or nature tours.

C&C Charters (800-733-SAIL, 410-827-7888; www.cccharters.com; 506 Kent Narrows Way N., Grasonville, MD 21638) Bareboat or captained charters; choice of fifteen to twenty vessels ranging in size from thirty-one- to sixty-foot powerboats or twenty-eight- to fifty-foot sailboats. One of the area's better-known companies.

Deep Reef Small Craft Rental (410-886-2545; www.toad.net/~jmathias; P.O. Box 170, Tilghman, MD 21671) Carolina skiffs with 25 hp engines and small sailboats (including a Hobiecat) available for rent. Half- and full-day rentals range from $110 to $185, a bit less for a smaller sailboat. Apr. 1–Oct.

Schnaitman's Boat Rentals (410-827-7663; 12518 Wye Landing Ln., Wye Mills, MD 21679) Crabbers gather here, where rowboats convertible to motor via a small engine go out on one of the Bay's best crabbing rivers. In all, eighty-five sixteen-foot, flat-bottom rowboats; you can row out or bring your own small motor (up to 25 hp). Also, six motorboats with 6 hp outboards. Crabbing supplies like dip nets for sale or rent; chicken necks, a favorite crabbing bait, also for sale. Fishing, too. Mid-May–Oct.

Tred Avon Yacht Sales and Charters (410-226-5000; 26106 Bachelor Harbor Dr., Oxford, MD 21654) Captained or bareboat, sail or power.

CRUISES & EXCURSION BOATS

Channel Charters (410-228-1645; www.channelcharters.com; 20 Algonquin Road, Cambridge, MD 21613) Ride aboard the Cambridge-built wooden workboat *Satisfaction* along with husband-and-wife captains Jeri and Randy Collins. Randy, a former local history teacher, also has taken a turn as a crabber, so he can detail all the sights along the way. The boat is often docked in Oxford by the Oxford-Bellevue Ferry for one- or two-hour cruises ($20 and $40), but trips elsewhere are available. Also, full or half days.

Dockside Express (410-886-2643; www.cruisinthebay.com; P.O. Box 803, located at the foot of Carpenter St. at Higgins Yacht Yard, St. Michaels, MD 21663) Narrated tour aboard the *Express Royale* includes natural history highlights of St. Michaels Harbor and area delivered by folks with deep Bay roots. Adults $20, kids under 12 $10. Sunset tours ($25) and other special cruises and charters available.

HM Krenz (410-745-6080; www.oystercatcher.com) The 1955 skipjack sails from St. Michaels. Check the web site, call for information.

Lady Patty (410-886-2215; www.sailladypatty.com; 5907 Tilghman Island Rd., Tilghman Island, MD 21671) Bay-built in Solomons by the M.M. Davis & Sons shipbuilders in 1935, the restored *Lady Patty* takes visitors out daily. Champagne sails, charters. Two-hour sails cost $30; call for other trips.

Lucky Dog Catamaran Co. (410-745-6203; www.luckydogcatamarancompany.com; 307 E. Chew Ave, St. Michaels, MD 21663) Sail aboard the high-speed catamaran *Sirius* on a two-mile cruise up the Miles River. Three or four trips a day, depending on the season. Call or check web site for times. $30 per person, Apr.–Oct. Docks at St. Michaels Marina on Mulberry St.

Patriot Cruises Inc. (410-745-3100; www.patriotcruises.com; P.O. Box 1206, St. Michaels, MD 21663) Perennially popular cruise of the Miles River with narration on local history. The 170-capacity *Patriot* departs at 11, 12:30, 2:30 and 4 daily, Apr.–Oct., from a dock off Mill Street near the Chesapeake Bay Maritime Museum. During the peak summer tourist months, prepare to wait in line. Adults $10, children under 12 $4.50. Special lunch cruises and evening charters are available.

Rebecca T. Ruark (Capt. Wade H. Murphy Jr., 410-886-2176; 21308 Phillips Rd., Tilghman, MD 21617) The oldest, prettiest, and fastest skipjack in the Bay's dwindling oyster fleet, captained by a man who has shown a talent for harvesting oysters and talking about the trade with visitors. Kids enjoy this tour. Two-hour tours; $30 per person for up to six passengers. Longer cruises can be arranged.

MARINAS

Chester

Castle Harbour Marina (410-643-5599; 301 Tackle Circle, Chester, MD 21619) 360 open slips. Located on the Chester River.
Piney Narrows Yacht Haven (410-643-6600; 500 Piney Narrows Rd., Chester, MD 21619) 279 slips, open and covered. Located on Kent Narrows, where the Chester River meets Eastern Bay.

Grasonville

Lippincott Marine (410-827-9300; 3420 Main St., Grasonville, MD 21638) 200 slips; transient slips available on Marshy Creek.
Mears Point Marina Kent Narrows (410-827-8888; www.mearspoint.com; 428 Kent Narrows Way N., Grasonville, MD 21638) Seven restaurants within walking distance, plus the happenin' Red Eye's Dock Bar. An impressive 600 slips; many powerboats live here, where the Chester flows into Eastern Bay.

Oxford

Crockett Brothers Boatyard (410-226-5113; www.crockettbros.com; 202 Banks St., Oxford, MD 21654) 74 slips. Pool, pump-out station, laundry. Located in center of town. Off the Tred Avon River in Crockett's Cove.
Oxford Boatyard (410-226-5101; 402 E. Strand, Oxford, MD 21654) Year-round. 76 slips, pump-out station. Located on the Tred Avon.

St. Michaels

St. Michaels Harbour Inn & Marina (410-745-9001; www.harbourinn.com; 101 N. Harbor Rd., St. Michaels, MD 21663) Open dawn to dusk, May–Oct., mostly serving transients. 56 slips along the Miles River. Water taxi, pump-out station, showers, and laundry. Morning coffee, newspapers; bike, kayak, and canoe rentals.
St. Michaels Marina (800-678-8980, 410-745-2400; 305 Mulberry St., St. Michaels, MD 21663) More than 50 transient slips on the Miles River. Bike rentals.

Stevensville

Bay Bridge Marina (410-643-3162; www.baybridgemarina.com; 357 Pier One Rd., Stevensville, MD 21666) Restaurant and small airport adjacent; shopping nearby. 310 slips, bathhouse, laundry, fuel. Located next to the Bay Bridge on Kent Island.

Tilghman

Knapp's Narrows Marina and Guest Quarters (410-886-2720; www.knapps narrowsmarina.com; 6176 Tilghman Island Rd., Tilghman, MD 21671) Swimming pool, laundry, showers, restaurants, motel. Deep-water harbor can accommodate boats up to eighty feet. 130 slips.

CANOEING & KAYAKING

The **Choptank River**, the largest of the Shore's twenty or so rivers, is fed into by **King's Creek**. Put in at Kingston Landing, accessible via Rte. 328 and Kingston Landing Road. The meandering creek runs past The Nature Conservancy's **Choptank Wetlands Preserve** and pristine marshes. South of this area, **Tuckahoe Creek**, which runs through **Tuckahoe State Park** in *Caroline County* before reaching the Choptank, is a popular Shore paddling spot. At the park, Tuckahoe Creek runs into **Crouse Mill Lake**, which has a dam at its lower end, after which the Tuckahoe continues its journey to the Choptank. The lake and the section of the creek north of it are freshwater; it's a good area for less-experienced canoeists. Below the dam, the Tuckahoe is tidal. From the dam to the landing in Hillsboro are 5.2 mi. miles of pleasurable canoeing, with great fishing for bass, pickerel, and bluegill. (Warning: Do not run the dam!) **Watts Creek**, entering the Choptank at **Martinak State Park** near *Denton*, makes for a pleasant two-hour paddle up and back. Go at high tide.

In Talbot County, put in at the public landing in *Whitman*. Stay on the peninsula side, running alongside Rte. 33, to enjoy beautiful farmland habitat, especially in the fall. From **Cummings Creek** into **Harris Creek**, there are some nice beaches along the way, and you'll pass through *Sherwood*, a neat little town. Follow the shoreline.

Enjoy **Marshyhope Creek**, a Nanticock River tributary; put in at Federalsburg (two boat ramps) and canoe downstream for some sunny open tripping, or upstream, ducking the brush on your way toward **Idylwild Wildlife Management Area**.

Outfitters rent craft and lead trips. They include:

Harris Creek Kayak (410-886-2083; 7857 Tilghman Island Rd./P.O. Box 41, Sherwood, MD 21665) Launching in spring 2002, with guided tours, custom moonlight tours, rentals, sales, certified ACA instruction. Singles, doubles. Recreational packages, including some with the owners' Moorings B&B. See their listing under "Lodgings" in this chapter.

Tidewater Kayaks (410-819-3284; Easton Point Marina, 975 Port St., Easton) Guided tours and rentals include tandem and solo craft for half or full days.

FISHING

BOAT RAMPS & FISHING PIERS

To obtain a free map of Bay access points, check "Landing & Boat Ramps" in Chapter Nine, *Information.*

Kent Island's piers include the long **Romancoke Pier** at the end of Route 8 S. (just east of the Chesapeake Bay Bridge) with fishing and crabbing from sunrise to sunset, May–Oct. Or check the **Matapeake Pier** on Rte 8 S. (410-974-2149). Small park, boat ramp.

As for boat ramps: In _Queen Anne's County_ (410-758-0835), there's a nominal, one-day permit fee for both residents and visitors. Try the ramps at Kent Narrows, Little Creek, Thompson Creek, Shipping Creek, Goodhand Creek, all on Kent Island, and Southeast Creek, Centreville, Crumpton, and Deep Landing in the northern part of the county.

The bridge that once spanned the **Choptank River** now serves as fishing piers on either side of the river, the dividing line between the Middle and Lower Eastern Shore. Crabbing and fishing, and a 25-acre park with waterside walking path on the Talbot County side. Fee. Located alongside Rte. 50 at the Frederick C. Malkus Bridge. Contact: **Choptank River Fishing Pier**, 410-820-1668; 29761 Bolingbroke Point Dr., Trappe, MD 21673.

A young mariner takes the helm.

Allison Blake

CHARTER BOATS & HEAD BOATS

Pintail Point (410-827-7029; 511 Pintail Point Farm Ln., Queenstown) Guided charters, including fly-fishers interested in learning from an Orvis guide.

Harrison's Sport Fishing Center (410-886-2121; www.chesapeakehouse.com; 21551 Chesapeake House Dr., Tilghman) Sportfishing central on the Bay, by an inn open since the last century's last decade. Sportfishers have been coming here since the late 1930s. Fourteen-boat fleet, plus a phalanx of on-call captains. Call for fees. Boat rentals, marina, and crab deck.

FITNESS FACILITIES

Cross Court Athletic Club (410-822-1515; 1180 S. Washington St., Easton) Four indoor and three outdoor tennis courts; exercise classes and equipment; child care and more. Guest fee for tennis, $5 plus court time; guest fee for health club, $10.

YMCA (410-822-0566; 202 Peach Blossom Rd., Easton) Two indoor swimming pools, 12 outdoor tennis courts, exercise and weight training equipment. Nonmembers, $10.

GOLF

The Easton Club (800-277-9800, 410-820-9800; 28449 Clubhouse Dr., Easton) 18 holes. Championship golf course in a waterfront community. Restaurant.

Hog Neck Golf Course (800-280-1790, 410-822-6079; www.hogneck.com; 10142 Old Cordova Rd., Easton) Public course; 27 holes, with an 18-hole championship course and a 9-hole executive course. Golf pros, pro shop, snack bar. Four stars from *Golf Digest*'s Places to Play.

Queenstown Harbor Golf Links (800-827-5257, 410-827-6611; www.mdgolf .com; 310 Links Lane, Queenstown) Two 18-hole courses. Very busy. Rated best public golf course in Maryland by *Golf Digest* in 1997. A beautiful setting on the Chester River.

Big Mario's Sport Center (410-822-7345; 9 mi. past Easton on Rte. 50 in Trappe) A driving range, heated and covered. Also batting cages, miniature golf.

NATURAL AREAS: STATE, FEDERAL AND PRIVATE PARKS/LANDS

Visitors trying to contact park management should be aware that some parks are satellite operations, managed from another park. For camping and picnic shelter reservations, call 888-432-CAMP, or visit www.dnr.state.md.us.

Adkins Arboretum (410-634-2847; located within Tuckahoe State Park, P.O. Box 100, Ridgely, MD 21660) For manicured walks through trails or a peek at native plants under cultivation, consider a stop here. Visitors center with rotating art shows, gift shop, books, plant sales.

Jean Ellen duPont Shehan Audubon Sanctuary (410-745-9283; www.audubon mddc.org; 23000 Wells Point Ln., Bozman, MD 21612) Located between St. Michaels and Tilghman, this new sanctuary is open to the public on Mondays, and features a variety of programs such as canoeing or birding at other times for National Audubon Society members. Mule wagon rides on Thurs. at this 950-acre farm.

Pickering Creek Audubon Center (410-822-4903; www.audubonmddc.org; 11450 Audubon Ln., off Sharp Road, Easton, MD 21601) Forest, fresh and brackish marshes, about a mile of shoreline along Pickering Creek. 400 acres. Canoe launch (canoes available to members), nature trails. Open to the public.

Idylwild Wildlife Management Area (410-376-3236, 410-820-7098; Houston Branch Rd., Federalsburg, MD 21632) Freshwater marsh and forest mean pileated woodpeckers, owls, and scarlet tanengers. Beavers in Marshyhope Creek. In all, 3,300 acres for hunting and hiking. Canoe access. Some trees down, but navigable for the most part.

Martinak State Park (410-820-1668; 137 Deep Shore Rd., Denton, MD 21629) A family-oriented 107-acre area along Watts Creek and the Choptank River featuring fishing, playgrounds. Four camper cabins; one full-service cabin. Picnic pavilions.

Horsehead Wetlands Center (410-827-6694; www.wildfowltrust.org; located off Rte. 8 at 600 Discovery Lane, Grasonville, MD 21638) Convalescing birds, such as owls, hawks, and bald eagles, live in large chain-link cages, making this a great up-close look at these marvelous creatures. Trails wind through a portion of the 500-acre center, operated by the Wildfowl Trust of North America. Canoe put-in, public programs. Closes promptly at 5.

Tuckahoe State Park (410-820-1668; 13070 Crouse Mill Rd., Queen Anne, MD 21657) A pretty 60-acre lake and lots of woods, including a marked fitness trail with exercises at each station. Fishing and boating on 20 acres of the lake. In all, almost 20 miles of trails for hiking or biking, including three miles on surfaced trails. Canoe, kayak, paddleboat rentals, Apr. 1–Oct. 31. Check for fees. Camping includes 33 sites, four camper cabins. Picnic pavilions.

Wye Island Natural Resources Management Area (410-827-7577; 632 Wye Island Rd., Queenstown, MD 21658) Primarily used for agricultural and natural resource management, this is 2,550 acres on a historic island paddlers like to circle. Access is not available from the island; try one of the Queen Anne's County boat ramps (info available in Chapter Nine, *Information*).

SPORTING GOODS & CAMPING SUPPLY STORES

Albright's Gun Shop (410-820-8811; 36 E. Dover St., Easton) Fishing and hunting gear, gunsmithing on premises; Orvis dealer.

Shore Sportsman (800-263-2027, 410-820-5599; 8232 Ocean Gateway, Easton) Hunting, fishing, bait, and tackle.

Chesapeake Outdoors (410-604-0446; 1707 Main St., Chester) Hunting, fishing supplies, archery pro shop.

Island Fishing and Hunting (410-643-4224; Exit 40A off Rte. 50 E., Kent Island) Bait, commercial and recreational crabbing supplies, tackle, hunting supplies, local sporting info. Open seven days a week.

SWIMMING

George W. Murphy Pool (410-820-7306; 501 Port St., off the Easton Bypass, Easton) Daily admission for 25-meter pool, plus smaller "zero" entry pool for kids. Mem. Day–Labor Day.

SHOPPING

Shops line St. Michaels' Talbot Street.

David Trozzo

ANTIQUES

Americana Antiques (410-226-5677; 111 S. Morris St., Oxford) A town fixture for 30 years, offering seventeenth-, eighteenth- and early nineteenth-century American art and artifacts.

Camelot Antiques Ltd. (410-820-4396; 7871 Ocean Gateway, Easton) Wide selection of antiques, including oyster plates and Quimper in huge shop on Rte. 50 through town.

Chesapeake Antique Center (410-827-6640; Md. 18 & Rte. 50, Queenstown) More than seventy dealers who almost entirely adhere to the 100-year rule in a vast exhibit space just east of Kent Island, behind Prime Outlets. Exceptions are made for any distinctly period, twentieth-century piece, such as Art Deco.

The Defender Collection I and II (410-822-0994; Maple Ave. and Main St., Trappe) Three buildings, antiques, furniture, collectibles, garden stuff in the tiny town of Trappe. Take Rte. 50 south of Easton.

Easton Maritime Antiques (410-763-8853; 27 S. Harrison St., Easton) Specializes in fine nautical antiques, including instruments, scrimshaw, ship models. Open Thurs.–Sat. 10–5:30 or by appointment.

Flo-Mir (410-822-2857; 23 E. Dover St., Easton) Popular local antiques shop, especially strong on china.

Foxwell's Antiques & Collectibles (410-820-9705; 7793 Ocean Gateway, Easton) With eighty dealers in one location, you'll find a variety of items from glassware to china to antique advertising in this eminently browsable shop on Rte. 50.

Janet K. Fanto Antiques and Rare Books (410-763-9030; 13 N. Harrison St., Easton) Early American silver, rare books, fine art.

Lanham-Merida/Bountiful Antiques and Interiors (410-763-8500; 218 N. Washington St., Easton) The best-quality English, Continental, and American furniture, plus paintings, silver, porcelain. Bountiful sells newer furniture, gifts, and accessories.

Lesnoff Antiques (410-822-2334; 7 N. Harrison St., Easton) French antiques and collectibles, much furniture.

Oak Creek Sales (410-745-3193; 25939 Royal Oak Dr., Royal Oak, off the road between St. Michaels and Easton) Eclectic selection of antiques and collectibles — the figurine saltshaker sitting next to the Depression glass. Across the street, an entire barn is devoted to antique and used furniture.

Pennywhistle Antiques (410-745-9771; 408 S. Talbot St., St. Michaels) Known for its exceptional decoys; antiques in one room after another.

Silver Chalice Antiques and Collectibles (410-745-9501; 400 S. Talbot St., St. Michaels) Specializes in Depression glass.

Stockley Antiques (410-822-9346; Mulberry Hill Farm, Rte. 50, Easton) Not a store, exactly, but a restoration shop and historic replica furniture maker. There's a barn full of interesting pieces, and they'll custom-build period furniture.

BOOKS

Book Bank: Crawford's Nautical Books (410-886-2230; 5782 Tilghman Island Rd.,Tilghman Island) Hundreds of fiction and nonfiction titles on all things nautical, from sailing to shipbuilding to seafaring. The store buys used books and sells nautical art.

Book Warehouse (410-827-8474; 429 Outlet Center Dr., Queenstown) Hardcovers and paperbacks below retail. Located at Prime Outlets.

The News Center (410-822-7212; Talbottown Shopping Center, 218 N. Washington St., Easton) Large paperback selection and fine section of regional writings. Also stocks the Shore's largest periodical selection, with more than 1,000 titles. A smaller News Center, without the books but with lots of magazines, is located in The Centre at Salisbury.

Unicorn Book Shop (410-476-3838; 3935 Ocean Gateway (Rte. 50), Trappe) Excellent rare and secondhand bookshop; bibliophiles will love this place. Antique map reproductions.

CLOTHING

Anastasia Ltd. (410-822-4814; 11 N. Harrison St., Easton) Classic women's clothing.

Bleachers (410-745-5676; 107 S. Talbot St., St. Michaels) Beachy boutique offers colorful, fun clothes for adults and children. Check out the shades.

Chesapeake Bay Outfitters (410-745-3107; Talbot St. & Railroad Ave., St. Michaels) Better sportswear, nautical apparel, Bay-oriented T's and sweatshirts, and boating and casual footwear for men and women.

Sailor of St. Michaels (410-745-2580; 214 Talbot St., St. Michaels) Souvenir shirts and sweatshirts from the Shore, women's and men's sportswear, and gifts.

Shaw Bay Classics (410-745-3377; 208 S. Talbot St., St. Michaels) Women's updated classic clothing and accessories. Geiger of Austria boiled wool collection.

Two on Talbot (410-745-0405; 105 S. Talbot St., St. Michaels) Fine-woven fabric jackets; other updated, stylish pieces for women. Also children's clothing.

FINE CRAFTS, GIFTS & GALLERIES

American Pennyroyal (410-822-5030; 5 N. Harrison St., Easton) A favorite among lovers of American folk art. Everything from baskets to pottery to rugs, quilts, and jewelry.

Artiste Locale (410-745-6580; 112 N. Talbot St., St. Michaels) Showcase for artisans from throughout the region.

Coco & Company (410-745-3400; 209 S. Talbot St., St. Michaels) Furniture, candles, garden items among the many goodies in this large design and gift shop.

Contemporary Tapestry Weaving Studio and Gallery (410-745-4303; by the Oxford-Bellevue Ferry, Bellevue) Swedish weaver Ulrika Leander's gallery brings expansive, brightly colored fabric art to the town's old post office. Urbane and contemporary — and most certainly not provincial. Open only by appt.

L'Atelier (410-763-8810; 9 Goldsborough St., Easton) High-end gift gallery featuring ceramics, porcelain, and glass.

Mind's Eye (410-745-2023; 201 S. Talbot St., St. Michaels) Contemporary craftworks include glass, chimes, and much more. Fun to shop.

Rugged Roses (410-820-9209; 137 N. Harrison St., Easton) Clothing and gifts.

St. Michael's Artisans Studio Co-Op (410-745-4125; Canton Alley at Freeman St., St.Michaels) Cool artists' co-op one block off the main street featuring artists who work in glass, textiles, photography, bronze, paintings, and more. Open Fri.–Mon. during the season; Sat.–Sun. in the off-season. Call for appt. to visit otherwise.

Troika Gallery (410-770-9190; 218 N. Washington St., Easton) Operated by three local artists at the Talbottown Shopping Center. Fine art.

JEWELERY

DBS Jewelers (410-745-2626; 111 S. Talbot St., St. Michaels) Resident goldsmith on-site for repairs and custom creations, or select from the updated or classic designs on display. Nice selection of gold Bay-inspired pieces, too.

Shearer the Jeweler (410-822-2279; 22 N. Washington St., Easton) Diamonds, colored gems, watches, and original designs.

Westphal Jewelers (410-822-7774; 19 N. Harrison St., Easton) Diamonds, gemstones, watches, and custom designs.

MARINE SUPPLY

Crockett Brothers Boatyard (410-226-5113; 202 Banks St., Oxford) Nautical supplies, boat repair, and pool.

L&B Marine Supply (410-643-3600; 124 Kent Landing, Stevensville) Discount marine supply.

OUTLETS

Prime Outlets-Queenstown (410-827-8699; 441 Outlet Center Dr., Queenstown) Notable destination among outlet shoppers, with more than fifty stores such as Nine West and Geoffrey Beene. The location, just over the Bay Bridge on the Eastern Shore, makes for a good stop. If you're hungry, the Chesapeake Gourmet there has good sandwiches.

SPECIALTY SHOPS & GENERAL STORES

The Christmas Goose (410-827-5252; Rte. 50, Queenstown) Handcrafted Christmas items like nutcrackers, ornaments, and more. Located across from the Chesapeake Outlet Center.

Crackerjacks (410-822-7716; 7 S. Washington St., Easton) Cool toy store in Easton's Historic District selling quality games, dolls, children's books, and stuffed animals. Many imported items.

Keepers at St. Michaels (410-745-6388; 300 S. Talbot St., St. Michaels) A full-line Orvis dealer with outdoor gear, clothing, plus antique and contemporary decoys.

Oxford Mews Emporium (410-820-8222; 105 S. Morris St., Oxford) Like an old-fashioned general store where you can buy anything. A good selection of Bay books and gifts, specialty food products, and biking and camping gear.

Rowens Stationery Inc. (410-822-2095; 8–10 N. Washington St., Easton) Along with all of its supplies for the office and art studio, the venerable Rowens houses a nice selection of glassware, from tumblers to martini glasses. Everything from gourmet cooking supplies to serving trays with waterfowl scenes.

Silent Poetry (410-226-5120; 201 Tilghman St., Oxford) Unusual gifts and works of art, including stemware and china, specialty food products, stuffed animals and toys, mood candles and fragrances, and much more.

Tidedancers (410-763-8630; 28272 St. Michaels Rd., Easton) Multiple cottages with imports and other fun items on the road to St. Michaels.

CHAPTER SIX
Water, Water Everywhere
LOWER EASTERN SHORE

Watermen farm cherrystone clams deep on Virginia's Lower Eastern Shore.

David Trozzo

The Choptank River broadens as it reaches the Bay, the longest of the Eastern Shore's tributaries and the start of the Lower Shore. Travelers on Rte. 50 cross its on-and-on bridge, formally known as the Frederick C. Malkus Bridge, to reach Cambridge, originally settled in 1684. Alongside run remnants of the bridge's Depression-era predecessor, now fishing piers. Sails, wakes, and the typical lowboard of Chesapeake workboats glint white from below, evidence that this is cruising paradise, or prime fishing grounds, with creeks detouring inland. Upon arrival in Dorchester County, visitors can reach Cambridge's Historic District behind the highway's commercial appearance, with grand homes lining a brick street, a couple of lodgings in grand old places, and a few places to eat. At Great Marsh Park, look out onto the Chesapeake and get a hint of the Lower Eastern Shore's primary draw. Pure and simple, it's nature.

Marshland blurs the distinction between land and sea in many parts of the Lower Eastern Shore, which runs 130 miles from the Choptank to the Virginia Capes, Charles and Henry, locus of the Chesapeake Bay Bridge-Tunnel.

Watermen and farmers live close to the earth and visitors are perhaps more likely to encounter a more authentic way of life here than Bay Country's other regions. Along Rte. 13 through the southern Delmarva Peninsula, you'll pass quaint towns and the bustling burg of Salisbury, but you'll also pass long rural stretches of farmland.

Antique shops are scattered along your way, and Eastern Shore seafood doesn't get any better than this, true fruits-du-mer, the much-heralded bounty of Chesapeake Bay that means three tiny fried soft-shell crabs on white bread are likely to trump fancier versions in city cafés. Fried food also is a must diet-buster if oysters inspire.

Nature-lovers cycle or paddle through the flat "Maryland Everglades," the marshland filled with rivers and twisting creeks, called "guts," that runs down the coast from Dorchester County south. Loblolly pine, tall green sentinels common to the area, stretch high. The endangered Delmarva fox squirrel lives here. Birders find nesting bald eagles throughout the area, along with an abundance of other nesters and avian visitors stopping along the Atlantic Flyway. Put in a boat and fish in Bay tributary rivers, or charter a fishing boat into prime Chesapeake fishing grounds in search of rockfish croaker, flounder and spot. From a pier, lower a net or string tied around a chicken neck to catch blue crabs.

Through these blackwater swamps that draw modern-day kayakers passed Harriet Tubman, the escaped slave who led some 300 slaves to freedom through this land. Born in captivity in Dorchester, "The Moses of Her People" is the subject of a local tour.

Salisbury, the Peninsula's business hub, is a few miles farther down the road, with its institution of higher education, Salisbury University, the Ward Brothers Museum — a standard in the world of bird carving — and the Salisbury Zoo. From here, many travelers turn east to the ocean beaches. To stay on a Bay Country course, drive farther south.

Scattered in Somerset and Worcester Counties are the historic towns marching toward the Atlantic Ocean. Princess Anne, founded in 1733 and named for King George II's daughter, is the Somerset County seat, its streets lined with Federal and Georgian houses.

Snow Hill, a royal port under England's William and Mary, once saw three-masted schooners and, later, steamboats arrive up the Pocomoke River. Now it's a reclaimed historical town drawing paddlers who stay in its updated Victorian B&Bs before heading out on the eminently enjoyable Pocomoke. Berlin, near the Atlantic Ocean, descends from colonial Burley Plantation, and is stylishly reclaimed.

Maryland's southernmost town is Crisfield, called Somers Cove until the mid- to late-1800s railroad arrived via the influence of a local lawyer named John Crisfield. The railroad's arrival touched off a true oyster boom, and by the late 1800s, the harbor was thick with watermen's vessels and people were getting rich on oysters. Crisfield was a noisy strip of brothels and saloons and street-brawl recklessness. The oyster boom faded long ago, but Crisfield remains an active, working watermen's port that has rebounded to boast of its standing as the "Crab Capital of the World." Word has it that oyster shells literally remain a foundation of the town.

Today, storefront businesses attend to the working folks, like hardware stores selling commercial crab pots. Visitors are well advised to check into one of Crisfield's few standard motels, or head out to Janes Island State Park for a cabin — either basic "camper" style (bathhouses nearby in the campground) or full-serve. This is also the place to take a ferry over to Smith or Tangier Islands, those final bastions of Bay island waterman life. If you've only got a weekend, plan to visit over Labor Day, when the Crisfield Hard Crab Derby or the nearby Deal Island Skipjack Races and Land Festival (highlighted under "Special Events") show folks what the waterman's life is all about.

Smith and Tangier both incubate a disappearing way of life, where crabbers and their families live by the crustacean's life cycle. Tangier, in Virginia, tends to have more for visitors than Maryland's Smith, which, with three towns, is larger. Time and tide erode the shores of both, and the white crab peeler sheds that line Tangier's shores have come ashore on Smith. If authentic Chesapeake intrigues, don't miss these islands.

Back on the mainland, Virginia beckons south. The old fishing town of Chincoteague promises beachside fun alongside oyster and clam beds, as well as the world-famous ponies living wild on nearby Assateague Island, ensured a future by three different parks or refuges. Farther down the highway stands Onancock, once the seventeenth-century port town of Scarburgh, named after a Native American village meaning "a foggy place." The fishing town has been reclaimed for boaters and tourists. Rte. 13 seems endless through here; tiny towns dot the terrain. At the tip of the peninsula, Cape Charles, the former railroad and ferry terminus town, is up and coming — but hasn't quite arrived. Still, B&B owners say they stay full much of the year with birders, kayakers and lovers of the small-town atmosphere. Turn-of-the-century houses are being renovated on almost every block, and newly "local" residents are the town's greatest boosters. Cape Charles' pavilion was the town's musical entertainment center back when people and goods came by train and steamboat to this transportation hub on the Chesapeake, which is sure to rise again.

LODGING

The Lower Eastern Shore offers a wide range of accommodations, from fixed-up farmhouses serving as B&Bs to more elegant, renovated Victorians to rustic cabins with million-dollar water views. Keep in mind that many lodgings have variable prices during the week or on weekends, during high season or low season. Two-night minimums are typical in high season. Check on cancellation policies, too. And, unless otherwise noted, leave the cigarettes and pets at home. Lodging price ranges are:

Inexpensive: Up to $75
Moderate: $76 to $120
Expensive: $121 to $150
Very Expensive: Over $150

Credit card abbreviations are: AE, American Express; CB, Carte Blanche; D, Discover; DC, Diner's Club; MC, MasterCard; V, Visa.

These lodging suggestions are arranged geographically (more or less) south from the Choptank River.

Cambridge, Md.

GLASGOW INN B&B
Owners: Louiselee Roche &
   Martha Ann Rayne.
888-373-7890, reservations;
   410-228-0575.
www.glasgowinncambridge
   .com.
1500 Hambrooks Blvd.,
   Cambridge, MD 21613.
Price: Moderate to Very
   Expensive.
Credit Cards: No.
Handicap Access: No.
Restrictions: Children
   allowed conditionally.

Grand Glasgow Inn was a private home from its construction around 1760 until Louiselee Roche and Martha Ann Rayne opened it to the public as a B&B during the 1980s. The main house retains its historic integrity, meaning seven large rooms include four with private baths. An adjacent building holds three more rooms arranged in colonial fashion around a central fireplace. Third-floor rooms are worth the long walk up the stairs for their cozy window seats, sloping eaves (and floors!), and queen-sized beds, though you'll have to share a bath. Careful development of the land in front of the Glasgow Inn as a modern Williamsburg-style subdivision hasn't hurt the view: You can still see the broad Choptank River from the front guest windows.

**HYATT REGENCY
   CHESAPEAKE BAY
   GOLF RESORT, SPA
   AND MARINA**
410-901-1234.
www.hyatt.com (search for
   "Chesapeake Bay").
2800 Ocean Gateway,
   Cambridge, MD 21613.
Price: Very Expensive.
Credit Cards: AE, D, DC,
   MC, V.
Handicap Access: Yes.

Opening in March 2002 is something completely different for this part of the Bay: an expansive resort overlooking the Choptank River. Guests will find 400 rooms, which include sixteen suites, and may partake in a range of activities, from golfing on the 18-hole championship course to settling in at one of six restaurants or lounges, or playing tennis at one of six lighted outdoor courts. Plans also call for a state-of-the-art spa with fitness center and spa treatments, jogging paths through an eighteen-acre wildlife refuge, and multilevel indoor and outdoor pools replete with waterfalls. Marina with 150 slips, kids' activities, and other fun such as boat charters.

Church Creek, Md.

LOBLOLLY LANDINGS AND LODGE
Innkeepers: Len and Marlene Slavin.
800-862-7452, 410-397-3033.
www.loblollylandingsbandb.com.
2142 Liners Rd., Church Creek, MD 21622.
Price: Inexpensive for bunkhouse and B&B; Expensive to Very Expensive for suite.
Credit Cards: MC, V.
Handicap Access: To main building, yes; to lodge and sleeping rooms, no.
Restrictions: No children under 5.

Outdoor lovers will be in heaven at this 170-acre getaway deep in the Dorchester lowlands. Watch birds, kayak Coles Creek, fish the stocked pond — or ask your hosts to arrange charters or hunting trips. Just as outdoor activities are plentiful, so the choice of accommodations range across tastes or vacation needs. Join your fishing buddies for $20 per night in the bunkhouse, with two baths for ten bunks and a sitting area and kitchen, or choose more typical B&B rooms (three rooms; two baths to share) inside the lodge, where windows reach nearly as high as the thirty-foot ceiling in the main room. Or, above the bunkhouse sits a countrified suite with a whirlpool tub and well-appointed kitchenette, a pullout couch, and even a grill on the deck. Bikes for rent, canoes, and a 3-D archery range (BYO equipment). Also here: Buster the friendly dog and six cats.

Princess Anne, Md.

WATERLOO COUNTRY INN
Owners: Theresa & Erwin Kraemer.
410-651-0883.
www.waterloocountryinn.com.
28822 Mt. Vernon Rd., Princess Anne, MD 21853.
Price: Expensive to Very Expensive.
Credit Cards: AE, D, MC, V.
Handicap Access: One room.
Special Features: Children welcome; pets OK in one room.

Theresa and Erwin Kraemer traveled from Switzerland several years ago to visit friends in Princess Anne. They saw a "For Sale" sign in front of this stunning 1750 Georgian-style mansion beside a picture-perfect tidal pond and decided that they had to stay. You'll be glad they did as soon as you check in. The two suites are luxurious, the four less-ornate rooms are still stylish. Outside there's a swimming pool, miles of country roads to cycle, and meandering streams to canoe (bicycles and canoe are complimentary). A paradise for nature lovers, Canada geese happily roam the landscaped lawns. Make arrangements with the Kraemers in advance and they'll be sure to have dinner ready for you, from a gourmet four-course meal to something simpler. The full breakfast includes freshly baked breads, eggs, fresh fruit, and, if you're of a European bent, cheese. The Kraemers may have settled far from their homeland, but they've imported a bit of Continental style into the Somerset County countryside.

Snow Hill, Md.

CHANCEFORD HALL
Innkeepers: Randy Ifft and
   Alice Kesterson.
410-632-2900.
www.chancefordhall.com.
209 W. Federal St. Snow
   Hill, MD 21863.
Price: Expensive.
Credit Cards: MC, V.
Handicap Access: No.
Restrictions: Children
   conditionally welcome.

As the last millennium ended, architect Randy Ifft and wife Alice left their busy Chicago life to move into this enormous 1759 Greek Revival manor house, and they've never regretted it. The boxwood-lined entrance walk draws visitors into this National Historic Landmark home located on a tree-lined back street. Once inside, elaborate crown moldings, mantels, and twelve-over-twelve windows holds visitors' attention. Four guest bedrooms, each with a private bath, offer sophistication, with handmade four-poster queen beds dressed in luxurious linens. Oriental rugs cover centuries-old polished wood floors. Each bedroom is outfitted with a generous stack of good books, mostly fiction, although bird-watchers can refer to Audubon and Sibley. Self-addressed mailers are provided for guests who can't bear to put down their book when they leave. A paved backyard terrace invites guests to sit and share a glass of wine or afternoon tea in the shade of the second-oldest black walnut in the state. In the morning, enjoy a gourmet breakfast served in the chandeliered dining room or at the huge, wooden farm table in the large, well-appointed kitchen. The house has ten working fireplaces, and a trellised lap pool covered with passionflower vines.

RIVER HOUSE INN
Innkeepers: Larry and
   Susanne Knudsen.
410-632-2722.
www.riverhouseinn.com.
201 E. Market St., Snow
   Hill, MD 21863.
Price: Expensive to Very
   Expensive.
Credit Cards: AE, D, MC, V.
Handicap Access: Yes, in
   the River Cottage.
Restrictions: Children at
   additional charge
   depending on age.

A profusion of flowers and black wrought iron gingerbread on the wide veranda greets guests entering this homey Victorian B&B, but the real treat is out back, where two-story screened porches invite guests to linger over the view down the long rolling lawn to the Pocomoke River. The inn offers three outbuildings on two acres of shaded lawn. While undergoing a major renovation, four suites are available. Some have fireplaces, all beds are queen- or king-sized, and baths are period-style with modern plumbing, appointed with fluffy white towels. The charming River Cottage, converted from an 1890 carriage barn, offers a private porch, minifridge, microwave, coffee maker and whirlpool tub.

Berlin, Md.

THE ATLANTIC HOTEL
Manager: Gary Weber.
410-641-0189, 800-814-7672.

Richard Gere slept here — or at least his character did in the movie *Runaway Bride*, filmed here in 1998. It was just one memorable moment in the

2 N. Main St., Berlin MD
21811.
Price: Moderate to Very
Expensive.
Credit Cards: AE, MC, V.
Handicap Access: Yes.

long history of the handsome brick Atlantic Hotel on Berlin's Main Street. The renovation of this 1895 hotel launched the town's vigorous revival, as residents gained a new pride in their unique surroundings and undertook the restoration of many buildings. The hotel's ten deluxe rooms and six smaller, substantially less-expensive standard rooms create a nineteenth-century feeling with their rich color schemes and antique furnishings. All have TVs, though you may find yourself more inclined to browse Berlin's boutiques and antique stores or wallow in Ocean City's Boardwalk extravaganza, just seven miles away. Breakfast is served downstairs, home to the Drummer's Café, a popular local meeting place, and the elegant formal dining room that built the Atlantic Hotel's reputation throughout the East Coast (See "Restaurants," later in this chapter). There's no better place to wind up a busy day than in one of the hotel's front-porch rocking chairs, a cool drink in hand and a view of charming downtown Berlin.

**MERRY SHERWOOD
PLANTATION**
Owner: Kirk Burbage.
410-641-2112, 800-660-0358.
www.merrysherwood.com.
8909 Worcester Hwy. (U.S.
113), Berlin, MD 21811.
Price: Very Expensive.
Credit Cards: MC, V.
Handicap Access: No.
Restrictions: Children OK.

Standing more than fifty feet tall, comprising twenty-seven rooms in over 8,500 square feet, the Merry Sherwood Plantation house is as impressive today as when it was completed in 1859. A jewel in classic Italianate style, set amid twenty acres of gardens featuring roses, topiary, and perennials, Merry Sherwood's grounds, designed by *Southern Living*, are almost enough to make you forget the rush of modern life. Inside the three-story house are seven rooms and one suite; two rooms share a bath in order to retain the building's integrity. Rooms are elegant and large, and the antique furnishings (including the Vanderbilts' former carved rosewood furniture) honor the mid-nineteenth-century Philadelphia affluence that created the house. A gourmet breakfast is served under an enormous chandelier. For a well-rounded visit, spend time on the fabulous sun porch perusing the photo album, which reveals the full marvel of the restoration that readied Merry Sherwood for guests in the mid-1990s.

Chincoteague, Va.

CHANNEL BASS INN
Owners: David & Barbara
Wiedenheft.
800-249-0818, 757-336-6148.
www.channelbass-inn.com.
6228 Church St.,
Chincoteague, VA 23336.

This simple frame house conceals a quiet, elegant décor, backdrop to a somewhat formal inn. Six guest rooms come with private baths and air-conditioning, most with queen- or king-sized beds triple-sheeted for luxury. Barbara has laid out a pleasant backyard garden, and full breakfast is

Price: Moderate to Very
  Expensive.
Credit Cards: AE, D, MC, V.
Handicap Access: No.

**ISLAND MANOR
  HOUSE**
Innkeepers: Carol &
  Charles Kalmykow.
800-852-1505, 757-336-5436.
www.IslandManor.com.
4160 Main St.,
  Chincoteague, VA 23336.
Price: Moderate to
  Expensive.
Credit Cards: AE, MC, V.
Handicap Access: No.
Restrictions: No children
  under 10.

served. The Channel Bass' tearoom functions as the island's only public tearoom and features Barbara's "world famous" scones.

Two brothers built a house in 1848, married two sisters, split the house, and moved half of it next door. Today, the two sections have been connected with a large garden room and redecorated in Federal style, making a most attractive place to stay. Eight rooms include six with private baths, some with water views. The friendly proprietors will be more than happy to share stories of their antique furnishings, books, and artwork, and guide you toward your own treasures as you shop the island. Expect a roaring fire in the winter and, in fair weather, breakfast on the secluded brick terrace with a fountain, surrounded by roses. Breakfast is large. Free bicycles and beach towels for guests.

Cozy in to the Inn at Poplar Corner in Chincoteague, Va.

David Trozzo

**THE INN AT POPLAR
  CORNER**
Innkeepers: Jackie & Tom
  Derickson, and Joanne &
  David Snead.
800-336-6787.
www.poplarcorner.com.
4240 Main St.,
  Chincoteague, VA 23336.

This welcoming inn with a wraparound veranda furnished with white wicker was once featured on TV's *Romantic Escapes*. No wonder. Floral-wallpapered rooms feature queen beds with ornate highback walnut headboards, marble-topped dressers and washstands. Each room is generously sized with a fine sitting area. Since this Victorian was built in 1996 as an inn, rather than a home, the rooms are

Price: Moderate to Very
  Expensive
Credit Cards: MC, V.
Handicap Access: No.
Restrictions: Children OK
  in the cottages; inquire
  about inns.

separated from each other and offer privacy. All have refrigerators, whirlpool bath, and shower. Guests may use bicycles, beach chairs, towels, and binoculars. The same people own the slightly less-expensive Watson House on the opposite corner of Main Street, with six rooms including the airy Sun Room. Rates include breakfast at the Inn at Poplar Corner. Cottage rentals (good for kids) available.

Onancock, Va.

COLONIAL MANOR INN
Owners: Ivonne and Hans
  Harenburg.
757-787-3521.
www.colonialmanorinn
  .com.
84 Market St., Onancock,
  VA 23417.
Price: Inexpensive to
  Moderate.
Credit Cards: MC, V.
Handicap Access: No.
Restrictions: No children
  under 6.

Your hosts left Germany to operate this 1882 Victorian, set back on two acres off Onancock's main street. The inn exudes a warm and friendly atmosphere. Children will find books and toys. Adults often find themselves in the living room around the inn's piano, joining impromptu sing-alongs. A gazebo out back prompts picnics and stargazing. Convenient to Onancock's attractions, the Tangier Island ferry, and beaches and nature preserves thirty minutes north at Chincoteague or south at Kiptopeake. Eight rooms have private or shared baths, comfortable furnishings, and in-room coffee and TVs. Full breakfast.

Cape Charles, Va.

**NOTTINGHAM RIDGE
  B&B**
Owner: Bonnie
  Nottingham.
757-331-1010.
www.nottinghamridge.com.
28184 Nottingham Ridge
  Lane, Cape Charles, VA
  23310.
Price: Moderate to
  Expensive.
Credit Cards: No.
Handicap Access: No.

From the private beach in front of Nottingham Ridge, you can see little but the blue Chesapeake and the Chesapeake Bay Bridge-Tunnel in the distance. This secluded home, built in 1974 but decorated like a colonial Williamsburg house, sits in a pine forest far removed from everyday hassles. Six miles south of Cape Charles and three miles north of the bridge, this is the perfect spot to overnight or get away from it all for a weekend. The B&B has three rooms and a suite, all with private baths, and in warm weather a full breakfast is served on the screened porch overlooking the Bay.

**STERLING HOUSE BED
  & BREAKFAST**
Innkeepers: Ned Brinkley
  and Steve Hairfield.

Just off the town's beach stands this tree-shaded Sears, Roebuck & Co. catalog house-turned-inn, a dream come true for bird-watching guests — and Cape Charles is nothing if not bird-watcher central.

757-331-2483.
www.sterling-inn.com.
9 Randolph Ave., Cape
   Charles, VA 23310.
Price: Moderate to Very
   Expensive.
Credit cards: V, MC.
Handicap access: No.
Restrictions: No children
   under 12.

Innkeepers Ned Brinkley and Steve Hairfield offer private natural history and birding tours, a great opportunity for amateur ornithologists since Brinkley is a professional international birding guide. Guests will find handmade mattresses — exquisitely comfortable — a substantial library, bicycles, and beach chairs. Guests also have access to a butler's pantry with microwave oven and a refrigerator stocked with beverages and ice. As for the rooms, four total include two with whirlpool tubs, including the popular Virginia Lee room, which expands into a suite with a sitting room that sleeps two more. A hot tub sits on an upstairs deck, almost in the treetops, perfect for soaking away sore muscles after a long day spent traipsing through marshes and creeks in search of a rare hawk. If that's not enough, Hairfield, an avid sailor, offers sunset cruises on his sloop, *Adhara*.

WILSON-LEE HOUSE
Innkeepers: David Phillips
   and Leon Parham.
757-331-1954.
www.wilsonleehouse.com.
403 Tazewell Ave., Cape
   Charles, VA 23310.
Price: Moderate to
   Expensive.
Credit Cards: AE, MC, V.
Handicap Access: No.
Restrictions: No children
   under 12.

Blooming oleanders and a wraparound porch welcome visitors into this 1906 Colonial Revival home, replete with attentive hosts and an eclectic style that means modern butterfly chairs share parlor space with Victorian settees. Period heirlooms come from the families of your hosts, who greet guests with conversation, maybe a cocktail, and a local tale or two. The six rooms, including one with a whirlpool tub, come with details such as portable CD players with clock radios. The Art Deco–style Virginia Wilson room, with its sunny southeastern exposure, queen-sized pencilpost bed, and cheerful peach wall, is especially popular. The Alyce Wilson room comes with a French iron canopy bed and twin wingback chairs. Your innkeepers are knowledgeable and enthusiastic, both about the house and about the town's rebirth. Full breakfasts feature goodies like crème brûlée French toast.

MOTELS/HOTELS

Maryland

Best Western, Salisbury Plaza (410-546-1300; 1735 N. Salisbury Blvd., Salisbury, MD 21801) Moderate to Expensive. Some rooms with microwave and data port. Outdoor pool. Continental breakfast. Handicap access.

The Washington Hotel And Inn (410-651-2525; 11784 Somerset Ave. (Rte. 675), Princess Anne, MD 21853) Inexpensive. Twelve rooms; owned by the same family since 1936. Built circa 1744; check out the double staircase: one for gentlemen, one for ladies in hoop skirts.

Somers Cove Motel (410-968-1900; Somers Cove Marina; P.O. Box 387, Crisfield, MD 21817) Inexpensive to Very Expensive. Forty serviceable rooms with balconies or patios. Pool. Expect prices to skyrocket for local festivals. Handicap access.

Virginia

Driftwood Motor Lodge (800-553-6117, 757-336-6557; 7105 Maddox Blvd./P.O. Box 575, Chincoteague Island, VA 23336) Moderate. Fifty-three rooms. Handicap access.

The Refuge Motor Inn (888-831-0600, 757-336-5511; 7058 Maddox Blvd./P.O. Box 378, Chincoteague Island, VA 23336) Moderate to Very Expensive. At the entrance to Chincoteague National Wildlife Refuge, seventy-two rooms with patios or balconies look onto loblolly pines. Whirlpool, sauna, exercise room, bike rentals. Handicap access.

Waterside Motor Inn (757-336-3434; www.watersidemotorinn.com; 3761 S. Main St./P.O. Box 347, Chincoteague Island, VA 23336) Moderate to Very Expensive. Private waterside balconies, refrigerators in rooms, fishing and crabbing pier, and tennis court. Handicap access.

Sunset Beach Inn (800-899-4786, 757-331-4786; 32246 Lankford Hwy./P.O. Box 472, Cape Charles, VA 23310) Moderate. Sixty-five rooms, eight suites, fifty-four RV sites on fifty beautiful acres, including a Bayside beach at the tip of the Delmarva Peninsula. Pool, restaurant, lounge, conference center.

RESTAURANTS

Two words to travelers of the Lower Eastern Shore: local seafood. Blue crabs — soft-shells, crab cakes, hard-shells — oysters, rockfish, clams. Indulge in these these Bay delights while you're on the Lower Shore, where they're as fresh as you'll find and the prices tend to be quite reasonable.

Restaurant pricing follows this range for entrée, appetizer and dessert:

Inexpensive: Up to $15
Moderate: $15 to 25
Expensive: $25 to $35
Very Expensive: Over $35

Credit card abbreviations are: AE, American Express; CB, Carte Blanche; D, Discover; DC, Diner's Club; MC, MasterCard; V, Visa.

Restaurants are arranged, more or less, in geographical order south from the Choptank River.

Hurlock, Md.

SUICIDE BRIDGE RESTAURANT
410-943-4775.
6304 Suicide Bridge Road, Hurlock.
Open: Apr.–Dec., Tues.–Sun.; Jan.–Mar., Thurs.–Sun.
Price: Moderate to Expensive.
Cuisine: Seafood/Eastern Shore.
Serving: L, D.
Credit Cards: D, MC, V.
Reservations: For parties of 10 or more only.
Handicap Access: Yes.

Located on a sturdy bit of rare upland in Dorchester County, this remote and surprisingly contemporary waterside restaurant offers decks, open stone and pine dining rooms, and a well-priced menu. Look for seafood and old-fashioned Eastern Shore cuisine kicked up, as Emeril says, a notch. Filet mignon or veal marsala aren't forgotten, but seafood lovers go for fried oysters or the Marylander, an English muffin topped with plenty of thinly sliced ham, a tomato, and lump crab mounded higher than any hummock on the Shore. The owner also operates Kool Ice and Seafood in Cambridge, a great local seafood market, which brings the fabulous seafood-to-price ratio into focus. The eighty-foot reproduction paddlewheeler *Dorothy-Megan* departs from here (call for departure times, including meal trips), and boaters ducking in from the Choptank River will find dockage. As for the legend of Suicide Bridge: The restaurant tells of devastated locals who flung themselves from this remote locale. A local explained that the bridge's natural curve, to accommodate the channel, had something to do with drivers failing to stay on course.

Hoopers Island, Md.

OLD SALTY'S RESTAURANT AND GIFT SHOP
410-397-3752.
2560 Hoopers Island Rd., Fishing Creek on the island.
From Cambridge, Rte. 16 West to Rte. 335 South to Hoopers Island.
Open: Thurs.–Sun.
Price: Inexpensive to Moderate.
Cuisine: American Homestyle.
Serving: L, D.
Credit Cards: No (personal checks OK).

Although the name "Old Salty's" suggests a roadside dive, it's not. And even through you drive through miles of winding marshland to reach this former schoolhouse, make reservations — especially if you want one of the evening's specials, which sell out early. Prime rib, a two-inch slab that could easily feed two people, is served on Fridays and Saturdays. Try the broiled flounder stuffed with crabmeat, or the crab cakes, which are puffy and lightly fried to golden. Each entrée comes with homemade yeast rolls and two vegetables. The mashed potatoes are rich, whipped and home-made. The candied yams are delicately sweetened with a brown-sugar syrup that doesn't overwhelm the natural flavor of the sweet potatoes. Afterward,

Reservations:
  Recommended, especially
  for the specials.
Handicap Access: No.
Restrictions: No alcohol
  served (OK to bring your
  own bottle of wine).
Special Features: Small
  video room for restless
  kids.

visit the antique and gift shop, with bargain-priced semi-antique ceramic pieces and hand-knitted clothing.

Taylor's Island, Md.

**TAYLOR'S ISLAND
GENERAL STORE**
410-221-2911, 410-397-3585.
Rte. 16, approx. 17 miles
  west of Cambridge.
Open: Daily, year-round.
Price: Inexpensive.
Cuisine: American.
Serving: B, L, D.
Credit Cards: No; cash only.
Reservations: No.
Handicap Access: No.

Scenic Bay byways meander through quaint towns or fingers of land poking into various bodies of water. Whether you're searching for historic sites, a place to launch your boat, or just exploring, eventually you'll end up on a road like Rte. 16, at a stopping place like Taylor's Island General Store — where you'll enter another time zone. A high-ceilinged general store is in the big front room, its shelves stocked with basic groceries and fishing tackle. The restaurant/bar area has Naugahyde booths, leaned-on tables that slope slightly, authentic advertising signs that must be worth a small fortune, as well as a view of the water alongside this fishing community's marina. The menu is fairly basic, but everything is fresh and portions are large. Whether you want breakfast before launching, beer and a sandwich at dusk, or a crab cake sandwich in between, Taylor's Island General Store will do nicely.

Salisbury, Md

CACTUS TAVERNA
410-548-1254.
2420 N. Salisbury Blvd.
  (Rte. 13).
Open: Daily.
Price: Inexpensive to
  Moderate.
Cuisine: Multiethnic,
  including Mexican and
  Mediterranean.
Serving: D.
Credit Cards: AE, D, MC, V.
Reservations: Yes.
Handicap Access: Yes.

First impressions of cactus, sombreros and bull-fighting pictures might brand Cactus Taverna a Mexican restaurant, but don't be fooled. Fajitas and tacos are joined on the menu by Peruvian-style ceviche (marinated fish), Spanish paella, robust roasted lamb shank, and delicately sauced grilled fish. The Lomo Saltado, sauteed beef and vegetables in a Peruvian brown sauce, is outstanding, as is the appetizer of breaded alligator chunks with raspberry jalapeno sauce. Hear out the specials; they're always intriguing. Sangria and white wine margaritas are nice accompaniments to whatever food you choose, and delicate flan and fried ice cream are fine finishes. Festive, busy, and featuring nightly live entertainment, this is an excellent place to linger over a meal with friends, or to bring small children.

Fruitland, Md.

ADAM'S THE PLACE FOR RIBS
410-749-6961.
219 N. Fruitland Blvd.
(Business Rte. 13, south of Salisbury).
Open: Daily.
Price: Inexpensive to Moderate.
Cuisine: American.
Serving: L, D.
Credit Cards: AE, MC, V.
Reservations: Yes.
Handicap Access: Yes.

If you're tooling along Rte. 50 and looking to stop someplace casual and comfortable for a bite, this edition of the Bay-area rib chain is the place. Civic club plaques and lacrosse championship photos from nearby Salisbury University mark this as a local hangout, but the massive blue marlin in the lobby, the signed NASCAR tire, and decorations evoking the great American outdoors make this a suitable dining spot for anyone. Adams' best charms aren't on the walls, though; they're on the menu. Signature baby back ribs are succulent and nicely sauced, served as a full or small rack. Less hearty appetites might enjoy the chopped barbecued beef brisket sandwich or pulled pork barbecue, both inexpensive and served with a pile of fries. Fans of Buffalo-style chicken wings will want to try Adam's version, hot and sweet at the same time. Located just a few feet off the highway, this is a perfect refueling stop for travelers.

Delmar, Del.

THE OLD MILL CRAB HOUSE & RESTAURANT
302-846-2808.
Rte. 54 West and Waller Rd.
(just over the Maryland state line).
Open: Daily, Mar.–Nov.
Price: Moderate to Expensive.
Cuisine: Seafood.
Serving: D.
Credit Cards: AE, D, MC, V.
Reservations: Available (and recommended) for parties of 10 or more Mon.–Thurs. only; otherwise, reservations are not accepted.
Handicap Access: Yes.

The Old Mill is where the locals go to eat crabs. They don't take reservations, unless you're one of a group of ten or more, and even then, only on weeknights. People come back anyway, to sit family-style at paper-covered tables, often with folks they've never met. The dining room is casual but substantial, with real knotty pine wood and stained-glass light fixtures. The all-you-can-eat crab special is priced according to the season, and for $4 more you can get unlimited steamed shrimp, too. Crabs are always local and good-sized, and come with fried hush puppies, fried chicken, fried clam strips, fried shrimp crisps, coleslaw, and steamed corn on the cob. Surely that's enough. A kids' menu (10 and under) starts with fries with a hot dog or drumstick with fries for $2.25.

Snow Hill, Md.

DAVID'S (A BISTRO!)
410-632-2811.
208 W. Green St., Snow Hill.
Open: Daily except Sun.
Price: Inexpensive to
  Expensive.
Cuisine: French/New
  American.
Serving: L Mon.–Sat.; D
  Thurs.–Sat.
Credit Cards: AE, MC, V.
Reservations:
  Recommended,
  especially on weekends.
Handicap Access: Yes.
Special Features: Live jazz
  and acoustic
  entertainment
  occasionally on
  weekends.

David's, a fine Salisbury restaurant that recently moved to Snow Hill, serves up classic French and New American food in a lively, earthy atmosphere at surprisingly reasonable prices. Expect flavorful, impeccably prepared food with fresh ingredients and unfussy attention to detail. The creamy, sherry-laced crab brie soup, thickened with brie, is a must-have. The portobello mushroom crepe is exquisite, with sautéed mushrooms, garlic, and shallots glazed with balsamic vinegar, wrapped in a crepe and covered with a red wine sauce. The buttery-textured salmon in champagne butter sauce is excellent. Grilled boneless duck breast, marinated in teriyaki, garlic, and ginger, is tender, and the flavors balance perfectly with the raspberry merlot sauce. Desserts, like the salad dressings and everything else, are made on the premises and landed Chef David recognition in the May 2000 issue of *Gourmet* magazine. Try the crème brûlée or the raspberry truffle, a pairing of raspberry sorbet and vanilla ice cream covered in a white- and dark-chocolate zebra-like shell in a drizzle of fresh berry sauce. The wine list is good, the martinis fun.

Berlin, Md.

THE ATLANTIC HOTEL
410-641-0189.
2 N. Main St.
Open: Daily.
Price: Inexpensive to Very
  Expensive.
Cuisine: American.
Serving: D only in dining
  room; L, D and late bar at
  Drummer's Café.
Credit Cards: AE, MC, V.
Reservations: Required in
  dining room; not
  accepted in café.
Handicap Access: Yes.

This is one of the Eastern Shore's nicest restaurants, with a dining room menu that draws the local elite alongside visitors to nearby Ocean City looking for something better than beach fare. The dining room is the place to go for special occasions, with its elegant atmosphere and discreet but flawless service. Caesar salad is prepared tableside, and a crab phyllo of sweet crabmeat, creamy cheese and crispy pastry is delectable. Main dishes include salmon bouillabaisse, the hotel's famous goat cheese-topped rack of lamb, and two large lump crab cakes. Diners are welcome to request menu variations to suit their tastes. Across the hall, in the Drummer's Café, the atmosphere is more relaxed but still special, and the expected menu of sandwiches and appetizers is supplemented with entrées like Cornish game hens and pecan-crusted catfish. The café features a piano player and singing waiter Wed.–Sat. in-season, weekends year-round. Additional seating is available on the hotel's front porch in the summertime. Be sure to save room for the Atlantic Hotel's desserts, all made on the premises.

Crisfield, Md.

WATERMEN'S INN
410-968-2119.
901 W. Main St.
Open: Wed.–Sun.
Price: Moderate.
Cuisine: American.
Serving: L, D (Also B on
   Sat. & Sun.).
Credit Cards: AE, D, MC, V.
Reservations:
   Recommended on
   weekends.
Handicap Access: Yes.
Special Features: Separate
   bar; early-bird specials;
   children's menu.

Sure, you can get soft-shell crabs at Watermen's; after all, Crisfield is the heart of watermen's territory. In fact, this is where local watermen go for a nice dinner out. But instead of typical soft-shells fried and flattened between slices of white bread, here, they're sauteed in butter with tomatoes and artichoke hearts. Last week they were, anyway — Chef Brian Julian changes the menu frequently so he and his many regulars will stay interested. And they do. This tiny, cheerful spot is always full of local couples, families, and well-heeled tourists. Your meal starts with fine bread: thick slabs of pumpernickel, raisin, and such. Appetizers include wild mushroom strudel or a waterman's mainstay, hot crab dip with a garlic overlay. A cream-based mushroom concoction is rolled within phyllo dough and baked. Nothing quite beats the earthy, rich taste of wild mushrooms, and the filet mignon with smoked wild mushroom sauce is irresistible. Another good choice is sauteed shrimp with grape tomatoes and scallions on lemon-pepper fettuccine in a garlic butter sauce. Some desserts are made on-site by co-owner Kathy Berezoski. Others — like the kajillion-layered Smith Island cake and the Smith Island banana cake — are made by "a local lady." The Smith Island banana cake is the stuff of legend. "On Smith Island," we overheard, "it used to be you were either asked to church, or asked to leave." Though islanders have lightened up a little, the cake hasn't lightened up at all: the cake and its frosting are outrageous, with the whipped cream on the side tame in comparison.

**SIDE STREET SEAFOOD
   RESTAURANT**
410-968-2442.
204 S. Tenth St.
Open: May–Sept. 30; hours
   vary.
Price: Inexpensive to
   Expensive.
Cuisine: Seafood/Eastern
   Shore.
Serving: L, D.
Credit Cards: D, MC, V.

This much-favored crab-crackin' deck serves its dozens aboard a bushel basket top, a twist on the usual serving devices: the red plastic serving tray or the endangered beer flat. The tops must be leftover from the baskets serving as light shades here, a typical Bay Country signal that you are in the right place for no-muss, no-fuss Eastern Shore seafood. Although "butter" is served in a plastic squirt bottle, we'll forgive that because Side Street is so honest about what a dozen fat medium-sized crabs cost late in a scarce season: a good $10 less (at

Reservations:
  Recommended.
Handicap Access: No.

least) from spots farther up the Bay. The restaurant sits atop a seafood market and looks out from a block or two away over Crisfield's hard-working harbor.

Wattsville, Va.

RAY'S SHANTY
757-824-3429.
Rte. 175.
Open: Thurs.–Sun.
Price: Inexpensive to
  Moderate.
Cuisine: Seafood.
Serving: L, D.
Credit Cards: MC, V.
Reservations: No.
Handicap Access: Yes.

Locals and tourists flock to this landmark on the road into Chincoteague from U.S. Rte. 13 primarily to eat steamed or fried shrimp, done just right, sold all you can eat or by the pound. Be prepared for a crowd on summer weekends. Landlubbers: steak's on the menu, too.

Onancock, Va.

**BIZZOTTO'S GALLERY-
  CAFFE**
757-787-3103.
41 Market St.
Open: Daily; closed Sun.
  Oct.–May.
Price: Moderate.
Cuisine: American with
  European overtones.
Serving: L, D.
Credit Cards: MC, V.
Reservations:
  Recommended.
Handicap Access: Yes.
Special Features: Craft and
  art gallery.

Perpetual window-shoppers, we were first drawn to Bizzotto's by the craftwork on display in the front windows. Then we saw the small menu, a hand-lettered sign created anew each day. When quality is this high, who needs more selections? The black bean soup with butter, cumin, cilantro, and diced bits of meat and red onion bursts with enough flavor to please the most passionate gourmet. Mussels Aljillo is positively fragrant with its tarragon, butter, garlic, and wine sauce. The chicken marsala, another seductive wonder, is tender enough to cut with a fork. Grilled salmon is presented in many ways, including with a wild and zingy red pepper and pineapple sauce — some great afterburn, yet not too strong for the fish. Veggies and sides, like the entrées, are rich, refreshing, homemade, and beautifully presented. Ditto for desserts such as pumpkin flan and a Bailey's cheesecake. Service is very good; ambience, lovely. Located in a historic storefront, the Caffe's high ceilings — crowned with pressed tin — complement hardwood floors and subdued lighting trained on artwork. The high-quality crafts, including jewelry, glass, and ceramics, as well as leather work by owner Miguel Bizzotto, are a pleasure to view during dinner. At Bizzotto's, the details rule; added up, they create a marvelous whole.

Cape Charles, Va.

HARBOR GRILL AND TAKE-OUT MARKET
757-331-3005.
203 Mason Ave.
Open: Mon.–Sat. in-season; Tues.–Sat. off-season.
Price: Inexpensive to Moderate.
Cuisine: Seafood/fancy luncheon sandwiches.
Serving: L, D.
Credit Cards: AE, MC, V.
Reservations: Strongly recommended for dinner.
Handicap Access: Yes.

With its sidewalk tables, this main street café offers an adventurous menu and a touch of sophistication that draw locals and visitors alike. The steamed harbor pot with veggies, clams, oysters, and shrimp remains on the menu, although dinner selections change daily. Chesapeake favorites include steamed clams and oysters. For something new, try the unusual three-cheese salad on tender greens with apples, onions, figs, and pecans in a delicious lemon poppy-seed dressing. Good desserts, interesting wines, and gourmet takeout.

Capeville, Va.

STING RAY'S RESTAURANT AT THE CAPE CENTER
757-331-2505.
26507 Lankford Hwy.
Open: Year-round, 5:30am–9pm during the week, until 9:30pm on weekends.
Price: Inexpensive.
Cuisine: Seafood/ American.
Serving: B, L, D.
Credit Cards: D, DC, MC, V.
Reservations: No.
Handicap Access: Yes.

The raft of 18-wheelers parked outside says truck stop. But make your way past the bags of smoked bacon, tacky lighthouse paperweights, and T-shirts to find a gourmet-quality restaurant with an interesting wine list, its menu posted on the blackboard wall. Order anything at all, from a hearty breakfast of eggs, grits, and country bacon (under $3) to a dinner of crabmeat-stuffed flounder. You'll be well pleased. If you dare, for dessert order Death By Chocolate, a flamboyantly large creation consisting of a fudgy brownie covered with a huge mound of vanilla ice cream, slathered with whipped cream. It's enough for two — or more. Some people say the Tennessee bread pudding with bourbon sauce is the best they've ever had. Or, more modestly, order the sweet potato pie with Damson plum sauce and discover why this establishment is packed with locals and tourists all year long. Chef Ray Haynie recently sold the place, but is staying on to make sure the cooking doesn't change. *Southern Living* devoted an article a few years ago to "Chez Exxon" and the fine food in this unusual establishment. Look for Eastern Shore seafood and very fresh produce in season.

FOOD PURVEYORS

CAFÉS/GIFT SHOPS

Globe Theatre (410-641-0784; 12 Broad St., Berlin, Md.) Coffee bar, deli, and wine shop located inside a historic theater offering live concerts, regional art, gourmet food items, books, cards, and gifts. Open daily; coffee served until closing, deli closes one hour earlier.

Bailey's Café (410-632-3700; 104 W. Green St., Snow Hill, Md.) A convenient sandwich lunch stop while visiting one of the many downtown antique stores.

Allegro (410-651-4520; 11775 Somerset Ave., Princess Anne, Md.) Good coffee, pastries, sandwiches, and soups, with a nice selection of gifts and tables so you can rest awhile.

Garden Café and Gifts (757-331-1600; 233 Mason Ave., Cape Charles, Va.) Cheerful café and enclosed courtyard offers crab salad with walnuts and Mandarin oranges topped with raspberry vinaigrette, or meatloaf with mashed potatoes, or grilled pork chops — all at very reasonable prices.

ICE CREAM

Muller's Old Fashioned Ice Cream Parlor (757-336-5894; 4034 Main St., Chincoteague, Va.) Fresh fruit sundaes, malts, ice-cream sodas, frozen yogurt, and yes, ice-cream cones, in an 1875 house with authentic Victorian atmosphere. Open 11–11 in summer.

PRODUCE MARKETS

How Sweet It Is (410-742-8600; southbound Rte. 13 at Somerset-Wicomico county line, Eden, Md.) Open daily from late spring until late Oct. for local strawberries, super-sweet white corn, giant pumpkins, and other produce, plants, flowers, and seafood.

Jack's Market (410-749-1889; westbound Rte. 50 near Hebron, Md.) Produce, preserves, candy, flags, country crafts, and an impressive array of lawn ornaments. Open daily 8–8 in summer; shorter hours rest of year.

SEAFOOD & FISH MARKETS

Kool Ice and Seafood Co. (800-437-2417, 410-228-2300; 110 Washington St., Cambridge, Md.) Dorchester-caught crabs and a fine selection of oysters, clams, lobsters, and fresh fish. Shipping available.

SPECIALTY MARKETS

Blue Crab Bay Co. (800-221-2722, 757-787-3602; 29368 Atlantic Dr., Melfa, Va.) Phenomenally successful specialty food maker with a worldwide mail-order business and a retail shop; features clam sauce for pasta, Sting Ray Bloody Mary mix, herb blends, gift baskets, and gifts. Open year-round, Mon.–Fri. 9–5, Sat. 10–4.

Healthful Habits (410-749-1997; 720 E. College Ave., Ste. 7, Salisbury, Md.) Organic and natural foods, herbs, and specialty items. Closed Sat.

Hotstuff! (757-336-3118; 6273 Cropper St., Chincoteague, Va.) Five hundred types of hot sauce, along with other hot stuff — including a carbonated fruit drink with chile pepper extract called Loco.

Pony Tails (757-336-6688; 7011 Maddox Blvd., Chincoteague, Va.) Saltwater taffy playfully named for the famous ponies is made daily in-season in an antique cutting and wrapping machine that you can see in operation. Closed Sun.

CULTURE

CINEMA

Cambridge Premiere Cinemas (410-221-8688) in Dorchester Square in *Cambridge* offers first-run films. Down *Salisbury* way, movies play at **Hoyts Cinema 10** (410-543-0902, 410-543-0905) in the Centre At Salisbury. *Chincoteague Island*'s **Roxy** (757-336-6301) at 4074 Main St. shows "Misty of Chincoteague" during Pony Penning for free; Misty stamped her hoofprints outside in concrete. Nightly movies in summer; four nights a week in the winter.

DANCE

Salisbury, Md.

SALISBURY UNIVERSITY DANCE COMPANY
410-543-6353.
Season: Mid-Nov.–Apr.
Tickets: 13 and older $9, seniors $7, 12 and under free.

A professionally run company at Salisbury University presents two productions. Performances in Holloway Hall Auditorium feature student choreography in the Fall Showcase; the Spring Concert highlights faculty, selected student works, and notable guest choreographers.

GALLERIES

Cambridge, Md.

**DORCHESTER ARTS
CENTER**
410-228-7782.
120 High St.
Open: Mon.–Sat. 10–2.

Housed on Cambridge's historic High St., the center showcases area artists and offers classes, weekend fine arts workshops, and performances. Gallery exhibits change monthly. The last Sun. in Sept. usually brings the Dorchester Showcase, a street festival with entertainment, a juried fine arts and crafts show, and food the length of High St.

Salisbury, Md.

**ART INSTITUTE &
GALLERY**
410-546-4748.
212 W. Main St.
Open: Mon.–Fri. 11–4.

The beautifully renovated former Woolworth's store on the Downtown Plaza is now called The Gallery Building, and among its fine tenants is The Art Institute & Gallery, showing works by local, Mid-Atlantic, and national artists in all media. National juried, professional, emerging, and solo artists shows. Fine gift shop.

**SALISBURY
UNIVERSITY**
410-548-2547.
Office of Cultural Affairs
and Museum Programs,
Fulton Hall.
Open: Tues.–Fri. 10–5,
Sat.–Sun. Noon–4 during
school year; otherwise,
call ahead.

Works by Joan Miró, Ansel Adams, Edward Hopper, and Yousuf Karsh have hung in this small but ambitious gallery in the university's fine arts building. Also here: student and faculty works, and pieces by regional folk crafters and artists. The Atrium Gallery, in the Guerrieri University Center, houses smaller exhibits and a gift shop; open Tues.–Fri. 11–4, Sat.–Sun. Noon–4.

HISTORIC BUILDINGS & SITES

Cambridge, Md.

**MEREDITH HOUSE AND
NEILD MUSEUM**
410-228-7953.
902 LaGrange Ave.
Open: Thurs.–Sat. 10–3.
Admission: Free to individ-
uals; large groups and bus
tours $2 per person.

This circa 1760 Georgian house with Greek Revival ornamentation is noted for Flemish bond brickwork and its devotion to county history — particularly the local contribution to the governorship. Seven Maryland governors resided in Dorchester County, including Thomas Holiday Hicks, who managed to suppress the state's strong secessionist element to maintain Maryland's Union status. The Neild Museum stands on the grounds, displaying the sickles, scythes, and yokes of the Lower Shore's yeoman class, as well as maritime tools used in oystering and crabbing. Look also — believe it or not — for memorabilia from one-time Cambridge resident Annie Oakley. The Goldsborough Stable (circa 1790), moved from a nearby site, houses a transportation exhibit, and a colonial-style herb garden stands near the Neild Museum.

Lloyds, Md.

SPOCOTT WINDMILL
410-228-7090.
Rte. 343.
Open: Daily 10–5.
Admission: Donations
   accepted.

One of the region's most enduring residents, the great boatbuilder James B. "Mr. Jim" Richardson took it upon himself to build this reproduction of a windmill destroyed here during the blizzard of 1888. "Mr. Jim," who passed away in 1989, kept his master builder's wooden boat workshop at his LeCompte Creek boatyard. His windmill, the only post windmill in Maryland, commemorates the twenty-three post windmills that once towered over the marshy countryside. Also open to the public are a colonial tenant house (circa 1800) and the 1870 one-room schoolhouse called Castle Haven. Lloyd's Country Store Museum opens on special occasions or by appt.

Princess Anne, Md.

TEACKLE MANSION
410-651-2238.
www.teacklemansion.org.
Mansion St.
Open: Apr.–mid-Dec.,
   Wed., Sat., Sun. 1–3 or
   call for appt.
Admission: Adults $4,
   children under 12 free.

Back before the Manokin River became so shallow, its deep water encouraged ships to travel upriver. Plantations and ports thrived along its banks, and Teackle Mansion is a well-preserved holdover. Probably the best example of neoclassical architecture on the Lower Eastern Shore, the 1801 mansion dominates the town with its 200 feet of pink brick and stylish symmetry. Built by Littleton Dennis Teackle, who moved from the Eastern Shore of Virginia with his wife, the house boasts his and her dressing rooms on either side of a central high ceiling, multiple stairways, and entrances by river or land. Outside are beautiful gardens. Teackle fell on hard times and lost nearly everything in the depression of 1821, but his mansion stands as testament to his one-time wealth.

Salisbury, Md.

**PEMBERTON
   HISTORICAL PARK**
410-860-0447, Wicomico
   Heritage Centre; 410-742-
   1741, Pemberton Hall.

One of the oldest brick gambrel-roofed houses in the Chesapeake region, Pemberton Hall was built in 1741 for Col. Isaac Handy, a plantation owner and shipping magnate who helped found

Pemberton Dr., about 2 mi. S.W. of Rte. 349 & U.S. 50.
Open: Pemberton Hall: May 1–Oct. 1, Wed., Thurs., Fri., & Sun. 2–4 and by appt.
Admission: Donations accepted.

what would become the city of Salisbury. Col. Handy's home is the centerpiece of a museum complex (operated by a handful of groups) that includes nearby Wicomico Heritage Centre, designed to resemble a colonial tobacco barn. This is also the Wicomico Historical Society headquarters, with a permanent collection of local historic memorabilia and rotating exhibits. Don't skip Pemberton even if the museums are closed. The park features several miles of nature trails through woods and along the Wicomico River. Lovely picnic area. Handy's Wharf here is the oldest wharf in Maryland.

Snow Hill, Md.

FURNACE TOWN HISTORIC SITE
410-632-2032.
3816 Old Furnace Rd., off Rte. 12 (Snow Hill Rd.).
Open: Apr. 1–Oct. 31, daily 11–5.
Admission: Adults $4, over 60 $3.50, 18 mos. through high school $1.50; does not include entry to special events.

The imposing Nassawango Iron Furnace looms over a swamp, a forest, and a small collection of buildings at this quiet echo of the bustling nineteenth-century village that once stood here. From 1832 to 1847, thousands of people lived and worked around this thirty-five-foot-high hot blast furnace in the forest, digging up bog ore and smelting it into pig iron. Around its remnants stand recreations of the old ways, including broom making, printing, blacksmithing, weaving, and gardening. Visit the museum, a gift shop, a picnic area, exhibit buildings, and many nature trails and boardwalks over the Nassawango Cypress Swamp. Come midweek to have the place to yourself, or visit when Furnace Town hosts one of many festivals, including the Worcester County Fair in Aug. and the Chesapeake Celtic Festival in Oct. A captivating spot.

Onancock, Va.

KERR PLACE
757-787-8012.
www.kerrplace.org.
69 Market St.
Open: Tues.–Sat. 10–4; closed Jan. & Feb.
Admission: Adults $4, children under 18 free.

Prosperous merchant John Shepherd Ker (original spelling) had the Kerr Place built in 1799 in this port town. His elegant Federal house has been restored as a museum and home to the Eastern Shore of Virginia Historical Society. Through period decorative arts, furnishings, and exhibits, Kerr Place gives visitors a glimpse of eighteenth-century Virginia plantation life. Bus tours welcome.

MUSEUMS

Cambridge, Md.

RICHARDSON MARITIME MUSEUM
410-221-1871.
401 High St..
Open: Apr.–Oct., Wed., Sat., Sun. 1–4 or by appt.
Admission: Donations accepted.

Dorchester County's maritime history and the accomplishments of Capt. Jim Richardson are celebrated in this former bank. Richardson built the Spocott Windmill and the re-created *Dove*, docked at St. Mary's City. Also here: a waterman's dock exhibit, workboat models built by their captains, examples of Bay boats, and a photo history on the building of the skipjack *Nathan of Dorchester*. Folks at the museum are knowledgeable and eager to educate visitors.

Crisfield, Md.

J. MILLARD TAWES MUSEUM
410-968-2501.
Somers Cove Marina at end of Ninth Street.
Open: Year-round; Mon.–Sat. 9–6, Sun. Noon–4:30 in-season; call for winter hours.
Admission: $2.50.

A Maryland governor and a famous pair of decoy-carving brothers hailed from Crisfield, along with a rakish late-nineteenth-century oyster gold rush. Catch a glimpse of it all at the J. Millard Tawes Museum, named for the Crisfielder who ascended to the Statehouse in the 1960s. The museum shows Native American artifacts, cultural and natural history of the Tangier Sound area, crabbing and oystering tools, and plenty on the mid-twentieth century's famed decoy-carving brothers, Lem and Steve Ward. The carvers lived and worked "Down Neck" on Sackertown Road, and their workshop is open by appt.

Salisbury, Md.

WARD MUSEUM OF WILDFOWL ART
410-742-4988.
www.wardmuseum.org.
Schumaker Dr.
Open: Mon.–Sat. 10–5, Sun. Noon–5.
Admission: Adults $7, seniors (62 yrs.+) $5, students $3. Family and other discounts available.

The legendary Ward brothers, Lem and Steve, elevated the pragmatic craft of decoy carving to artistry, and their name symbolizes the decoy-as-art-form. This may be the region's most extensive public collection of antique decoys, and a lovely showcase of wildfowl art. The evolution of decoys is traced from the Native American's functional, twisted-reed renderings to the latest lifelike wooden sculpture. View the personal collection of the Ward brothers, including their own favorites among their earliest and latest efforts. The Ward Foundation, established in 1968, hosts the annual World Championship

Carving Competition and a wildlife art exhibition and sale. The building and gift shop are on a four-acre site overlooking a pond. A must-see for decoy-lovers.

Snow Hill, Md.

JULIA A. PURNELL MUSEUM
410-632-0515.
208 W. Market St.
Open: Apr.–Oct., Tues.–Sat. 10–4, Sun. Noon–4; tours by appt. in off-season.
Admission: Adults $2, children $.50.

At the age of eighty-five, Snow Hill's Julia A. Purnell (1843-1943) fell and broke her hip. In place of her formerly active lifestyle, she completed more than 2,000 needlepoint pieces, documenting Worcester County's homes, churches, and gardens. Her son, William, was so proud that he opened a museum of her work one year before her death. The place is informally known as "the attic of Worcester County" for all of the everyday items and artifacts here. About five percent of what is on display is the lady's original work.

Parksley, Va.

EASTERN SHORE RAILWAY MUSEUM
757-665-RAIL.
18468 Dunne Ave.
Open: Mon.–Sat. 10–4, Sun. 1–4; closed Wed. Nov.–Mar.
Admission: Adults $2, children free.

Before the Chesapeake Bay Bridge and the Chesapeake Bay Bridge-Tunnel opened the Delmarva Peninsula for travelers coming by car, most people and goods came from the north — by train. Stop by to check out exhibits that include an antique auto display, to which collectors loan unusual classics. The museum celebrates the area's rail heritage with model trains, railcars, and railway artifacts, including a turn-of-the-century crossing guard shanty.

PERFORMING ARTS

Salisbury, Md.

COMMUNITY PLAYERS OF SALISBURY
410-543-ARTS.
Tickets: Prices vary.

Noteworthy among the Lower Eastern Shore's community troupes, this one is over sixty years old. Performances at locations in and around Salisbury usually include a musical, a drama, and a comedy each season.

SALISBURY SYMPHONY ORCHESTRA
410-543-ARTS, 410-548-5587.

Based at Salisbury University and funded by the Salisbury Wicomico Arts Council and the Maryland State Arts Council, the symphony performs a holiday performance in Dec. and a spring

Season: Winter and spring concerts; occasional special events.
Tickets: Prices vary; call for information.

concert in May, both in Holloway Hall Auditorium. The SSO membership includes faculty, students, professionals, and community players, and enjoys enthusiastic regional support.

**SALISBURY
UNIVERSITY
PERFORMANCES**
410-543-6030.
Tickets: Prices vary.

The theater stage in Fulton Hall hosts drama, comedy, and musical productions put on by faculty and students throughout the school year. Call for schedule.

SEASONAL EVENTS & FESTIVALS

Cambridge, Md.

You'll find no more hard-core celebration of Lower Eastern Shore country living than the **National Outdoor Show** deep in Dorchester County's marshland. You can compete in the muskrat-cooking contest if you bring your own 'rat, but stand back and watch the natives vie for honors in the muskrat-skinning contest. Come Fri. night to watch the crowning of Miss Outdoors; Sat. brings exhibits, local crafters, food, and log-sawing races. The Outdoor Show is held the last full weekend in Feb. South Dorchester School in Golden Hill; take Rte. 16 S. from Cambridge; at Church Creek, go left on Rte. 335; proceed two miles to school on the left. Contact: 800-522-TOUR, 410-397-8535; www.tourdorchester. Admission fee.

Cape Charles, Va.

Hawks, songbirds, and other migratory birds cruising down the eastern seaboard en route to the tropics converge on the Delmarva Peninsula's southern tip every fall, an annual event now celebrated by the **Eastern Birding Festival**. One recent year, alert birders spotted 175 different species at Kiptopeke State Park, Sunset Beach, and other sites in and around Cape Charles. Also sighted here: Mississippi kites, a white-faced ibis, a rare cave swallow, and a swallowtail. Experts consider the Cape Charles area, where the Bay and Atlantic Ocean meet, to be one of the East Coast's best bird-watching spots. Held in early Oct., the festival features tours, presentations, exhibits, and workshops. Contact: 757-787-2460 or www.intercom.net/nop/esvabirding.

Chincoteague, Va.

Legend says Assateague Island's wild ponies descended from Spanish horses that swam ashore after a long-ago shipwreck. Scientists suggest that they descended from ponies that grazed on this outpost island in centuries

An Authentic Day on the Bay

Maybe it's the name — "watermen" instead of "fishermen" — or maybe it's the romance of the disappearing skipjacks, old wooden rake-masted sailboats aboard which watermen still dredge (in Maryland, by law) for the depleted Chesapeake oyster. Whatever it is, you'll hear plenty about both in your Bay travels. For a taste of the real thing, head deep into the Lower Shore over Labor Day for two authentic hometown festivals. **The National Hard Crab Derby & Fair** in Crisfield (800-782-3913, 410-968-2500), launched in 1948, gives top billing to the annual Governor's Cup Race — a crab race with entrants from as far away as Hawaii. But we'd direct you to the workboat docking contest on Sunday at the Crisfield City Dock. Smith and Tangier Island watermen come over to participate, and, as one fellow from down Virginia tidewater way remarked, the locals have the thing locked up. Also featured: a crab-picking contest, a crab-cooking contest, the "Miss Crustacean" beauty contest, a carnival with rides and games, a 10K race, a parade, live entertainment, and, of course, plenty of excellent eating. It all ends Sunday night with fireworks over the harbor. Overlapping this weekend is the Deal Island-Chance Lions Club's **Skipjack Races and Land Festival**, with rides, food (great soft-shell crabs), Smith Island skiff races, carnival games for the kids and "Little Miss Skipjack." The **Labor Day Skipack Races**, dating to 1959, take place out in Tangier Sound, and the thin crowd watching from the beach is both a joy and a crime. Who's out there supporting Maryland's historic state boats? Since this is an easy daytrip from Annapolis or the St. Michaels area, or even Washington or Baltimore, come see the real deal, the skipjacks that go out oystering. Bring binoculars, and catch another round of workboat docking contests. Contact: 800-521-9189.

past. Whatever the case, Chincoteague's annual **Pony Penning** is an event to see. Always held the last Wed. and Thurs. of July, it starts when members of the sponsoring Chincoteague Volunteer Fire Co. corral the ponies and send them swimming across the channel from Chincoteague National Wildlife Refuge to town. The swim attracts tens of thousands of visitors; for a more intimate experience, preview the ponies in a corral on Assateague Island on Tues. or stick around for the return swim on Fri. The pony sale, held on Thurs., is a long tradition to raise funds for the fire company, which officially owns the ponies in Virginia. A firemen's festival stretches for a couple of weeks leading up to Pony Penning. If you (and your ten-year-old Misty-loving daughter, granddaughter, or niece) really want to attend, make reservations months in advance. Contact: Chincoteague Chamber of Commerce, 757-336-6161; 6733 Maddox Blvd., Chincoteague Island, VA 23336.

The **Chincoteague Oyster Festival** is held on the Sat. of Columbus Day weekend, one of the Bay's hottest tickets for serious oyster lovers. Famed Chincoteague oysters are slightly salty and considered by many to be the Bay's best. Tales tell of folks who get clear to Chincoteague on festival weekend only to find it sold out, so call the island's Chamber of Commerce (757-336-3131) to get your advance tickets. Held at the Maddox Family Campground.

David Trozzo

Oyster shucking at the popular Chincoteague Oyster Festival.

The **Eastern Shore Seafood Festival** is the Virginia Shore biggie, with so much good food and socializing (including state politicians) that bus tours include it on their spring itineraries. Steamed and raw clams, steamed and raw oysters, fried fish, and plenty of sides, including French-fried sweet potatoes, fill the menu at this all-you-can-eat feast. Held the first Wed. in May at Tom's Cove Campground in Chincoteague. Call the Eastern Shore Chamber of Commerce (757-787-2460) for tickets

TOURS

The "Moses of her people," Harriet Tubman led more than 300 slaves north to freedom along the Underground Railroad. See her birthplace and take a tour through Dorchester County's rich African-American history via **HomeTowne Tours**, operated by the Harriet Tubman Organization, 410-228-0401. Headquartered in the Underground Railroad Gift Shop with its little museum, 424 Race St., _**Cambridge**_.

If you're interested in the architecture of these little Lower Eastern Shore towns, don't overlook their walking tour brochures; most are easily available at local businesses or visitor centers.

Hidden well behind the dull commercial strip along U.S. 50 stands _**Cambridge**_, with abundant history, beautiful waterfront, and fine old buildings. The seventeenth-century Nanticoke River town of _**Vienna**_ also is worth a ramble to see the town's cemeteries, homes, and churches. Both are located in

Dorchester County. In Worcester County, stroll **_Snow Hill_**, a peaceful town of brick sidewalks on the banks of the Pocomoke River, known for its numerous historic houses. None are open to the public, but you can admire the architecture from the street. Contact: Julia A. Purnell Museum, 410-632-0515. Historic **_Princess Anne_**, established in 1733 and named in honor of the daughter of King George II, is distinguished by many Federal-style and mid-to-late Victorian houses and commercial structures from the turn of the last century. Note the oldest dwelling in the town, the circa 1755 William Geddes House, and the circa 1850 Boxwood Garden on Somerset Avenue. At the southern tip of the Eastern Shore stands **_Cape Charles, Va._**, laid out around 1883 as the southern terminus of a new railroad line that soon linked this remote town with New York and Philadelphia. Most of the once-thriving town, devastated by the Depression and the end of ferry and steamer service, now is a historic district. The fine homes of its heyday remain intact, and the town is poised to become a golfing destination with a regional and national draw.

RECREATION

Climb to the top of Assateague Lighthouse at Chincoteague National Wildlife Refuge, Virginia.

David Trozzo

BASEBALL

The **Delmarva Shorebirds** play at Arthur W. Perdue Stadium (named for poultry magnate Frank Perdue's father) at 6400 Hobbs Road, just east of Rte. 50 and the Rte. 13 bypass in Salisbury. The Class-A Baltimore Orioles affiliate draws a crowd, particularly for Saturday fireworks in the summer Contact: 410-219-3112 for tickets; www.theshorebirds.com for tickets/directions/schedules, etc.

BICYCLING

David Trozzo

Bike riding along Bay Country's flat terrain is a favored pastime.

The flat country roads through marshland or near the Chesapeake's many rivers (or even the Bay itself) make bicycling a favored visitors' pastime on the Lower Eastern Shore. In *Dorchester County*, the **Blackwater National Wildlife Refuge** means flat roads through spookily stunning swamps, where one easily catches sight of bald eagles or hawks. For a map of recommended cycling trails, contact: Dorchester Tourism, 800-522-TOUR; 203 Sunburst Hwy., Cambridge, MD 21613. Farther south, in *Worcester County*, relatively light traffic makes for some good riding on the main roads. (Beware the overcast day, however; heavy traffic often heads inland from the Atlantic beaches.) A good ride starts in **_Berlin_**, a historic town with some interesting shops and a couple of worthy cafés, then heads down Evans Road. Wander west along Bethards Road to Patey Woods Road, then pedal down Basket Switch Road to Taylor Road. This route is about nineteen miles and brings you to a good choice of destinations: go left and head to Chincoteague Bay, or go another four miles west to **_Snow Hill_**, a pretty, historic town along the Pocomoke River.

Serious cyclists should mark their calendars for early Oct., when the 100-mile **Sea Gull Century** takes more than 6,200 riders from Salisbury to the ocean and back in the largest century in the East. Call months ahead for a registration packet (410-548-2772). Hundreds of riders also enjoy the **Between the Waters Bike Tour** on the fourth Sat. in Oct., which takes advantage of the unique position of Virginia's Eastern Shore between the Bay and Atlantic Ocean. Rides from 25 (popular with families) to 100 miles wind past scenic stops overlooking the Bay, seaside marshes, and the barrier islands protecting the Shore from the sometimes stormy Atlantic. For info, call Citizens for a Better Eastern Shore at 757-678-7157, or check www.cbes.org.

LOCAL CYCLING SHOPS

BikeSport (410-543-BIKE; 1013 S. Salisbury Blvd., Salisbury, Md.).
Salisbury Schwinn Cyclery & Fitness Center (410-546-4747; 1404 S. Salisbury Blvd., Salisbury, Md.).

BIRD-WATCHING

Bald eagles thrive on the Lower Eastern Shore, where the parade of good birding sites equals the long list of parks and recreational areas along the lower portion of the Delmarva Peninsula. At the top of the Lower Shore, spot the largest nesting population of bald eagles north of Florida at **Blackwater National Wildlife Refuge** (410-228-2677; 2145 Key Wallace Dr., Cambridge, MD 21613) in Maryland's Dorchester County, with its endless (and we do mean endless — make sure your gas tank's full) winding roads through marshland and open water. Other possible sightings: yellow-billed cuckoos, Bewick's wrens, and northern goshawks down toward nearby Hooper's Island. It's said birds there include 15,000 ducks, 35,000 wintering geese, and hawks by the dozen. At Assateague Island, along the Atlantic, **Chincoteague National Wildlife Refuge** (757-336-6122; 8065 Beach Rd./P.O. Box 62, Chincoteague, VA 23336) carries a blue-ribbon birding reputation. Piping plovers scratch their near-invisible nests in the sand, and man-made lagoons offer a natural stopover on the Atlantic Flyway for skimmers and coots. At Delmarva Peninsula's end, **Kiptopeake State Park** (757-331-2267; 3540 Kiptopeke Drive, Cape Charles, VA 23310) has a hawk observatory and is home to the Eastern Shore Birding Festival each Oct. Depending on the time of year, see gannets and oystercatchers on the man-made islands along the seventeen-mile long **Chesapeake Bay Bridge-Tunnel** (757-331-2960; www.cbbt.com; Dept. 001; P.O. Box 111, Cape Charles, VA 23310), where, with permission, you can stop. Take your binoculars to any of the parks listed under "Natural Areas" later in this section and look for all these avians.

BOATING

CRUISES & EXCURSION BOATS

Cambridge Lady **Cruises** (410-221-0776; Corner of Gay St. and Court Ln., Cambridge, MD 21613) Tour the Choptank River aboard this yacht.

The Nathan of Dorchester (410-228-7141; Dorchester Skipjack Committee, 526 Poplar St., Cambridge, MD 21613) Two-hour sunset cruises offered aboard this sailing ambassador, a skipjack built in 1994. Cruises on the second and fourth Sat. in June, July & Aug. Reasonable fees.

Capt. Dan II (Purchase tickets through The Refuge Motor Inn, 757-336-5511; 7058 Maddox Blvd., Chincoteague Island, VA 23336) Guided tours of the Chincoteague/Assateague area. Mid-June–Sept.; adults $12, children $7. Reservations needed. Daily fishing trips, too.

MARINAS

Cambridge Municipal Yacht Basin (410-228-4031; Mills and Water Sts., Cambridge, MD 21613) Located on the Choptank River. City-run docks next to Historic District in area known as Port of Cambridge. Borrow a bicycle to get around ashore. 196 slips.

Somers Cove Marina (800-967-3474, 410-968-0925; Broadway and Water Sts., Crisfield, MD 21817) Huge marina right in town on Tangier Sound. 450 slips. Owned & operated by the state Dept. of Natural Resources.

Port of Salisbury Marina (410-548-3176; 506 W. Main St., Salisbury, MD 21801) Full-service marina; free bike use. 112 slips. Located downtown on the Wicomico River.

CANOEING & KAKAKING

Water trails have arrived to direct paddlers through some of the Lower Shore's many waterways, and these maps and guides are more than a fun convenience. In areas such as Dorchester County's wild marshes — known as "Maryland's Everglades" – they're a godsend. Make no mistake, it's easy to get lost in these winding waterways. Obtain the guides to the Island Creek Trail and Transquaking River Loop Trail in the **Fishing Bay Wildlife Management Area** by contacting Regional Coordinator, MD DNR — Nature Tourism Program, Janes Island State Park, 26280 Alfred J. Lawson Drive,

Crisfield, MD 21817; DESMITH@dnr.state.md.us. Or contact: Director, Dorchester County Dept. of Tourism, 2 Rose Hill Place, Cambridge, MD 21613; 800-522-TOUR; info@tourdorchester.org. In addition, three color-coded trails of 8, 3.5, and 2.5 miles were being developed at deadline for the **Blackwater National Wildlife Refuge.** Call the refuge (410-228-2677) for info on purchasing the guides for a nominal fee. The refuge's waterways are only open during spring and summer.

Assateague Island National Seashore (410-641-3030; 7206 National Seashore Lane, Berlin, MD 21811) A good place to canoe in the marshes and interior bays, although wildlife protection regulations must be followed. Canoe rentals.

Janes Island State Park (410-968-1803; 26280 Alfred J. Lawson Drive, Crisfield, MD 21817) Color-coded water trails meander through the island "guts," or channels of this wonderful lowland paradise. Backcountry camping.

Pocomoke River Canoe Co. (410-632-3971; 312 N. Washington St., Snow Hill, MD 21863) Knowledgeable outfitter rents canoes and kayaks every day, Apr.–Dec. Well worth contacting even if you're going out with your own canoe. Company will drive you and your rented canoe to a put-in; canoe back to Snow Hill.

Tangier Sound Outfitters (410-968-1803; 27582 Farm Market Rd., Hopewell, MD 21838) Delivers to Janes Island State Park, conducts other trips, including full-moon tours. Knowledgeable help navigating the area's wild and winding creeks.

Southern Expedition (888-62-MARSH; www.sekayak.com; 32218 Lankford Hwy., Cape Charles, VA 23310) Kayak tours, from two hours to several days. You can even go fishing or clamming. Specialty tours; located just north of the Chesapeake Bay Bridge-Tunnel entrance.

Survival Products (410-543-1244; 1116 N. Salisbury Blvd., Salisbury, MD 21801) Canoe and kayak rentals from knowledgeable people who cruise area waterways.

FAMILY FUN

Science- and math-loving kids who grew up to be engineers and scientists started the **Excel Interactive Science Museum** (410-546-2168; 2300 N. Salisbury Blvd., Salisbury, Md.) in their spare time to interest a new generation of children in topics like rocketry, physics, and electronics. The museum in the Centre at Salisbury is filled with fun and educational, interactive exhibits. Classes; call for schedule. Open Noon–5 during the season; call for off-season hours.

An outpost of the **NASA Goddard Space Flight Center**, the **NASA Wallops Flight Center** (757-824-2298; Rte. 175, Wallops Island, Va.) is a beehive of scientific activity closed to the public. You can get a glimpse, however, at the goings-on in the visitor center, which features programs like model rocket launches and exhibits on spaceflight past, present, and future. Gift shop, picnic area. Free. Open Mar. –June and Sept. –Nov., Thurs.–Mon. 10–4; July 4–Labor Day, daily 10–4. Open in the winter for group tours by appt. **[closed since 9/11; still closed at presstime.]**

Hailed as one of America's finest small zoos, the **Salisbury Zoological Park** (410-548-3188) has distinctive and well-conceived animal exhibits. Free, but donations welcome. Picnicking area and concessions outside. Open year-round. Located E. of Rte. 13 and S. of U.S. 50.

FISHING

Fish or crab along the piers that once were the Choptank River Bridge. Alongside Rte. 50 and the current bridge in Cambridge. Contact: 410-820-1668.

Boat Ramps

Check Chapter Nine, *Information,* for information on obtaining free maps of Bay access. Also,

Fishing Bay Wildlife Management Area (410-376-3236), **Taylor's Island Wildlife Management Area** (410-376-3236), **Janes Island State Park** (410-968-1565), and **Taylor's Island Boat Ramp** (410-221-2911).

Charter Boats & Head Boats

Chincoteague, Va.

The **Chincoteague Island Charterboat Association** publishes a brochure listing licensed professional charter boats. Contact: Chincoteague Chamber of Commerce, 757-336-6161; P.O. Box 258, Chincoteague, VA 23336. Or visit www.chincoteague.com and click on the link for the Charterboat Assoc.

Chincoteague Hunting & Fishing Center (888-231-4868; 3801 Main St., Chincoteague, VA 23336) The bays behind Virginia's barrier islands offer good fishing. In-season, catch spot, flounder, and other edible species in sheltered waters; offshore, albacore, tuna, and shark are among the favorites. Guided waterfowl hunting with Capt. Pete Wallace is also available.

Crisfield, Md.

For the best list of the many charter boat captains operating out of the fine fishing grounds near Crisfield, contact Somers Cove Marina, operated by the **Maryland Dept. of Natural Resources**: 800-967-3474, 410 968-0925; P.O. Box 67, Crisfield, MD 21817.

Wachapreague, Va.

Wachapreague Hotel & Marina (757-789-3222; 17 Atlantic Ave./P.O. Box 360, Wachapreague, VA 23480) Bottom and deep-sea fishing from several charter craft. They also rent small boats. The Island House Restaurant is located by the marina.

GOLF

Bay Creek Golf Club (757-331-9000; 2037 Old Cape Charles Rd., Cape Charles, Va.) 18 holes, open to the public. An Arnold Palmer-designed course, surrounded by farms and woodlands, is bounded by the Chesapeake Bay and Plantation Creek.

Captain's Cove Golf and Yacht Club (757-824-3465; www.captscove.com; 3370 Captain's Corridor, Greenbackville, Va.) 9 holes; public. Open water on four holes.

Eastern Shore Yacht and Country Club (757-787-1525; 14421 Country Club Rd., Melfa, Va.) 18 holes. Private club available to visitors by reciprocal agreement with other clubs. Reservations required. Open year-round.

Nassawango Country Club (410-632-3114, 410-957-2262; www.nassawango.com; 3940 Nassawango Rd., Snow Hill, Md.) 18 holes; semiprivate championship course. Pro shop.

Northampton Country Club (757-331-1180; P.O. Box 267, Cape Charles, Va.) 18 holes; public.

Nutters Crossing Golf Course & Driving Range (410-860-4653; 30287 Southampton Bridge Rd., Salisbury, Md.) 18 holes; semiprivate.

Winter Quarters Golf Course (410-957-1171; 355 Winter Quarters Dr., Pocomoke City, Md.) Public. Two separate sets of tees make a front nine and a back nine.

NATURAL AREAS: STATE AND NATIONAL PARKS AND REFUGES

Many expansive natural areas are the best part of the Lower Eastern Shore, where the endangered Delmarva fox squirrel resides and the exotic Sika deer can be spotted. These large dog-sized deer got loose decades back, and provide intriguing animal sightings alongside plentiful bird species.

A couple of notes while perusing the natural area entries:

Assateague Island stretches 37 miles between the Atlantic Ocean and Sinepuxent Bay, and straddles the Maryland-Virginia border amid one state park and two federal ones: Assateague State Park and Assateague National Seashore in Maryland, and Chincoteague Wildlife Refuge in Virginia. Among the 44 mammal species seen there are bottlenose dolphins offshore and gray

David Trozzo

Sika deer, related to the elk, were introduced to the Lower Eastern Shore decades ago and are often seen in the wild.

seals, born here at the southernmost point in their birthing range. Birds include northern bobwhites, least bitterns and indigo buntings, and more exotic seagoing passersby. This is also home to the famous wild ponies, most likely descended from horses grazed here by seventeenth-century settlers. They're generally mild-tempered and will leave you alone if you leave them alone.

Dorchester County's lowlands, known as "Maryland's Everglades," include nearly 55,000 acres between Blackwater National Wildlife Refuge and Fishing Bay Wildlife Management Area, located farther southwest and more remote. Bald eagles nest through this marshy territory, with its flat roads that make for great cycling, and creeks for paddling — but do take advantage of the new waterways guides and maps (see "Canoeing and Kayaking"). It's not hard to get turned around and lost in these marshy creeks; pay attention to winds and tides.

Assateague Island National Seashore (410-641-3030; 7206 National Seashore Lane, Berlin, MD 21811) Thirteen miles of barrier island. Backcountry camping (register for a backcountry permit), stretches of isolated beach, shellfishing, crabbing, canoeing, hiking. Spectacular seashore wilderness.

Assateague State Park (410-641-2120; 7307 Stephen Decatur Hwy., Berlin, MD 21811) This is the "beachier" portion of this 37-mi.-long barrier island, and by that we mean the part with sun worshipers, families, and beachcombers. Two miles of ocean beach.

Blackwater National Wildlife Refuge (410-228-2677; 2145 Key Wallace Dr., Cambridge, MD 21613) 26,000 acres south of the tiny town of Church Creek include lowlands, forests, flat roads for cycling and short walks, creeks for paddling. Birds aplenty, and you might even glimpse the Chesapeake's endangered Delmarva fox squirrel, its territory reduced to just four counties. Take the six-mile driving loop, with its minimal cost for cars and cyclists. Good nature center.

Chincoteague National Wildlife Refuge (757-336-6122; P.O. Box 62, Chincoteague, VA 23336) Ten miles of beach. Bird-watcher central.

Eastern Shore of Virginia National Wildlife Refuge (757-331-2760; 5003 Hallett Circle, Cape Charles, VA 23310) 750 acres; visitor center with wildlife exhibits. Located just above the Chesapeake Bay Bridge-Tunnel.

Fishing Bay Wildlife Management Area (410-376-3236; S. of Cambridge off Bestpitch Ferry Rd.) 28,000 acres located 14 mi. south of Cambridge. Paddlers' trails (see "Canoeing and Kayaking" for water trail info), boating, in-season hunting, bird-watching, and boat ramp. Habitat supports the Asian Sika deer, bald eagles, osprey, shorebirds, and waterfowl. Fishing and crabbing. The WMA's entrance is down Bestpitch Ferry Rd. Get there by going south on Bucktown Rd from Cambridge.

Janes Island State Park (410-968-1565; 26280 Alfred Lawson Dr., Crisfield, MD 21817) One of the coolest parks anywhere, comprised of a mainland portion with marina, camping, and cabins, and a 2,800-acre island. Rent a small boat to explore the guts of the island, marked into water trails. Boasts a lovely beach on the island's far side along Tangier Sound.

Kiptopeke State Park (757-331-2267; 3540 Kiptopeke Drive, Cape Charles, VA 23310) Birders' paradise, 3 mi. N. of the Chesapeake Bay Bridge-Tunnel. Trails through upland or boardwalks through the sand, beach for swimming Mem. Day-Labor Day, camping, boat launch, lighted fishing pier. Nominal fees; 450 acres, handicap access.

Pocomoke River State Park (410-632-2566; 3461 Worcester Hwy., Snow Hill, MD 21863) Two discrete areas make up this intriguing, 14,753-acre park, with its cypress swamp and blackwater paddling on the Pocomoke River. Milburn Landing is 7 mi. N. of Pocomoke City; Shad Landing is 3.5 mi. S. of Snow Hill. Cabins, boating, paddling, fishing, walking trails, swimming pool at Shad Landing.

SPORTING GOODS & CAMPING SUPPLY STORES

Assateague Market (410-641-3380; Stephen Decatur Hwy./Rte. 611, Berlin, Md.) From doughnuts to camping supplies.

Buck's Place (410-641-4177; 11848 Assateague Rd., Berlin, Md.) Groceries, bait and tackle, souvenirs, takeout subs and seafood.

Dave's Sport Shop (410-742-2454; 23701 Nanticoke Rd., Quantico, Md.) Everything for the hunting season, deep in the heart of Wicomico's best hunting territory.

Tommy's Sporting Goods (800-236-0295, 410-228 3658; U.S. 50, 300 Sunburst Hwy., Cambridge, Md.) Serving hunters and fishers for more than forty years.

SWIMMING

Assateague State Park (410-641-2120; 7307 Stephen Decatur Hwy., Berlin, Md.) Ocean swimming and beachcombing. Also check the Assateague Island National Seashore next door (410-641-3030).

Dorchester County Pool (410-221-8535; 106 Virginia Ave., Cambridge, Md.) Where the locals go, especially after the sea nettles arrive in the Bay. Adults $2, students $1. Open daily, Mem. Day–Labor Day.

Great Marsh (contact Dorchester County Tourism, 410-228-1000; Somerset Ave., Cambridge, Md.) Boat ramp, picnicking, pier, and playground. Swim in early summer, before the sea nettles arrive.

Pocomoke River State Park (410-632-2566; 3461 Worcester Hwy., Snow Hill, Md.) Swimming pool at the Shad Landing portion of the park, 3.5 mi. S. of Snow Hill.

TENNIS

Salisbury City Park (410-548-3188; E. Main St. & S. Park Dr., Salisbury, Md.) A few public courts located in a tree-shaded park featuring a summer bandstand. Sun. concerts, playground, paddleboats, and riverside walking trails.

NEARBY RECREATION

Ocean City, Md.

Ocean City is within easy driving distance of Salisbury, Berlin, and Assateague — in fact, many would consider these a natural and worthy grouping of travel destinations. The sprawling beach town's major attraction is a ten-mile-long strip of golden sand that often is packed blanket-to-blanket on summer weekends. Over the years, the government has engaged in a lengthy (some might say fruitless) battle to keep the beach in place by importing tons of sand from offshore to replace what nature and the ocean wash away.

None of that worries visitors much, though. They come for the sun, the sand, the carnival rides, the "World Famous French Fries" sold on the boardwalk, the shops and restaurants, and the fishing, including the big-money, white marlin tournament.

You can reach Ocean City, or "O.C.," from the Bay via three routes. Enter the oldest, southernmost part of the city on U.S. 50 from the west; or take Md. 90 across the Assawoman Bay Bridge to what has become the city's center; or from the Delaware beach towns of Rehoboth, Dewey, and Bethany Beaches to the north (highly worthwhile destinations) via Rte. 1, which becomes the Coastal Hwy., Md. Rte. 528, once you reach Maryland. Contact: Ocean City Convention and Visitors Bureau, 800-OC-OCEAN, 410-289-8181; www.oc ocean.com, www.ocean-city.com.

SHOPPING

Due to the spread-out geography of the Lower Shore, we've arranged shops in geographical order. Antique lovers, in particular, will find other shops besides these we suggest along the area's multitudinous wandering back roads.

ANTIQUES

Newspaper sculpture artist Mama Girl, Mary Onley, runs her Painter, Va., gallery Tues.–Sat.

David Trozzo

Packing House Antiques (410-221-8544; 411 Dorchester Ave., Cambridge, Md.) Recommended by those in the know; more than 100 dealers.

Bay Country Antique Co-Op (410-228-3112; 415 Dorchester Ave., Cambridge, Md.) Furniture and collectibles.

Holly Ridge Antiques (410-742-4392; 1411 S. Salisbury Blvd./Business Rte. 13, Salisbury, Md.) Specializing in eighteenth- and nineteenth-century furniture and accessories under the strict 100-year rule. Appraisals and refinishing.

Town Center Antiques (410-629-1895; 1 N. Main St., Berlin, Md.) Antiques and collectibles from more than seventy dealers are spread out in a big building. Snack bar.

Deadrise Enterprises, Inc. (757-787-2077; 3 & 5 North St., Onancock, Va.) Antiques and collectibles from nauticals to books, furniture, and more. Upstairs find the North Street Gallery, showcase for local and regional fine art.

Charmar's Antiques (757-331-1488; 211 Mason Ave., Cape Charles, Va.) A little bit of everything, from a fine old Eastern Shore corner cupboard to antique tools. Rare items such as scythes and snaths are common. (For the uninitiated: a snath is the handle of a scythe.) Unusual and stylish lamps. Ask owner Margaret Carlson to open the small museum next door, where she's set up a complete store as it might have looked in 1900 — filled with the owner's collection and many local artifacts.

BOOKS

Atlantic Book Warehouse (410-548-9177; 2734 N. Salisbury Blvd., Salisbury, Md.) This cavernous bookstore offers a huge selection of books discounted anywhere from ten to eighty percent. Plus calendars and magazines.

Henrietta's Attic (800-546-3744, 410-546-3700; 205 Maryland Ave., Salisbury, Md.) Aisles of antique and used books, watched over by bookseller Henrietta Moore and the bookstore's cat. Browse as long as you like, or ask for Moore's help. Collectibles, glassware, china, and genealogy materials are also packed into this "anything goes" place.

GALLERIES

Salisbury, Md.

The Gallery (410-742-2880; 625 S. Division St.) Regional works in all media. Regular one-person shows and an annual Christmas exhibit featuring four or five local artists. Custom framing and a range of gifts and crafts, such as decoys and shorebirds.

Salisbury Art & Framing (410-742-9522; 213 North Blvd., Waverly Plaza) Works by local and nationally known artists, from Eastern Shore seascapes to abstracts. Prints, pottery, handmade jewelry, and custom framing.

Chincoteague, Va.

Island Arts (757-336-5856; 6196 Maddox Blvd.) Owned by local artist Nancy West, the shop specializes in woven clothing and unique jewelry offerings. Also featured are Nancy's oil paintings, which have been exhibited nation-wide.

Lott's Arts & Things (757-336-5773; 4281 Main St.) Features the silk screens of Welsh native Hal Lott, known to poster collectors for his works commemo-rating Pony Penning.

Onley, Va.

Turner Sculpture & Gallery (757-787-2818; Rte. 13) The drive down Rte. 13 gets a little long through Virginia's Eastern Shore until you stumble upon this fascinating foundry and art display, where Dr. William Turner and his son David, both nationally known wildlife sculptors, create great blue herons, beluga whales, and even a draft horse. Their wildlife sculptures are displayed throughout the U.S. While you're there, take a look at the magnifi-cent glass-topped dining and coffee tables offered for sale. The glass is sup-ported underneath by an interconnected bounty of sculpted undersea creatures, including silver-plated fish. If you're lucky, they'll show you the foundry on a day when bronze is being poured.

CRAFT GALLERIES, GIFT SHOPS & GENERAL STORES

Cambridge, Md.

Bay Country Shop (410-221-0700; 2709 Ocean Gateway Dr.) Rustic and goose-oriented Shore items; lots of gifts.

Salisbury, Md.

The Country House (410-749-1959; 805 E. Main St.) At 16,000 square feet, it's the largest country store in the East and an overwhelming experience for nonshoppers who accidentally wander inside. Everything country that you could hope to find, plus collectibles, Christmas, and candles, and more for the kitchen, bath, and household.

Chincoteague, Va.

Marsha Carter Gifts (757-336-3404; 6351 Cropper St.) A boutique filled with handcrafted products like hand-blown glass, quilts, embroidered cotton lingerie, paintings, jewelry, pottery, and local bird carvings.

Onancock, Va.

Herbal Instincts (757-787-7071; 141 Market St.) Owner/gardener Christine Porco stocks everything imaginable in the herb line, scented vinegars, oils, teas, soaps, and dried herbs in bulk. Handcrafted items include teapots and cups. Organic food items also available, including fresh vegetables in season. Her elegant bungalow-turned-showroom is graced outdoors with colorful perennial borders and, naturally, herbs.

Cape Charles, Va.

Watson's Hardware (757-331-3979; 225 Mason Ave.) Step back in time and browse though this hardware store that looks like a hardware store must have looked in Cape Charles' early days. Owner Chip Watson stocks most anything hardware, plus all manner of fascinating implements for opening tasty local crabs, oysters, and clams. Find metal openwork clamming buckets to try your luck at digging the elusive mollusk, or simply to use for decoration. On fair-weather days, find the owner sitting out on the sidewalk greeting passersby from a wooden rocking chair.

JEWELRY

Princess Anne, Md.

Bailey White Jewelers (410-651-3073; 30400 Mt. Vernon Rd.) Probably the best handcrafted, Bay-inspired Chesapeake designs around, including a crab, a skipjack, and an oyster with its pearl, each rendered in 14K or 18K gold.

Salisbury, Md.

G.B. Heron & Co. (410-860-0221; 1307 Mt. Hermon Rd.) Custom-designed jewelry and a store full of high-quality pieces. Watch and jewelry repair by goldsmiths on the premises.

Kuhn's Jewelers (410-742-3256; 107 Downtown Plaza) Diamonds and watches; full line of quality jewelry from a company established in 1853.

MALLS & OUTLETS

Crisfield, Md.

Carvel Hall Factory Outlet (410-968-0500; Md. 413) Along with the famous Carvel Hall cutlery (serious crab pickers use their knives), there's crystal, silver, pewter, and housewares, much available at discount prices.

Salisbury, Md.

The Centre at Salisbury (410-548-1600; 2300 N. Salisbury Blvd.) A major mall with four anchor department stores (Boscov's, The Hecht Co., Sears , and J.C. Penney), dozens of small stores, a food court, and a ten-screen cinema.

Salisbury Pewter Outlet (800-824-4708, 410-546-1188; 2411 N. Salisbury Blvd.) Watch workers create the pewterware pieces sold in this "outlet," where first-quality pieces sell for less. Save more with seconds, factory overruns, and discontinued items. Factory tours by appt. Salisbury Pewter has a second outlet on U.S. 50 in Easton (410-820-5202).

SMITH & TANGIER ISLANDS

The boat schedule rules the time visitors can ramble on Chesapeake's last two inhabited islands, the remote crabbers' communities on Smith and Tangier Islands. Promptly, the boats depart Crisfield, and just as promptly, the boats pull away from the island docks, 12 miles away, to return to the mainland. It was therefore impossible to partake of the evening activity inside the fire station at Ewell, the largest of Smith Island's three towns, on that day not long before Thanksgiving. Through the open door stood tables covered with layer cakes, perhaps as many as 12 thinly sliced layers each. These were the offerings for the evening ahead here, where neighbor seems to know neighbor as most siblings know their own. On the mail boat back to Crisfield, a fellow headed home for the holiday carried a box. Inside was a cake — a Smith Island layer cake, delicious evidence of a place where folks do things their own way.

Visitors will quickly discover so. There's no ATM, credit cards are generally not accepted, and the islands, bastions of an old-style brand of Methodism, are dry. For many, an afternoon peek at island life via the tourist ferries may be enough. Those who stay overnight will notice how many island businesses open and close as the tour boats arrive and depart.

Part of a chain of shifting, sinking, eroding islands, Tangier and Smith lie only three feet above sea level — and sometimes far less. On tiny Tangier in Virginia, half of the three-mile island is livable; the rest is tidal marsh. Smith Island, in Maryland, is far larger, at eight-by-four miles. The two share similarities, but they are different, too. Erosion threatens their lives, and precarious crab populations, their livelihoods. After a day or two cycling the narrow streets where Smith Islanders barely bother with license plates and Tangier's residents prefer golf carts, where grave markers in front yards repeat old names like Crockett or Parks, outsiders know this isn't a place where folks forget their past. Folks say the islanders' distinct accents descend from Elizabethan forebears who settled here.

The white crab shanties that once lined Smith's "Big Gut," the channel into Ewell, have come ashore, to the crab co-op in Tylerton, but still line the channel into Tangier. Just as you wouldn't waltz into a businessman's private office without an invitation, so a visit to a Tangierman's crab shack comes at his behest. Shallow wooden "tanks" line the interior, filled with crabs moving toward a molt, the final step toward producing a valuable soft-shell.

Three towns are settled on Smith Island: Ewell, Rhode's Point, and Tylerton. Tylerton, reputedly the most devout of the three, is separated from the island proper by a channel, and therefore accessed only by boat. It is fronted by docks, with well-kept houses and its own general store. A bike ride out the main road from Ewell, the island's largest town, takes visitors into tiny Rhode's Point, teetering on the edge of the Bay. Upon finishing a ride, only a stop at Ewell's nearly century-old general store, called Ruke's for the current owner of more than 40 years, will do. Order up soft-shell crabs; you won't find finer in any city's fancy restaurants. And, of course, indulge in a slice of Smith Island layer cake.

Tangier hosts just one town, but visitors immediately see its bustle. Golf carts manned by tour guides line up to meet the tour boats, and a "tour buggy" tour is quick but thorough, covering the gift shops lining the main road, the school, and the Methodist church. On poles are boxes akin to bluebird boxes, which open to those honest enough to plop in a couple of quarters in exchange for an island recipe, often featuring crab.

Travelers should understand this is not Chesapeake Disneyland. Tangier has a bit more for tourists to do, including a three-mile beach on the far side of the island, and an airstrip. But Smith draws its own, such as those who want to visit the fabled Ruke's or the lovely Inn of Silent Music in Tylerton, operated by former city dwellers who understand why you're ga-ga over being this far from civilization.

Finally, three practical bits of advice: Although the islands are dry, most innkeepers don't mind if you bring your own libation — but do be discreet, as some islanders dislike drink. Ask your innkeeper. Also, Nantucket and the Vineyard these are not. Much of what you're looking for is clustered near the dock where your boat lands. If you have any questions at all, just ask somebody. And remember: no ATM, and credit cards generally not accepted.

GETTING TO THE ISLANDS

Take a seasonal ferry for tourists, or travel year-round as the locals do, via mail boat, usually from Crisfield. Be sure to leave enough time to secure parking — especially if you're going to be gone overnight — and note that not all boats departing Crisfield leave from the City Dock. For general questions about the boats and their schedules, contact the Somerset County tourism office: 800-521-9189.

Smith Island Cruises (410-425-2771; 4065 Smith Island Rd., Ewell, MD 21824) Sail from Crisfield's Somers Cove Marina aboard the *Capt. Tyler* daily from Mem. Day through Oct. A la carte lunch available at The Bayside Inn at the dock in Ewell. Departs Crisfield 12:30pm, returns 5:15pm; adults $20. The company also operates a ferry from Point Lookout, Md., at the mouth of the Potomac River in St. Mary's County. (See "A South-of-Town Outing" in the "Annapolis" chapter.)

Tangier Island Cruises (410-968-2338; 1001 W. Main St., Crisfield, MD 21817) The *Steven Thomas* runs daily, May 15–Oct., departing from 10th Street in Crisfield at 12:30pm, returning about 5:15pm; adults $20, kids 7–12 $10. The company also operates the *Capt. Rudy Thomas*, which takes overnight cruises to Norfolk and Portsmouth May–Oct. Reservations required for that trip, which costs $275 per couple, including lodging.

Tangier-Onancock Cruises (757-891-2240; 16458 W. Ridge Rd., Tangier, VA 23440) Leave daily from Onancock's historic Hopkins & Bro. General Store aboard the sixty-five-foot *Capt. Eulice* at 10am. A guide meets passengers at the Tangier dock for a tour. Lunch at the famed Hilda Crockett's Chesapeake House for an added fee, if you like. Runs Mem. Day weekend–Oct. 15; adults $20, kids 6–11 $10. Group reservations required.

Mail Boat to Tangier Island (757-891-2240; 16458 W. Ridge Rd., Tangier, VA 23440) The *Courtney Thomas* travels year-round between Crisfield and Tangier. Leaves Crisfield Mon.–Sat. at noon, and Tangier at 8am. From Nov.–mid-Apr., the boat adds a Sunday afternoon run, leaving Tangier at 3 and Crisfield at 4. $10 one-way.

Mail Boats to Smith Island. The *Captain Jason* (410-425-4471 or -5931; 4132 Smith Island Rd., Ewell, MD 21822) travels year-round to Ewell, then Tylerton, on Smith Island, with one of the Capt. Laird brothers at the helm. Departs the island at approximately 7am and 4pm, and Crisfield daily at 12:30. Or depart Crisfield at 12:30 aboard the *Island Belle II* (410-968-1118; 20915 Somers Rd., Ewell, MD 21824) with Capt. Otis Tyler. Tickets cost about $15; might be small added charges for freight, such as bikes.

WHAT TO DO, WHERE TO STAY

SMITH ISLAND

Rent golf carts ($8 for a half-hour, $10 for an hour) or bikes ($5 for an hour, $3 for a half-hour, $5 for an hour), or climb aboard a bus at the Bayside Inn at the dock in Ewell for a $2 tour of the island. This is also home to a seasonal gift shop.

Orient yourself to island life at the **Smith Island Center** (410-425-3351: www.intercom.net/npo/smithisland; Caleb Jones Rd. at the county dock), which tells of boats, oystering, crabbing, and Joshua Thomas, the famed "Parson of the Islands" who spread Methodism here in the nineteenth century. Open May–Oct., Noon–4 daily; Wed. & Sat. during the winter.

Food and Lodgings

Bayside Inn Restaurant (410-425-2771, 4065 Smith Island Road, at the dock in Ewell) Open Mem. Day–Oct., 11–4 daily; buffet, family-style, or a la carte. Serves up big platters of Southern-style seafood, as well as famed Smith Island layer cake — up to ten layers! — for dessert.

Ewell Tide Inn (410-425-2141; 4063 Tyler Rd., Ewell, MD 21824) Reasonably priced and very homey, in a former captain's house. Four rooms share two baths. Owner Steve Eades also runs the nearby Driftwood General Store, and can arrange fishing charters. Continental breakfast. Inexpensive. AE, D, MC, V. No handicap access.

Inn of Silent Music (410-425-3541; www.innofsilentmusic.com; 2955 Tylerton Rd., Tylerton, MD 21866) Hosts Sharryl Lindberg and LeRoy Friesen escaped D.C. several years ago and set up this unique waterside getaway, with its soft colors and peaceful ambiance. Three guest rooms come with private baths. Gourmet breakfast, and a seafood dinner for an added $15 (plan on it — there's no dinner-hour restaurant in Tylerton). Canoes, a kayak, bikes. Moderate to Expensive. No credit cards. No handicap access.

Ruke's (410-425-2311; 20840 Caleb Jones Rd., Ewell) Don't pass up the opportunity to eat a crab cake or soft-shell crab here at Ewell's general store, with its tables in back. Locals drop by for coffee and you can find a few antiques and ice cream, too. Open summer 11–5, then again from 6–8 daily; winter, 11–4 Mon.–Sat. Inexpensive to Moderate.

TANGIER ISLAND

Full-, half-day or hourly golf cart rentals, $35, $25, or $10, from **RB Rentals** (757-891-2240). The office is located at the dock. While you're there, ask about the 6pm eco-cruise if you're staying overnight. Rent a bike from the **Waterfront Restaurant** (757-891-2248; 16125 Main St.), $3 for up to three hours, $5 all day, or $7 overnight.

Clamber aboard a "tour buggy," one of the fleet of golf carts lined up to meet the tour boats. There's no need to make arrangements in advance. Also, there's a three-mile beach on the far side of the island.

Six gift shops reside along Tangier's main street, where visitors can buy T-shirts, shell wreaths, homemade afghans, and the like. Hours, like all things here, conform to the island's schedule: about 10:30–4 during the spring-fall season when tour boats operate, then they re-open about 7pm so the townspeople can shop. Distinguishing itself from the competition is **Sandy's** (757-891-2367; 16227 Main St.), with a small museum in the back of the store. Among the treasures: notebooks bulging with newspaper clippings of Tangier events, such as engagements, going back generations. Shelves are full of island memorabilia.

Food and Lodging

Hilda Crockett's Chesapeake House (757-891-2331; Main St./P.O. Box 194, Tangier Island, VA 23440) Family-style seating at this island institution, 11:30–6. Breakfast is available 7–9. Also, there's lodging here from Apr. 15–Oct. 15. No credit cards, alcohol, or pets.

Fisherman's Corner Restaurant (757-891-2900; 4419 Long Bridge Rd.) Operated by four island woman, this homey restaurant serves the kind of indigenous seafood people travel a lifetime to find. Soft-shells, crab claws, crab cakes, and other Bay specialties available. Moderate. Open May–Sept.

Shirley's Bay View Inn (757-891-2396; www.tangierisland.net; P.O. Box 183, Tangier Island, VA 23440) Walking distance to gift shops, beach, and airport. In all, eight "cottages" in back and two rooms in the main house. One cottage is a "family" cottage, with one full, one twin and bunk beds. Enjoy the gazebo and look out toward the water. Full breakfast. Moderate. No credit cards or pets.

Sunset Inn (757-891-2535; www.tangieronline.com/rooms.htm; 16650 W. Ridge Rd., Tangier Island, VA 23440) Next to the beach. Ten rooms in an addition, four inside the house with decks overlooking the water. Fridges in room. Continental breakfast. Inexpensive. No credit cards; personal checks OK.

Waterfront Restaurant (757-891-2248; 16125 Main St.) You can't miss it, right where the tour boats come in. Sit on the deck and eat soft-shells and crab cakes. Open May–Oct. Inexpensive to Moderate.

CHAPTER SEVEN
Virginia's Treasures: Rambling Roads and a Home to History
NORTHERN NECK/MIDDLE PENINSULA

David Trozzo

Boathouses line the Bay's many rivers and creeks.

The side street along Urbanna Creek deadends near a marina. We pulled in, parked, and figured we'd find out where to rent a boat at the marina. A fellow pulling a red wagon carrying a battered old battery trundled by. "Excuse us," we said. "Do you know where we can rent a small boat around here for tomorrow?" He stopped. "Well," he responded. "I have a paddleboat you could borrow."

For all of their abundant U.S. history, Virginia's rural tidewater peninsulas seem most remarkable because the people are just so disarmingly *nice* — from the lifelong locals who trace their roots back to the founding settlers to recently arrived retirees. Visitors can easily navigate the area simply by asking.

Chesapeake tributaries bound the Northern Neck and Middle Peninsula; the first, just below Maryland, is defined by the Potomac and Rappahannock Rivers; the second is bounded by the Rappahannock and York Rivers. Besides the upper-Northern Neck birthplaces of George Washington, Robert E. Lee, and James Madison, perhaps the best-known landmark here has been The Tides Inn, a Northern Neck-end resort launched just after World War II.

At the top of the Northern Neck lies Colonial Beach, a former casino and steamboat town with a thin Potomac River beach, located near the Potomac River birthplaces of Washington and Lee. Surprisingly, their ancestral homes, Popes Creek Plantation and Stratford Hall, sit close to one another. The original Popes Creek house is long gone, destroyed by fire, but the memorial house there is lovely and you won't find finer waterside grounds for enjoying a picnic. Stately brick Stratford Hall, built in 1723 by Thomas Lee, where his pair of Declaration of Independence–signing sons lived and descendant Robert E. was born, is worth touring to see the wood-paneled Great Hall with its view across the bluffs to the Potomac. Montross, home to the plant that bottles Northern Neck Ginger Ale (try some — you can taste the ginger!) is the "big city" hereabouts.

Waterman Catherine Via with a selection of soft crabs.

David Trozzo

From here, the road rambles to peninsula's end; farmland dominates unless the famously endless creeks of Chesapeake Bay tuck in, sometimes bearing a marina with a homestyle seafood restaurant where it's hard to go wrong on cuisine. At the "northern" tip of the Chesapeake end of the Northern Neck stands Reedville, looking like a New England village, with its Main Street lined with stately Victorian homes. Yankees in search of new menhaden fishing grounds moved here, founding the local fishery in the latter half of the nineteenth century. Fishermen should plan to join a charter into the rich Chesapeake fishing grounds nearby.

Farther south, on the Rappahannock side of the peninsula, the villages of Lancaster Courthouse, Kilmarnock, Irvington, and the one-stoplight village of White Stone cluster near one another (well, as near as you get in this land of rural rambling roads), offering amenities for visitors seeking comfort, history, and maybe some fun on the water. The Mary Ball Washington Museum in Lancaster, named for George Washington's mother, who was born nearby, includes a genealogical library. Closer to Irvington stands the famed colonial Christ Church, built in the 1730s and financed by the Northern Neck's colonial baron, planter Robert "King" Carter. His name is still invoked here, where folks know their roots. Irvington is undergoing a renaissance that's oft-discussed in the letters to the editor section of the local *Rappahannock Record*. Newcomers like the arrival of a handful of upscale shops and ambiance; old-timers complain about new development and traffic. It's a debate familiar to anyone who's lived in a transitional old seaside town.

Across the Rappahannock lies Urbanna, one of Bay country's most delightful towns, established in 1680 as a customs port by the colonial Virginia government, and beloved by cruisers. With its eighteenth-century brick buildings and cluster of good restaurants, it retains a vigorous year-round community — 525 people strong. Down the highway stands Deltaville, with its boaters, and further toward the Bay, rural Mathews County. Among the creative surprises here is The Poddery, a tucked-away pottery (operated by a couple named Podd) with a rambling wood showroom displaying Chesapeake marine life in stoneware.

On the far side of the lower Middle Peninsula, getting on toward the York River and the cradle of American colonialism, is Gloucester County, first settled about 1644. This was tobacco country, with magnificent plantations — some now converted to inn status for modern visitors. Be sure to visit the small brick historic district at Gloucester Courthouse, and consider coming in April for the Daffodil Festival, hailing a floral resident that arrived with early English settlers in the 1600s and spawned an industry here.

Westmoreland, Northumberland, and Lancaster Counties on the Northern Neck offer much of what's covered in this chapter in that area, while Middlesex, Mathews, and Gloucester Counties comprise much of the Middle Peninsula coverage.

LODGING

From renovated watermen's homes to drop-dead gorgeous colonial estates, Virginia's Bay country offers delightful B&Bs and small inns. Virtually none allow smoking inside the house; tobacco-users should ask if they are allowed to smoke outside. Also ask about two-night minimums, typical during high season, and check on cancellation policies when you make reservations. If you're traveling with Fluffy and your inn says no to pets, as most do, your innkeeper may be able to recommend a nearby kennel. Ask about other policies that can change.

Lodging price ranges:

Inexpensive: Up to $75
Moderate: $76 to $120
Expensive: $121 to $150
Very Expensive: Over $150

Credit card abbreviations are: AE, American Express; CB, Carte Blanche; D, Discover; DC, Diner's Club; MC, MasterCard; V, Visa.

NORTHERN NECK

Colonial Beach

Once the summer home of Alexander Graham Bell's family, the Bell House Bed and Breakfast overlooks the Potomac in Colonial Beach.

David Trozzo

THE BELL HOUSE BED & BREAKFAST
Innkeepers: Anne and Phil Bolin.
804-224-7000.
www.thebellhouse.com.
821 Irving Ave., Colonial Beach, VA 22443.
Price: Moderate.
Credit Cards: No.
Handicap Access: No.
Restrictions: Children 14 and older OK with own room.

Alexander Graham Bell's family summer home, built by a Civil War general's son in 1882, offers soaring Victorian peaks and widow's walks that open onto the Potomac River, thirty miles from the Chesapeake Bay. This former casino town retains an old-style, beachy feel, with a few local seafood places and some rummage-worthy antique shops. The Bell House maintains a bygone sensibility, too, with lots of original stained glass topping original windows. Four rooms — all with attached baths — offer queen-sized beds. In a couple, fireplace mantels have become headboards, an art nouveau mirror topping one. Look up through a glass ceiling panel in the third floor to see how the pointed wood cupola was built. Upstairs is a library with local history and fiction. Full breakfast. This is also home to *Apolonia*, a sturdy motor yacht that provides Sun. daytrips, Sat. dinner cruises, and Fri. champagne and dessert cruises, May–Nov. Call for prices and reservations.

Kinsale

A cozy room for two at The Skipjack Inn in Port Kinsale.

THE SKIPJACK INN
Innkeeper: Kathy Morse.
804-472-2044.
www.portkinsale.com.
Port Kinsale Marina & Resort.
347 Allen Point Ln./ P.O. Box 280, Kinsale, VA 22488.
Price: Inexpensive to Moderate.
Credit Cards: AE, D, MC, V.
Handicap Access: No.
Special Features: Children and pets OK in the cottage.

Pots of mandevilla hang from the wraparound porch at this rescued oysterman's home on the Yeocomico River, fresh with a white coat of paint and black shutters. Inside, visitors find a restored vision of what this home might have been, with wood-planked floors and Victorian furniture in the downstairs parlor (replete with fireplace and movies via VCR), and three comfortable rooms upstairs, each named for a skipjack. The green Virginia W comes with a queen-sized bed on the water-facing wall; renovations give all the rooms new baths. The HM Krenz comes with two quilt-covered daybeds, an old-style radio, and pretty carved oak rockers. The blue Wilma Lee means a white and brass bed. Besides the reasonable rates, one of the nice things about The Skipjack Inn is the updated but old-style feel. Continental breakfast served; bikes available. Thin beaches line the riverside, and the marina restaurant stays open into winter. Also here: the contemporary waterside Oyster Reef Cottage with accommodations for two couples — and their pets.

Montross

'TWEEN RIVERS BED & BREAKFAST
Innkeepers: Rayne and Roy Debski.
804-493-0692; 800-485-5777.

If settling into a rocking chair and whiling away the afternoon over a game of Yahtzee on a lovely side porch is your idea of relaxation, 'Tween Rivers may be for you. Located on a main road through

www.tweenrivers.com.
16006 Kings Hwy (Rte. 3),
  Montross, VA 22520.
Price: Moderate.
Credit Cards: AE, MC, V.
Handicap Access: No.
Restrictions: No children
  under 12.

the Northern Neck in Montross (though set back, with fine gardens in back), this homey B&B sits within driving distance of Stratford Hall, Popes Creek Plantation, and other "northern" Northern Neck attractions. Three upstairs rooms and recently renovated touches to the 1920s home combine to make a comfortable, easygoing place. Full breakfasts by candlelight, and hosts who will even drop you and a canoe off at a nearby lake. This is country comfort for the twenty-first century.

Lancaster

INN AT LEVELFIELDS
Innkeepers: John Dunn and
  Charlotte Hollings.
800-238-5578, 804-435-6887.
www.calmwatersrowing
  .com.
10155 Mary Ball Rd.,
  Lancaster, VA 22503.
Price: Moderate to
  Expensive.
Credit Cards: MC, V.
Handicap Access: No.
Special Features: Kids and
  pets OK with prior
  approval.
Added attractions: Guests
  may join the crew school
  for $110 a day; prices
  subject to change.

This landmark antebellum home north of Lancaster Courthouse has turned yet another page in its long history, and now hosts a rowing school — although anyone is welcome to stay here. The former women's varsity crew coach at Cornell University and his wife, a former world rowing champion, searched for two years for an appropriate site before buying the lake down the street, and then found this venerable inn for sale. The Williamsburg colors remain, and three rooms upstairs, with their seven-foot showers and high ceilings, remain available for guests. Three large, brick-walled rooms have been added downstairs. Much about the 1857 house remains from its previous B&B era, but there's still a new air about the place. A widescreen TV, for instance, used for critiquing videoed daily rowing performance, is ensconced in a high-ceilinged parlor painted a Williamsburg rose. Why does this feel like a fancy dorm lounge? Come for a three-, four-, or seven-day rowing vacation, or join the scullers for a per-day fee. Contact the rowing school, called Calm Waters Rowing, via the inn's contact information.

Reedville

THE GABLES
Innkeepers: Barbara &
  Norman Clark.
804-453-5209.
859 Main St./P.O. Box 148,
  Reedville, VA 22539.
Price: Moderate to
  Expensive.

Built by one Capt. Fisher, former schooner captain and early partner in the booming menhaden industry, The Gables is endlessly interesting to architecture buffs, with one of his schooner's three masts erected through the home's third and fourth floors. A carriage house next door is being renovated to add four rooms and, possibly, a tea-

A schooner captain erected his ship's mast through the top two floors of his home, The Gables, now a B&B in Reedville.

David Trozzo

Credit Cards: MC, V.
Handicap Access: No.
Restrictions: No children under 13.

room. Whether guests stay in the house or carriage house (known as the Coach House Inn at the Gables), they will be able to tour the house. The Gables sits at the foot of Reedville's Main Street.

Irvington

THE HOPE AND GLORY INN
Co-owners: Bill Westbrook and Peggy Patteson.
800-497-8228, 804-438-6053.
www.hopeandglory.com.
65 Tavern Road/P.O. Box 425, Irvington, VA 22480.
Price: Expensive to Very Expensive.
Credit Cards: AE, MC, V.
Handicap Access: No.
Restrictions: Children and pets in the cottages only.

This inn hits a perfect note of hip whimsy with an outdoor bath tucked behind a high stockade fence, complete with a claw-foot tub and a big sunflower-sized shower head. You'll find it after rounding the garden path out back, past four cottages (with kitchenettes and/or sitting rooms), folk art birdhouses, and a ballerina sculpture. The circa 1890 schoolhouse-cum-inn is enormous fun, with unexpected touches throughout, from a green-and-white, painted block lobby floor to a white picket fence used as a headboard in one of the rooms. The seven rooms are all different. Among our favorites: a tiny study in white with a huge gilded mirror. The bathrooms tend more toward functional than

Once a schoolhouse, the Hope and Glory Inn in Irvington embodies charm, style, and whimsy.

David Trozzo

fancy, but it all works. Guests find easygoing comfort, like overstuffed furniture and a TV in a sitting area downstairs. Coffee and muffins are out at 6am; full breakfast at 9. Browse the gift shop in the lobby, and feel free to inquire about any activity or amenity you may seek in the area. A classic powerboat and catboat can be booked for guests who want to motor or sail. Managing partner Peggy Patteson spent many years as an executive at the nearby Tides Inn and knows the territory. An upscale, increasingly recognized retreat.

THE TIDES INN
Owners: Sedona Resort
   Management.
800-843-3746, 804-438-5000.
www.thetides.com.
King Carter Dr., Irvington,
   VA 22480.
Price: Very Expensive.
Credit Cards: AE, CB, D,
   MC, V.
Handicap Access: Yes.
Special Features: Pets
   allowed in certain rooms
   for extra charge.

Change has been afoot at the tony Tides Inn, a grande dame resort recently sold by the family that ran it for three generations. A winter 2001–2002 renovation was slated to bring the number of guest accommodations to 106 and update the inn's appearance. But the longtime list of amenities won't change: a day spa, saltwater pool, two freshwater pools, golf, tennis, and dining in casual or upscale comfort. The venerable yacht *Miss Ann* remains a familiar sight cruising local waterways. Marina dockage is available.

MIDDLE PENINSULA

Champlain, near Tappahannock

**LINDEN HOUSE BED &
BREAKFAST
PLANTATION**
Hosts: Ken & Sandy
Pounsberry.
800-622-1202, 804-443-1170.
www.lindenplantation.com.
Rte. 17 S./P.O. Box 23,
Champlain, VA 22438.
Price: Expensive to Very
Expensive.
Credit Cards: AE, D, MC, V.
Handicap Access: Partial.
Restrictions: No children
under 12.

Bluegill, bass, and catfish live in the sizable fish pond dug by the Pounsberrys, evidence of the industrious work-in-progress your hosts have made of this former plantation. This 1750s planter's home eight miles north of the Rappahannock River crossroads town of Tappahannock is inspiring. Guests find two suites and five rooms, including a suite and two rooms with an upstairs balcony in a newish carriage house. Upstairs in the old home (with two fine porches), the Davis Room exemplifies the accommodations, with a fireplace mantel discovered in the old barn (in pieces) and a whirlpool in the bath just steps from the bedroom door. Everything about this inn seems thoughtful and well considered, from a decision to incorporate the existing columns into a sun room to the footpaths on the 200-acre spread. Breakfast in the old part of the house is plentiful, and the service most gracious and warm. Dinner by request. A retreat unto itself.

Urbanna

Tucked behind Urbanna's main street is Atherston Hall Bed and Breakfast.

David Trozzo

ATHERSTON HALL
Owner: Phyllis G. Hall.
804-758-2809.

Lots of B&Bs come with antiques — a walnut dresser from here, a mahogany armoire from there — but how many boast a box in the hallway

250 Prince George St./P.O. Box 757, Urbanna, VA 23175.
Price: Moderate.
Credit Cards: No; checks OK.
Handicap Access: No.
Restrictions: Inquire about children.

that once was the backpack for a samurai's armor? Four rooms here include two rooms sharing one floor and one bath. They're on the second floor of this nineteenth-century home; one with twin beds and one with an antique rice bed once owned by Gen. John Hunt Morgan of Morgan's Raiders. Atherston Hall tends toward a "home stay," but you're in the midst of one of Cheapeake's most lovely and uncluttered historical towns. In the new section of the house, visitors will find two modern rooms with queen beds, attached baths, and individual entries. Full breakfast; bicycles available. Public pool and tennis courts nearby.

THE INN AT URBANNA
Owners: Lora Rudisill & Robert Harwell.
888-758-4852, 804-758-4852.
www.urbannainn.com.
250 Virginia St./P.O. Box 861, Urbanna, VA 23175.
Price: Inexpensive to Moderate.
Credit Cards: AE, DC, MC, V.
Handicap Access: Yes.
Special Features: Restaurant, raw bar, outdoor dining in warm weather.

Urbanna's midcentury Coca-Cola bottling plant has been a motel for decades now, where travelers will find thirteen guest rooms in a building behind a fine restaurant and lively raw bar. Stay here if you're looking for a reasonably priced, central location that means you can walk back to your room from dinner, and expect more of a motel than an inn. Prices are reasonable, and rooms come with coffee pots. The front desk opens at 9am. For breakfast, visit the nearby **Boathouse Café** or the **Virginia Street Café**.

Port Haywood, Mathews County

INN AT TABB'S CREEK
Innkeeper: Catherine Venable.
804-725-5136.
Turpin Lane/P.O. Box 219, Port Haywood, VA 23138.
Price: Moderate to Expensive.
Credit Cards: MC, V.
Handicap Access: No.
Restrictions: Kids on approval; pets OK in one room.

Folks in search of comfort and tradition mixed with creative surprises are in for a treat here, where ceiling fans circle on the screened porch looking out on Tabb's Creek, and Oriental rugs cover the sunroom and dining room floors. Contemporary artworks include many by Innkeeper Catherine Venable, a painter who seems to embody the traditional/contemporary theme of her B&B with her paintings that include creative depictions of quilts. Classical statues stand by the pool, and a poured aluminum branch birdbath done by a sculptor friend sits in the English gardens, which lead to the outbuilding where two suites and a room carry on the surprises. Enjoy the dalmatians marching amid yellow tulips along the painted border atop one suite, or the lavender sink and black toilet in another. Columns rescued from an old nearby cottage create a four-poster bed in one suite; the cobalt-and-white bathroom tiles come from New Mexico. Another suite is located upstairs in the house. Give this place a medal for combining the eclectic with the traditional, and enjoy those Adirondack chairs on the dock at water's edge. Canoes and bikes available.

Gloucester

INN AT WARNER HALL
Innkeepers: Theresa and Troy Stavens.
800-331-2720, 804-695-9565.
www.warnerhall.com.
4750 Warner Hall Rd., Gloucester, VA 23061.
Price: Expensive to Very Expensive.
Credit Cards: AE, D, MC, V.
Handicap Access: Yes.
Restrictions: Ask in advance about kids under 8.

A massive renovation has restored the mansion located at George Washington's great-great-grandfather's seventeenth-century plantation, culminating in a classy inn full of modern creature comforts that surely make this one of the Bay's best. Eleven rooms are painted chic colors and/or swathed in gorgeous Shumacher fabrics and wallpapers, with four-poster (or similarly luxe) beds covered by down comforters and feather beds. Furnishings tend toward reproductions, although surprises may be in store, such as a pair of antique Chinese wooden chairs. Ceilings reach ten feet, whirlpool baths or fireplaces make lounging fun, and Virginia's Severn River stretches out before many windows. As with most ancient homes, fire and fate have conspired to destroy old parts of the house, resulting in varied periods. Much of this inn — the center hall — dates to 1895-1903. However, the old plantation school in the east wing, where two guest rooms stand, dates to sometime between 1690 and 1720. Augustine Warner, George's great-great-grandpa, may have been here at the same time. Tuck into the comfortably renovated boathouse along the Severn (named the same as the river that flows past the Naval Academy in Annapolis) for an afternoon or take a kayak out for a paddle. With dinner served beneath a crystal chandelier in the dining room, breakfast on the glass veranda out back, and even a midday meal by request, guests may find little reason to stir from the thirty-eight-acre grounds. Prix fixe dinner for guests or the general public; call for prices.

NORTH RIVER INN
Innkeepers: Mary and Breck Montague.
877-248-3030, 804-693-1616.
www.northriverinn.com.
P.O. Box 695, Gloucester, VA 23061.
Price: Moderate to Very Expensive.
Credit Cards: MC, V.
Handicap Access: No.

Bay Country is full of old estates, but rarely do mere mortals get to enjoy those dating back to the days of early royal grants. North River Inn, comprised of eight rooms in three fine twentieth-century outbuildings at the seventeenth-century estate known as Toddsbury, is an exception. This is an outstanding waterside option for folks looking to escape to another time, and, with its range of rooms and prices, it's a good value, too. Drive down a long maple-lined drive, and turn left into Toddsbury Cottage, where you'll check in. Guests staying here find three rooms, including a small and reasonably priced downstairs twin bedroom with a Franklin stove. Down the lane, the Creek House offers four guest accommodations, some with French doors opening onto the water. Romantics, however, will never forgive themselves for missing the brick Toddsbury Guest House, with built-in shelves packed with Virginia or maritime history and a fireplace in the cozy, wood-paneled living room downstairs. The upstairs bedroom looks over the North River, and the bed's done up with a floral chintz canopy and bedskirt. Talk about a classy retreat. Continental breakfast in your cottage, or head over to Creek House for a full country breakfast. The Montague family, which owns the inn, resides in the old estate house on the property.

HOTELS/MOTELS

Best Western (804-333-1700; 4522 Richmond Ave., Warsaw, VA 22572) Thirty-eight rooms; Inexpensive to Expensive in high season.

Comfort Inn, (804-695-1900; 6639 Forest Hill Ave., Gloucester, VA 23061) Seventy-nine rooms located just off Rte. 17, including six mini-suites. Inexpensive to Very Expensive, depending on the season. Coffee, ironing boards, Continental breakfast, nice staff.

Deltaville Dockside Inn (804-776-9224; Rte. 33/P.O. Box 710, Deltaville, VA 23043) Twenty-three rooms. Inexpensive to Moderate. Efficiencies with small refrigerators and microwaves. The only motel around this part of the Middle Peninsula.

Holiday Inn Express (800-844-0124, 804-436-1500; 599 N. Main St., Kilmarnock, VA 22482) Sixty-eight rooms, including some suites. Inexpensive to Expensive. Continental breakfast.

Windmill Point Resort (804-435-1166; end of Va. Rte. 695; P.O. Box 368, White Stone, VA 22578) Sixty-one rooms, many with Bay views, in this resort complex. Inexpensive to Moderate. Restaurant, bar, beach, 150-slip marina, tennis, pool, golf.

Whispering Pines Motel (804-435-1101; P.O. Box 156, White Stone, VA 22578) Twenty-nine rooms. Inexpensive to Moderate. Quiet, centrally located .5 mi. N. of White Stone on Rte. 3. Swimming pool; coffee and doughnuts in the am.

RESTAURANTS

Restaurant pricing follows this range for entrée, appetizer and dessert:

Inexpensive: Up to $15   Expensive: $25–$35
Moderate: $15–25   Very Expensive: Over $35

Credit card abbreviations are: AE, American Express; CB, Carte Blanche; D, Discover; DC, Diner's Club; MC, MasterCard; V, Visa.

NORTHERN NECK

Kinsale

Don't pass up this sign outside Port Kinsale, home to the Good Eats Café.

David Trozzo

GOOD EATS CAFÉ
804-472-4385.
Rtes 202 & 203.
Open: Thurs.–Sun.; closed mid-Dec.–Mar. 1.
Price: Moderate to Very Expensive.
Cuisine: World-beat New American/Updated Chesapeake.
Serving: D.
Credit Cards: MC, V.
Reservations: Accepted for groups of 8 or more only.
Handicap Access: Yes.

Here we have a genuine off-the-beaten track gem shining a bit brighter than most because everything about it is a surprise — down to the fact that it's even here. Former big-city chefs Steve Andersen and Sally Rumsey, he with credits in kitchens ranging from French to New American and she with a Johnson & Wales degree, opened this, their second Northern Neck restaurant, in a former gas station several years ago. With lit stars in the windows and orange and yellow faux-painted walls, there's nothing overtly Chesapeake-y about Good Eats except for the local seafood dishes on the menu. We opted for an artichoke dip that went well with the café's trademark rosemary-touched bread sticks; a scorcher of a pork loin with jalapenos and tomatillos served as a nightly special; and turbans of salmon stuffed with crab imperial (at $17.95, the menu's priciest item). Perhaps best of all were mid-August's seasonal veggies — fresh green beans, yellow squash and tomatoes — roasted, we thought, but in reality sautéed at very high heat. Tempted by the unique "sweet eats," we ended with a Mudslide. Yowza! Rich and wonderful coconut-covered ice cream in a cinnamon-tinged Mexican cajeta sauce is better than a Mounds bar on steroids. Like the menu, the café is tinged with a hipster back-on-the-heels kind of style. A nice change of pace, or a useful transition if you're stopping by en route back to real life in the city. Try the updated fried oysters Sun. nights during the cold-weather season.

Mollusk

CONRAD'S UPPER DECK RESTAURANT
804-462-7400.
1947 Rocky Neck Rd.
Open: Mar. 1–Oct. 31, Fri. & Sat. 5–9.
Price: Inexpensive to Expensive.
Cuisine: Seafood.
Serving: D.
Credit Cards: Not accepted.
Reservations: No.
Handicap Access: No.
Special Features: Dockage for boaters.

Isolated at the end of a back road on the Rappahannock River and Greenvale Creek, Conrad's Upper Deck is no secret to Lancaster County residents and regulars who flock by car, pickup, and powerboat, parking on the oyster shell lot or tying up at the bulkhead. The specials board outside the front door suggests such regional delicacies as sugartoads, which, according to the waitress, taste like chicken. Soft-shells, crab cakes and a seafood platter (fried flounder stuffed with crabmeat, two pounds of snow crab legs) appeal to tastes gone less fully native. An all-you-can-eat buffet, recommended only if you're starving, offers steamed shrimp, fried scallops, oysters, clams, crab balls, baked fish, ribs, fried chicken, corn on the cob, and hush puppies. Landlubbers can find beef and chicken entrées, and kids can order burgers, fries, and chicken tenders. Dessert? If you still have room, succumb to a slice of Gale Conrad's homemade German chocolate pie, with two forks. Milton Conrad opened the restaurant in 1985 atop E.J. Conrad & Sons seafood, which his father launched a half-century earlier. It's easy to find from River Rd. (Rte. 354) at Mollusk. Just turn onto Rocky Neck Rd. and drive two miles to the end. It's worth the trip.

Kilmarnock

LEE'S RESTAURANT
804-435-1255.
Main Street.
Open: Mon.–Sat.
Price: Inexpensive to Moderate.
Cuisine: Seafood/Luncheonette.
Serving: B, L, D.
Credit Cards: No; personal checks OK.
Reservations: Not accepted.
Handicap Access: Partial.
Restrictions: No alcohol.

Here we have your downtown everytown restaurant, where apple pie comes with crispy crusts and toothpicks roll, one-by-one, out of the toothpick dispenser by the cash register. Order up eggs with toast or biscuits, bacon or sausage, coffee or juice for under $5, or a $3.75 crab cake sandwich for lunch. Seafood platters come broiled or fried, and you won't pay much more than $10 for the most elaborate on the menu, with trout, shrimp, scallops, and a crab cake. Landlubbers can dig into beef liver or a Delmonico steak. Knotty pine paneling lends an old-fashioned air to the place. Harry

Lee started the restaurant in 1939 as Central Lunch; the family still operates the place.

Irvington

THE TRICK DOG CAFÉ
804-438-1055.
4357 Irvington Rd.
Open: Tues.–Sun.
Price: Expensive.
Cuisine: Seafood/
　Asian/Continental.
Serving: D Tues.–Sat.;
　brunch on Sat. & Sun.
Credit Cards: AE, DC, MC,
　V.
Reservations: Only for
　parties of 6 or more
　before 6:30; otherwise, no
　reservations.
Handicap Access: Yes.

It's the hottest new restaurant in the Northern Neck. The food is superb, but be prepared for the check. It's probably also the priciest — but well worth it. The restaurant is the brainchild of Bill Westbrook, an advertising executive turned Irvington developer who once told *Business Week* that Irvington would be the Hamptons of the twenty-first century. He may be on to something.

Chic and modern, the Trick Dog seems to cater to the area's elite and features a stunning, well-attended bar with an ambitious Scotch selection. The menu, which changes some each month, features superb veal paillard served over caramelized onion mashed potatoes ($20), as well as delicious leg of lamb ($18) and hoisin and plum glazed tuna filet with shrimp and ginger wontons ($25). Three nightly specials range from grilled wild sturgeon with procini and chanterelle risotto ($28) to wild king salmon with morel truffle sauce and shaved truffles ($30).

The fried calamari served with tarragon remoulade and salsa verde is a superb appetizer and enough for at least two. And don't forget the desserts, which include a molten chocolate Godiva cake as well as delicious crème brûlée. Specials also are available.

Since the restaurant takes no reservations, it's best to arrive before 6:45 to be seated immediately. Otherwise, the wait can be quite long. In good weather, there's a lovely outside patio. The Trick Dog is not to be missed. You won't find anything else like it for miles.

White Stone

ROCKET BILLY'S
804-435-7040.
851 Rappahannock Ave.
Open: Mon.–Sat. 6:30–3:30
　year-round.
Price: Inexpensive.
Cuisine: Local
　Seafood/Takeout.
Serving: B, L.
Credit Cards: No; local
　checks accepted.

Rain pelted furiously the morning we awoke early in White Stone's lone highway motel, the day's first foggy thought floating to mind: where to get good coffee? Ah, surely at Rocket Billy's. A bright red-and-white-striped canopy has been added to the 8-by-16 Wells Cargo trailer takeout stop in recent years, and the breakfast crowd was huddled beneath. Given the fine fried oysters here, we gambled on a salt trout breakfast specialty if

Reservations: N/A.
Handicap Access: N/A.

only to live like a local. You've got to admit, this breaded and fried item is the sort of thing that should be limited in a daily diet. But the authenticity speaks to other seafood here: fresh oysters, fish, crabcakes, and curried seafood bisque. One local man huddled beneath the canopy waiting for breakfast called the steak and onions the best thing on the menu; a local woman said, simply, "everything" — including the prices. Eat up.

MIDDLE PENINSULA

Urbanna

THE BOATHOUSE CAFÉ
804-758-4046.
41 Oyster Rd. on the
 Urbanna waterfront.
Open: Tues.-Sun.
Price: Inexpensive.
Cuisine: Gourmet Tavern
 Fare.
Serving: B, L, D, SB.
Credit Cards: No; personal
 checks accepted.
Reservations: No.
Handicap Access: Yes.

Silver paint peels from the corrugated sheet metal on the façade of Urbanna Creek's former Texaco fuel dock, now a stylish, small eatery that lists ever so authentically to port. For breakfast, lunch or an early dinner, fresh gourmet ingredients go into The Boathouse's meals, and the results have the locals talking. Pull up a heavy mosaic garden chair to one of four indoor tables, or settle in at the umbrella-shaded tables on the deck. Shrimp salad comes with potatoes, carrots, and basil-lemon mayo; marinated portobello mushroom sandwiches are made with roasted red peppers, black olive tapenade, and mozzarella. As our waitress promised, the peppery cream of chicken soup was "awesome," and a hot turkey sandwich with brie and a honey mustard went down easy. From croissant to focaccia, choose your sandwich bread. Breakfast ranges from muffins to eggs rancheros with black beans at $4.25. Tie up at the Urbanna Creek dock if you've sailed or motored in, and give a call to see what they're serving in the off-season.

JIMMIE'S GRILLE
804-758-5213.
230 Virginia St.
Open: Daily.
Price: Inexpensive to
 Moderate.
Cuisine: Tavern
 Fare/Seafood/American.
Serving: L, D, SB.
Credit Cards: V, MC.
Reservations: No.
Handicap Access: Yes.

Locals flock to Jimmie's, where crisscrossing beer flags line the ceiling, a sporting event usually fills the TV screen, and live music often plays on weekends. The casual T-shirt and shorts atmosphere is welcoming, the food is terrific, and the prices couldn't be better. When proprietor David McDaniel's not dropping by to say hi, he's bussing tables or back in the kitchen cooking. The restaurant is always full, but, somehow, you rarely have to wait for a table.

For lunch, the crab cake sandwich — all crabmeat, no filler, and quite large — with Jimmie's fries is excellent at $6.95. During the season, Jimmie's has a soft-shell crab sandwich — a delicious choice on a sandwich bun. Other delights: a smoked salmon sandwich with Allouette cheese for $5.95, jumbo shrimp on a pretzel roll (also with Allouette cheese) for $6.25, and a terrific grilled Reuben or burger. The menu even features a vegetarian sandwich — three cheeses with lettuce, tomato, onions, black olives, artichokes, and garlic mayonnaise. Dinner remains casual, and entrées range from crab cakes ($12.95) to fine fried oysters ($12.95) or even a grilled filet mignon ($16.95). Starters include a tempura vegetable medley with wasabi dip, barbecued shrimp, excellent she-crab soup, or mesquite chicken quesadillas.

The restaurant is named for David's father, Jim McDaniel, the unofficial mayor of White Stone just across the Rappahannock. Jim runs the River Market, which features excellent takeout, an upscale wine and beer selection, fine meat, and other gourmet goodies. Both he and his wife, Mary, are excellent chefs, and they've obviously passed the talent on to their son. A second Jimmie's Grill opened in Kilmarnock in 2002. Call 804-435-7799.

Deltaville

TOBY'S
804-776-6913.
220 Jack's Place Rd.
Open: Bar opens daily at
  3pm; dinner daily
  starting at 5pm
Price: Moderate.
Cuisine: American.
Serving: D.
Credit Cards: AE, MC, V.
Reservations: Suggested on
  weekends and holidays.
Handicap Access: Yes.
Special Features: Provides
  free shuttle transportation
  to/from local marinas.

It takes an adventuresome soul to head to Toby's in Deltaville, especially at night. The adventurer drives past boats, Evinrude signs and Brown's Marine on a narrow gravel lane. The heart races in anticipation at what lies ahead, but Toby's lights eventually shine a bright welcome. Looking like a veranda that somehow became separated from the main house, Toby's requires a strong sense of curiosity. First-time visitors walk past a languishing flower bed and climb a sloping ramp to the porch, where the reward is a large blackboard advertising the night's specials. A typical sampling includes crab imperial, rockfish with crabmeat and hollandaise sauce, spadefish with tomatoes and capers, and barbecued ribs.

Toby's front room, painted in inviting persimmon, dispels any last doubts as guests are shown to linen-covered tables adorned with fresh flowers. Warm, soft bread, baked daily on the premises, is served while the entrées are being prepared. Welcoming first courses include freshly prepared soups such as crab bisque and seafood gumbo, both rich in taste and texture. Crisp salads with distinctive homemade dressings ranging from Greek vinaigrette to Parmesan peppercorn are a pleasing second course. The seafood specials were not only perfectly cooked, but perfectly seasoned — a rare blend of fresh fish and crab complemented, not overpowered, by spices. The seafood used in the specials, the manager proudly asserts, is chosen fresh from boats daily.

Taste-tempting desserts, made on-site daily, are available for anyone who still has room. Locals rave about the homemade ice cream — the flavor each day "depends on what my husband feels like," the manager says. In short, Toby's is a pleasing reward at the end of an off-the-beaten path.

Gwynn's Island

SEABREEZE RESTAURANT
804-725-4000.
2 Old Ferry Rd.
Open: Year-round; closed Mon.
Price: Inexpensive to Moderate.
Cuisine: Local Seafood.
Serving: B, L, D.
Credit Cards: No.
Reservations: No.
Handicap Access: Partial.
Restrictions: No alcohol.

The floor slopes toward the water here at the inner edge of Gwynn's Island, just across Milford Haven via the Gwynn's Island Bridge, where the Seabreeze has held forth since 1979. Prices still reflect those days, what with hamburgers for $1.45. But old-fashioned fried seafood is the reason to visit, as well as some of the best brewed iced tea you'll ever find. A fried soft crab sandwich costs $4.95; a fat fried seafood platter goes for $12.95. Ask for a seat in the waterfront room and enjoy down-home seafood in a blast-from-the-past dining room.

Ordinary, near Gloucester

SEAWELL'S ORDINARY
804-642-3635.
3968 George Washington Memorial Hwy.
Open: Tues.-Sun.
Price: Moderate to Expensive.
Cuisine: New American/Seafood.
Serving: L, D, SB.
Credit Cards: AE, DC, D, MC, V.
Reservations: Required on weekends.
Handicap Access: Partial.

Local lore contends that George Washington and the Marquis de Lafayette planned the encirclement of Lord Cornwallis at this 1757 tavern, known in colonial parlance as an ordinary. If true, folks who recall their American history know this means Seawell's Ordinary could rightly be enshrined at the Smithsonian, what with the Revolution ending after Cornwallis was surrounded (and surrendered) down the road at Yorktown. Modern-day diners can enjoy updated cuisine at this fine on-the-road stop. We tucked into lunch at a corner table in the tavern, one of two dining rooms, right next to a charred scar on the pine floor where the Marquis allegedly dropped his burning pipe one night. The lunch menu brings a series of upscale sandwiches, such as the popular crabmeat and baby shrimp on a toasted English muffin or a chicken salad seasoned with red grapes, walnuts, and dill. Dinner is more ambitious, with a nice range of specialty salads (spinach goat cheese and walnut; oak-smoked Chilean salmon salad) and entrées running from roasted garlic filet mignon to oysters volcano, fried oysters on a white wine cream sauce with diced tomatoes and pesto sour cream. The wine list is varied, and dessert may include a seasonal specialty such as peaches or blueberries.

Gloucester Point

RIVER'S INN
804-642-9942.
8109 Yacht Haven Rd.
Open: Daily, except Mon.
  from Oct.-Mar.
Price: Moderate to
  Expensive.
Cuisine: Seafood.
Serving: L, D, SB.
Credit Cards: AE, MC, V.
Reservations: Encouraged.
Handicap Access: Yes.

Expansive decks run alongside River's Inn, a rambling place along the York River where boaters dock for their meals. It's hard to imagine a lovelier summer afternoon (or evening) than one spent here, perhaps on a bar stool topped by a cushion just like you'd find on a speedboat. A more casual menu running to gussied-up sandwiches and salads or raw bar offerings is served outside. Inside the split-level dining room, the fare slides up the scale a tad and includes such offerings as a wine special. The night we visited, three Ravenswood zinfandels and reds from Napa, Somona, and Amador arrived in half-full glasses for our palate's inspection. As for the food: a special appetizer of roasted "Jingle Bell" peppers filled with crab imperial topped with a dill hollandaise got our table's "awesome" award. A pistachio-crusted flounder fillet came over a mango sauce, and the overloaded Chesapeake Blue Plate offered a huge Caesar salad, a brothy she-crab soup, and a baked crabmeat imperial in pastry that left us fully overdosed on crab imperial. The food is fancier than standard Chesapeake seafood offerings, but we remind readers: the deck, the deck, the deck.

FOOD PURVEYORS

FARMER'S MARKETS

The roadside farmstand is a way of life in Virginia's tidewater peninsulas, just as it is elsewhere in Bay Country. You'll never forgive yourself if you don't stop for fresh sweet corn and tomatoes. In addition, check the **Irvington Farmer's Market** on the green on King Carter Drive. Held 8am–noon the first Sat. of each month from Apr.–Dec., featuring everything from herbs to flowers, baked goods to produce.

GOURMET SHOPS

Kelsick Gardens (804-693-6500; 6604 Main St., Gloucester) Wines, cheeses, gift baskets, gourmet foods. Lunch service includes build-your-own sandwiches. Wine tastings and dinners; takeout. Smaller version in Kilmarnock (804-435-1500).

The River Market (804-435-1725; 1 Rappahannock Dr., White Stone) Run by Jim and Mary McDaniel, the market also specializes in such dinner treats as prime rib, a real bargain at $12.95, steak tips and shrimp, mixed grill seafood, and more. You can't beat the price or the quality. Gourmet takeout; varied wine selection.

White Stone Wine and Cheese (804-435-2000; 572 Rappahannock Dr., White Stone) The Wine and Cheese, as its called locally, now serves eat-in or take-out dinner Wed.–Sat. Large wine selection, fresh baked baguettes, free wine tasting every Fri. from 4 to 7pm.

SEAFOOD MARKETS

Captain's Choice Fresh and Frozen Seafood (804-435-6750; 839 Rappahannock Dr., White Stone) A good place to look first for local seafood, located right before (or after) you cross the Rappahannock River.

Cockrell's Creek Seafood & Deli (804-453-6326; 567 Seaboard Rd., Fleeton, outside Reedville) Crab cakes and soft-shell sandwiches to go and a variety of other fresh seafood. Closed Jan.–mid-Mar.

J&W Seafood (804-776-6400; Rte. 33 E., Deltaville) Fresh seafood in this outpost fishing and sailing town. Peeler tanks in back.

WINERIES

Ingleside Winery (804-224-8687; 5872 Leedstown Rd., Oak Grove) Located near the "top" of the Northern Neck, the 50-acre property was once a Civil War garrison and a courthouse. The Flemer family bottles sparkling wine (Virginia Brut) as well as premium wines served in many local restaurants. Look for tastings and jazz at the winery, as well as the new Blue Crab series of wines. Mon.–Sat. 10–5, Sun. Noon–5.

CULTURE

HISTORIC BUILDINGS

Gloucester

GLOUCESTER COURTHOUSE CIRCLE HISTORIC DISTRICT
Contact: Gloucester Parks, Recreation and Tourism. 804-693-0014, 866-VISITUS. www.co.gloucester.va.us/court1.htm.

Colonial and early-U.S. architecture buffs who find themselves deep on Rte. 17 north of Williamsburg will be disappointed if they don't stop to see this collection of eighteenth- and nineteenth-century buildings. Set inside a circular, walled green are the Debtor's Prison, Old Jail, Colonial Courthouse, and more. Plaques bow to Pocahontas, who reportedly saved John Smith near

P.O. Box 157, Gloucester, VA 23061.

here, and Nathaniel Bacon, the rebel buried not far away. Interestingly, some of these old structures are adapting to contemporary times — the Old Jail's façade bears a small sign: "DIT Technical Support." A gem.

ROSEWELL
804-693-2585.
5113 Old Rosewell Ln., Gloucester, VA 26061 (turn on Rte. 614 from Rte. 17).
Open: Mon.–Sat. 10–4, Sun. 1–4.
Cost: Adults $2, children $1.

The past never really departs in Virginia, as evidenced by the patiently preserved ruins of Rosewell, a brick colonial burned in 1916. The four chimneys and portions of walls of the classic house still stand. Begun in 1725, the house was home to John Page, a young patriot and Thomas Jefferson's friend. Picnic tables, visitor's center. Oct. barbecue and silent auction; "Picnic in Past Times," with eighteenth-century re-enactors, in spring.

Irvington

David Trozzo

Completed in 1735, Historic Christ Church near Irvington exemplifies fine Georgian architecture.

HISTORIC CHRIST CHURCH
804-438-6855.
420 Christ Church Rd., Irvington, VA 22480.
Hours: Museum, Mon.–Sat. 10–4, Sun. 2–5.
Church, daily 9–4:30 (except Christmas and New Year's).
Services: 8am Sundays, Mem. Day–Labor Day.

Built in 1730 by the dominant colonial planter Robert "King" Carter, the Historic Christ Church is a study in symmetrical period architecture. Vaulted ceilings, three-foot walls, and perfectly pointed brick, as well its original, boxed high-backed pews and a triple-decker pulpit make this a beautiful, peaceful place to visit. A church was first built on this site in 1670. A museum tells more about this National and Virginia Historic Landmark.

Stratford (Westmoreland County)

Robert E. Lee's infant crib still sits in Stratford Hall, birthplace of the Confederate general and the ancestral Lee family home in Stratford.

David Trozzo

STRATFORD HALL PLANTATION
804-493-8038, 804-493-8371.
www.stratfordhall.org.
45 mi. E. of Fredericksburg, Rte. 214, Stratford, VA 22558.
Open: Museum, daily 9–4.
Admission: Adults $8, seniors $7, children 6 and older $4, children under 6 free.

"Light Horse Harry" begat Robert E., the best-known member of the illustrious Lee family, who was born here. Their historic home features a 1,670-acre working plantation and Great House (circa 1738), and is considered one of the finest museum houses in America. It was built in 1738 by an ancestral Lee named Thomas, one-time acting governor of the colony and father to eight children, including six sons, almost all of whom went on to distinguished careers. Two, Richard Henry Lee and Francis Lightfoot Lee, were the only brothers to sign the Declaration of Independence. "Light Horse Harry," their cousin, was a friend to George Washington and lived here for more than twenty years. Built of brick made on-site and timber hewn nearby, the H-shaped manor house features the twenty-nine-square-foot Great Hall, renowned as one of the finest colonial rooms still in existence. Visitors can see the crib where the Confederate general slept as an infant in 1808. More than three miles of trails lead through the working farm, and at a reconstructed mill, the millstones still grind barley, wheat, and corn, which are sold at the plantation store. Robert E. Lee's birthday is celebrated every Jan. 19.

Washington's Birthplace (Westmoreland County)

The Memorial House salutes the birthplace home of George Washington, destroyed by fire in 1779, at the George Washington Birthplace National Monument along Popes Creek and the Potomac River.

David Trozzo

GEORGE WASHINGTON BIRTHPLACE NATIONAL MONUMENT
804-224-1732.
www.nps.gov/gewa.
1732 Popes Creek Rd., Washington's Birthplace, VA 22443.
Rte. 3 to Rte. 204, 38 mi. E. of Fredericksburg.
Open: Daily 9–5.
Admission: $3, free for children 16 and under.

It didn't all start at Mount Vernon, as visitors here will soon discover. Colonial history and the Washington family headline the Popes Creek Plantation complex on Popes Creek off the Potomac River. The home where Washington was born burned in 1779, but archaeologists have outlined the footprint of the U-shaped house in oyster shells. The brick Memorial House here was built in 1931. A colonial garden stands alongside, amid a gorgeous stand of cedars. The park has hiking trails, one of the most delightful waterside picnic areas around (replete with more huge cedars), and a visitor's center showing a film about the plantation. Look for special holiday events, such as the Christmas celebration and George Washington's birthday celebration.

LIBRARIES

The long-settled Northern Neck offers a couple of good places to spend time on historical research. In _Heathsville_, the **Northumberland County Historical Society** (804-580-8581; Rte. 360) offers a collection of genealogical and historical documents. Open Tues.–Thurs. 9–4, Sat. by appt. Also, the **Mary Ball Washington Museum and Library** (804-462-7280; 8346 Mary Ball Rd.) in _Lancaster_ offers a historical lending collection, genealogical sources, and research facilities, including an extensive collection of Lancaster County records dating to

1651. Named for the mother of our country's father, born nearby, the property also includes displays in the old clerk's office and jail. Open Thurs.–Sat. 10–4.

MUSEUMS

GLOUCESTER MUSEUM
804-693-1236.
6538 Main St., Gloucester.
Open: Mon.–Fri. 11–3, Sat.
  Noon–4.

Quartered in the old Botetourt Building, built in 1774, the museum offers a glimpse of Gloucester County and other area history with its changing monthly exhibits. Recently, one looked at George Washington.

**REEDVILLE
  FISHERMEN'S
  MUSEUM**
804-453-6529.
www.rfmuseum.com.
504 Main St., Reedville.
Open: Daily 10:30–4:30 in
  summer; call for winter
  hours.
Admission: $2, children
  under 12 free.
Handicap Access: Yes.

Reedville looks like a New England fishing village, and no wonder. Nineteenth-century menhaden barons came south and launched the fishery here. Stop in at this little museum and gift shop, originally culled from neighborhood attics and homesteads, to view a photographic explanation of purse seining for menhaden or to see the restored 1922 "buyboat," as the boats that went around purchasing oysters from skipjacks were called. Appropriately enough, visitors have been known to arrive here by water, rowing or motoring in by dinghy to the museum dock. The boats docked outside, including the restored netting boat *Elva C*, are especially fun. Tiny Reedville has produced a well-done museum.

MUSIC

Irvington

**CONCERTS ON THE
  COMMONS**
Sponsored by the Irvington
  Chamber of Commerce &
  Village Improvement
  Assoc.

Look for concerts performed by groups such as the Air Force bands or the eighteen-piece big band The Continentals from Richmond on the first Fri. or Sat. of the month to coincide with the monthly farmer's market. Right in the middle of town. For information, call 804-438-5447 or 804-438-6230.

Kilmarnock

**RAPPAHANNOCK
  FOUNDATION FOR
  THE ARTS**
804-435-0292.

The community's arts supporters — bringing programs to the schools and supporting visual artists — offer a fall-spring, six-performance series featuring professional artists. Artsits have included

Tickets: $105 for recent season subscription; about $20 per individual performances.

the Dukes of Dixieland and the Philadelphia Brass. There is also an annual concert by the Virginia or Richmond Symphony, dance, and other performances, too. Call for ticket cancellations, often available to the heavily subscribed series, or call for a schedule in the spring if you're planning to be in the area. Performances held at the Lancaster County Middle School, 191 School St.

Mathews

DONK'S THEATER
804-725-7760.
Tickets: Adults $10, children under 12 $2.

Home of Virginia's "Li'l Ole Opry," this is Tidewater's capital of country music. Hometown musicians and stars alike show up on stage. "We've had the big ones," we were once told by Harriet Smith Farmer, one of the many Smith family members who lease the place. "We had Dolly. She was here in 1977." The former movie theater at Rtes. 198 and 223 is an appropriate venue for families (no alcohol sold), who may want to check out the Smith Family Christmas Show the first week of Dec. Number of musical Smiths? "It's a bunch," said Harriet. Shows every other Sat. night.

SEASONAL EVENTS

Daffodil Festival and Show (804-693-2355; follow tourism links at www.co.gloucester.va.us; Gloucester County Parks and Recreation Dept., 7406 Carriage Court/P.O. Box 157, Gloucester, VA 23061) Celebrate the annual daffodil harvest with tours of a county daffodil farm. Includes a parade, arts and crafts show, 5K- and one-mile run, historical exhibits, live entertainment, food, children's games, and rides. Held the first Sat. in Apr.

Urbanna Oyster Festival (804-758-0368; www.urbannaoysterfestival.com; Urbanna Oyster Festival Foundation, Drawer C, Urbanna, VA 23175) Population 525 Urbanna grows upwards of 100,000 over the first Fri. and Sat. of November when folks converge for the oyster festival, launched in 1958. Try oysters raw, roasted, sautéed, fried, stewed, frittered, or souped. The town crowns a queen and Little Miss Spat (the name for a baby oyster), and on Friday night the Fireman's Parade marches through. Crafters, artists, and waterfront educators. Make hotel reservations early.

Mathews Market Days (804-725-7196; Mathews Market Days Committee, P.O. Box 296, Mathews, VA 21308) Held in early- to mid-September, craftspeople and artists show their wares; local organizations and others staff the food booths. Music, games, and other community exhibitors at the courthouse area.

RECREATION

BIRD-WATCHING

All of the Bay area's birds, including osprey, herons, and passing ducks can be found in the region's parks and refuges (see "Nature Preserves," below). Bald eagles, back from endangered status, are likewise found hereabouts, but if you're interested in seeing the state's largest concentration of our national avian, schedule a stop at Caledon Natural Area along the Potomac River. Bus tours control access to the eagle's favorite spot. Advance registration; contact Caledon for info: 540-663-3861; 11617 Caledon Rd., King George, VA 22485.

BOATING

CHARTERS & BOAT RENTALS

Classic Cruising and Charters (804-438-1212; P.O. Box 158, Irvington, VA 22480) Two classic yachts, a motoring 1931 Elco 32 and a 1925 catboat, take folks for ninety-minute cruises. $30. Departs from Rappahannock Yachts.

Deltaville Yachts Charter (804-776-7575; www.deltavilleyachts.com; P.O. Box 775, Deltaville, VA 23043) Sailboat charters aboard thirty-two- to forty-six-foot Beneteaus. Captain service available. Located at Rtes. 33 and 631.

Smith Island and Chesapeake Bay Cruises (804-453-3430; 382 Campground Rd., Reedville, VA 22539) A native Smith Islander, Capt. Gordon Evans once oystered aboard the skipjack *Ruby Ford*. He knows his way through the inland waterways, creeks, and canals that lace the cluster of islands collectively known as Smith Island, and now he's shown the way to his son, Capt. Greg Evans. Depart on the ninety-minute trip from the family's KOA Campground and Resort in Reedville to dock at Ewell, the largest of this island's three villages. Visitors can bring picnics, but many like to stop at one of a couple of island eateries. Weather conditions may dictate your trip. No credit cards. Departs 10am, returns 3:45pm, May–Oct. Adults $21, children 3-12 $10. Reservations requested, not required. (See Smith and Tangier Island section in Chapter Six, *Lower Eastern Shore.*)

Tangier and Rappahannock River Cruises (800-598-2628, 804-453-2628; www.eaglesnest.net/tangier; Rte. 1, Box 1332, Reedville, VA 22539) Daytrips to windswept Tangier Island. Also ask about day cruises of the Rappahannock River. May–Oct. Reservations required.

Landings & Boat Ramps

See Chapter Nine, *Information*, to find out how to order a free Bay access map. Some communities require permits for use of the ramps; usually the locations where you can buy one are posted at the boat ramp.

Marinas

Coles Point

Coles Point Plantation (804-472-3955; 307 Plantation Dr.) Fuel dock, boat ramp, beach, seafood restaurant, 110-site campground, and a 575-ft. fishing pier for guests. 132 slips; transients welcome. Located on the Potomac River.

Deltaville

Deltaville Yachting Center (804-776-9898; Rte. 33 at Broad Creek) Formerly Dozier's, the 87-slip marina offers a pool, clubhouse, private showers and heads; laundry and restaurants within walking distance. Transient slips available.

Fishing Bay Harbor Marina (804-776-6800; www.fishingbay.com; Rte. 1104) Pump-out station, gas, café, and pool. About 10 transient slips available on Fishing Bay Harbor.

Kilmarnock

Chesapeake Boat Basin, Inc. (804-435-3110; 1686 Waverly Ave.) Ship's store, ice, showers, fresh water, transient slips. Located on Indian Creek, just above the Rappahannock.

Kinsale

Kinsale Harbour Yacht Club (804-472-2514; Rte. 203 at Kinsale Bridge) Fuel, fresh water, pool, tennis courts, showers, laundry, launching ramp, and restaurant. 99 slips; transient slips available. Located on the Yeocomico River.

Port Kinsale Marina & Resort (804-472-2044; www.portkinsale.com; 347 Allen Point Ln.) Pool, campground, bathhouses, B&B, restaurant, fuel. 86 deepwater slips; transient slips available. On the Yeocomico River.

David Trozzo

Recreational boats at Port Kinsale Marina await the next adventure.

Lancaster

Yankee Point Marina (804-462-7018; yankeepointmarina.com; 1303 Oak Hill Rd.) Full-service marina on the Corrotoman River. Charters, sailing school, 101 slips, fuel, travel lift, showers, laundry.

Lottsburg

Olverson's Lodge Creek Marina (804-529-6868, 800-529-5071; www.port-star-board.com/marina; 1161 Melrose Rd.) Fuel dock, pump-out station, boat ramp, pool, showers. Open year-round. 209 open and covered slips; about 30 transients. Located off the Yeocomico and Potomac Rivers on Lodge Creek.

CANOEING & KAYAKING

Bay Trail Outfitters (888-725-7225, 804-725-0626; www.baytrials.com; P.O. Box 6500, Onemo, VA 23130; located on Rte. 609 in Mathews County) Kayak sales, rentals, and guided tours like the lighthouse island and blueberry picking tour; fossil hunt and haunted woods. $30 per person for tours; homemade pound cake when they end. Rentals: $15 for single, $25 per double for two hours.

Belle Isle State Park (804-462-5030; 1632 Belle Isle Rd., Lancaster, VA 22503; located off Rte. 354 on Rte. 683) Nice paddling in a protected creek off the Rappahannock River, where you can rent canoes for a nominal fee. Take Rte. 3 to Rte. 354, then Rte. 683 near Litwalton to the park. Guided trips in summer.

FISHING

FISHING CHARTER BOATS

For a roster of licensed Coast Guard captains located throughout the Northern Neck, Middle Peninsula, Lower Peninsula, and Eastern Shore, check www.fishva.org, or write the **Virginia Charter Boat Association, Inc.**, P.O. Box 1217, Gloucester Point, VA 23062.

Heathsville

Betty Jane (804-580-5904; www.christopher-family.com/charters; Buzzard's Point Marina, 227 Crosshills Rd., Heathsville, VA 22473.) Capt. E. Wayson Christopher has been at it for years. Licensed for six passengers.

Capt. Billy's Charters (804-580-7292; Ingram Bay Marina, 545 Harvey's Neck Road/P.O. Box 270, Heathsville, VA 22473) Sail out of Ingram Bay aboard *Liquid Assets*, a forty-foot vessel designed for fishing parties and sightseeing. Reservations required.

Crabbe's Charter Fishing (804-453-3251; 51 Railway Rd., Heathsville, VA 22473) Licensed for twenty-six passengers.

Port Royal

Port Royal Landing (804-742-5820; 136 Main St., Port Royal, VA 22535) Fish for catfish here in this freshwater portion of the Rappahannock River. Guides available. Rent a canoe, johnboat or kayaks at reasonable rates. Or sit at the picnic table out back and pick crabs, enjoying the river view. Located one mile north of Rtes. 17 & 301.

Reedville

Pittman's Charters Inc. (804-453-3643; 2998 Fairport Rd., Reedville, VA 22539) Head out aboard the forty-six-foot *Mystic Lady II*. May–mid-Dec.; $60 per person, $420 minimum. Night trips vary; call for prices. Also home to Pittman's Bait and Tackle. On Cockrell's Creek.

Topping

Locklies Marina (804-758-2871; Rte 621, Topping, VA 23169) About twelve charter boats take fishers into the Bay or the Rappahannock from this marina.

Wicomico Church

Jimmick Jr. III (804-580-7744; 95 Long Cove Lane, Wicomico Church, VA 22579) Everything-supplied fishing and catered cruises for up to twenty-five passengers. Capt. Jim Deibler, a full-timer since 1986. Reservations required.

FAMILY FUN

WESTMORELAND BERRY FARM
800-997-2377, 804-224-9171.
www.westmorelandberry farm.com.
1235 Berry Farm La., Oak Grove, VA 22443.
No entry admission; pay per pound of fruit picked.
Hours: May–Labor Day, 8–7; after Labor Day until the end of Nov., 9–5.

Groups from local schools and day care centers make it a point to visit this family-friendly farm, and if you're in the area with a backseat full of kids, you should, too. (Once overheard from an employee: "I can handle the eighteen four-year-olds." Need we say more?) Located along the Rappahannock River, the farm boasts historic, European-invasion roots dating to 1641. In all, 1,600 acres include 800 acres in the adjoining Vorhees Nature Preserve as well as the farm. Not only can kids pick a bushel of different fruits, but there's a "goat walk," an arcing wooden bridge where goats and their kids pick their way across the horizon. The carefully planned, seasonal wave of harvests brings strawberries in May, followed by cherries, black and red raspberries, blueberries, and peaches. By October, kids are picking apples. Everyone is assigned a particular plot upon which to pick. There's a kid-friendly food stand in the market area and a broad veranda with picnic tables. Best berry months: June–mid-July. Best days to pick: Tues.–Thurs. The river runs alongside, and there's a pier. Open daily in-season.

GOLF

Bushfield Golf Club (804-472-2602; Rte. 711, Mount Holly) 9 holes; par 72. Golf carts, driving range, pro shop, snack bar. Located at the historic Bushfield Plantation.

Gloucester Country Club (804-693-2662; Golf Club Rd., Gloucester) 9 holes; public. Good for beginners. Located twelve miles north of York River Bridge.

Golden Eagle Golf Course (800-843-3746, 804-438-5501; P.O. Box 480, Irvington) 18 holes; championship course. A par 3 for guests. Part of The Tides Inn. Restaurant, professional instruction, and driving range.

Hobbs Hole Golf Course (804-443-4500; 1267 Hobbs Hole Dr., Tappahannock) 18-hole course, pro shop, fine restaurant.

Piankatank River Golf Club (804-776-6516; Rte. 629, Hartfield) 18-hole public golf course. Also home to the Steamboat Grill.

Tartan Golf Course (804-438-6200; 633 St. Andrew's Ln., Weems) 18 holes. Formerly owned by The Tides. Pro shop, restaurant, grill room, practice facilities.

The Village Green Golf Club (804-529-6332; 17390 Northumberland Hwy., Callao) 9 holes; public. Pro shop and restaurant year-round.

NATURAL AREAS: STATE, PRIVATE, & FEDERAL PARKS

Beaverdam Park (804-693-2107; follow links from Parks, Recreation and Tourism at www.co.gloucester.va.us; near Gloucester Courthouse at end of Rte. 616, 8687 Roaring Springs Rd., Gloucester, VA 23061) A 635-acre freshwater lake with largemouth, channel cat and crappie fishing is the centerpiece here, which also includes a nature trail (11 mi. one-way to the second entrance). Programs offer adventures such as night canoeing and owl walks

Belle Isle State Park (804-462-5030; 1632 Belle Isle Rd., Lancaster, VA 22503; located off Rte. 354 on Rte. 683) Seven miles along the Rappahannock River — along with access to Greenvale Creek — offer fine fishing and trails. Rent skiffs with 9.9 hp outboards ($10/hour; reduced hourly rate for half-days). Also, rent bikes and canoes for nominal fees. Two nice picnic areas with water views; boat launch; between four and five miles of trails; guided trips. Birds here include eagles, osprey, red-tailed and red-shouldered hawks. Bottlenose dolphins may be spotted feeding in late summer. Also available: rental of the Overnight Area, a bureaucratic name for the 1942 Bel Air mansion and guest house on a private 33-acre peninsula. TV, working fireplace, kitchen. Sleeps 14 total; rates are reasonable. For reservations, call 800-933-PARK.

Bethel Beach Natural Area Preserve (For information, call the Mathews County Visitor and Information Center, 804-725-4229. The park is located at the end of Route 609 outside Mathews). Fifty-acre preserve with sandy beach and salt marsh along the Chesapeake Bay. Dozens of bird species and the rare northeastern beach tiger beetle.

Chesapeake Nature Trail (W. of Kilmarnock on the south side of Rte. 3) A 1.6-mile trail that passes the west branch of the Corrotoman River.

Hickory Hollow Nature Preserve (804-692-0257 or the Northern Neck Audubon Society, P.O. Box 991, Kilmarnock, VA 22482) Located on Route 604 outside Kilmarnock en route to Lancaster. Walking trails up to 1.8 mi. long.

Westmoreland State Park (804-493-8821; State Park Rd., Montross, VA 22520) Almost 1,300 acres along almost two miles of the Potomac River. Fish, swim in the Olympic-sized pool (no swimming from the beach), or rent a kayak or other small boat. Located off Rte. 3 E. outside Montross. Visitors may discover washed-up sharks' teeth, vestiges of life from an ancient, Miocene sea.

ROWING

Calm Waters Rowing (800-238-5578, 804-435-6887; www.calmwatersrowing.com; at the Inn at Levelfields, 10155 Mary Ball Rd., Lancaster, VA 22503) A recent addition to the area, offering athletic vacations and instruction sessions of different lengths. Check the Inn at Levelfields listing under "Lodgings" for more information.

SPORTING GOODS & FISHING SUPPLY STORES

J&W Seafood (804-776-9740; Rte. 33, Deltaville) Fishing licenses and tackle.
Pittman's Bait & Tackle (804-453-3643; 2998 Fairport Rd., Reedville) On Cockrell's Creek, near wide-open fishing grounds.
B&H Fishing and Hunting (804-725-2699; Rtes. 198 & 223, Hudgins) Fishing licenses. Full-service bait and tackle. Closed mid-Jan.–Mar.
Winter Harbor Seafood (804-224-7779; Rte. 3, Oak Grove) This may be a seafood market, but it's also the place to get hunting and fishing gear and licenses. Game checking.

SWIMMING

Westmoreland State Park's swimming pool fronts the Potomac River.

David Trozzo

Gloucester Point Beach Park (804-642-9474; Rte. 17, on the York River next to Coleman Bridge/York River Bridge, Gloucester) Fishing pier, picnic area, horseshoe and volleyball courts, and swimming. Concession stand, rest rooms open seasonally.

Westmoreland State Park (804-493-8821; State Park Rd., Montross) Olympic-sized pool alongside the Potomac River. Located 5 mi. W. of Montross, off Rte. 3 E.

SHOPPING

ANTIQUES

Holly Hill Farm Antiques (804-695-1146; Rte. 17, Gloucester) Open Fri.–Sun. 10–5.

Kilmarnock Antique Gallery (800-497-0083, 804-435-1207; www.virginia-antiques.com; 144 School St., Kilmarnock) Open daily. Approximately 80 dealers. More extensive than most.

Plantation Antique Mall (804-695-1410; 7032 George Washington Memorial Hwy., Gloucester) Open daily except Wed.

Urbanna Antique Gallery (804-758-2000; 124 Rappahannock Ave., Urbanna) Variety of vendors peddling all kinds of stuff, from Coca-Cola boxes to unique lighters.

BOOKS

Book Nook (804-435-3355; 53 W. Church Street, Kilmarnock) Fine selection of local-interest and even fishing books. In business for more than 30 years.

Twice Told Tales, Ltd. (804-435-9201; 75 S. Main St., Kilmarnock) Centrally located and easy to find, with a range of books, including quality activity books for kids. Also located in Gloucester at Main St. & York Ave. (804-639-9209).

CLOTHING

Cyndy's Bynn (804-758-3756; 311 Virginia St., Urbanna) Look for the black awning along Virginia St. Inside find a very nice shop featuring seasonal gifts and jewelry, fine women's clothing, and a nice little selection of children's and baby's gift items.

Khakis of Irvington (804-438-6779; 4345 Irvington Road, Irvington) Clothing and gifts for men.

Pepper's (804-436-9606, 538 Rappahannock Dr., White Stone) Five of us spent a Saturday morning in here one April day; nobody was at a loss over what to buy. Great women's clothing.

The Dandelion (804-438-5194; 4372 Irvington Rd., Irvington) Four proprietors shop the designers in New York and Atlanta — and it shows. Even a famously restless shopper wished that she'd had more time. Great women's clothing, from designer upscale to closer to home. Well worth a stop — or even a special trip.

GALLERIES

Mathews Art Group (804-725-3326; Main Street, Mathews) Nice gallery with a range of work — pottery, stained glass, fine art, prints — from group of about forty local artists. Open 10–4 daily, year-round.

Nimcock Gallery (804-758-2602; 31 Cross St., Urbanna) In this little custom frame shop, Santas are painted on crab-shell ornaments and set in a tray amidst antiques, collectibles, paintings, and prints.

The Poddery (804-725-5956; Rte. 660, Foster) Surprises live down the long country lanes in Mathews County, and The Poddery is one. Operated by potters Karen and Rob Podd, the pottery looks like summer camp, with its rambling wooden showroom/studio and green-roofed shelters displaying Bay-inspired stoneware. The main showroom is chockablock with useful and artful wares alongside small crabs, mollusks with sea grass, or realistic fish made from molds of fish brought by neighboring watermen. Buy them individually for a kitchen or bathroom backsplash, or affixed to pots crafted for various cooking duties. Open year-round; special open houses the weekends before and after Thanksgiving. Showroom open 10–5 daily.

Rappahannock Art League Studio Gallery (804-436-9309; 19 Main St., Kilmarnock) About fifty artists. A good place to look for a range of different artwork, including paintings, jewelry, pottery, turned wood.

GENERAL STORES

R.S. Bristow Store (804-758-2210; Virginia & Cross Sts., Urbanna) As much a stop on the local history walking tour as your vacation shopping trip, this 1898 dry goods store offers nice clothing and much, much more. R.S. Bristow Sr. opened his first retail shop in 1876.

Sibley's General Store (804-725-5857; 1 Main St., Mathews) An "old-timey" country store where you can find whatever it is that you can't find anyplace else. Oil lamp parts and new decorative flags.

SPECIALTY SHOPS & CRAFT GALLERIES

Duncan & Drake (804-438-5447; 81 King Carter Dr., Irvington) Carries an eclectic collection of decorative home items, linens, baby gifts, and toiletries. One just doesn't know what you'll find here, but there's plenty to see.

Make Thyme (804-758-2101; 260 Prince George, Urbanna) Dried and fresh herbs of many varieties, fragrant gift items in the two-room house/shop. Larry Chowning, a Bay writer noted for his work on the lives and lore of local watermen, owns this shop with his wife, Dee.

Maybebaby (804-438-5611; 4351 Irvington Road, Irvington) Retirees are moving into the Northern Neck, and their grandkids are in for some great gifts. Gourmet baby clothes.

Papeterie (804-758-0046; 260 Virginia St., Urbanna) Lots of fun stuff to see, from whimsical glass fish Christmas ornaments to fine papers.

Rappahannock Jewelry Co. (804-758-3003; 230 Virginia St., Suite 3, Urbanna) Chesapeake-themed jewelry and gifts.

River Birch Gifts (804-758-8814; Rte 33, Locust Hill) Design-oriented gift shop in back of nursery. Bay items, custom gift baskets.

The Tides Inn Gift Shop (804-438-4440, 804-438-5000; 480 King Carter Dr., Irvington) Fine gifts, men's and women's resortwear.

Time to Cook (804-438-6691; 4349 Irvington Road, Irvington) Cooking utensils to specialty foods.

Wood-A-Drift Art Shop (804-438-6913; 4474 Irvington Rd., Irvington) Homey and long in residence, this little shop offers nautical gifts ranging from small knickknacks to drawings.

CHAPTER EIGHT
The Urban Bay
BALTIMORE & OTHER URBAN ATTRACTIONS

Ice skaters enjoy winter at Baltimore's Inner Harbor.

Baltimore, whose world-famous Inner Harbor set a standard for urban rejuvenation, is reinventing its downtown once more. New hotels, attractions, shops, and restaurants continue to spread along the waterfront, transforming neighborhoods into hot destinations. Elsewhere in urban Chesapeake Country, the massive World War II-era battleship *Wisconsin* is docked outside Norfolk's NAUTICUS maritime center, while the formerly placid Tidewater region between Richmond and Williamsburg continues to grow. New residents include world-class golf courses near the Williamsburg-Jamestown-Yorktown area.

BALTIMORE

More than two decades after Baltimore turned a moribund waterfront into the internationally acclaimed **Inner Harbor**, the city's "second renaissance" has rapidly expanded attractions well beyond the harbor basin. A $1 billion-plus development blitz that began in the mid-1990s has added a huge waterfront hotel, a new football stadium (home to the 2001 Super Bowl champion Baltimore Ravens), the world's first Walt Disney–designed children's museum, and a major retail and entertainment complex inside a long-dormant power plant. The energy of the Inner Harbor also has spread to other neighborhoods, including **Federal Hill, Fells Point, Canton,** and **South Baltimore**. A weekend is hardly enough to catch all the city's charms.

A good place to start is the Inner Harbor and the twin glass pavilions of **Harborplace**, with all manner of shops and restaurants. The once-dormant **Power Plant**, a former steam-generating plant, has been transformed into a hip, neon-emblazoned entertainment and retail spot overlooking the harbor. It features three mega-attractions: the world's first ESPN Zone, interactive and much-loved by sports fans (including those who gather after Baltimore's Preakness, stop two in horse racing's Triple Crown), a grand **Barnes & Noble** that demands attention with its inventory, trendy café, and a 30,000-gallon saltwater fish tank, and the ever-popular **Hard Rock Café**. In front, diners sit at restaurants on two floating barges. The high-voltage Power Plant is also a fine complement to longtime Inner Harbor attractions such as the **National Aquarium in Baltimore** and the **Maryland Science Center**, an interactive science museum with **IMAX Theater** and **Davis Planetarium** (410-685-5225, 24-hour information line; 601 Light St.; open daily; admission).

Just a few blocks northeast of the Inner Harbor, the former city Fishmarket has been transformed into **Port Discovery,** the first children's museum with exhibits designed by the Walt Disney Company.

But Baltimore is not only the Inner Harbor. The city's cultural heart beats at **Mount Vernon**, while **Little Italy** continues to romance with its cozy eateries. **Fells Point**, an eighteenth-century fishing village, charms by day with its unique shops and galleries, but at night it transforms into a Soho of sorts; if you're ever in Baltimore during Halloween, be sure to visit the neighborhood to check out the outrageous costumes. **Federal Hill** has grown into a hot, restaurant-filled neighborhood, with the acclaimed **American Visionary Art Museum** (800 Key Hwy.), which features works by artists outside the mainstream. And in once-industrial **Canton**, former canneries, tin factories, and fertilizer plants have been converted into restaurants, bars, offices, shops, and some of the hottest real estate in the city. Just a few blocks from an expansive waterfront park and promenade, Canton's O'Donnell Square provides a gathering spot perfect for strolling, people-watching, shopping, eating, and drinking.

Food is also big in Charm City, and its public markets are legendary. The most famous is **Lexington Market** (400 W. Lexington St.), established in 1782, with about 140 merchants offering abundant and fresh foods of all kinds at unbelievable prices; a sandwich here can go for $2, and fresh produce sells at well below supermarket prices. Such markets are located throughout the city, the most gentrified being **Cross Street Market** (between Charles & Light Sts.) in Federal Hill. The **Broadway Market** (last two blocks at south end of Broadway) in Fells Point offers fresh gourmet bread, as well as no-frills breakfasts.

For more refined tastes, **Charles Street** is Baltimore's "Main Street," which leads to picturesque **Mount Vernon Square**, home to many fun and trendy shops such as the furniture store **Nouveau** (519 N. Charles St.), and restaurants like the hot spot **Sotto Sopra** (409 N. Charles St.), a classic building with a great bar but expensive drinks. Among the city's cultural jewels here are the nation's first monument to **George Washington**, **The Walters Art Museum**, with its expansive collections, and the famed **Peabody Conservatory of Music**, the oldest American music school. Farther up the street, in Charles Village, look for the **Baltimore Museum of Art** adjacent to the sprawling Homewood campus, the main campus of **Johns Hopkins University**.

American history lovers also will enjoy Baltimore, once home to Babe Ruth and Edgar Allan Poe. The **Babe Ruth Birthplace and Museum** (216 Emory St.) is just a home run away from **Oriole Park at Camden Yards**, the city's trend-setting, retro baseball park, well worth a visit even for those who aren't baseball fans. For Baltimore Orioles game information, call 410-685-9800. Next to the ballpark is the sprawling $220 million, 69,084-seat home of the Baltimore Ravens, PSINet Stadium (tickets, 410-261-RAVE; other info, 410-547-8100).

Catch the Baltimore Ravens, 2001 Super Bowl champs, at PSINet Stadium.

David Trozzo

Easily accessible by Interstate 95 (I-97, if you're headed north from Annapolis), this eminently livable city is easy to navigate by car, by foot, or by scenic water taxi for as little as $5 for a day-long ticket. Contact: Baltimore Area Convention and Visitors Association's Visitors Center (800-282-6632, 410-837-4636; www.baltimore.org; 301 E. Pratt St., Baltimore, MD 21202).

BALTIMORE ATTRACTIONS

BALTIMORE MUSEUM OF ART
410-396-7100.
www.artbma.org.
10 Art Museum Dr., Baltimore, MD 21218.
Open: Wed.–Fri. 11–5, Sat.–Sun. 11–6; closed Mon., Tues.
Admission: Adults $7, seniors and full-time students $5, children 18 and under free; all visitors free on Thurs.

Maryland's oldest and largest art museum unveiled eight thematic galleries in April 2001 after a two-year, $4 million renovation and expansion. A new Interpretive Gallery includes the first public display of many works from the museum's best-known collection, The Cone Collection, artwork from two Baltimore sisters who amassed one of the world's great selections of Matisse paintings (and caught up with their friend, former JHU medical student Gertrude Stein, in Paris as she presided over the unfolding of the great era of Modern painting in the early 1900s). The BMA also displays American painting and decorative arts; European painting and sculpture; art of Africa and Asia; and modern and contemporary art.

BALTIMORE ZOO
410-366-5466.
www.baltimorezoo.org.
Druid Hill Park, Baltimore, MD 21217.
Open: Daily 10–4; call for extended spring and summer weekend hours.
Admission: Adults $10, children 2–15 and adults 62 and older $6.

The 161-acre Baltimore Zoo, the nation's third-oldest, features an African Watering Hole, where the rhinos roam; the Leopard Lair, where a new African leopard lives; and the acclaimed Children's Zoo, a walk-through, interactive display of Maryland's habitats and species.

FORT McHENRY NATIONAL MONU-MENT AND HISTORIC SHRINE
410-962-4290.
www.nps.gov/fomc.
E. Fort Ave., Baltimore, MD 21230.
Open: Daily 8–4:45; extended summer hours, 8–7:45.
Admission: Adults $5, children 16 and under free.

The star-shaped Fort McHenry is known throughout the world as the birthplace of "The Star-Spangled Banner." Inspired by the American flag still flying after British bombardment of the fort, Marylander Francis Scott Key wrote the words to the U.S. national anthem during the War of 1812. Situated in the industrial neighborhood of South Baltimore, Fort McHenry's expansive grounds, brick fort, and ramparts lie adjacent to the Baltimore harbor. A peaceful setting, the vast, green grounds provide a perfect picnic spot and a haven for joggers and cyclists. The fort allows visitors opportunities to explore a variety of exhibits; don't miss the free sixteen-minute movie, shown every thirty minutes in the visitor center.

NATIONAL AQUARIUM IN BALTIMORE
410-576-3800.
www.aqua.org.
501 E. Pratt St., Baltimore, MD 21201.
Open: July–Aug., daily 9–8; Mar.–June and Sept.–Oct., Sat.–Thurs. 9–5, Fri. 9–8; Nov.–Feb., Sat.–Thurs. 10–5, Fri. 10–8.
Admission: Adults $16, seniors $13, children 3–11 $9.50.

Get caught in the mist in the Tropical Rain Forest at the Inner Harbor's popular National Aquarium. Or check out the Coral Reef, where a winding, downward path takes you up close to a huge tank containing the reef, with its sharks, tortoises, and other colorful inhabitants. The Amazon River Forest re-creates a section of a blackwater Amazon River tributary, where visitors can spy schools of dazzling tropical fish, giant river turtles, and a giant anaconda. The Marine Mammal Pavilion features performing dolphins, with shows usually on the hour. The aquarium's biggest drawback is its crowds. Lines start forming early on the weekends, and the crush of people can make viewing the exhibits a bit uncomfortable. Try visiting on Fri. evenings during the summer.

PORT DISCOVERY
410-727-8120.
www.portdiscovery.org.
35 Market Place, Baltimore, MD 21202.
Open: Labor Day–Mem. Day, Tues.–Sat. 10–5, Sun. Noon–5; Mem. Day–June 30, 10–5 daily; July and Aug., Sat.–Thurs. 10–6, Fri. 10–8.
Admission: Adults $11, children 3–12 $8.50.

The first children's museum with exhibits designed by the creative maestros at Walt Disney beckons with a three-story, interactive wonderland. Kids can slide, jump, and swing through an "urban treehouse"; travel back in time to the land of the pyramids to search for a lost pharaoh's tomb; and try their tiny hands at inventing stuff at R&D Dreamlab. Outside, visitors can soar 450 feet above the city in the gondola of a helium balloon, tethered by a steel cable.

THE WALTERS ART MUSEUM
410-547-9000.
www.thewalters.org.
600 N. Charles St., Baltimore, MD 21201.
Open: Tues.–Sun. 10–5; first Thurs. of each month 10–8.
Admission: Adults $8; seniors $6; college students, young adults 18–25 with ID $5; children 17 and under free.

With a collection of 30,000 pieces spanning three wings, the Walters presents buildings as impressive as the masterpieces they contain. These include the landmark Italian Renaissance Revival 1904 Gallery building, the four-story 1974 "Centre Street" building, and the Hackerman House, a separate Greek Revival mansion. The museum has recently completed a $24 million renovation to the largest and most modern of the group, the so-called 1974 building. The Walters is one of only a few museums worldwide to present a comprehensive history of art from the third millennium B.C. to the early twentieth century. The Walters also boasts a fine collection of ivories, jewelry, enamels, and bronzes, and a spectacular reserve of medieval and Renaissance illuminated manuscripts. Also featured: highly regarded collections of Egyptian, Greek and Roman, Byzantine, Ethiopian, Western medieval, Renaissance, and Asian works. Acclaimed exhibits have included such shows as "Manet: The Still-Life Paintings," which opened at the Walters after premiering at Paris' Musee d'Orsay, the great home to so many famed Impressionist paintings.

BALTIMORE LODGINGS

For visitors who prefer quaint lodgings to mega hotels, consider a sampling of the city's inns and B&Bs. More accommodations can be found by contacting the reservation service, Amanda's (443-535-0008).

Rates may vary according to season or day of the week, and cancellation policies may vary from inn to inn. Always check. Rate ranges are as follows:

Inexpensive: Up to $75
Moderate: $76 to $120
Expensive: $121 to $150
Very Expensive: Over $150

Credit card abbreviations are: AE, American Express; CB, Carte Blanche; D, Discover; DC, Diner's Club; MC, MasterCard; V, Visa.

THE ADMIRAL FELL INN
Owner: Dominik Eckenstein.
800-292-4667, 410-522-7377.
www.admiralfell.com.
888 S. Broadway, Baltimore, MD 21201.
Market Square at Thames St.
Price: Very Expensive.
Credit Cards: AE, DC, MC, V.
Handicap Access: Yes.
Special Features: Smaller dogs or pets allowed on first floor with prior arrangement.

Long before the cult television cop drama "Homicide: Life on the Street" put Fells Point on the map, there was The Admiral Fell Inn, aptly named after the man responsible for this quaint, yet sometimes rowdy, part of Baltimore. The city's original port retains much of its eighteenth-century charm with Belgian brick streets, tugboats, salty taverns, and red brick row houses. This elegant inn, once a boardinghouse for sailors, embodies that charm with finely appointed rooms furnished with custom-crafted Federal-style pieces. The inn's formal restaurant, Hamilton's, is considered one of the state's best.

CELIE'S WATERFRONT BED AND BREAKFAST

Owner: Celie Ives.
410-522-2323.
www.baltimore-bed-breakfast.com.
1714 Thames St., Baltimore, MD 21231.
Price: Expensive to Very Expensive.
Credit Cards: AE, D, MC, V.
Handicap Access: No.

Tucked amid brick row houses and shops lining Thames Street, just across the cobblestone street from tugboats moored in the harbor, sits this oasis. The three-story inn's airy rooms come with harbor or courtyard views, and are filled with antiques, collectibles, comfortable wicker chairs, and, in some, king-sized beds, fireplaces, and whirlpool tubs. Two have private balconies. All seven rooms have TVs, VCRs, desks, coffee makers, terry robes, and updated tiled baths. Owner Celie Ives or her innkeepers serve a "deluxe" Continental breakfast either in the cozy, country-style dining room or at wrought iron tables in the brick courtyard garden out back. A rooftop deck offers views of the harbor and city. Centrally located in Fells Point.

THE INN AT HENDERSON'S WHARF

Owner: Bob Gunn.
410-522-7777, 800-522-2088.
www.hendersonswharf.com.
1000 Fell St., Baltimore, MD 21231.
Price: Expensive to Very Expensive.
Credit Cards: AE, DC, MC, V.
Handicap Access: Yes.

Expect the amenities of a big hotel and the intimacy of an inn at this former Baltimore & Ohio Railroad tobacco warehouse built in 1893 at the edge of Baltimore's harbor in Fells Point. The inn's thirty-eight rooms occupy the first floor of the six-story, red brick building on a quiet, cobblestone street just a block from the neighborhood's bustle. Spacious harbor-view rooms with exposed brick walls look out to a boardwalk-style promenade and a marina beyond, and each have two wrought-iron queen-sized beds. Smaller rooms, with one queen bed each, offer views of a brick courtyard garden with fountains. All rooms feature oak furnishings, a muted beige-and-blue décor and touches such as feather beds, terry robes, cordless telephones, TVs, and coffee makers. Rooms have spacious tiled baths and walk-in closets as well. A Continental-style buffet breakfast is served in an elegant lobby with polished hardwood floors, Oriental rugs, and a fireplace. Free parking and exercise room, too. Located a short walk away from the Baltimore Water Taxi, which makes stops around the Inner Harbor.

MR. MOLE BED & BREAKFAST

Owners: Paul Bragaw & Collin Clarke.
410-728-1179.
www.mrmolebb.com.
1601 Bolton St., Baltimore, MD 21201.
Price: Moderate to Expensive.

Elegantly appointed in English-country fashion, the 1860s town house in historic Bolton Hill boasts marble fireplaces, fourteen-foot ceilings, and scores of eighteenth- and nineteenth-century antiques. The owners take obvious pride and personal interest in their guests. Each of five rooms comes with its own style and name, and all of them include spacious and crystal-clean, white bathrooms with hair dryers and terry cloth robes. A breakfast of

Credit Cards: AE, D, DC, MC, V.
Handicap Access: No.

SCARBOROUGH FAIR BED & BREAKFAST
Owners: Ellen & Ashley Scarborough.
410-837-0010.
www.scarborough-fair.com.
1 E. Montgomery St., Baltimore, MD 21230.
Price: Expensive to Very Expensive.
Credit Cards: A, D, MC, V.
Handicap Access: No.

sliced meats, cheeses, fresh fruit, and homemade baked goods is served each morning. The inn is a bit removed from the tourist areas of Baltimore, and guests should drive or take a cab at night.

This gem in rejuvenated Federal Hill boasts not only stellar accommodations, but also a location that other inns would envy. Walk to the Inner Harbor or Fells Point (a longer hike), and dine at Federal Hill's exceptional restaurants. The Scarboroughs offer today's comforts amid yesteryear's charm. They opened the inn in 1997 and have gone above and beyond in refurbishing the stately brick house at Charles and Montgomery Sts., distinctive with its gabled roof and Flemish bond bricks. Six beautifully renovated rooms are offered, all with period and reproduction furnishings, four with gas fireplaces and two with whirlpool tubs. The décor and style varies from room to room, one with a brass bed and red wing chair, another with a Victorian bed and marble-topped nightstand. Updated, spacious private baths in each room have touches such as antique sink vanities. TV in the cozy library. Hearty, unique breakfasts daily in the traditional French blue and yellow dining room. Off-street parking is included.

And for well-located Baltimore hotels, try:

Baltimore Marriott Waterfront Hotel (410-230-0368; 700 Aliceanna St.).
Harbor Court Hotel (410-234-0550; 550 Light St.).
Hyatt Regency Baltimore (410-528-1234; 300 Light St.).
The Tremont Plaza (410-727-2222; 222 St. Paul St.).

BALTIMORE RESTAURANTS

AMICCI'S
410-528-1096.
231 S. High St.
Open: Daily.
Price: Moderate.
Cuisine: Italian.
Serving: L, D.
Credit Cards: AE, CB, D, DC, MC, V.
Reservations: Accepted for parties of 6 or more.
Handicap Access: No.

Baltimore's Little Italy is just a long bocci ball toss from the Inner Harbor — which makes the neighborhood a popular dinner destination for locals and tourists alike. Great pasta can be had at any of the neighborhood's many eateries, but it's difficult to find a casual dining room where it won't cost you your last lira to eat well — unless you know about Amicci's.

Amicci's bills itself as a "very casual" Italian joint. And it is just that. The brightly colored dining room adorned with framed movie posters is usually crowded and conducive to a great meal. The house salad is a perennial bargain. A bowl of greens, onions, tomatoes and cucumbers tossed in a tangy-sweet vinaigrette is simple, tasty, and enough for two. Don't miss the restaurant's signature appetizer, the "panne rotondo," a bread boule filled with jumbo shrimp swimming in garlicky cream sauce. Polish off one of these and you may find dinner unnecessary.

But you should save room for one of the many pasta choices. Shrimp Fra Diavolo features some more of those great big, perfectly cooked shrimp in a spicy tomato sauce. Pasta with white clam sauce is delicious and loaded with the tasty bivalves. Lasagna, tortellini, penne — there's something for every pasta-lover's taste. Wrap up your repast with one of Amicci's fantastic cannolis. According to our waitress, the cannoli shells come from a nearby pastry shop. The house blends ricotta with powdered sugar and chocolate chips to create a nearly perfect version of this favorite Italian confection.

CHARLESTON
410-332-7373.
1000 Lancaster St.
Open: Mon.–Sat.
Price: Very Expensive.
Cuisine: Sophisticated Southern.
Serving: D.
Credit Cards: AE, CB, D, DC, MC, V.
Reservations: Essential.
Handicap Access: Yes.

In the booming Inner Harbor East development you'll find Charleston — an oasis of Southern-influenced cuisine served in a stylish setting that has quickly become one of the city's premier restaurants. National food and wine media have begun to take notice, including internationally known oenophile Robert Parker, who tabs Charleston as his favorite dining spot in Baltimore.

The Southern influence in Chef Cindy Wolf's cuisine is evidenced primarily in the ingredients. Peruse the menu and you'll find dishes incorporating Southern staples such as andouille sausage, cornmeal, stone-milled grits and fried green tomatoes. But with your first bite, it's evident that this isn't mom's home cooking. Dinner here is meant to be leisurely and luxurious. Whether you order off the a la carte menu, or are tempted by the "tasting" menu that changes daily — think multiple courses.

Start with seafood. Crispy cornmeal oysters seal in the shellfish's succulence. An upscale BLT features giant scallops seared to perfection and balanced atop applewood smoked bacon, fresh tomatoes and frisee. Move on to a light summer salad of cucumbers, tomatoes, red onions and mint. Another, featuring mango, kiwi and micro greens, is a perfect prelude to a main course.

A veal chop served simply with chopped asparagus and tomato tarragon butter should satisfy meat-lovers. Seafood gets very creative treatment. Grilled tuna arrives settled among the contrasting colors of swirls of fresh pesto, a smattering of olives, slices of grilled cucumber and a beautiful round slice of yellow tomato.

Take your pick of fresh cheeses from the selection of twenty or so on the cheese cart. Sample the fresh-fruit sorbet, or dig into a delicate chocolate mousse-crisp cookie concoction swimming in a pool of creme anglaise. When the meal is over, it will be easy to see why so many Baltimoreans travel frequently to Charleston.

CRAZY LIL'S
410-347-9793.
27 E. Cross St.
Open: Mon.–Sat.
Price: Moderate.
Cuisine: Pub/New
  American.
Serving: L, D.
Credit Cards: AE, D, DC,
  MC, V.
Reservations:
  Recommended for
  weekend dinner.
Handicap Access: Yes, in
  smoking area.

Here's the perfect way to pretend you're a local. Wander a few blocks south of the Inner Harbor. Stop in at Nick's Seafood in Cross Street Market for a bucket of beer, a glass of wine, and oysters on the half shell. Then head around the corner to Crazy Lil's.

Outside — and in — the tiny storefront restaurant looks like a typical neighborhood bar. An odd mishmash of posters and celebrity photos that wouldn't look out of place in a frat-house basement line the walls. But ever-present owner Tony Guarino and his staff dish up food that transcends pub grub. Sure, you'll find exemplary burgers and buffalo wings. But you'll also find grilled pizza with chicken, onions and roasted corn salsa, and New York strip with roasted garlic demi-glace.

Catch shrimp night on Tuesday and dig into a half-pound of steaming, already peeled jumbo shrimp. Or make it a Baltimore theme night and start off with the restaurant's pastry-topped crock of crab bisque. Follow that with Crazy Lil's version of Baltimore's ubiquitous crab cake. The generous patty features lots of lump crabmeat and little filler. But the kitchen can be creative too, as evidenced by the orange roughy fillet with bananas and melon beurre blanc — as well as numerous nightly specials. Grab dessert at Spoons coffeehouse on the other side of Cross Street and you're living la vida local.

EURASIAN HARBOR
410-230-9992.
711 Eastern Ave.
Open: Tues.-Sun.
Price: Expensive.
Cuisine: Pan-Asian.
Serving: D; takeout lunch.
Credit Cards: AE, CB, D,
  DC, MC, V.
Reservations:
  Recommended on
  weekends.
Handicap Access: Yes.

You've finished sightseeing at Baltimore's Inner Harbor and you're ready for a relaxing dinner. Confronted with the packed chain eateries dotting the waterfront, however, that may seem impossible. Fortunately, just a pedestrian bridge away from this well-trod restaurant path you'll find Eurasian Harbor.

This newcomer dishes up stylish Asian-influenced cuisine in a sophisticated setting. The menu offers something for just about everyone on just about any budget. There's a wide range of sushi and appetizers — or "First Tastes," as the restaurant puts it. Order up several of these small plates with salad or soup and you've got a meal. Don't miss the blackened sea scallops, delicately perched atop a briny mound of sea-weed salad amid a swirl of mango lemon butter. Scrumptious. For the somewhat less adventurous, chicken and shrimp potstickers are a modern take on the Chinese favorite. Eurasian Harbor's are pan-fried and drizzled with a just-sweet-enough sauce made of pineapple and star fruit.

For a main course, seafood lovers could opt for fresh salmon wrapped in a delicate rice paper crust with a lime-ginger soy sauce, accompanied by perfectly cooked jasmine rice and bok choy. Among an array of poultry dishes, you'll find citrus-glazed crispy duck. The juicy slices of duck fanned out over a bed of curried couscous could win over the toughest Peking duck aficionado. Stir-fry, noodle dishes, even an Asian seafood bouillabaisse round out the menu.

And whatever you do, don't miss Eurasian Harbor's delicious and visually stunning desserts.

WASHINGTON, D.C.

The nation's capital stands at the edge of Bay Country (though firmly within its watershed region, which spans Virginia and Maryland and reaches clear to New York), about thirty miles west of Annapolis along the tidal portion of the Potomac River. The city hosts an impressive number of free museums and performances, as well as good restaurants, and is particularly elegant in early spring, when the delicate cherry blossoms burst forth, and into October, when the trees turn color and the famously oppressive humidity of summer has faded.

The United States Capitol in Washington, D.C.

David Trozzo

There's a ton to see here: the **Washington Monument**, the **Lincoln** and **Jefferson Memorials**, the **National Gallery of Art**, the **Kennedy Center for the Performing Arts**, the museums of the **Smithsonian Institution**, and, of course, the **White House**, the **Capitol**, and the **Mall**. These are just the traditional highlights. Visitors do well to also see the nonfederal parts of the city beloved by residents: neighborhoods such as upscale **Georgetown**, with its great shopping and restaurants; funky-but-going-gentrified **Adams-Morgan**, home to much good nightlife; and cultured and gay-friendly **DuPont Circle**, with myriad good restaurants, shops, and the marvelous **Philips Collection** for those who love early modern art. If you've got kids in tow, don't miss the **National Zoo**, with a zillion wonderful animals and its stars, giant pandas Mei Xiang and Tian Tian. They moved in after the 1990s deaths of the much-mourned Ling-Ling and Hsing-Hsing, who launched the region's romance with their species in 1972.

The city's **Metro** system is a safe and dependable way to get around (though, curiously, it has no Georgetown stop). The diverse dining scene, with world-class chefs such as Michel Richard holding forth at his **Citronelle** at Georgetown's The Latham Hotel, just keeps getting better. For information on all the nation's capital has to offer, start with the **Washington Convention and Visitors Association** (202-789-7000; www. washington.org; 1212 New York Ave. NW, Suite 600, Washington, DC 20005). The *Washington Post* web site (www.washingtonpost.com) also should prove useful; click on the "Travel" section.

HISTORIC TRIANGLE: JAMESTOWN, YORKTOWN, WILLIAMSBURG

Perhaps all of America should visit this area, truly the cradle of our colonial history. Before the Pilgrims ever arrived in Massachusetts, the *Susan Constant, Godspeed* and *Discovery* sailed into **Jamestown**. These first English settlers arrived in 1607 and began their explorations of the Chesapeake Bay. In 1699, Virginians moved their capital from Jamestown to **Williamsburg,** where it remained until moving in 1780 to Richmond. Nearby, the final shots of the Revolutionary War rang out in 1781 when George Washington led the colonists and French in defeat of the British at the Battle of **Yorktown.**

Current-day visitors to the region are blessed with the very lovely Colonial Parkway, a wonderful way to explore the Virginia Peninsula, as the area is known. Travelers can drive from Jamestown to the west, along the James River, then tunnel under the historic district of Colonial Williamsburg. The road reaches its end at Yorktown to the east, alongside the York River. Under the auspices of the National Park Service, the Colonial National Historical Park operates significant historical sites throughout the area, such as the Yorktown National Battlefield. To contact the park service: 757-898-2410; www.nps.gov /colo; P.O. Box 210, Yorktown, VA 23690.

JAMESTOWN

The Jamestown Settlement combines indoor gallery exhibits with outdoor living history to tell the tale of the early colonists who came here. Docked along the riverbank are three full-sized replicas of the square-riggers *Susan Constant, Godspeed* and *Discovery*, and onboard sailor-interpreters tell of the four-month voyage by these early English settlers. A fort and Powhatan Indian village complete the interpretive tale. A significant expansion is under way, developed in anticipation of the colony's 400th anniversary in 2007. A new visitor's center and café will be joined by a theater and special exhibition hall, with other changes to follow. The settlement is located six miles west of Williamsburg, just off Rte. 31. Visitors also can visit **Jamestown Island,** home to the first settlers. The National Park Service, along with the Association for the Preservation of Virginia Antiquities, operates 22.5 acres at the western end of the island (the **Jamestown National Historic Site**), replete with archaeological sites. The park service runs the rest of the 1,500-acre island.

YORKTOWN

The same foundation that operates Jamestown Settlement presides over the historically rich **Yorktown Victory Center**. Five hundred different Revolutionary War artifacts are on view, and the museum offers a re-created history of the era, with costumed interpreters and hands-on exhibits. Also stop at the **Yorktown National Battlefield**, where visitors can take a seven-mile driving tour through the site where the War for Independence ended. Two years later, England signed the Treaty of Paris, ratified farther up the Bay in Annapolis. Information on both national sites is available through the Colonial National Historical Park, 757-898-2400; www.nps.gov; P.O. Box 210, Yorktown, VA 23690.

WILLIAMSBURG

Williamsburg is a great town in any season, with fireplace wood smoke and bayberry candle aromas filling winter's air, and daffodils and dogwood bursting forth come spring. **Colonial Williamsburg** nestles within the town of Williamsburg proper, alongside The College of William and Mary (a historical treat in itself), located midway between Richmond and Norfolk, off I-64.

Restored in 1926 with the aid of John D. Rockefeller Jr., **Colonial Williamsburg**, Virginia's original 1699 capital city, truly takes visitors back in time as they stroll the old streets and take in everything from the Governor's Palace to nearby museums. At the Governor's Palace, formal English gardens are restored to period symmetry and perform double duty for families with children, who will love the boxwood maze. People in period costumes are everywhere. If they're not demonstrating the fine craft of smithing, they're marching in a fife-and-drum corps.

Along Duke of Gloucester Street stand the restored homes and workshops of the eighteenth century, manned by docents in colonial garb. This is also home to three historic taverns (Josiah Chowning's Tavern, King's Arms Tavern, and Shield's Tavern) prepared to serve to twenty-first-century diners with a colonial meal and perhaps a song. Nearby, on Waller Street, Christina Campbell's Tavern holds forth with its seafood fare. (Dinner reservations for the taverns are a must. For Chowning's, stop by to make reservations the day you want to dine; for the others, call 1-800-HISTORY.) In all, eighty-eight original buildings stand among the 500 structures that comprise Colonial Williamsburg proper.

Visitors who are staying more than a day are well-advised to check out ticket packages. For instance in 2001 a day pass cost $16 for children age 6–17 and $32 for adults, while year passes cost $19 for kids and $38 for adults. Information is available by contacting 1-800-HISTORY; www.colonialwilliamsburg.org. The Colonial Williamsburg Visitor's Center is located off Colonial Parkway at 100 Information Center Dr., Williamsburg, VA 23187.

Visitors also will want to check out a variety of other fun options. Nearby stands family entertainment from the **Busch Gardens** theme park and **Water Park USA**, shopping at three outlets on Richmond Road (Rte. 60) at the edge of town, the upscale Duke of Gloucester Street shops at **Merchant's Square**, and the enormous bargainland known as the **Williamsburg Pottery Factory.**

Golfers, too, will be in paradise. Among their options: Courses designed by Pete Dye, Arnold Palmer, Curtis Strange, and Robert Trent Jones Sr. For more information, request an annual Virginia Golf Guide from the Virginia Tourism Corp. by calling 800-786-4484 or clicking the "Publications" menu item at www.visitva.org.

Gourmets know to check out the famed cuisine at the **Trellis Restaurant,** with its equally famed Death by Chocolate dessert (Merchant's Square; 757-229-8610). Allow us to also recommend breakfast or lunch at the small and reasonably priced **Williamsburg Drug Co.** (Merchant's Square; 757-229-1041). The soda fountain and booths in the back, where milkshakes and grilled-cheese sandwiches are favorites, recall life as it used to be. The simple menu also features a turkey club, a BLT, or a veggie sandwich on basil bread. Takeout available. Also consider **Berret's Restaurant and Raw Bar** (Merchant's Square; 757-253-1847) for lunch or dinner, an eatery happy to divide entrées. The elegant menu features local cuisine such as a Virginia ham and crabmeat combination swooning in a puff pastry topped with a lemon dill hollandaise, or the she-crab soup. Red beans and rice arrive with a sprig of rosemary, with little-neck clams spicing this old-style, deep South/Caribbean staple. The restaurant's intimate dining areas include a brick patio with tables in view of the College of William & Mary. There's an outdoor raw bar, too. Also keep in mind the rustic **Williamsburg Winery** (757-229-0999; 5800 Wessex Hundred), with its vineyards, gift shop, and **Gabriel Archer Tavern**. Enjoy a cheese platter, French bread, and wine offered during the midday meal with a side salad of baby lettuce and mixed field greens with balsamic vinaigrette — with a treat: brown-sugared pecans and dried cherries. Sandwiches such as fresh mozzarella and roasted red peppers on artichoke hearts, and smoked salmon with capers, onions, and dill sauce arrive on basil focaccia and French baguettes. While you're there, try a winery offering, such as the Two-Shilling Red or a chardonnay. Outdoor picnic tables with a vineyard view are pleasant in warm weather. Tavern customers can take part in a winery tour that starts in the gift shop, where you can also purchase wines. Call ahead for tour reservations.

Lodging suggestions for the region include the **Kingsmill Resort** (800-832-5665, 757-253-1703; www.kingsmill.com; 1010 Kingsmill Rd., Williamsburg, VA 23185), or the **Best Western Patrick Henry Inn** (757-229-9540, 800-446-9228; York & Page Sts., Williamsburg, VA 23187). National chain hotels also operate within the area. For abundant tourist information, contact the Williamsburg Area Convention & Visitors Bureau, 800-368-6511, 757-253-0192; www.visit williamsburg.com; P.O. Box 3585, Williamsburg, VA 23187.

URBAN VIRGINIA TIDEWATER: HAMPTON, NORFOLK & NEWPORT NEWS

Virginia's Tidewater officially includes the entire tidal shoreline of the Bay, but many refer to the cities near the mouth of the Bay simply as "Tidewater." Here, the Chesapeake meets its final tributary, the James River, and joins waters with the Atlantic Ocean. The naturally secure harbors have drawn not only commercial vessels, but the U.S. Navy as well. Military residents include Naval Station Norfolk, the world's largest naval station.

Of 100 exhibits at the **Virginia Air & Space Center** (800-296-0800, 757-727-0900; www.vasc.org; 600 Settlers Landing Rd., Hampton), highlights include a weather exhibit (try playing with a tornado funnel), a chunk of moon rock brought back by the 1969 Apollo 17 mission, and the Apollo 12 command module. There's also an IMAX theater, which shows a new movie every four months or so. Norfolk's **NAUTICUS** (800-664-1080, 757-664-1000; www.nauti cus.org; Waterside Dr., Norfolk), on the city's waterfront, offers aquariums and interactive simulators that let visitors check out life beneath the sea or aboard a naval battleship. The World War II–era battleship *Wisconsin*, at more than 877 feet, docks alongside. Art-lovers will want to see the **Chrysler Museum of Art** (757-664-6200, www.chrysler.org; 245 W. Olney Rd., Norfolk), with its collection that includes Tiffany glass and French (Gaugan, Renoir, Degas) and Italian (Cavallino, Filippino Lippi) paintings. A must-see for anyone interested in the sea: the impressive and copious exhibits at the **Mariners' Museum** (800-581-SAIL, 757-596-2222; www.mariner.org; 100 Museum Dr., Newport News), with a center devoted to the famed *USS Monitor*, the historic Civil War ironclad whose artifacts are being slowly brought ashore. Its 1862 Bay battle with the Confederate *Virginia* ended the era of wooden naval ships. Also: spot-lit cases and magnifiers highlight the miniature ship collection of August F. Crabtree, and a Chesapeake Bay Gallery devoted to its maritime history includes watermen and shipbuilding on up to these recreational days. Boat-lovers should see the indigenous craft from around the world, from a seventeenth-century dugout canoe to a Venetian gondola.

For more information on the area, including dining and lodging, contact the Newport News Visitor Center (757-926-3561, 888-493-7386; www.newport-news.org; 13560 Jefferson Ave., Newport News, VA 23603) or the Norfolk Convention and Visitors Bureau (800-368-3097, 757-664-6620; www.norfolkscvb.com; 232 E. Main St., Norfolk, VA 23510).

VIRGINIA BEACH

East Coast revelers flock to Virginia Beach, perched along 28 miles of ocean beach and another ten miles of Bay. Sun, fish, surf fish, or stroll Atlantic Avenue, the main thoroughfare fronted by a three-mile boardwalk, prime people-watching territory. For more information, contact the Virginia Beach Visitor and Information Center (800-822-3224; www.vbfun.com; 2100 Parks Ave., Virginia Beach, VA 23451).

CHAPTER NINE
The Right Connections
INFORMATION

From the air, Annapolis' baroque-style circles are evident, from the Maryland Statehouse dome and the St. Anne's Church spire.

David Trozzo

Consider this an abbreviated encyclopedia of Bay-related information that will help you move more easily through the area. This chapter provides guidance on the following subjects:

AMBULANCE & EMERGENCY INFORMATION

For police, fire and ambulance emergencies, dial 911. Via cell phone, report accidents or other highway emergencies by calling #77 or 911. On the water, the U.S. Coast Guard responds to VHF marine radio Channel 16.

Maryland

Maryland Department of Natural Resources Police Emergency Dispatch (410-260-8888 in Annapolis, or 911 and ask to be connected to the DNR police; 877-620-8367, general information).
Maryland State Police (410-486-3101).
U.S. Coast Guard Activities Baltimore (410-576-2558, general questions; 410-576-2525, search and rescue).
U.S. Coast Guard Station Annapolis (410-267-8108).

Virginia

On the water, the U.S. Coast Guard directs your calls as follows: For threat to life and limb, contact the **U.S. Coast Guard Hampton Roads Group,** 757-484-8192. For threat to property, the **U.S. Coast Guard's Marine Safety Group** out of Hampton Roads can be reached at 757-483-8567. If you're farther north, from Smith Point (near Reedville) to the York River, call **U.S. Coast Guard at Milford Haven,** 804-725-2125.

For boating information or to report environmental hazards (during weekday business hours): **Department of Game and Inland Fisheries**, 804-367-1000; 4010 W. Broad St., Richmond, VA 23230.

To reach the **Virginia State Police**, contact 804-674-2000. For state road conditions: 800-367-ROAD.

AREA CODES

In **Maryland**, callers must always dial the area code, even if it's not a long-distance call. Most Chesapeake area numbers are 410, except for St. Mary's County, in Southern Maryland, where it's 301. **Virginia** area codes are as follows: Hampton Roads/Tidewater region, 757; Northern Neck, 804; Richmond, 804. The 703 area codes in this book serve northern Virginia telephone numbers in the Washington, D.C. metropolitan area. Washington, D.C. is 202.

BIBLIOGRAPHY

BOOKS YOU CAN BUY

CHILDREN'S BOOKS

Cummings, Priscilla. *Chadwick the Crab*. Tidewater Publishing, 1986.
Henry, Marguerite. *Misty of Chincoteague*. Rand, 1947. Many editions and publishers; this is the original.
Holland, Jeffrey. *Chessie, The Sea Monster That Ate Annapolis*. Oak Creek Publishers, 1990.
Voigt, Cynthia. *Homecoming*. Fawcett Juniper, 1981.

COOKBOOKS

Kitching, Frances, and Susan Stiles Dowell. *Mrs. Kitching's Smith Island Cookbook*. Tidewater Publishers, 1981.
Shields, John. *Chesapeake Bay Cooking with John Shields: A Companion Cookbook to the Public Television Show*. Bantam Doubleday Dell Publishers, 1998.

FICTION

Barth, John. *The Sot-Weed Factor*. Doubleday, 1987.
————. *Tidewater Tales*. Fawcett, 1987.
Chappell, Helen. *Giving up the Ghost: A Hollis Ball/Sam Westcott Mystery*. Dell Publishing, 1999.
————. *Ghost of a Chance: A Hollis Ball/Sam Westcott Mystery*. Dell Publishing, 1998.
Michener, James A. *Chesapeake*. Random House, 1978.
Styron, William. *A Tidewater Morning: Three Tales from Youth*. Random House, 1993.

HISTORY, MEMOIR & LORE

Brown, Alexander Crosby. *Steam Packets on the Chesapeake: A History of the Old Bay Line Since 1840*. Cornell Maritime, Tidewater Publishers, 1961.
Brown, Philip L. *The Other Annapolis, 1900-1950*. The Annapolis Publishing Co., 1994.

Brugger, Robert J. *Maryland: A Middle Temperament, 1634-1980.* Johns Hopkins University Press, 1988.

Burgess, Robert H. *This Was Chesapeake Bay.* Cornell Maritime Press, 1963.

Carr, Lois Green, Philip D. Morgan, and Jean B. Russo. *Colonial Chesapeake Society.* University of North Carolina, 1988.

Chowning, Larry S. *Chesapeake Legacy: Tools & Traditions.* Tidewater Publishers, 1995.

Davison, Steven G., et al. *Chesapeake Waters: Four Centuries of Controversy, Concern, and Legislation.* Tidewater Publishers, 1983, 1997.

De Gast, Robert. *The Lighthouses of the Chesapeake.* Johns Hopkins University Press, 1973.

Dize, Frances W. *Smith Island, Chesapeake Bay.* Tidewater Publishers, 1990.

Freeman, Roland L. *The Arabbers of Baltimore.* Tidewater Publishers, 1989.

Horton, Tom. *An Island Out of Time: A Memoir of Smith Island in the Chesapeake.* W.W. Norton & Co., 1966.

Jander, Anne Hughes. *Crab's Hole: A Family's Story of Tangier Island.* Literary House Press, Washington College, 1994.

Keiper, Ronald R. *The Assateague Ponies.* Tidewater Publishers, 1985.

Middleton, Arthur Pierce. *Tobacco Coast: A Maritime History of Chesapeake Bay in the Colonial Era.* Johns Hopkins University Press, 1984.

Mills, Eric. *Chesapeake Bay in the Civil War.* Tidewater Publishers, 1996.

————. *Chesapeake Rumrunners of the Roaring Twenties.* Cornell Maritime Press, 2000.

Shomette, Donald. *Pirates on the Chesapeake: Being a True History of Pirates, Picaroons, and Sea Raiders on Chesapeake Bay, 1610-1807.* Tidewater Publishers, 1985.

————. *Ghost Fleet of Mallows Bay and other Tales of the Lost Chesapeake.* Tidewater Publishers, 1996.

————. *Lost Towns of Tidewater Chesapeake.* Tidewater Publishers. 2000.

Wennersten, John R. *The Oyster Wars of Chesapeake Bay.* Tidewater Publishers, 1981.

Whitehead, John Hurt III. *The Watermen of the Chesapeake Bay.* Tidewater Publishers, 1979.

NATURAL HISTORY & FIELD GUIDES

Hedeen, Robert A. *The Oyster: Life and Lore of the Celebrated Bivalve.* Tidewater Publishers, 1986.

Horton, Tom. *Bay Country.* Johns Hopkins University Press, 1987.

————. *Turning the Tide: Saving the Chesapeake Bay.* Island Press, 1991.

Lawrence, Susannah. *The Audubon Society Field Guide to the Natural Places of the Mid-Atlantic States: Coastal.* Pantheon Books, 1984.

Lippson, Alice J., and Robert L. Lippson. *Life in the Chesapeake Bay.* Johns Hopkins University Press, 1984, 1997.

Meanley, Brooke. *Birdlife at Chincoteague and the Virginia Barrier Islands.* Tidewater Publishers, 1981.

Sherwood, Arthur W. *Understanding the Chesapeake: A Layman's Guide.* Tidewater Publishers, 1973.

Taylor, John W. *Birds of the Chesapeake Bay.* Johns Hopkins University Press, 1992.

Warner, William W. *Beautiful Swimmers: Watermen, Crabs and the Chesapeake Bay.* Penguin Books, 1976.

White, Christopher P. *Chesapeake Bay: A Field Guide.* Tidewater Publishers, 1989.

Williams, John Page, Jr. *Chesapeake Almanac: Following the Bay Through the Seasons.* Tidewater Publishers, 1993.

PHOTOGRAPHY & ESSAY

Cushard, Carol, and Jane Wilson McWilliams. *Bay Ridge on the Chesapeake: An Illustrated History.* Brighton Editions, 1986.

Harp, David W., and Tom Horton. *Water's Way: Life Along the Chesapeake.* Johns Hopkins University Press, 2000.

Meyer, Eugene L., and Lucien Niemeyer. *Chesapeake Country.* Abbeville Press, 1990.

Snediker, Quentin, and Ann Jensen. *Chesapeake Bay Schooners.* Tidewater Publishers, 1992.

Warren, Mame. *Then Again . . . Annapolis, 1900-1965.* Time Exposure, 1990.

Warren, Marion E., with Mame Warren. *Bringing Back the Bay.* Johns Hopkins University Press, 1994.

RECREATION

Gillelan, G. Howard. *Gunning for Sea Ducks.* Tidewater Publishers, 1988.

Shellenberger, William H. *Cruising the Chesapeake: A Gunkholer's Guide.* International Marine Publishing Co., 1990.

TRAVEL

Anderson, Elizabeth B. *Annapolis: A Walk Through History.* Tidewater Publishers, 1984.

Arnett, Earl, Robert J. Brugger, and Edward C. Papenfuse. *Maryland, A New Guide to the Old Line State.* Johns Hopkins University Press, 1999.

Wiencek, Henry. *The Smithsonian Guide to Historic America, Virginia and the Capital Region.* Stewart, Tabori & Chang, 1989.

BOOKS YOU CAN BORROW

Bodine, A. Aubrey. *Chesapeake Bay and Tidewater.* Bodine and Assoc., 1954. 3d ed., 1980. Classic black-and-white photographs by noted *Baltimore Sunday Sun* photographer.

Burgess, Robert H. *This Was Chesapeake Bay.* Tidewater Publishers, 1963. Compendium of historic accounts of watermen and Bay vessels.

Byron, Gilbert. *Early Explorations of the Chesapeake Bay.* Maryland Historical Society, 1960.

Capper, John, et al. *Chesapeake Waters: Pollution, Public Health, and Public Opinion, 1607-1972.* Originally published by the EPA, contains historic account of Bay pollution. Republished by Tidewater Publishers, 1983.

Chapelle, Suzanne Ellery Greene, et al. *Maryland, A History of Its People.* Johns Hopkins University Press, 1986.

Earle, Swepson. *The Chesapeake Bay Country, 1923.* Reprinted by Weathervane Books, 1983.

Fiske, John. *Old Virginia and Her Neighbours.* Houghton, Mifflin & Co., 1897. Old-style account of the founding of Chesapeake colonies.

Footner, Hulbert. *Rivers of the Eastern Shore.* Rinehart & Co., Inc., 1944.

Gibbons, Boyd. *Wye Island.* Johns Hopkins University Press, 1977. History and natural history of unspoiled island surrounded by Wye River on Maryland's Eastern Shore.

Hildebrand, Samuel F. *Fishes of Chesapeake Bay.* TFH Publications, 1972.

Klingel, Gilbert C. *The Bay.* Tradition, 1966. Natural history essay.

Lippson, Alice Jane. *The Chesapeake Bay in Maryland: An Atlas of Natural Resources.* Johns Hopkins University Press, 1973.

Metcalf, Paul. *Waters of Potowmack.* North Point Press, 1982. Natural and social history of the Bay's most famous tributary

Schubel, J.R. *The Life and Death of the Chesapeake Bay.* University of Maryland, 1986.

Tawes, William I. *God, Man, Salt Water and the Eastern Shore.* Tidewater Publishers, 1967.

Wilstach, Paul. *Tidewater Maryland.* The Bobbs-Merrill Co., 1931. Funky classic. Reprinted several times.

BICYCLING BASICS

Both Maryland and Virginia staff offices to assist cyclists. In Maryland, call the bicycle coordinator's office at 800-252-8776 or 410-545-5656; www.sha. state.md.us; 707 N. Calvert St., C 502/P.O. Box 717, Baltimore, MD 21203. Ask for maps or other information. Keep in mind that you can't cycle across many major bridges, such as the Chesapeake Bay Bridge near Annapolis.

In *Virginia,* contact: Dept. of Transportation's Bicycle Coordinator, 800-835-1203; e-mail: vabiking@vdot.state.va.us; 1401 E. Broad St., Richmond, VA 23219.

BOATING

What the heck is a "bareboat" charter? It's captaining a charter boat on your own — and if you don't know how, you'll need to take a course to do so. It's also one way to get out on the water. The following definitions will help you choose which option is best for you and your travel companions.

Charter boats are what you want if you plan to sail or power for more than a day — often a week — which you'll do with a captain or by yourself (aka bareboating). Charter agencies will want to see your boating résumé and to check references. Keep in mind that "chartering" means a range of things: you can charter the fifty-foot yacht you're thinking of buying and take yourself to the Caribbean, or you can charter a weekend sailboat with skipper and relax on deck. Although technically it's conceivable to charter a boat for a day, you're more likely to encounter two-day minimums and weekend prices starting around $800 to $850. Prices range widely depending on the boat, prices may drop the longer you're out on the boat, and you can split the cost with friends. Chartering's a great way to see the Bay. Local boating schools offer courses to get you certified to handle someone else's prized vessel, and can usually rent or charter craft once you're certified. They, too, will want to see your sailing résumé.

David Trozzo

Boats dock in the Sassafras River on the Upper Eastern Shore.

Cruise and excursion boats take folks out for a ride, and your vessel may be anything from an authentic Chesapeake skipjack to a reproduction schooner to the equivalent of a waterborne bus. These are good get-acquainted options, perfect for an afternoon outing, and your crew often narrates the history (either natural or man-made) of the passing shoreline. **Water taxis** can stand in for an excursion boat, providing fun (and usually cheap) point-to-point rides across the harbor to a good restaurant or other destination.

Boating schools supply all you'll need to learn to handle a jib, navigate by the stars, or take a safe spin through crowded waters aboard a powerboat. Some folks plan vacations around weeklong sailing lessons.

Rent a daysailer, skiff, windsurfer, Jet Ski, rowboat, canoe, or kayak! Go out for as little as an hour or as long as a day. Your outfitter is in charge of how much experience you'll need to take the boat out and will ask all the necessary questions. Many marinas host vendors who rent various craft.

Good sources for more information include the about-town freebie *Spinsheet* (www.spinsheet.com; 301 Fourth St., Annapolis, MD 21403) and the *PortBook*, also distributed free at boating outlets that advertise (www.port book.net; P.O. Box 462; Belfast, ME 04915; specify "Annapolis"; $3 per mail-ordered copy).

CLIMATE & WEATHER

Expect relatively mild weather in Chesapeake country. Fahrenheit averages bring January highs of 40 degrees at the top of the Bay in Chesapeake City (22 degrees low) and, nearly 240 miles south, at the mouth of the Bay in Norfolk, average highs of 47 degrees (30 degrees low). July can often bring temperatures in the upper 80s to both the Upper and Lower Bay regions. Annapolis, located mid-Bay on its western shore, generally expects January high into the 40s and lows in the 20s, while July temperatures can range into the 80s during the day and drop into the 60s at night.

But averages tell only part of the story. Proximity to the 3,700-square-mile Bay often brings high humidity during the months of July and August, which can bring furious afternoon and evening thunderstorms in late summer, when daytime temperatures easily top 90 degrees. Take these storms seriously; people have been struck and killed by lightning on and around the Bay. Even on the calmest day, boaters must always keep an eye on the windward sky (and an ear on the marine weather forecast).

By early September, humidity often has dropped considerably, although temperatures in the 80-degree range tend to continue well into the month. Chesapeake's average fall temperature is 62 degrees. Sailors love it; a steady breeze blows in the 10- to 15-knot range.

Chesapeake winters usually bring mild temperatures, with an average of fewer than ten inches of snowfall. Windchill near the water, however, can make the air seem considerably colder and may even produce dangerous chilling or frostbite.

On the open Bay, rays are magnified by the water's surface, increasing the risk of sunburn and sunstroke. A hat, lip balm, and sunscreen are always recommended. Also, keep in mind that alcoholic beverages are best consumed after your voyage. Enforcement of drunken-boater laws can be stringent.

To obtain updated weather reports, check any local newspaper (or their web sites), or The Weather Channel's weather.com. In **Virginia**, call 757-877-1221, Newport News; 804-268-1212, Richmond.

ENVIRONMENT

"**S**ave the Bay" is a rallying cry around the Chesapeake Bay, the focus of a massive cleanup effort by state and federal agencies since the late 1970s. If you really want to get into the issue, there's plenty to learn — and plenty of information. Local libraries often stock scientific studies on the Bay. Or you can contact the following organizations:

The **Chesapeake Bay Foundation** (410-268-8816, Annapolis office; www.cbf. org; Philip Merrill Environmental Center, 6 Herndon Ave., Annapolis, MD 21403). Headquartered out of a new "green" building in Annapolis, with other offices elsewhere throughout the Chesapeake watershed region in Delaware, Pennsylvania, and Virginia, this is the leading nonprofit "Save the Bay" organization, which actively educates the watershed region about a range of Bay-related environmental issues at stops up and down the Chesapeake. Contact them if you're interested in environmental education programs in the field (or, for that matter, on a boat).

The multiagency umbrella that oversees the government cleanup, the **Chesapeake Bay Program**, has a hot line (800-YOUR-BAY). The **Chesapeake Regional Information Service**, or CRIS (800-662-CRIS; e-mail acb@ari.net), is the 24/7 hot line to call for facts and figures on the Bay or to report an illegal dumping. Sponsored by the Alliance for the Chesapeake Bay (www.acb-online.org).

FISHING

From marshy creeks to wide-open water, the Chesapeake and its tributaries comprise one of the greatest anglers' destinations anywhere. Catch and release fishing is popular, and fly-fishing has caught on. Seventeen species of game fish live in the Bay, pursued from riverbanks, piers, skiffs, head boats and charter boats. Among the favorite finfish: bluefish, striped bass (known locally as rockfish), sea trout, white and yellow perch, spot, striped bass, catfish, and summer flounder.

Then there is the Maryland blue crab, wildly popular and the focus of considerable political attention as both Maryland and Virginia wrestle with how to manage the up-and-down populations of recent years. Some blame overharvesting; others cite problems including the natural life cycle of any species, loss of their grass bed habitat, and predation by finfish whose populations have recovered. Whatever the reason, be kind and resist the urge to catch a couple dozen for yourself alone. Some people think that it would be a good idea not to catch females, which have rounded, U-shaped aprons, unlike the pointed aprons of the males.

Fishing licenses are widely available at fishing and sporting foods stores, but are not required if you are under age 16. A saltwater fishing license issued by Maryland or Virginia is good in either state, although there are some limits when it comes to fishing certain tributaries. You won't need a license in Maryland if you are fishing from a chartered boat or if you are fishing as a nonpaying guest from private property. In addition, the Maryland Department of Natural Resources can tell you about free fishing areas. Ask about nonresident licenses for consecutive days of fishing — probably a bargain if you're visiting the region. Prices are generally reduced for fishers over age 65.

In Maryland, licenses for recreational crabbers are required for anyone using a trotline, or anyone who wants to catch more than two dozen crabs. In Virginia, recreational crabbers need a license if they're using more than two crab pots.

Other rules may apply and regulations may change; check at bait stores or contact the states for more information on fishing or crabbing.

Keep in mind that you can partake of the fine art of "chicken necking." Tie a chicken neck to a string, tie the string to a piling, and when it tenses up, slowly ease the bait up into sight, a crab or two hanging on to feed, and scoop with a long-handled dip net. Keeps the kids happy for hours!

A new map of the Bay shows all its public access points, and is available free by calling 800-YOUR-BAY. In addition, Maryland publishes a list of boat ramps, *A Fisherman's Guide to Maryland Piers and Boat Ramps*, which also provides license details, creel limits, and seasonal limits for each species. To obtain the guide, or get information on both fresh- and saltwater fishing licenses or other needs, contact: Maryland Department of Natural Resources, Fisheries Service, 800-688-FINS (3467) or 410-260-8200; www.dnr.state.md.us; 580 Taylor Ave., Annapolis, MD 21401. For information on Virginia freshwater fishing, contact: Department of Game and Inland Fisheries, 804-367-1000; www.dgif .state.va.us; 4010 W. Broad St./P.O. Box 11104, Richmond, VA 23230. Virginia saltwater anglers, contact: Marine Resources Commission, 757-247-2200 or 800-541-4646; www.state.va.us/mrc/homepage.htm; 2600 Washington Ave./P.O. Box 756, Newport News, VA 23607.

HANDICAPPED SERVICES

In *Maryland,* the free *Destination Maryland* guide notes entries with accessibility for disabled persons. Contact: Maryland Office of Tourism Development, 800-543-1036, 410-767-3400; www.mdisfun.org; 217 E. Redwood St., Baltimore, MD 21202.

In *Virginia, The Virginia Travel Guide for the Disabled* is a free comprehensive guide for the disabled that goes beyond whether or not a wheelchair-bound visitor can get in and out of doors. Contact: Virginia Tourism Corporation, 800-742-3935, 804-786-4484; www.virginia.org (keyword "handicapped accessible"); 901 E. Byrd St., Richmond, VA 23219.

HOSPITALS & HEALTH CARE

Should a serious health problem arise, you are, fortunately, near some of the nation's top medical facilities.

Baltimore, Maryland

The Johns Hopkins Hospital (410-955-2280 main emergency, 600 N. Wolfe St.; Johns Hopkins Children's Center, located in the hospital, 410-955-5680 emergency; Johns Hopkins Bayview Medical Center, 410-550-0350 emergency, 4940 Eastern Ave.).

University of Maryland Medical Center University Hospital (410-328-6722 adult emergency; 410-328-6677 pediatric emergency; 22 S. Greene St.).

Washington, D.C. area

Georgetown University Hospital (202-784-2000; 202-784-3111 emergency services; 3800 Reservoir Rd. NW, Washington, D.C.).

The George Washington University Medical Center (202-715-4000; 202-715-4911 emergency room; 901 23rd St. NW, Washington, D.C.).

Washington Adventist Hospital (301-891-7600; 301-891-5070 emergency; 7600 Carroll Ave., Takoma Park, Md.).

Norfolk, Virginia

Children's Hospital of the King's Daughters (757-668-7000; 757-668-7188 emergency; 601 Children's Lane).

Richmond, Virginia

Medical College of Virginia Hospitals (804-828-9000; 804-828-9151 emergency; 401 N. 12th St.).

The following local hospitals offer comprehensive medical services. All operate emergency rooms twenty-four hours a day, seven days a week, unless otherwise noted.

ANNAPOLIS

Anne Arundel Medical Center (443-481-1000; 443-481-1200 emergency; www.aahs.org; 2001 Medical Parkway, off Rte. 50, Annapolis).

THE UPPER BAY

Kent & Queen Anne's Hospital, Inc. (410-778-3300; 100 Brown St., Chestertown) Ask for the emergency room, or, if an operator is unavailable, ext. 2500.
Union Hospital (410-398-4000; 410-398-1400 emergency; 106 Bow St., Elkton).

MIDDLE EASTERN SHORE

Memorial Hospital at Easton (410-822-1000; 219 S. Washington St., Easton).

LOWER EASTERN SHORE

Dorchester General Hospital (410-228-5511; for emergency room, dial 8, then 525 or 526; 300 Byrn St., Cambridge).
Edward W. McCready Memorial Hospital (410-968-1200, ext. 3300; 201 Hall Hwy., Crisfield).
Peninsula Regional Medical Center (410-546-6400; 410-543-7101 emergency; 100 E. Carroll St., Salisbury).

NORTHERN NECK/MIDDLE PENINSULA

Rappahannock General Hospital (804-435-8000; 804-435-8545 emergency; 101 Harris Dr., Kilmarnock, Va.).
Riverside Walter Reed Hospital (804-693-8800; 804-693-8899 emergency; 7519 Hospital Dr., north of town on Hwy. 17, Gloucester, Va.).

LANDINGS AND BOAT RAMPS

A terrific map of the Bay shows all its public access points, and is available free by calling 1-800-YOUR-BAY or visiting www.chesapeakebay.net. In addition, Maryland publishes a list of boat ramps, *A Fisherman's Guide to Maryland Piers and Boat Ramps.* Contact: Maryland Department of Natural Resources, Fisheries Service, 800-688-FINS (3467) or 410-260-8200; www.dnr .state.md.us; 580 Taylor Ave., Annapolis MD 21401. Small charges apply at some ramps; usually the locations where you can obtain a permit are posted at the ramp.

LATE-NIGHT FOOD & FUEL

ANNAPOLIS

Chesapeake Exxon (410-266-7475; Rtes. 50 & 450, Annapolis) Open 24 hours; fuel.

THE UPPER BAY & MIDDLE EASTERN SHORE

Dutch Family Restaurant (410-778-0507; Rtes. 301 & 291, Millington) Open 24 hours; food, fuel, and full-service restaurant.
Fast Stop (410-822-3333; 9543 Ocean Gateway Dr., Easton) Open 24 hours; food and fuel.
Faulkner's Exxon (410-822-8219; 8147 Ocean Gateway Dr., Easton) Open 24 hours; fuel.
Royal Farm Store (410-778-0646; 301 Maple Ave., Chestertown) Open 24 hours.
Royal Farm Store (410-479-3422; 5th & Market Sts., Denton) Open 6am-midnight; food.
Trailways Truck Stop (410-758-2444; Rtes. 301 E and 304 E, Centreville) Open 24 hours; centrally located on the Eastern Shore; clean, relatively new.

LOWER EASTERN SHORE

Dunkin' Donuts (410-228-6197; Sunburst Hwy., Cambridge) Open 24 hours.
Shore Stop (410-548-3385; 811 Priscilla St., Salisbury) Open 6am-11pm; food and fuel. Keep an eye out for the **Shore Stop** stores, which are convenience store/gas stations scattered along the Delmarva Peninsula — often a welcome sight for weary travelers heading through the sparse Lower Eastern Shore. Among those open 24 hours along the Virginia shore:

Cape Charles (757-331-4008; 22177 Lankford Hwy.).
Chincoteague (757-336-6380; Church & N. Main Sts.).
Nassowadox (757-442-5170; 7410 Lankford Hwy.).

NEWSPAPERS & MAGAZINES

The Chesapeake's proximity to major cities means that folks deep in Chesapeake country are as likely to read the *Washington Post* as their local paper. Still, the local papers are filled with information about everything from tides to VFW oyster roasts.

Maryland

Bay Weekly (410-867-0304; P.O. Box 358, Deale, MD 20751) Eclectic free weekly features entertainment, nature, and other topics of interest to Bay readers. Look for it around Maryland's Western Shore. Published Thurs.

The Capital (410-268-5000; www.capitalonline.com; 2000 Capital Dr., Annapolis, MD 21401) The state capital's daily newspaper. Also publishes a comprehensive Fri. entertainment section focusing on Annapolis-area events.

Chesapeake Bay Magazine (410-263-2662; 1819 Bay Ridge Ave., Annapolis, MD 21401) A monthly magazine featuring stories about the Bay, boating, fishing, and other water-related issues.

The Daily Banner (410-228-3131; 1000 Goodwill Rd./P.O. Box 580, Cambridge, MD 21613) Published Mon.-Fri.

The Daily Times (410-749-7171; www.thedailytimesonline.com; 115 E. Carroll St., Salisbury, MD 21801)

Kent County News (410-778-2011; 217 High St./P.O. Box 30, Chestertown, MD 21620) Published Thurs.

The Star-Democrat (410-822-1500; www.stardem.com; 29088 Airpark Dr., Airport Industrial Park, Easton, MD 21601) Published Sun.–Fri.

The (Baltimore) Sun (800-829-8000, 410-332-6000; www.sunspot.net; 501 N. Calvert St., Baltimore, MD 21201) Blanket coverage of Maryland, as well as a weekly entertainment tabloid on Thurs.

Washington, D.C.

The Washington Post (202-334-6000; www.washingtonpost.com; 1150 15th St. NW, Washington, DC 20005) The national morning daily includes a Fri. Weekend section focusing on events in and around Washington, D.C., and often, on the Bay.

The Washington Times (202-636-3000; www.washtimes.com; 3600 New York

Ave. NE, Washington, DC 20018) Morning daily includes a weekly entertainment section published on Saturdays.

Virginia

The Daily Press (757-247-4600; www.dailypress.com; 7505 Warwick Blvd., Newport News, VA 23601).

The Gazette-Journal (804-693-3101; 6625 Main St./P.O. Box 2060, Gloucester, VA 23061) A local weekly. Published Thurs.

The Northern Neck News (804-333-NEWS, 804-333-3655; Court Circle St./P.O. Box 8, Warsaw, VA 22572) Published Wed.

The Virginian-Pilot-Ledger-Star (800-446-2004, 757-446-2000; www.piloton line.com; 150 W. Brambleton Ave., Norfolk, VA 23501) Tidewater's major daily.

PARK BASICS

In each chapter, we've suggested parks, but to find out more contact the **Maryland** Dept. of Natural Resources toll-free at 877-620-8DNR; www. dnr.state.md.us. For camping and cabin reservations, call 888-432-2267. Write the department at: 580 Taylor Ave., Annapolis, MD 21401. In **Virginia,** contact the Dept. of Conservation and Recreation by calling 800-993-PARK or 804-786-1712; www.dcr.state.va.us. You can download a state park guide from the site. For cabin and campground reservations, call 800-933-PARK. To write: 203 Governor St., Suite 213, Richmond, VA 23219-2094.

ROAD SERVICE

Annapolis: Darden's 24-Hour Towing (410-269-1046; 211 West St., Annapolis).

The Upper Bay: Morgan's Auto Repair & Tow Service (410-398-1288; 668 W. Pulaski Hwy., Elkton) Towing 24 hours.

Middle Eastern Shore: Mullikin's Auto Body, Inc. (410-820-8676; 9277 Ocean Gateway Dr., Easton).

Lower Eastern Shore: Adkins Towing (410-749-7712; 2207 Northwood Dr., Unit 8A, Salisbury).

Northern Neck/Middle Peninsula: Curtis Texaco Station (804-580-8888; 7043 Northumberland Hwy., Heathsville, Va.) Towing 24 hours.

Dickey's Auto Recycling (804-693-4244; Hwy. 17, Ark, Va., near Gloucester) Towing 24 hours.

TIDES

If you're going for a sail or leaving your crab pot in the water for a few hours, you may want to check the tide. Typical Chesapeake tide falls are only 1.5–2 feet, but it can make a big difference in the Bay's shallow waters. Keep an eye out for extra high tides if a storm is in the forecast. For information, check local newspapers, broadcast weather reports, or the monthly *Chesapeake Bay Magazine*. On the Western Shore, look for *Bay Weekly*, and around Chestertown, look for *The Tidewater Trader*. Both freebies publish information about tides. Information is also available at any marina or bait and tackle shop.

TOURIST INFORMATION

Both Maryland and Virginia offer extensive tourist information services. In addition, local tourism offices have considerably increased their offerings in recent years. For information, contact:

Maryland Office of Tourism Development (800-543-1036, 410-767-3400; www.mdisfun.org; 217 E. Redwood St., Baltimore, MD 21202).
Virginia Tourism Corporation (804-786-4484, 800-VISITVA; www.virginia.org; 901 E. Byrd St., Richmond, VA 23219).

ANNAPOLIS SOUTH TO THE POTOMAC RIVER

Annapolis and Anne Arundel County Conference and Visitors Bureau (410-268-8687, 410-280-0445; www.visit-annapolis.org; 26 West St., Annapolis, MD 21401).
Calvert County Department of Economic Development (800-331-9771, 410-535-4583, or 301-855-1880; www.co.cal.md.us/cced/tourism.htm; Courthouse, 175 Main St., Prince Frederick, MD 20678).
St. Mary's County Chamber of Commerce (301-884-5555; www.smcchamber.com; 28290 Three Notch Rd., Mechanicsville, MD 20659).

THE UPPER BAY

Discover Harford County Tourism Council (800-597-2649, 410-272-2325, or 410-575-7278; www.harfordmd.com; 3 W. Belair Ave., Aberdeen, MD 21001).
Kent County Chamber of Commerce (410-810-2968; www.kentchamber.org; 400 S. Cross St., Chestertown, MD 21620).

MIDDLE EASTERN SHORE

Caroline County Commissioner's Office (410-479-0660; 109 Market St., Rm. 109, Denton, MD 21629).

Queen Anne's County Office of Tourism (888-400-RSVP, 410-604-2100; www.qac.org; 425 Piney Narrows Rd., Chester, MD 21619).

Talbot County Office of Tourism (888-BAY-STAY, 410-770-8000; www.talbot county.md; 11 North Washington St., Easton, MD 21601.

LOWER EASTERN SHORE

Chincoteague Chamber of Commerce (757-336-6161; www.chincoteague chamber.com; P.O. Box 258, Chincoteague, VA 23336).

Dorchester County Office of Tourism (800-522-TOUR, 410-228-1000; www.tourdorchester.org; 2 Rose Hill Pl., Dorchester, MD 21613).

Eastern Shore of Virginia Chamber of Commerce (757-787-2460; www.esva tourism.org; P.O. Box 460, Melfa, VA 23410).

Somerset County Tourism Office (800-521-9189, 410-651-2968; www.skip jack.net/le_shore/visitsomerset; 11440 Ocean Hwy./P.O. Box 243, Princess Anne, MD 21853).

Wicomico County Convention & Visitors Bureau (410-548-4914; www.wicomicotourism.org; 8480 Ocean Hwy., Delmar, MD 21875).

NORTHERN NECK/MIDDLE PENINSULA

Gloucester Chamber of Commerce (804-693-2425; www.gloucestervacc.com; 6688 Main St./P.O. Box 296, Gloucester, VA 23061).

Mathews Chamber of Commerce (804-725-9029; www.mathewschamber.com; P.O. Box 1126, located at Faye's Secretarial Service downtown on Main St., Mathews, VA 23109). Closed Wed.

Northern Neck Visitor Information Line (800-453-6167; Rte. 301, Dahlgren, VA 22448).

IF TIME IS SHORT

It's hard to pick and choose among the Bay's many activities, but here are some suggestions:

In _Annapolis_, sit in the gardens at the **William Paca House** (410-263-5553; 186 Prince George St.), perhaps the best spot in the Historic District. Dine at **O'Leary's Restaurant** (410-263-0884; 310 Third St. in Eastport), the Wild Orchid Café (410-268-8009; 909 Bay Ridge Ave., Eastport) or **Joss**, for sushi (410-263-4688; 195 Main St.). Check to see if **Watermark Cruises** is running a "blues cruise" one evening and plan on that (410-268-7600; Annapolis City Dock).

On the _Upper Shore_: Wander Chestertown's historic streets. Go to **Eastern Neck Wildlife Refuge** (410-639-7056; 1730 Eastern Neck Rd.), a peninsula past Rock Hall, to look for good birds. Eat dinner in the other direction, eight miles out of Chestertown at the **Kennedyville Inn** (410-348-2400; 11986 Augustine Herman Hwy.). And stop by the **Galena Antiques Center** (410-648-5781; 108 N. Main St.) in Galena, and seriously consider buying a handmade barnboard table.

On the _Middle Eastern Shore_: Go canoeing on the Wye or Corsica rivers. In addition to having way cool names, their shorelines are as pretty as they get, with tucked-away (mostly) houses and habitat full of green herons, osprey or bald eagles. Go out aboard the _Rebecca T. Ruark_, the Bay's oldest skipjack, out of Tilghman's Dogwood Harbor with **Capt. Wade Murphy** (410-886-2176; 21308 Phillips Rd., Tilghman). Dine at the **Tilghman Island Inn** (410-886-2141), or any of the trendy new Goldsborough Street restaurants in Easton.

On the _Lower Eastern Shore_: Rent a camper cabin at **Jane's Island State Park** near Crisfield (410-968-1803; 26280 Alfred J. Lawson Dr.). Canoe, kayak, or motor through the marshy guts. Eat crabs at **Side Street Seafood Restaurant** (410-968-2442; 204 S. Tenth St). Ferry over to Tangier Island, take a nickel tour of the watermen's village aboard a golf cart, then stop at any restaurant to eat the only truly great (except if you're on Smith Island) soft-shells mere mortals ever find.

On the _Northern Neck and Middle Peninsula_: Honestly? Read the chapter and do everything! This area's magic. If you have time only for one spot, hit Urbanna just to soak in the laid-back Tidewater style and have a meal at **Jimmie's Grille** (804-758-5213, 230 Virginia St.), one of the Bay's great restaurant values, or on the water at the funky **Boathouse Cafe.** (804-758-4046; 41 Oyster Rd.). If you're inclined toward a colonial waterside plantation experience overnight, consider the **North River Inn** (877-248-3030) or the **Inn at Warner Hall** (800-331-2720), near Gloucester.

Index

LODGING BY PRICE CODES

Price Codes
Inexpensive: **Up to $75**
Moderate: **$76 to $120**
Expensive: **$121 to $150**
Very Expensive: **Over $150**

ANNAPOLIS area (incl. Solomons Island)

Moderate–Expensive
Back Creek B&B, 90–91
Eastport House B&B, 36
Jonas Green House, 39

Moderate–Very Expensive
Comfort Inn/Beacon Marina, 91
Holiday Inn Select, 91
Loews Annapolis Hotel, 40
Solomons Victorian Inn, 91

Expensive
The Barn on Howard's Cove, 35
The Dolls' House B&B, 36

55 East, 37

Expensive–Very Expensive
Chez Amis, 36
Harbor View Inn, 38
Historic Inns of Annapolis, 39
1908 William Page Inn, 34
Two-O-One, 41

Very Expensive
Annapolis Inn, 34
Annapolis Marriott Waterfront, 35
Flag House Inn, 38
Schooner *Woodwind*, 40

BALTIMORE

Moderate–Expensive
Mr. Mole B&B, 267

Expensive–Very Expensive
Celie's Waterfront B&B, 267

The Inn at Henderson's Wharf, 267
Scarborough Fair B&B, 268

Very Expensive
The Admiral Fell Inn, 266

LOWER EASTERN SHORE

Inexpensive
The Washington Hotel & Inn, 189

Inexpensive–Moderate
Colonial Manor Inn, 188

Inexpensive–Very Expensive
Loblolly Landings and Lodge, 184
Somers Cove Motel, 190

Moderate
Driftwood Motor Lodge, 190

DINING BY CUISINE

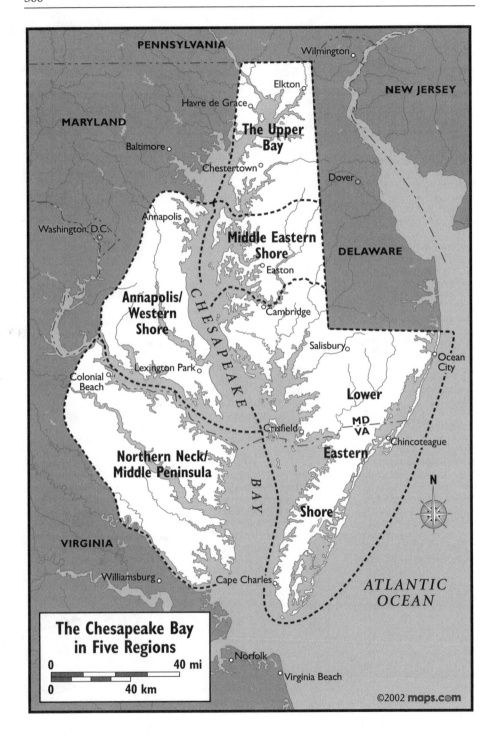

The Chesapeake Bay in Five Regions

0   40 mi

0   40 km

©2002 maps.com

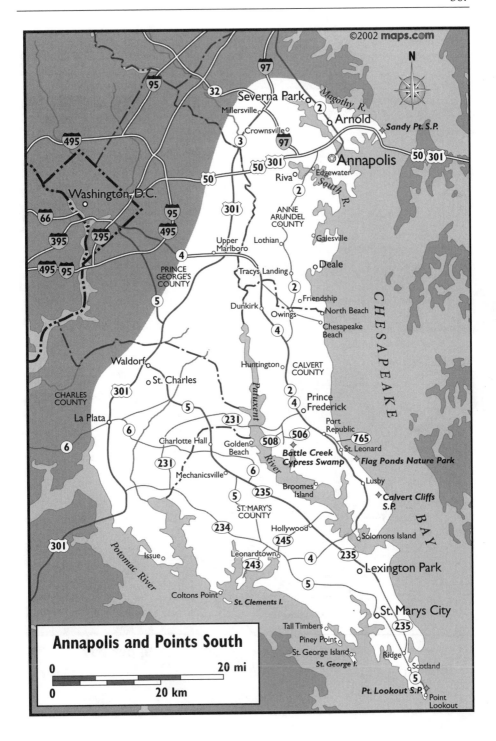

©2002 maps.com

N

Annapolis and Points South

0   20 mi

0   20 km

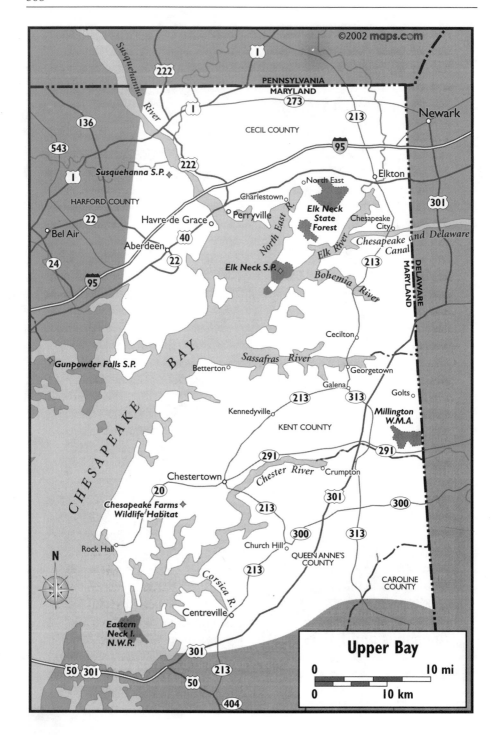

©2002 maps.com

Upper Bay

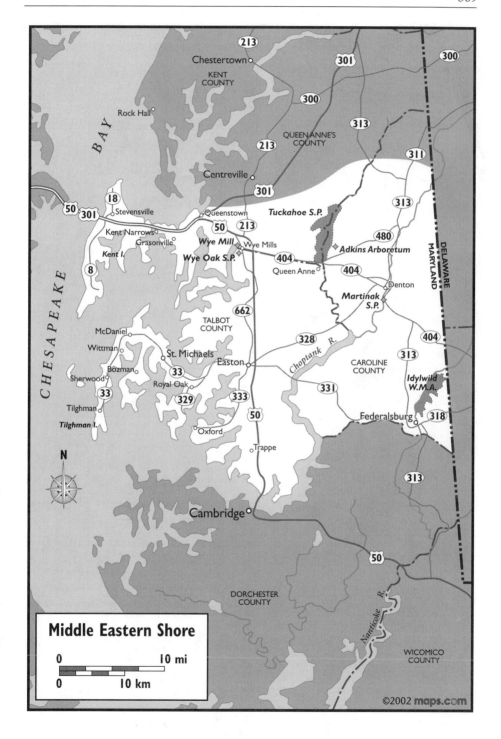

Middle Eastern Shore

0   10 mi

0   10 km

©2002 maps.com

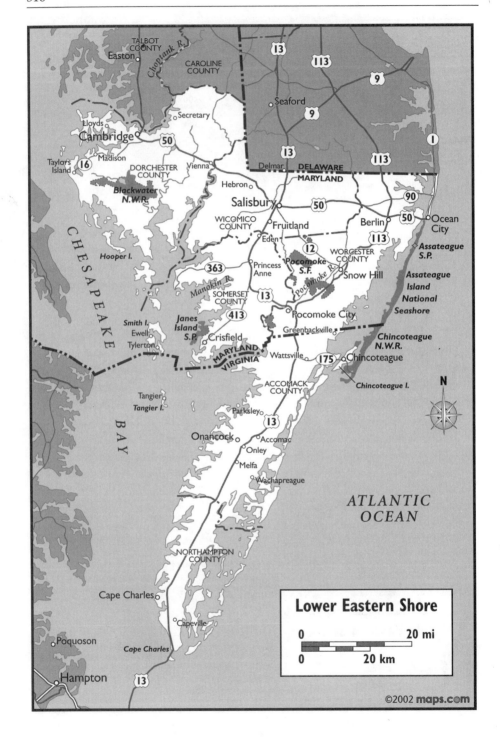

Lower Eastern Shore

0   20 mi

0   20 km

©2002 maps.com

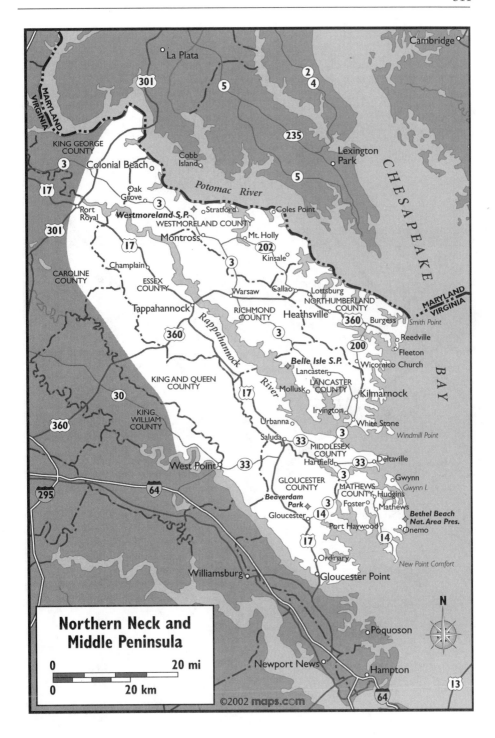

Northern Neck and Middle Peninsula

0   20 mi

0   20 km

©2002 maps.com

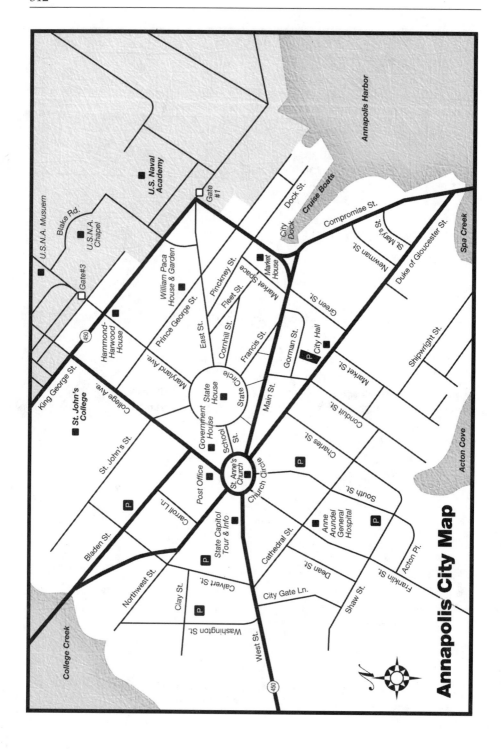

Annapolis City Map